Bikers

Bikers

❖

Dave Ebert

Library of Congress Control Number:		2010908870
ISBN:	Hardcover	978-1-4535-0535-9
	Softcover	978-1-4535-0534-2
	Ebook	978-1-4535-0536-6

This book was printed in the United States of America.

To order additional copies of this book, contact:
Xlibris Corporation
1-888-795-4274
www.Xlibris.com
Orders@Xlibris.com
76380

CONTENTS

I dedicate this book in the loving memory of;
Maynard (Kebus) Ebert and Bobby Graber,
"Rest in Peace my Brothers"

INTRODUCTION

One percent Bike Clubs have always flourished after every American war. Post World War II produced a couple of the earliest and largest Outlaw Motorcycle Clubs the WORLD knows today. It would seem any time club membership falls into growth doldrums, the United States finds itself involved in another foreign war, or what it may affectionately call "A Conflict" and club growth returns. Not to say some clubs don't grow during peace time, but my story is concentrated on one club and its relationship between the U.S. military and the wars the two have shared by their members. Although I never served in the U.S. Armed Forces, it's easy for me to see there's something about being in a Combat Zone one day, then on the Home Front the next, as much too sudden for some. I suppose there is a freedom in unregulated violence, to find a "Place in Time," where all we know and all we have ever been taught about compassion is converted into primordial instincts, casting away all moral and governmental laws. Probably one grows to love maybe not so much the danger, but the freedoms of war. A freedom of not having to answer for his mistakes or even so much as mood swings. The freedom of doing whatever he wants whenever he wants, provided it's cloaked under the "War Effort" and has a host government support that behavior. Not to say an American war zone is undisciplined rape, but many have told me the first man they killed in Vietnam was followed by the fear of prosecution. These men were raised in a nonviolent society governed by strict laws prohibiting violence, and then to have a medal pinned to them from the kill produced an almost invincible feeling. As they killed more, that feeling matured and they evolved into an educated "Cave Man" type of being! When returned to the

United States and told to act as if they had never been to war and seen its horrors became the one "Lie" most U.S. veterans would not adopt! To some, Harleys Davidsons and Bike Clubs became the answer; they found truth in "Brotherhood."

A. B. A.
-Clutch-

CHAPTER ONE

STEP 'N' FETCH

Its 1969, the Vietnam War rages on without any end in sight, declared by our government, not the people from within. Death and destruction, unpopularity, fought hard by brave Americans, sadly, many of whom are tagged with the name "Baby Killer" upon their uncelebrated Homecoming. It is the "Age of Nixon." Over half the Americans killed in Vietnam died during the first four years of the Nixon administration! Our cities are ablaze! They burn as rioters battle police and National Guardsmen in the congested, smoke filled streets, littered with rubble and badly beaten bodies! Black Panthers scream-out, "Destroy them!" College campuses' have been overtaken by the Radical Youth Movement and are being held hostage in protest of our government and its involvement in Southeast Asia! The U.S. is in much disorder . . . Mayhem! The civil rights movement and the radical youth are at war with the government, and in-between them is a wealth of hard narcotics and hallucinogens mixing up the rest! Cell phones, flat screen TVs, and the Internet have yet to make their debut. Computers are here, but not like we know them today. They have Green Screens and DOS. No digital television, no digital music, and eight-track tape players have only recently arrived. One hundred channels on your TV, unheard of! There is one thing however that has been heard of, and has been since 1903, the Harley Davidson. Along with the Harley Davidson has come the "Age of the Biker." Their fast, carefree lifestyle has spawned a very select group that was Born Free, Born Wild, and Born to Ride. They are One Percent of the Bikers, and they were offered No Choice, they were Born That

Way, and they will Die That Way. My biological Father and Brother happened to be part of that Chosen Few, selected not by Choice, but by Circumstance, and Birth.

"One Percenters" have been here since man learned to walk upright, maybe longer. This number is being used symbolically, not for its numeric value. They are the restless ones, those who can never find peace or love for any length of time. In that respect, there is never any consistency in their lives. They are the Cowboys and the Loners, wildly drifting in and out of history. They appear in our history books as Jesse James, and you'll find their name to be Edward Teach, alias Black Beard. They are the Pirates sailing free, and they are Bikers riding free. Jesse James was no doubt a one percenter. RIP. Like most, he was born into that group, but it took a war between the states to fuel the desire that blossomed into what he was, and like me, he had No Choice. Black Beard also was born a one percenter, calmed through youth, but restless by nature. It took an English war to light his fuse, and out of the explosion, matured one of the world's deadliest men, swinging his sword, wild on the attack! Could you imagine what power he and Jesse could have created together, "Flying Colors," screaming down our highways, riding side by side on Harleys? Trust me, they're here; but only as one percenters and answering to different names.

U.S. Special Forces are also one percenters. They are one percent of the military that hates having to shave and hates doing all the stupid bullshit the military requires. The dumb shit like burying your cigarette butts and being made to act as if you're a complete moron because you did something completely against regulations, like eating before you were told that you were hungry. But their nonconformity is offset by their willingness to do the tough work, the dangerous and dirty work, and they love doing it. It's when they returned from war to the United States, took off their uniforms, and put on Club Colors that the government began to worry. Not that these men are traitors to our country or subversives; quite the contrary, they are Heroes! In fact, they love the United States of America more so than most. Remember, they fought hard for it. But because our government knew when it trained one percent of its military population to kill in perfect Art Form and they would always be one percenters, and dangerous. It formed a team of federal agents in the hopes of controlling and keeping these men down. It did not work out as planned; these federal "Watch Dogs" only fueled the rage in these one percent hearts. There began a war within our own country between the government and war veterans. Many of our war heroes climbed on Harley Davidson's, flew their Colors wide open, and became the most deadly "Outlaws" the world has ever known. And I confess, I'm one of them, and here's my story.

It's late summer of '69. I'm fourteen years old as I stand in front of my older brother's Harley, holding his Colors. It's a risk I'm willing to take. If caught, I know he'll beat the shit out of me for touching his Rag. I can't help it, I love looking at them! I love the patches and all the pins. I even know what most of them mean. Like the number 13. That's the thirteenth letter in the alphabet, what do you suppose that stands for—Marijuana, Motorcycles or Murder? And the one percent, 1%, which means they're one percent of Bikers that don't conform. You know, those coined "The Bad Ones." But there's a small Death Head with crossed bones that I have no idea about. It is very secret among all the members of this gang. Excuse me, "Motorcycle Club!" From what I can see, only a few in each Chapter wear this Nazi SS-looking Death Head Patch. It strikes me as curious—always the largest, meanest, most deadly ones, like my older brother, Kebus, hmmm? Anyhow, I'll get back to that later. Let me continue. Once my brother found me sitting on his Hog, which is in itself a big No-No, and wearing his Colors, Ta Boot! I think I was pretend revving the throttle while making Vroom-Vroom sounds. It goes without saying; it was the worst beating I've experienced to date.

I live on an old one hundred acre farm just outside a small town that's not too far from a major city. My brother's Motorcycle Club has many parties out here. I love it. I'm usually Step 'N' Fetch or Beer Boy. They call me Clutch. My brother gave me that name because whenever I do something stupid, he always says, "Your clutch must be slip'in!" There's a huge party planned soon. They never say when, but I've learned the signs. For example, a bunch of Porta-Potties showed up here earlier today. Firewood has been collected in mass quantities, and the famed "Horse Trough" used as a beer/ice container has been flipped upright and cleaned. In itself, that sucker holds enough beer to get the entire U.S. Army drunk! The reason I know this one is going to be big is this time a beer truck has been rented. You know, with the tappers on the side. I think there are ninety kegs of beer in that sucker. There's an old pigpen that now has six live pigs oinking around in it. To eat, not to pet! Yep, it looks like a big one.

There's always some sort of incident, a happening, during these parties. I think it's cool; I just sit back and watch the excitement. Last party, a Club member, Chains, tried to run through the bonfire drunk. He tripped and fell face first into it! Two other Bikers quickly grabbed his feet and drug him out. They dumped beer on his head—laughing of course, while saying, "We gotta put-out the fire, Bro!" I've been punched in the face a few times during these parties, but because of who I am, I can usually weasel my way out of any problem. The trick is, Don't Drink. Once, they gave me 151 rum. I ended up puking on one of the Harleys! You guessed it. "Pow," right in the "Soup Coolers!" If I complain, then it's said I'm Sniveling, and "No Sniveling Allowed!" Or worse, "Snitching"—you guessed it again, for Snitching "Double Pow!" They say they're trying to make me tough, but sometimes I think they're trying to make me dead! Uh-oh, I must be careful because right now I'm stepping dangerously close to Sniveling. Yesterday I saw members wearing Colors from a bunch of different states I didn't even know the Club was in! Yep, this one's gonna be a huge party!

Well, here it is, Friday, 6:00 p.m. Labor Day weekend. I'm standing beside a never-ending column of Harleys riding two abreast. They're slowly moving down our long driveway and have been off and on all day long. The heat, the deep thunderous sound created by hundreds of Harleys, the Colors, I swear I love it! Right now my job is to reach into the Horse Trough and hand every member an ice-cold beer as they pass. I may only be fourteen years old, but the girls on the back of these bikes keep my hand busy at night! Sorry . . . ? Police helicopters have been circling overhead off and on all day long also.

I hope I'm allowed to stay up with the party tonight. Sometimes they run me off; they tell the prospects to keep me away from the actual party. I hate prospects. But don't tell them I said that because some of them become members, but then they change and usually treat me pretty cool. I'm not sure what they do to prospects, but for sure, they always look miserable! One thing for sure, I don't ever want to be one, but I don't think there's a choice, that's the only way in.

Here's how it works, after you "Hang Around" the Club long enough, they vote to see if they want you. If they vote yes, you're a prospect. Oh yeah, first you must sign your Harley over to the Club. If you quit, they keep it. After you prospect for a while, your first advancement comes in the form of a Bottom Rocker. It's called that because it's shaped like the mouth of a smiley face or the bottom of a rocking chair, get it, a Rocker. This patch shows territory. It reads the town or state you're in. Clubs have gone to war over that one! Now you just keep prospecting. In other words, you do anything asked of you and keep your mouth shut. Next you receive your Center Patch. That's sorta the Club's logo, very artistic; they always look cool! It's sewn on your Rag directly above the Bottom Rocker. And finally, after Hell Week, you get your Top Rocker, that harbors the Club's name. It's an upside down smiley face, sewn above the Center Patch. This entire process can take years! You're now a Full Patch Holder—a Brother. It's rumored during this prospect period one must commit a felony for the Club—take a guess which one?

Anyhow, back to the party. In order to be here, I must have a ribbon pinned to my chest which reads Guest. Can you believe it? I'm a guest at my own house! The ribbon they say keeps me alive, so I guess I'll wear it! There's gonna be bands here this weekend. They have brought in a huge flatbed trailer to be used as a stage, but first the bikini and wet tee shirt contest. Yeah! Then followed by the Marshmallow Race—you'll never believe this one!

With the exception of one Brother, this is for Prospects only. Now the race track obviously has a start and finish line; it has very narrow side-to-side boundaries, so it's a long, skinny rectangle. In this race, all contestants pull their pants and undies down to their ankles then cram a marshmallow into their butt. While racing, if the marshmallow falls out, they must stop until it is returned to that Unforgiving Zone. A prospect could never consider winning this race over the Full Patch Holder. That would hold very unpleasant consequences for him. Very unpleasant indeed. So knowing he's gonna win and untouchable, the Brother is not moving very fast down the approximate center of the racetrack. He's only there to fuck with the Prospects by moving slow, stopping whenever, and sipping a beer of course. A Prospect can't win over the Brother, but he can't lose either. Did I mention, the loser must eat all the other contestants' marshmallows? Yuck! If he pukes while eating them, he must puke into his boot and then drink it after he's finished eating! No wonder Prospects always look so miserable!

There are some very large Prospects. They're all pushing and punching one another as they hobble down the track; they'll do anything not to be last. At the finish line, however, they're all trying not to be first. One must be sure he's not shoved across the finish line in front of the slow-moving Brother. One can't really fall out of the side-to-side boundaries because the entire racetrack is shoulder to shoulder Brothers, yelling, drinking, and laughing. But if a Prospect does get pushed out, he must go back to the Starting Line and begin again, not a big deal unless the contestants are nearing the finish line. A Prospect wins this race by not losing. Second place is fine, fourteenth is fine also, as long as he's not last.

In the case of a Prospect knocking out another Prospect, the only Patch Holder in the race merely stops until the unconscious Prospect is revived and back in the race. It really turns into quite the brawl. I hope I never have to compete in the Marshmallow Race.

The one I like, and a little calmer I must say, is the Harley Race. Last one across the finish line wins. This one's for Brothers only, so it's to see who can ride the slowest without putting his feet down. That one's cool! Then there's Bobbing for Beer. That one's for Prospects only also. If you hold a strong fear of drowning, you're in for a long stroll through hell in this competition. But you'll have to wait for a few more chapters in my book to hear about this miserable invention composed by drunken, sadistic Brothers! But I will say this, the winner, if one can be considered a winner, is rewarded by being dragged around an open field tied to a rope behind a Harley! I won't go into what happens to the losers right now, but like I said, no wonder Prospects always look so miserable!

The party rages on for three days! I try to remain anonymous, snaking through the crowd of Brothers, watching, learning, and Coppin' a view of the Hot-lookin' Women whenever possible! I watch some Brothers pound the fuck out of a Hang-around. Although curious, I keep my distance; it's a serious beating and none of my business. Bikers in this Club never administer a light beating. Once they start, the person receiving it is usually beaten almost to death. That's called a Thumpin'!

The party never really ends at any given time; it simply tapers off little by little until our farm is void of Harleys, Brothers, and the Hot-lookin' Women they surround themselves with.

Well, it's been three weeks since the big party, turns out it was the Club's National Run! Heavy-duty security was pulled during that one. It wasn't secure enough to prevent me from taking a few more hits to the head though. I broke my "Don't Drink" rule, only this time I didn't puke on a Harley—I knocked one over! It fell into another bike and almost created a chain reaction. This would have sealed my fate. But the Club's not stupid. Anytime hundreds of scooters are parked in a tight line side by side, they park one bike forward and the next one backward. This way the kickstands are on opposite sides of each bike, and a falling motorcycle must work harder at creating the Domino Effect. Anyhow, I survived! A few Brothers spent the weekend in jail and one was hospitalized from a bike crash, but all in all, the run was considered a great success. Cleanup sucked; some Prospects and I got that job.

Today is my birthday, and I'm fifteen years old. Earlier a Brother, Big Tony, came by and gave me a motorcycle! Can you believe it? Not a Harley, but who cares, it's mine! A Triumph, Bonneville 650! All it needs is a carburetor and cleaned up some. I haven't been able to get off it all day long! One of the Prospects said he had a Bonneville years ago and still has some parts he'll give me. He said he may even have the Amal Carburetors I need, new in the box! I have all winter to get this Bad Boy up and running. I'm gonna put it in my bedroom and begin rebuilding it tomorrow. I have boxes of parts in there already, some Harley and some Limey! Hidden in one box is a large-caliber handgun! A .45 automatic! I found it cleaning up after the National Run. I haven't heard anything about it and probably won't because it's a sin for a Brother to lose his gun! My brother, Kebus, has tons of .45 caliber ammo. While he's at work, I'm gonna take it out and fire it.

I was also given my first Cut-off. A Brother named Fingers gave me the jean jacket and showed me how to cut-off the collar and sleeves. Oh yeah, it's got to be a Levi and is. I have a bunch of pins, and some really cool patches and such Brothers have given me over the years, and have already begun decorating my Rag. Fingers is cool; I like him. He was given that name because his fingers were blown off in an explosion. Another Brother gave me a

Buck Knife with a locking blade. He said the knife is not the entire gift, it's what goes with it; he's also going to teach me how to Knife Fight! He was in "Special Forces" and said, "You'll need it when the Russians attack!" He always says that though. Once, when I was getting him a beer, I asked why he had so much beer. The shit was stacked to the ceiling. He told me, "I'll need it when the Russians attack! Won't be able to get any then." I'm not sure but I think he's just clowning around by saying that. Anyhow, so far I've done very well this birthday.

Well, even though it's my birthday, my older brother Kebus has me outside digging a long, narrow ditch. With beer in hand, he antagonistically yells to me, "Don't worry, Clutch, digging this ditch isn't your only birthday gift. I got another one even better than this!" Then he laughs insanely. I have no idea what he means by that, but I hope he's just fooling around. I've heard rumors he has spared no expense on my gift this year, so I'm eager to see what it is he has for me, but this ditch must come first!

I'm digging a ditch from where our long driveway meets the road to the house, and that's quite a distance. The house sits back from the road at least a third of a mile, and there is nothing but woods between it and the road. Our long drive gently snakes its way through the woods, past the house, all the way to an old run-down barn. There's a large turnaround area there and a few smaller outbuildings. The ditch I'm digging is for burying a cable that will be used to connect a closed circuit television camera Kebus recently acquired. He traded some Harley parts for it and this huge wooden spool of underground cable I'm now sitting on. We are going to hook up the camera and an intercom system from down at the Iron Gate to a monitor and two-way intercom speaker at the house. The Iron Gate has a security light and can be locked up tight, barricading our long driveway from the county road we live on. Very high tech for this day and age I must say. I'm very anxious to see how it's all going to work. It should be cool as hell. We'll now be able to watch any activity at the gate from our house, day or night.

I have a prospect here that's supposed to be helping, but he's done little of that! He treats me as if I'm his prospect. He orders me around and makes me do all the work. He slips off and sleeps in the woods whenever possible, and has me watching and warning him whenever Kebus comes around checking on our progress. This guy immediately jumps up and grabs a shovel, then pretends he's been working all along. That's okay, because the truth is Kebus has a wonderful birthday gift for me. It's just I do not get it until this camera and intercom are hooked up; I want to finish the job before nightfall, but that Prospect is definitely slowing down my progress.

I spend the better part of my day on the Ditch Project, but when it's finally done and I'm coming out of the shower heading for my bedroom, Kebus calls to me from the living room. "Clutch!" he sharply yells. "Get your ass in here. Now!" I quickly change paths and make my way to him! The only thing I'm wearing is a towel wrapped around my waist; with one fist clenched tight, I hold it together at my hip as I stand in front of my brother dripping wet, wondering what he wants.

"What's up, Kebus?" I ask. Kebus is kicked back in our comfortable recliner chair, his feet extended up and out. He's not wearing a shirt; his upper torso is rich with inked graffiti. On his right pectoral is a 1% tattooed inside a diamond-shaped geometric design, and on his other is the mysterious Death Head! His left shoulder adorns a beautiful tattoo of the Club's three piece patch, an arched Top Rocker, a Center Patch, and finally an arched Bottom Rocker! His forearms and stomach are lined with deep running scars received from a knife fight. They are testament he swore his allegiance to the Biker lifestyle many years ago; he's busting with muscles! Kebus is a huge, powerful man. He looks at me and stares emotionlessly for a long time, analyzing my development as his younger brother. I hate when he does this. I don't know if I'm going to receive a compliment or an Ass-Beating!

Finally he says, "Do me a favor, go out to my car and in the trunk is a box, bring it to me! But first, I need another cold beer!" He holds up the empty beer bottle he's been drinking from and rocks it back and forth as proof of its emptiness.

"Sure," I quietly say, unimpressed by the two new chores I've just been assigned. After fetching Kebus a cold beer, I slowly walk barefoot to his car still holding the wet towel around my waist. I'm not very motivated. The ditch has drained most of my energy. But when I get to his car and hear something moving around in the trunk, I immediately perk up. "Whata heck?" I pop the trunk lid open, and there is a pure-bred Rottweiler puppy staring up at me!

"Ahhhh . . . It's Beautiful!" I lean down and scoop this little girl up; she's licking all over my face! I struggle to hold both the squirming puppy and the towel, as I exuberantly turn to make my way back, I find Kebus is standing tall directly in my pathway!

In his deep voice he explains the rules, "That Clutch, is your new Best Friend. You have total responsibility for her. Feeding, watering, naming, everything. I will not tolerate any neglect from you when it comes to caring for this dog. I want her bathed and groomed regularly. I want her properly trained. If she ever Shits in the house, I'm not gonna rub her nose in it; instead, I'm gonna rub your nose in it!" Kebus slowly takes a swig off his beer, as his head tilts back his eyes never leave mine. One side of his mouth accommodating the beer bottle; the other accommodates a large smile! I pause for a brief second acknowledging Kebus's warning, knowing the threat is mostly in jest, that's just his way.

I smile then cheerfully say, "What a beautiful gift, Kebus, Thank You! I'm gonna call her Tikki!" I reach up to give my older brother a one-armed hug. I'm trying to hold the squirming puppy, the towel, and hug Kebus all at the same time, but it doesn't work out, and the towel drops to the ground, leaving me standing Bare-Ass naked!

When this happens, Kebus quickly jumps back one step and jokingly says, "Put that towel back on, you little faggot!"

Two years to the day have passed since Kebus gave me Tikki, it's my seventeenth Birthday. I have found a deep love for this dog; she follows me everywhere I go while I'm at home! She sleeps in my bedroom beside my bed while I sleep. While I shower, she lies just outside the bathroom door. And whenever I have one of my two limey motorcycles out riding, she will wait by the Iron Gate for my return, then follow me to the house by running alongside the bike. She'll then lie between the front tire and frame guarding it while I'm inside. She's a perfect dog, a great companion, and my "Best Friend!"

With the help of many Club Members, I have restored the Bonneville 650 Big Tony gave me on my birthday two years ago; I also picked up a Norton 750, Combat Commander! Fingers helped me acquire this bike; I make monthly payments to him for it and a complete set of "Whitworth" tools he sold me. This is a ten-and-a-half-second machine through the quarter mile. It has a ten over front end with Pull-Back Ram Horn type handlebars.

Although the bike has only been painted black by spray paint cans, all in all, it really doesn't look too bad. Fingers says the last thing we'll do after the bike is completely together the way I want, is tear it totally down, do some mold work, then give it a beautiful paint job. I'm running a Sportster tank and a Fishtail rear fender, there is no front fender! I mounted a small rigid solo seat that took its design from the original Harley "Buddy seat," with the chrome Hand Rail that borders its backside. The frame is somewhat stock, less the rake that's there to accommodate the ten over front end. Also the swing arm has been modified; with the help of a few Brothers, I have converted to stock Harley shocks and a stock seventeen inch Harley rear tire. I'm also running "Lake Fuel Injection!" My Carbs and intakes have been polished and sent out for a liquid oxygen treatment against scratches, compliments of Fingers. I took this bike to an amateur drag race and that's where I ran mid tens without the aid of a Wheelie Caster. Not bad, huh! Although, I must confess, the speed achieved by this machine is a Team Effort. Just about every member of the Chapter has donated in one form or another. With that being said, let me say this, that bike gets worked on even when I'm not around. Many times, when I come home from school, two or three Brothers will have it pulled out and will be drinking beer while turning wrenches!

But today when I get home my life is greatly changed for the worse. I am not greeted at the gate by Tikki and her usual Greeting Ritual. This is very concerning to me. When I reach the house, still no sign of her. I have a very bad feeling about this. "Where in the hell is Tikki?" I call and call as I walk endlessly throughout our property, "Tikki . . . Tikki . . . Come here, girl!" Finally I jump back on my Norton and begin riding up and down the county road we live on, looking and calling for her. About a mile from the house, I see our new neighbor standing in his driveway; he only moved in a month ago. I pull into his drive so I can introduce myself and ask if he's seen Tikki.

"Hello," I say as I climb off my 'Snort'in Norton!' This guy doesn't answer; just blankly stares at me as if I'm intruding. He tightly grips the Marlin thirty-thirty lever action rifle he holds. I stop for a brief second, analyzing the situation, then say, "I stopped to welcome you to the neighborhood, and also ask if you've seen a Rottweiler, she's two years old but still thinks she's a puppy!" I chuckle and grin, hoping to provoke a positive response from this obviously rude Farmer-Type individual.

This guy takes a couple steps back and assumes a defensive posture then boldly replies, "Yeah, I seen her, she's lying over there!" He points to a swampy area behind his mobile home!

"What?" I demandingly ask.

He says, "She's dead! . . . . I shot her!" At first I think he's only joking, but as I prepare to reprimand his lousy sense of humor, I realize he's serious! My heart sinks! About this time a Brother named Buttons is riding by on his Shovel Head. Seeing me, he pulls into the drive and slowly putts up to us. I'm now showing visual signs of distress.

I walk to Buttons, as he shuts off his machine I turn and blast out an angry threat to my new neighbor. "If you killed my dog, I'm gonna kill you!" Realizing there is a serious problem, Buttons immediately jumps off his bike and rapidly approaches this Punk.

Chest out, he demands, "Wat da fuck is goin' on, pal?"

Again this guy takes a step back, then boldly answers, "Nothing! I shot this kid's dog . . . . that's all!" Buttons stands shocked when hearing this. Like me, he too loves Tikki!

Buttons angrily leans toward this Punk and shouts, "You shot Tikki? Why!"

Showing no remorse, my new neighbor replies, "I'm not gonna stand here and discuss it any longer. If you want the dog, it's over there!" He once again points back at the swampy area.

It takes Buttons and me over an hour to collect Kebus and his truck then return and remove Tikki from the swamp where she so disrespectfully lay dead, and then back to our place where we bury her. I do it with tear-drenched eyes. During this entire process, I could see Buttons and Kebus ready to explode with violent anger, along with me. Kebus never spoke a single word the entire time. But as we were loading Tikki into the truck, I saw Kebus wave to the Neighbor Punk who was watching from his trailer window. As big as Kebus is, I was going to risk a punch in the gut by bitching at him for waving hello to this guy, right up to the point I realized he was not waving Hello . . . He was waving Good-Bye—and all that insinuates!

Tikki was a beautiful animal. She was full of life, love, and loyalty. She definitely was a member of our family, and no doubt, that's going to prove to be a major problem for this Farmer type who killed her, because our family is one hundred percent, a 1% Outlaw Motorcycle Club, and all that insinuates!

It's been a month since my Punk Neighbor murdered Tikki, even though I vowed vengeance. Both Kebus and Buttons have calmed retaliation by saying, "Vengeance is a dish best served on a platter Cold!" But tonight the Punk Farmer sacrifices himself to us. "Finally!"

I'm sitting in a bar not far from home, Papa-Dadieo's, where I work part-time cleaning up and stocking beer, when in staggers the dude that killed Tikki. He is about thirty years old, six feet tall, one hundred and eighty pounds, somewhat muscular, and drunk as hell. This guy is first-generation off the farm. And that's all he knows! He was raised by the Television and two parents that never made it past the third grade! His high school graduating class did not exceed over ten students, and they too were Farmer raised! Nothing against Farmers, but without any social skills, this one is rude and does not understand respect. His uneducated parents, although somewhat hardworking, learned early-on how to engineer Government Farm Subsidies to the point they became better skilled at filling out forms than agriculture itself. They never missed a meal! As the huge city grew, their government-bought farm became surrounded by housing developments and strip malls; the property value soared until it was valued well into the millions of dollars! Where their house and barn once stood, now sits a huge shopping mall. Now this punk lives off his aging parents' somewhat meager handouts while eagerly awaiting their death so he can collect the inheritance, "The Mother Load!" He gauges his daily accomplishments by the amount of money he scams from his parents—some days are better, others worse!

This bar he just entered into is a one hundred percent Biker bar, and generally frequented by Club Members, but that doesn't stop this drunk-ass Farmer type from staggering to the bar and loudly demanding a beer. He is cocky, arrogant, and very disrespectful. He obviously thinks he's much better than anyone here, and much tougher than he really is. He also believes Bikers to be lowlife characters, and weak punks. Well, it's time to educate him.

I pull my hat over my eyes and tip my head down as this drunken Piece of Shit passes me, zigzagging his way to the bar. I want to remain anonymous so he has no idea I'm here and plotting against him. Although just a kid, he knows I'm part of the Biker Clan he sees coming and going from our house.

This guy told another neighbor of ours, a good man and also a Farmer, he's not afraid of any Bikers. If need be, he'll shoot a Biker as easy as he shot Tikki. Now fueled by alcohol and the false feeling of confidence that has matured through the misconception he has escaped retribution for Killing Tikki. He stands challengingly, beer in hand, chest out, slowly panning his view around the bar, analyzing the clientele and smirking. His Beer Muscles are bulging; he's ready for action! In his drunken hick mind, he thinks by putting on a tough-guy act nobody will bother him, but in this bar, it's quite the opposite . . . Stupid Fuckin' Farmer!

With one hand holding the bar, he supports his drunken self as he stands weaving from side to side. Fearing he may fall, he eventually pulls a bar stool toward himself to sit, knocking over his beer in the process. Buttons quickly but nonchalantly slips into the booth where I sit.

He nods at my drunk neighbor then smiles and says, "Looks like Christmas just came early! Ready for some Payback, Clutch?" I'm so fucking mad right now I can't even enjoy the idea of Setting this guy up.

Impatient, I only want to stand and beat him to death. "Right here, right now!"

Buttons says, "Be cool, Clutch! We're gonna Take Care Of Business tonight, but it must be done right to avoid the law! So sit here and do as I tell ya, okay?" I collect myself, calmed in the trust that Buttons is a Hard Core 1% Outlaw Biker and a veteran to this kind of activity. Myself, this will be my first felony!

Buttons motions Big Tony over and quietly explains, "That's the guy who shot Tikki! Here's ten bucks. I'm gonna take Clutch and split. We're gonna arrange a little coming-home party for his drunk ass! Do me a favor, buy him some drinks and keep him here until I call ya. It shouldn't be over an hour! After I call, tell Papa to cut him off, then you nicely send him home, okay?" Big Tony pauses for a while, analyzing what was just said. Once understood, he grins and takes the ten-dollar bill.

Big Tony looks at me and says, "This night belongs to Tikki!" Just like the rest of us, he too loved her. He stands and slowly moves toward the Farmer Fuck. As he does, he turns and gives me a strong smile!

Big Tony is about six foot two and pushing near three hundred pounds. He has a long black ponytail with a full jet-black beard, and even though it's nighttime and the bar is dim, he still wears his dark wraparound shades. Although he's not wearing his Colors, with two buck knives strapped side by side on one hip, along with a chain wallet looped around the other hip, all held securely by a chrome Primary Chain belt, and arms busting with tattoo covered muscles, it's easy to peg him as a 1% Biker!

I've been around this Bike Club my entire life, but this is the first time I've ever seen them In Action. They're slick as hell, I'm impressed!

Big Tony sits down beside his intended target, smiles and pats him on the back, saying, "Howdy, wats ya drinkin' Partner?" As he does, Buttons softly motions for me to follow him outside. We anonymously slip through the exit door!

Once outside, Buttons anxiously says, "Let's go, Clutch!" We ride a hundred miles per hour straight back to my house and tell Kebus what's going on.

Kebus releases a sadistic smile and through punishing eyes looks directly at me then says, "Clutch, it's time to pop your Cherry! Tonight you're gonna witness the way we Take Care Of Business! You follow me and Buttons to that Punk's house and do exactly as you're told! After we're done, you and I must have a long talk, okay?"

I reply, "Kebus, I will do as you tell me and will never speak a word about it to anyone!"

Kebus growls, "You do, and you'll receive a little of the same!" He then hands Buttons a pair of gloves and a ball bat and says, "Make the call!"

Buttons calls Big Tony at the bar and says, "Party's over!"

Big Tony tells Papa, the bartender and owner, "Cut the Farmer off," then very politely helps the inebriated farmer to his car, saying, "Better head straight home. It was nice meeting ya, hurry back!"

The drunken Farmer thinks he just made a new friend and in a loud slur, thanks Big Tony . . . . Stupid Fuckin' Farmer!

The three of us walk to the neighbor's house; we all have black hooded ski masks, gloves, and ball bats! When we arrive, Kebus lifts me onto the roof and tells me to cut the phone line. This mobile home was purchased new and is one of the first offered with vaulted ceilings, so I tightly grip the edge of the roof with one hand as I carefully climb to the phone line. But just before cutting it, I'm briefly drawn away from my mission by the sound of crickets and the sight of lighting bugs. I pause and look around at this beautiful countryside. The weather is perfect, the sky is clear, displaying trillions of stars, a quarter moon proudly shines—it's Picture Perfect. A falling star streaks across the sky followed by a long glowing tail; an owl hoots in the distance. I turn and focus on the sound of many bullfrogs communicating in their deep voices; they're telling each other the swamp is free from predators. They too are enjoying this beautiful night. It's all somewhat relaxing until I return from this humble moment, remembering that's the same swamp we pulled Tikki from. I violently cut the phone line!

After the line is cut, we stand behind the house-trailer patiently waiting. I wonder what Kebus and Buttons have in mind for our up-and-coming attack. Are they planning to kill this guy? Or maybe beat him so badly he recovers as a retard? Maybe they won't beat him badly at all, just enough to teach him a lesson. I hope we beat him to Death!

The Farmer pulls in his drive; he's driving horribly! He staggers from his car mumbling, but when he tries to unlock his front door, he fumbles with the key until finally getting mad and busting the door open with his shoulder. He then falls onto the couch where he instantly passes out.

Kebus signals us to follow him; he moves slowly, crouched along the side of the trailer then looks through a window and finds the Farmer Fuck out like a lamp. Once he knows the Farmer is incapacitated, he stands tall and hurries into the living room where he presses me into a tight corner and motions for me to stay put. First, he and Buttons explore the entire trailer to be sure it is in fact empty. Next, they quietly lift the coffee table, moving it into the kitchen, giving full range of accessibility to the couch where the Farmer lies face up and loudly snoring. Now they return and stand shoulder to shoulder in front of their victim. Kebus slowly raises his ball bat high above his head then violently comes straight down with a mighty blow onto the Farmer's chest. Wham! One second later, Buttons does the same, striking a solid blow into the knee cap. Crack! I swear, it sounds like the bat hitting a tree trunk. Then Kebus returns another into the rib cage and then Buttons into the other knee cap. With each blow the Farmer lets out a loud moan, but this does not deter the two Bikers from unleashing their retribution, a continuous pounding, one after the next.

The beating lasts a long time. Crack! Pow! Boom! The sounds of bones crushing. I stand stunned, watching the two raising their bats then delivering powerful downswings. For a brief second, almost like a movie, it turns into slow motion for me. They look like two demons slowly dancing ritualistically over the Farmer while pulling life from his body, then converting it into energy and devouring it for themselves—A Satanic Feast.

When the two finally finish, Kebus turns to me.

Peeling off his black hood, he says, "It's your turn!" He's sweating and out of breath! Buttons is also sweating and out of breath. He steps back, opening a clear pathway to the now badly beaten, very bloody Farmer Fuck who is obviously unconscious but still moaning. I take a deep breath while searching my heart for the hatred it holds for this Farmer. Now focused on that, I waste no time stepping up to bat! But just before I land a Home Run Hit, Kebus grabs the bat held high above my head and quietly says, "Not in the head!" This guy looks bad, maybe even dead, but that doesn't stop me in the least! I reposition my intended swing and begin pounding one after the next into his arms, legs, and ribs! With every blow I think about Tikki and how I loved her and how I found her that day alone and dead in the swamp. Pow! Pow! Pow! I can't get enough! The rhythm of my swings is not as calculated and precise as were Buttons' and Kebus', rather fast and furious! I am still swinging away when Kebus finally stops me by once again grabbing the ball bat and holding it strongly with one hand!

I swear, I can do this all night long. "That miserable Piece of Farmer Dog Shit!"

Buttons and Kebus grab the near-dead Farmer by the arms and drag his badly beaten, blood-covered body out of the trailer, through the backyard and down to the mosquito-infested swamp where he's thrown into the stinky leach-filled water! Exactly where he left my girl Tikki.

As we walk home nobody speaks a word. I'm hoping the Farmer is dead! Kebus is hoping we didn't overdo it and kill the Farmer! And other than any legal implications, Buttons is indifferent.

We return home and throw the ball bats, our boots, and every bit of clothing we're wearing, less our skivvies, into a quick-made fire I build. Then one by one, we all shower!

While Buttons and I stand in our undies watching our clothes burn and Kebus is first in the shower, Buttons says to me, "Congratulations, Clutch, you just entered into a Brotherhood with me! What we did here tonight could land all of us in prison for a very long time. We now share that secret with each other. It's a Tight Bond we shall all take to the grave. This, Clutch, is what true trust is all about. Ten years from now nobody can ever tell me you are not to be trusted, because I'll always know what happened here tonight . . . as will you!"

I focus directly into Buttons' eyes and nod my head in agreement, assuring him I understand his mentorship, then pop my chest out and ironically say, "I wonder if that Piece of Shit will ever shoot another one of my dogs."

Buttons laughs and replies, "After tonight, I guarantee ya if he does, he won't be squeezing the trigger with his right hand! Coz I busted that one into many, many very small pieces!" I smile with pleasure.

The following day, Kebus tells me to fire up his Harley and bring it to the porch, along with one of my bikes. "We're going for a ride!" We pull onto the road and give our bikes hell. I know my Snortin' Norton will eat his Seventy-Four Inch Harley alive through the first quarter mile, but Kebus is impossible to keep up with in the corners, so I don't challenge him by Passing. Oh yeah, and the main reason I don't pass him is, he's flying his Colors! Kebus will not even allow me to ride side by side with him while he's Flying Colors. "It's a Biker thing!" I must always trail shortly behind, so passing him is out of the question anyhow.

We ride out to a National Forest where Kebus spends the better part of an hour coaching me on what we did to the Farmer Fuck. He says, "Clutch, understand this is exactly why you never call the cops on anyone for any reason. Had you called the cops on the Farmer for shooting Tikki, at best all he would have received is a smack on the wrist and you would have to finish the job in

Civil Court! If that didn't work out to your satisfaction and you ball-batted the Farmer Fuck anyhow, then the cops would have probable cause for a strong motive. Clutch, do not ever talk to anyone about anything you do. If you are ever questioned by the cops, don't say a word, call an attorney! I don't know if you will ever want to join our Motorcycle Club, but you'll never make it if you don't learn at a young age to keep your mouth shut! I'm your older brother, and I love you very much, but if you ever get us thrown in jail because you ran your mouth, you better hope we don't get locked in the same cell!"

Kebus always runs little threats on me, but they're usually followed by a slight grin or chuckle, but this time there is no smile, and he is too big to argue with. So I don't bother with reassurances. I just sit and listen and nod my head in agreement and keep my mouth shut.

A month has passed since the farmer's beating. I feel elevated in the presence of the Club now! I feel like the surrounding Members know I did something illegal, something Hard-Core, and I feel I'm being treated with a bit more Respect because of it.

Today as I rode past the Farmer Fuck's house trailer, I noticed a "For Sale" sign posted. "Huh . . . . imagine that!" Immediately following his beating, Kebus had a Club Mama from a distant Chapter send flowers to his hospital room; the bouquet consisted of two different color roses, exactly the same two colors that are the Club's Colors! Oh Yeah, and a 'Get Well Soon' card, ironically printed in those same two contrasting Colors. The card was signed, "Tikki."

CHAPTER TWO

PROSPECT

Bad news! Federal and local cops raided the Clubhouse in the city late last night. My brother Kebus is in County Jail awaiting arraignment along with several other members and affiliates. I'm eighteen years old now and a legal adult. Its mid-November 1972 and I'm still at the farm. If my brother goes to prison, I'll be able to stay out here. My house filled up with Full Patch Holders shortly after the raid. I'm still "Step and Fetch," but only if no prospects are around. Club business is only discussed during the meetings they call "Church." But tonight, a Summit Meeting, "Emergency Service," is to be held. I've been told to help with security and I gladly comply. This shows I'm greatly trusted by the Club—well, this Chapter of the Club. I use an electronic device that checks the house for hidden microphones—Bugs. What it does is look for radio waves, and everything checks out okay. Another problem is, whenever anybody talks indoors, their voice vibrates the glass windows of the house. The Feds have laser beams they shoot from great distances onto the glass. The laser will detect any vibrations from the voice, and a computer translates it back into speech. I turn music on loud so the speakers vibrate on the windows, masking our voices. It's all admissible in court. Might as well figure the Grand Jury sat down many moons ago and voted the Club's constitutional rights away.

It's funny because the early news reports are greatly exaggerated. I mean greatly! "Huge raid, hundreds of Bikers arrested! Guns, drugs, explosives!" . . . etc . . . etc . . . Mostly all bullshit! An FBI spokesman said they have seized many files and that the Club has more information about the police than the police have about the Club. Of course, there may be a small bit of truth to that one!

What the feds did was send in a pretty girl via one of the Club's bars. She had been Hanging Around for months, working as a bartender, Suckin' 'n' Fuckin'. Finally, one night she made it into the Clubhouse. Once inside, she claimed she was abused, Attempted Rape! A total lie, this is the same Cunt that Pulled Train on ten different Brothers one week earlier while lying on her back across a pool table in the back room of a Club bar. Now the cops have an open door to come through and do whatever they please. I swear the cops are no different from any other organized criminals. No one is going to believe the cops planted evidence that set up a Biker with a prior felony. Trust me, this is common. Some citizens may believe it happens, but accept it under the "You gotta fight fire with fire" rule! I wonder if the police know when to stop though. That same citizen may very well be next. Anyhow, now that they have raided the Clubhouse, no telling what high-tech listening devices were planted. That could be the entire reason for the raid. For sure, that Clubhouse is through.

At the meeting, I was called in and asked about my brother's finances, which made me very suspicious. My brother is President of this Chapter and I know they have plenty of bail money. What possible charges could he have received for the Club to think they may not be able to afford his bail? After the meeting, "After Church," Fingers told me I am the only nonmember that has ever been in a Club Meeting, ever. Even though it was only for a small portion of the meeting, it tells me I'm being accepted as a part of this organization. If I prospect, I think it may go easier for me because I was born and raised by the Club. I say born because my biological father was one of the earliest members. He was murdered when I was very young. I have a poster of him hanging on my wall. He's wearing his Colors and standing beside his 47 Knuckle Head, arms crossed and looking very mean. He was a Korean War Vet and a decorated War Hero. Korean War Vets got the same kind of Fuckin' the Vietnam Vets received from the U.S. Government! There weren't many Ticker Tape Parades for either of those War Vets!

A year has passed since the police raid on the Clubhouse. It's early winter 1973; my older brother was set up by false evidence collected and sentenced to life for a murder he didn't commit. The

Kennedys get away with murder. Bikers don't, even when innocent of the Deed! He is still in the appeal process, and we hope to see his release soon. Oh yeah, that Clubhouse mysteriously burned down shortly after the raid.

Today I'm as nervous as a long-tailed cat in a room full of rocking chairs. I told the Club's Vice President, Crusher, I wanted Club Colors! The entire Chapter is in Church now, voting on whether or not to let me prospect. I guess I always knew I would, but was reluctant. I've seen what happens to Prospects! I feel as if I've been groomed for this my entire life and could never be a whole man without a Patch. Shit, is it possible they could turn me down? I guess I never considered that possibility! I don't know why they would, I'm a pretty tough guy, and loyal to the Club. However, being tough is not enough; it requires discipline, intelligence, emotional fortitude, and the ability to commit your entire life to the Club without exception. There are members that have died. There are members that have gone to jail for life. If you are not prepared to risk that and give it all, 110 percent, then stay home!

I thought this was a good time for me to enter the Club—well, prospect for the Club—because lately I've had numerous negative encounters with members from other Chapters. I don't want politics to drive a wedge between me and the organization, splitting apart the only thing I love. Many of the older members are gone now, and I don't know many of the newer ones. At one time, there was a huge age difference between me and most of the members. Now at nineteen years old that difference is less obvious. I detect jealousy from many Prospects these days. There's one Prospect, Brock, which had me pissed-off enough to kill! Doing a Hit on a Prospect isn't a good idea, and I never would. I will say this however; if he doesn't make it into the Club, that son of a bitch is mine.

I picked up a '65 Pan Head a year or so ago; it's a Police Special. The last three years of the Panhead are 1963, '64, and '65. They are the only Panheads with overhead oilers. My '65 is cool because it's the first year with an electric start and it also kept the kick start. For the most part, this bike is a stock Duo-Glide, but since Harley Davidson gave it an electric start and a twelve-volt charging system, they renamed that model the Electra Glide. Therefore, my 1965 Panhead is the first year Harley Davidson introduced the model Electra Glide, and this model will live on forever. I have kept the bike stock, less a custom paint job. I gave it a cop theme; there has been airbrushed along its front fender, tank, and rear fender a highway scene that depicts police cruisers giving chase to Brothers on Harleys, all flying Colors! I had to get permission from the Club to put a small, no detailed version of the Club's Patch on the back of each rider. You pretty much can't see the name, Center Patch or Bottom Rocker, but the two colors are right! Anybody in the know has to know what Club is being represented in this paint job. A Brother in this Chapter, Buttons, painted it and he did an excellent job. Every Member of this Club that sees my bike loves it. I think it's not only because of the beautiful paint job Buttons achieved, but also, they can all relate to the paint job's theme of Brothers being chased by the cops. Not to mention, it's simply a beautiful scooter. The pink slip is in my pocket ready to sign over to the Club. No problem, I'll be getting it back along with my Top Rocker soon enough. I'll sign it over, but still hold possession of the scooter. In fact, while prospecting, my only allowed means of transportation will be my bike. No matter how cold, no matter how hard it rains, no matter what the season, I ride. Therefore, I better be able to keep my Putt running.

Well, Church has ended and my bike is signed over to the Club, temporarily, and I'm now "A Prospect." My first Patch is small and to be worn above the left pocket of my Rag. It obviously reads "Prospect." However, it's my first Patch, and I like it. All my pins and such had to be removed; only Club Patches can be on your Cut off while prospecting. I think that's a dumb rule, but the truth is, it's there to protect the Prospect, because a Brother has the right to take just about anything he wants away from a prospect, even a treasured decorative pin displayed on his Colors!

Well, it's already started. A member of the Chapter that dislikes you the most will be assigned as your sponsor. Your sponsor is your Mentor, your Go-Between to work between you and the Club whenever there's a problem. In most cases, by the time a prospect gets his Top Rocker, his sponsor is his closest Brother, but it never begins that way! The gig is, the Club will do whatever it can to try to make me quit while finding my Breaking Point.

My new Sponsor has only been in the Club a few years, and has only been with this Chapter half of that. He "Patched Over" from another Club that was affiliated for many, many years. Patched

Over means he willingly traded his Colors from the Club he first belonged to for our Patch; he never had to Prospect for this Club! But you can bet your bottom dollar, he earned it. This guy is a retired Special Forces Team Member; he served Active Combat in Vietnam for many years! He is huge, and mean as hell.

I don't think this guy likes anybody; for the year or so that I've known him, today's the first time he ever spoke to me. After Church, I traded my bike title for the Prospect Patch and the Vice President told me Hillbilly is my Sponsor. "Oh boy, Hillbilly!" Hillbilly walked me outside alone and said he didn't want to be my Sponsor and that he argued hard not to be, but now that he is, I should make it easy on myself and quit. I made the mistake of rebutting his statement by telling him, "Maybe you're the one that should quit!" He immediately pushed me up against the outside wall of the Clubhouse, held my throat with his left hand, and put a knife to my eye with his right hand.

He warned, "If you ever speak to me again, I'll cut out your eyeball!"

The Club likes to put Prospects in a 'Trick Bag,' so you're damned if you do and damned if you don't, to see how you respond. Now I'm in a huge Trick Bag. I can't even talk to my Sponsor!

"Fuck! Nobody is gonna make me quit!" This is where I belong; it's all I've ever known! The Club is about Brotherhood, its family, its love for your Brothers, but right now, I'm a little confused on that issue. Of course, I'm not a Brother yet! I can usually see through their games. Problem is, I don't think Hillbilly is playing one. He is just one big mean Motherfucker, and it's easy to believe he hates everything and almost everyone. Oh yeah, he wears the Death Head Patch!

Hillbilly came from the same Chapter that Prospect Brock is prospecting for. That's the Chapter he originally Patched Over to, and Prospect Brock is the one I hate. Hillbilly may not talk much, but you can bet he knows exactly what's going on between Brock and me. You can also bet Hillbilly and the rest of the Club will be pitting Brock and me every chance they get. When two Prospects feud, one must hope the other doesn't get his Top Rocker first, because then he'll have the power! Although I know I never will, I do enjoy plotting Brock's murder. Just contemplating it makes me feel better. That would be against everything the Club is about.

If I did kill him however, and the Club found out, for sure I'd go next.

The biggest thing Brock has going for himself is his Ol' Lady, Nikkei. She is beautiful. I mean a stone-cold fox! Not to mention her father was in the Club, and like me, she too was raised by it. That's probably the single biggest thing I hate about Brock, the fact that he has her. She is about one year younger than me, and I think I'm in love with her. Maybe not 100 percent in love, but for sure, I'm intoxicated by her looks. Dark hair, dark eyes, sort of Hispanic looking, nice skin tone with a perfect body and a gorgeous ass. She looks so good in tight blue jeans and a black leather jacket. I see her dressed casually that way, her beautiful dark hair, long and flowing, capturing her sexy broad shoulders, knowing that she has put forth no effort toward that look, her beauty just comes naturally. I have no defense against her. She makes me Cream My Jeans. God, I do love her.

Her father and my father grew up together. They both served in the Korean War and they started these two Chapters. They're legends in this Club. They were both murdered by a rival club while riding their Harleys side by side, screaming down the highway, machine gunned off their bikes by cowards shooting from a passing car. She and I always shared that connection, a powerful bond between us.

Nikkei and I got along great up until Brock. He has done all he can to turn her against me. Before Brock, I used to see her all the time. Once she and I were drinking together at a Biker swap meet. She pulled her pants down to her ankles and exposed that perfect ass. She was wearing Club thongs! God, she looked good! Anyhow, with a felt marking pen I wrote "Property of Clutch" on her ass cheek! Just doing that gave me a three-hour woody! For the rest of that day, anytime someone would flirt with her, male or female, she would pull her pants down just far enough to expose the writing on her ass and say, "Sorry, I belong to Clutch!" What a turn on! The entire time I was growing up, I always felt like someday she would belong to me and me to the Club. But right now, in order to fulfill that dream, I must concentrate on prospecting and receiving my Top Rocker, and then I'll concentrate on getting Nikkei.

Prospecting sucks! The days go by very slowly, as do the hours, minutes, and seconds! I've been prospecting for six months now, and I must say there's nothing about it I like. Initially, I thought it might go easier on me because of who I am. Bull fucking shit! This is bad, I mean really, really bad! "And I'm not Sniveling, so Shut the Fuck Up!" All I can say is, "No way I'm Quitting!" Problem is, I'm just getting started. This could last for a couple of more years! "Two more years, fuck!" I'm not sure I can handle two more years of this shit! At one time, my bike was top priority in my life. It meant everything to me! Now it's not even in the equation. We steal so many, they're so easy to come by, and from all the tricks I've learned from the Club, I could replace my scooter in a week's time! Other than a really bad Thumpin' and the loss of my bike, I could be out of this shit and a free man in one day, a Loner again. What I mean to say is, giving up my scooter no longer means anything to me. It's just a possession. Giving up the Club means everything. It's my life and I will not quit!

After a Prospect receives his Top Rocker and is now a Brother, the Club has been known to 'Pull His Patch' if he fucks-up bad enough. That means they physically cut or tear the Top Rocker off his Colors! This generally comes with a heavy-duty ass kicking because nobody gives up their Patch easily after all this. They'll fight until beaten unconscious! Once the Patch has been 'Pulled' he's a Prospect again.

"Well, fuck that! I'd rather be dead! Or fuck me, anyone will die trying to Pull My Patch!" I'll just follow Club rules and hold onto my Colors with both hands!

Sorry about all the exclamation points, but right now my blood is running hot. I just had a Brother, a drunken Brother, pull a knife on me and slice twenty-five stitches worth of cut into my right forearm. It was obviously a defensive wound, yet the hospital patched me up, accepting my lame explanation, "I fell on a sharp piece of metal!" Yeah, right. The reason he was so pissed-off was, I took the rhythm from a top forty song and changed the lyrics to my own liking and own design. The new song, my song, went like this: "The whole . . . world . . . sucks, my dick!"

I was not even singing loudly when the Brother got square in my face and said, "Motherfucker, I never sucked your dick!"

With all my wisdom and diplomacy, I simply replied, "Well, don't be impatient honey, I'll make time for ya" as I reached for the zipper on my Levi's and slowly unzipped them. I was only joking around but that was all it took. Out came the knife and El'Sliceo! Luckily, I moved fast in this crisis situation, only receiving twenty-five stitches in the arm! It could have been twenty-five stitches in the neck! Ouch! Oh well, needless to say, he just made 'The List.' Problem is, I'm beginning to think the entire Club is going to be on that List before this whole prospect thing is over!

Once again, I can't say anything about it to anyone or I'll either be Sniveling or Snitching!

The truth is, I'm not really thinking of quitting. It's just I'm really pissed-off over the twenty-five stitches I received. The Club is always running games on prospects. Once the Brother that cut me sobers up, his game will be sending people to me asking what happened to my arm. Then they'll report back on whether or not I'm snitching or sniveling on or about him! But I'm ready for it, I'll just tell them the same story I told the hospital.

It's late Saturday morning on this beautiful sunny April day, 1974. The temperature is high, humidity low, and the sky is clear and blue. I'm at the Clubhouse doing my Prospecting thing; running full blast to fetch beer for Brothers, lighting cigarettes, and being made to do push-ups.

Suddenly Hillbilly yells to me, "Prospect! Come!" I snap to attention and sprint to him. I don't want to explain the cut on my arm so I'm wearing a long-sleeved shirt in this early spring heat. I get to him fast—I have to. Prospects can't dillydally, they must run full bore everywhere they go! He's standing with Crusher behind a 1968 Ford Mustang; the trunk lid is open. Hillbilly ask me if I'm claustrophobic; I nod my head yes. He tells me to watch carefully because he'll only show me this once. He points to the trunk lid's interlocking mechanism and shows me how to unlock it from the inside. As soon as he does, Crusher puts his hands behind his back and then turns around. Hillbilly produces a pair of handcuffs and cuffs Crusher! With Hillbilly's help, Crusher climbs into the trunk and Hillbilly closes the lid!

Although Crusher's time in the trunk is not monitored, he could not have been in there for more than a minute when the trunk lid opens and he climbs out, unhandcuffed! Hillbilly says, "Not bad, Crusher, you may have beaten your own record!" He then turns to me and strengthens his tone.

"Clutch," he says, "You must learn to overcome your claustrophobia. There could come a day your life depends on it! I first want you to learn to escape from the trunk. Then second, you must learn to escape from the trunk handcuffed. Are you ready for round 1?" I can't answer aloud because I'm still not permitted to speak to him. Therefore, I just nod yes and reluctantly climb into the trunk. God, I hate that big Mother Fucker and this small dark trunk I'm in! Hillbilly always says in order to overcome a bad situation, you must take your mind totally to another place, one that is pleasant to you, and give it 100 percent focus. So I'm thinking of sex! However, that does not completely take my mind off being in this small, dark, dirty and claustrophobic coffin of a place! One thing for sure, I must have my Top Rocker. So I must do exactly as I'm told, and if I freak out, they may give me the Boot instead of a Patch. I will have no problem killing Hillbilly for putting me in this trunk if I become trapped for any period of time. That anger spawns the desire to beat this Big Mother Fucker! I won't give him the satisfaction of freaking out. "Fuck him!" The only thing I'll give that Fucker is a bullet. Fueled by this growing anger toward Hillbilly, I get busy and concentrate on the latch and what he showed me only moments ago. Suddenly the lid opens! Ahh, fresh air! That really wasn't very hard at all.

Hillbilly says, "Good job, Prospect, now do it again!" as he slams the lid shut, almost hitting my head. This time it was easy and I open the lid in half the time it originally took. Once again, immediately after I open the lid, Hillbilly slams it shut and says, "Now do it again, Prospect!" This time I open the trunk even faster! Now Hillbilly says, "Get out of the trunk, Prospect. The next time you go in, you'll be wearing handcuffs!" That struck deep fear into my heart. I hate being confined in small spaces. In addition, I hate having my hands bound; now Hillbilly's suggesting both! I already decided, Club or no Club, if that Big Mother Fucker traps me inside a car trunk, he better hope I die in there. Because if and when I get out, he's dead!

Hillbilly says, "Prospect, you go with Crusher. He has something to show you!" He then starts his Harley and rides off.

Crusher and I go into the Clubhouse. I am relieved Hillbilly has left; well, actually I'm ecstatic with joy. We sit alone in the kitchen and Crusher says, "Here's an old Biker trick!" He removes his Colors and shows me at the bottom, near the middle inside of his rag, is a small incision along the seam. Inside of that is sewn a Smith & Wesson handcuff key which is exactly what the cops use! I stare speechlessly. Here I thought when he escaped from the trunk, he was wearing trick handcuffs.

Crusher shows me how to sew the key into my Colors. As he does, he explains that few people, cops or our enemies, are looking for this. But only use it to save your life or the life of a Brother, and practice until I can get out of cuffs as fast as him! He said I must learn to open all trunk lids, to always be examining any new locking mechanism. He also tells me the handcuff key in the back of my Colors will not do me any good if my hands are cuffed in the front.

He says, "The way to avoid that is to act somewhat threatening, and the cops will always cuff your hands behind your back!" Crusher was being extremely accommodating; he was also coaching me on my relationship with Hillbilly. He says, "Clutch, I could see your anger, almost hate in your eyes towards Hillbilly when he ordered you into the trunk. Listen to me, he likes you. He sees himself in you fifteen years ago. That guy has big plans for you, Clutch, so stick it out with him. He's planning on forging you into one of our top Brothers. So when he's extra tough on you, remember, that's why!"

What a cool trick Crusher just showed me! I'm pleased I'm trusted enough to be shown this possible life-saving secret! I'm confident through practice I can overcome my claustrophobic fears and become as fast as Crusher is at getting out of handcuffs. As far as killing Hillbilly goes, I was wrong to feel that way. I should be thanking him for teaching me these Old Biker Tricks. I hope that he has many more to share with me. He has already shown me many different things I never considered, and they will all make me a better man and Biker. Therefore, I know it's wrong to fantasize about killing him, but he fucks with me so badly, the idea of murdering him just comes natural!

As a prospect, I must run full speed everywhere I go when asked to do something by a Brother. If a Brother asks—well, demands a beer—then I must sprint to the cooler, grab a beer, and sprint back, careful not to shake it up, open it, and then respectfully hand it to him. Same thing with food, cigarettes, drinks, anything. A prospect always carries a few lighters with him; he never lets a Brother light his own cigarette. Never. Can you imagine a three-day party, with hundreds upon hundreds of Brothers, what a prospect must go through? I'm not sniveling, only explaining. For three days a prospect will never sleep, he runs everywhere he goes, fetching beers and lighting cigarettes. Anytime he's too slow or fucks up in any way he's ordered to do push-ups, or worse, receives a punch to the chops!

Then there are the head games, and oh my God, they never end, and a prospect must stay on top of them. He must do anything asked by any Brother, but what does he do when asked to do something by two different Brothers that totally conflict with each other? Uh-oh, he just entered into a Trick Bag. So he's damned if he does and damned if he doesn't! A Brother generally wears his name above the right pocket of his Colors, and if he is an officer, that title will be displayed above his left pocket. Each Chapter has four officers, President, Vice President, Sergeant at Arms, and Secretary Treasurer. Just like the military, one must follow the chain of command. If the Trick Bag a prospect is in consists of being told to do two different things by two different Brothers and one of them is an officer, a President, then that's who he must follow! Problem is, he just pissed off the other Brother.

Example: a Brother, who is a President named Giggles, demands, "Prospect, bring me a beer!" So the prospect sprints to the cooler.

But when he gets there, a Brother standing beside the cooler, who's not an officer, says, "Beer's gone, Prospect!" As he puts his foot on top of the cooler's lid! Now what the fuck does the prospect do, call him a liar by trying to lift the lid to get a beer? . . . Good luck!

Or maybe go back empty-handed and tell that President "Beer's gone,"! Once again, good luck! Remember, it doesn't take much to receive a hard punch to the gut, or worse, one to the snout! Either of those could happen in this Trick Bag. Problem is, he knows there's plenty of beer in that cooler because the Brother that told him it was empty, said it just after reaching in and taking one out for himself. Diplomacy will not completely solve this problem, but when this exact scenario happened to me.

I simply said, "I know the beer's gone, but it must only be gone for me, because I was sent by Giggles and he told me there's plenty of beer here for him as long as I give you this." I pulled a joint out of my pocket, lit it, and passed it to him.

He puffed it a few times then removed his foot from the cooler and said, "Okay, Prospect, help yourself." Now that may not seem too tough, but had I not convinced him to allow me a beer, I would have had to answer to the entire Club as to why I'm asked by a President for a beer and return empty-handed. Ass-Kicking Time!

For three days, these kinds of games never end. Some are easier than others, some are almost impossible to get through. One Brother tells you to stay and another tells you to go. One says do it, and another says don't do it! After three days, you're going nuts, ready to totally flip out. If anyone of them sees your frustration, they will always default to the formula statement, "If you don't like it, Prospect, quit!"

Here's a common game the Club will run on a prospect. One Brother gives him a beer, and it would be an insult not to drink it. By the way, one insult equals one ass kicking.

Then another Brother says, "Oh, you'll drink with him but not me, huh?" Well, down goes another beer. This goes on all weekend long, and the worst thing a prospect can do is to find himself drunk. Oh boy, that would be bad for him.

Then the Club would be asking his sponsor, "Wat Da Fuck?" All the beer, absolutely no sleep and running everywhere he goes; then on Monday, back to work and having to perform.

"It sucks!" However, that's a typical weekend, and an easy weekend. A prospect must really want that Patch, because the Harley he'll lose by quitting doesn't seem all that important now, but that's really simple shit as far as the games go. The trick to beating that game is learn to pretend you're drinking, but dump out as much as you can as often as you can, without detection.

They run the drinking game on prospects because that's exactly what an enemy will do; he'll fuck you up via a bottle of rum served by a sweet-looking female. Once drunk, or passed out, you become an easy mark. Next, you wake up in the hospital, or wearing handcuffs, duct taped to a chair in a dark, wet basement, kidnapped. Or worse, you don't wake up at all. A Brother must always watch for any outsiders, male or female, who insist he drinks more than just a few!

The games it seems never end; there are thousands of them. A Prospect will advance from no more than a 'Prospect Patch' to that plus his 'Bottom Rocker.' Then those two, plus a 'Center

Patch,' and then finally the Prospect patch is removed and a 'Top Rocker' is added. Now he has a three-patched vest! Well, as he advances, the games also advance; they increase in their intensity. At first, they are somewhat petty and designed to introduce Club methods. However, after a Prospect receives his Center Patch, the smaller games go away for the most part, but they are replaced with much tougher ones! Games that are introduced as tests, tests of his manhood, his honor, and his loyalty. They will test his bravery, his ability to think clearly after two or three days without sleep while drinking, snorting, and running everywhere he goes! Games that are designed to find out if he's working for the Feds or another Club. Many of these games are of a life-or-death nature, and most are impossible to detect.

Not all the games played are designed to fuck with a Prospect in the attempt to find his Breaking Point or to see if he'll Quit. Some are orchestrated to teach a Prospect what to watch for by the Club's enemies. When a man puts on a Patch, he puts on a target! One must be smart and streetwise to the games not just the cops play, but also his enemies. And an Outlaw Motorcycle Club has many enemies.

Speaking of enemies, our Club is at war with another Club. Yep, it happened about two weeks ago. I'll get into that in my next chapter, but for now all I can say is if I bring my Club one of our enemy's Colors, I get my Top Rocker free. When I say bring my Club an enemy's Colors, what I'm really saying is first I must kill him! Then cut his Colors from his body! I've already been shown how to remove the Colors. You cut the Rag on both sides above the dude's shoulders from the neck opening to the opening of the arms. Then off they come, quick and easy! Quicker than skinning a snake. So guess how I spend most of my spare time? Yep, I'm out hunting! I'd do anything to have my Top Rocker and not have to prospect, and I do mean anything!

I know a cute little girl, Cindy, who has been to the house of a member of the club we are at war with. She says the Dude wants to fuck her very much. That has Set-Up written all over it! Now I just have to figure, am I using her to set him up, or is he using her to set me up? It's dangerous; this is life or death, you gotta be smart. Number 1, we are at war so I must follow any lead I can for the Club. Number 2, there may be a Patch in it for me. Either way, I'll work hard toward killing this punk. It would be easier if I had more free time and help from my Club, but I don't want to tell them that. I'm afraid if ordered to make the Hit, it will be considered prospecting and I may not receive my Top Rocker.

I got Cindy's roommate Nancy helping me also. I've been fucking them both for years; Cindy will do anything I say. In fact, Cindy, Nancy, and I have many threesomes together. Yeah, I go over there and whichever one is home, I fuck! If they're both home, I fuck 'em both! Of course, Cindy doesn't know Nancy is helping. It's kind of covert that way, but that's working out well. It's easier to cipher the truth with one watching the other then reporting back to me. Of course, neither one can know the real reason for their help. The best way, and how I'm trying to work it, is neither girl knows she's being used for any reason. After the Hit, the cops will figure it came from our Club, but done right, the girls won't have a clue.

The cops would be very happy if they could see two birds killed with one stone. One Biker dead and the other doing life for it. Oh, they'd love that! We are always under the microscope. The cops want to know all they can about us. So obviously, I must be extremely careful, but the truth is, this Hit can and will be done by me alone. Patch!

At this point, no one knows we're at war. Both Clubs want to keep it that way so the cops stay back and we can move freely against each other. We both know eventually it will get back to the cops. When it does, they will be watching prospects very closely, more so than any of the members. Prospects are used as a buffer between Club members and the law; they always do the dirty work. So in that respect, this is a very good time for me. If I can make this Hit, I'll be in the Club before the 'Shit Hits the Fan,' sort of speak.

There is a federal agency contrived and solely dedicated to the removal of all Outlaw Bike Clubs. Maybe you've heard of them—BET. That's an acronym for Biker Enforcement Team. They are a Task Force from the ATF. I will definitely be talking more about these Fuck Sticks. They were put together a couple years back over a war between two clubs. The truth is they were instrumental in starting that war. They call it, "Stirring the Pot." Oh yeah, they go to one club and give out the legal names and addresses of their rival club members, then go to the other club and do the same. Stirring the Pot! These people are dirty! It's funny because they say the reason they're so dirty is because we're so dirty, and one must fight fire with fire! And we say, the reason we're so dirty is because they're so dirty. When our own government is doing it, why can't we? It's a cyclic dilemma.

You know, "What came first, the chicken or the egg?"

Now that we're at war, one of my jobs as a prospect is to start all the members' cars. This way, if the car has been wired with a bomb, I blow up, not a valued Patch Holder. I've learned a few Biker Tricks along the way to try and protect myself. One I use quite frequently is I rub a small strip of Scotch Tape across the hood of the car where it meets the front fender, half on the hood and half on the fender. If the hood has been raised, the tape will be torn, indicating the car has been tampered with. A thin strip of clear tape is almost impossible to detect unless one knows it's there! And if an assassin is planting a bomb in that vehicle, I don't want him to know the tape is there or he may find a different location to plant the device.

When a Brother's car is initially parked, I put tape on it. Then before starting the vehicle when he returns to leave, I check to see if the tape has been torn. If it has, I know the hood has been opened, so I carefully check to find out why. I also tape along the doors. One problem though, if the car is dirty the tape will not stick well, and if I clean an area for the tape, it becomes obvious because of the contrast, little clean spots on an entirely dirty car. So if the car is extremely dirty, I will not use tape. I use a single match from a paper matchbook. I fold the match in half and gently slide it into the small space between the hood and fender, same as the doors. Problem with that technique is the match does not always hold securely, a heavy wind could blow it away. When I return to the vehicle to start its motor, if the match is missing, I must determine if it's a false reading from a loose-fitting match or someone has opened the hood. This is life or death, so for my sake, I must read it correctly.

Brothers from up north tell me during winter in the freezing cold, tape will never stick to a car's hood or doors. An excellent system to compensate for this problem is a thin piece of clear monofilament fishing line held on either side of the hood or doors by a single droplet of water delivered from an eyedropper. The water will immediately freeze, securely holding the fishing line.

In addition, I always lie on my back and wiggle beneath the car looking for bombs, even if it's parked over a puddle of water!

Then finally, when I do start the car, I leave all the doors open and as much of my body as possible outside of the car. Unless I need to pump the gas pedal to start the vehicle, I'll always stand outside the car and lean in. This way, if a bomb detonates, the doors being open will lessen the pressure of the explosion inside the car's compartment. Obviously, the farther my body is from the car, the better. If I need to give the motor some gas to start it, I always leave at least one leg out of the car. However, there have been times when I'm so fucking beat up and tired from Prospecting, I don't exercise any of the above precautions.

I simply close my eyes and start the car, saying, "Fuck It!"

CHAPTER THREE

GRAVEYARD RUN

Not to move too quickly away from the war we're now involved in with another Outlaw Club or our ongoing problem with the cops, I'll tell you what just happened and you'll see how the battle with both has escalated.

Last weekend our Club went on a Graveyard Run. This is when twenty or more Chapters meet up and ride to the burial site of a fallen Brother to pay respect. Last weekend was Rudy's first death anniversary. Approximately four hundred Club members and affiliates surprised Rudy's small hometown about five hours from here. We all rode to the cemetery. The prospects clean his headstone, mega amounts of beer is consumed, and lastly, it's all followed by the Brothers firing their guns into the air! Cops hate it, but they know it would be very ugly to interfere. After the graveyard, everyone rides into town and fill up the bars, then to Rudy's house where his wife and kids reside to spend the night. So that's a brief rundown of the weekend's itinerary. Now, let me give you the, "Rest of the story!"

It started for me Friday afternoon. I was coming home from work about four o'clock, I pulled down my long driveway and guess who was standing on my porch? If you guessed Hillbilly, you guessed right. Fuck! I was thinking. Now what? I still can't speak to him although there are times I feel a Fuck You or a Fuck Off is in order. Anyhow, there was a half dozen or so other Top Rockers standing around the porch with him, mostly all from my Chapter. I slowly shut off my Harley and climbed from the bike carefully surveying the situation; all their eyes were upon me.

Hillbilly, in his typically hateful tone, bellowed out, "Prospect Clutch, follow me!" He waved his right arm in a circular motion as he walked from the porch, directing me to the spacious unmown backyard. I trailed behind him followed by all the Brothers. I'm thinking, Shit, I've done nothing wrong, but it looks like for whatever reason they think I have! I figured I was gonna receive some sort of Ass-Kickin' or something. Starting with his back to me, Hillbilly slowly turned, making visible a Bottom Rocker held in his left hand. This big son of a bitch gave me a shit-eating grin and said, "Come and get it . . . Prospect!" I know the way it goes; you must fight for it. You have to physically take it from your Sponsor. I didn't even hesitate, I just went for it. I ran directly at him, and in a half-wrestling, half-football tackle, I hit him at waist level. To my disbelief, I knocked this big Fucker down! That did as much for my adrenaline rush as seeing my Bottom Rocker! We wrestled around for a while. At one point, I must have been losing my mind in anger or maybe it was the frustration of trying to take my Rocker from Godzilla. Either way, all I remember is briefly catching the glance of the Vice President as I was being flipped; he was clearly warning, "Don't hit him, Prospect!" I must have been making it obvious I was thinking of punching Hillbilly. Understand, prospects can't hit Brothers for any reason, in any situation. Finally, I got hold of the Rocker and stood up as fast as I could. I backed up looking at this thing of beauty. Holding it up with both hands, I wiped the sweat and blood from my eyes with my forearms. With my legs spread wide, I raised it high into the sky, the sun's rays bursting from around it.

I let out an endless yell that could be heard for miles, "FUCKIN AAAA!" One by one the Brothers patted my back and shook my hand, congratulating me. It's impossible to explain the emotion I experienced at that moment.

And then in complete out-of-character behavior, Hillbilly gave me a hug and said, "Sew it on your Rag, get your Harley, and meet me at the bar in one hour . . . . Prospect." I gave him an understanding nod yes and headed for the house to sew on my new Rocker. I was practically running!

The bar I was summoned to is named Papa-Dadieo's; it's twenty minutes outside of this small town and one of our Chapter's regular watering holes. As I wheel in, I see my Sponsor's bike

already there. It is backed up to the outside wall directly in front
of a large window and under an outside security light, making it
visible from both inside and outside the bar. This place is a kind of
back-woodsie-type dive bar, you know a, beat'em-up joint. I backed
my bike in beside his, shut it off, and cautiously entered the bar. It
was so fucking cool flying my Rag with a Rocker. My dick was hard
and I was walking ten feet tall.

Hillbilly and I sat at a small round table in the back corner of
the dimly lit bar, both our backs to the wall. He told me I had the
rest of the day off. "Day Off" in Biker terms, means a prospect
can party and behave as if he is a Full Patch Member. A Brother.
And when in public, a Brother is never wrong! Any other Brothers
present, no matter what he says or does, must defend him to the
death. So I can say what I want to whomever I want, even Hillbilly,
Providing it's done respectfully to him. Some prospects have been
known to go crazy during their Day Off. I've heard the stories.
Only one very large problem exists, the next day they're a prospect
again! Oops, hope they didn't piss off too many members during
their drunken craziness. I already decided on my way to the bar
if Hillbilly gives me a Day Off, which generally follows receiving a
Rocker, I'm going to stay sober.

Now as an acting Brother I can speak to Hillbilly and say
anything I want. He and I sat in that bar together all night long; we
drank until closing. I found a man in him I never saw before. This
guy is as cool as anyone I have ever met. Actually cooler! No shit,
I mean I began to love him like a Brother. His ownership of such
wisdom simply dazzled me. There is such a wealth of knowledge
to be learned from him. I'm so pleased he's my sponsor. What a
privilege to be sitting here beside this truly great man! Before this
day, I would put my life at risk for him because I had to. Now I'll
do it because I want to—gladly. If I ever hear anyone disrespect
Hillbilly, I will rearrange their face.

I told him about my dad and my life growing up with the Club.
He talked about his life in Special Forces and how they were
trained to be Force Multipliers. That's where he would be dropped
into a "Hot Zone" anywhere in the world and begin training and
supplying the local militia to fight for the American agenda. Two
or three Special Force Teams can build a small army of their
own without using a single American soldier. He said the entire

Chapter in the Club from which he Patched Over from were all in Special Forces and had all seen active combat in Vietnam. What a tough Chapter that had to be! In that Club's Center Patch was sewn a large knife, and I always thought that Club's Center Patch looked so fucking cool, very artistic. However, until tonight what I didn't know is, the knife is there to represent the knife given to a Special Forces graduate at his graduation. The knife is not there because of so many Special Forces men in that Club, but because that Club was founded by Special Forces men. Wow, how cool is that? These men have been trained to kill in many different ways. They're experts in demolition and small arms. They speak several different languages, and like a chameleon changing its color to blend, they too can adjust to whatever environment is needed to Take Care Of Business. They are, indeed, True Warriors. You know, now that it's been explained, I've been thinking, our Club has its share of Special Forces members also. Hmm . . . . I wonder if that's what the small Death Head Patch is all about, Special Forces? No, because my blood brother, Kebus, wears the Death Head and I know he wasn't Special Forces. As we sat and talked, I could see Hillbilly's eyes watching mine as I looked at his small Death Head Patch in curious wonder. I've had dumb moments, especially after a few beers, but I knew enough to keep my big mouth shut on that subject.

Saturday started out fucked up. I had to be at the Clubhouse in the city an hour ago and my bike wouldn't start. The Vice President and my Sponsor pulled into my driveway riding in a nice Cadillac. Of course, they were bitching at me before they were even out of the car.

"Where the fuck you been, Prospect?" They told me to get into the Cadillac and we'd go get the parts needed for my Harley. Without thinking, I jumped into the backseat with my Colors on! Just as I realized I fucked up, the Vice President sprang from the driver's seat and violently opened my door. He grabbed my Colors and pulled me to himself, then without hesitation punched me in the mouth. Wham! He hit me so hard I saw stars, you know, the purple with white twinkly things you see from the inside out as your knees buckle and you're going down for the count. Understand, Colors are to be flown! Never disrespectfully pressed between your back and a car seat. This Club definitely has a way of making sure prospects don't forget what they've been taught. In other words, they translate 'The School Of Hard Knocks' in a literal sense.

I got my bike running, and then over the course of two hours' riding time, our Chapter met up with ten other Chapters at a large truck stop. We're about one hundred and seventy miles from our destination. Of course, I still don't know where we're going, or why. Prospects are always on a Need-to-Know basis. For security purposes, we came this far riding together in no more than sets of two with our Colors on under our leathers. This way if you go down, you go down with your Colors on. I rolled into the truck stop with one Brother, Lead; we gassed up then parked our Harleys with the other bikes, nearly two hundred motorcycles at this point! Bikes kept pouring in two at a time. It's about noon thirty. The plan is we leave together at one o'clock sharp. This is a good time to take a piss and grab some grub. But not for me only, I must prospect! So I run throughout the herd of Bikers, lighting cigs, fetching beers from our supply trucks, and pumping gas—how I hate it!

Back on the road, and we're now running in a full pack, two abreast and riding fast in a tight, well-disciplined formation, almost Military Fashion. We are all flying Colors! This to me is what it's all about. My heart is pumping fast and hard, adrenaline is flowing. There are a couple of vans behind us hauling Brothers with guns, pulling security. And behind them some trucks with trailers, to quickly load any bikes that may break down along the way, and then a small caravan of cars and such carrying a melting pot of members, affiliates, mamas, and Ol' ladies.

Riding fast is a defensive tactic. It's like this, if you're riding fast, maneuvering through traffic, it becomes obvious if someone is trying to follow you, because in return, they too are also dangerously cutting through traffic. Our column of Harleys is exceeding the speed limit excessively so that any vehicle pulling past the end vans will be very noticeable. Not to say a car couldn't pull past and take a potshot at one of the Bikers, but without a doubt, it would be suicide. The overpasses are where we really want to watch, especially at night. For the most part, we have them covered though. At the overpasses without on/off ramps, a couple of Bikers are sent ahead to sit and watch for trouble. One by one, as we ride under overpasses with entrance ramps, additional Chapters that have been waiting on the bridges above join us. As we cruise under the overpass, they ride down the ramp and become part of the whole. The bridges with Chapters waiting to join the column have prospects holding huge Club Banners draped over the side of the bridge facing our oncoming army of Bikers. The column keeps growing longer and longer. It's so fucking cool! A lot of planning goes into these runs, and this one, by comparison, is not very large.

By now, the State Police are aware of this huge column of "One Percenters" flying their Colors down the highway. They have dispatched helicopters along with many patrol cars. We are definitely the main topic on every police radio. The State Police turn on their beacons and block traffic for us wherever possible. BET, Biker Enforcement Team, may or may not be around, but one thing for sure, the cops will be taking as many pictures of us as they possibly can, and BET will collect as many of them as possible for their ongoing intelligence file. Sadly, they don't see us as anything other than enemies of the state that must be removed! . . . "Fuck'em!"

No citizens in the small town we're now approaching is expecting this oncoming army of Bikers to show up on this nice, clear, sunny afternoon. Our Club is now at war, and for security purposes, this Graveyard Run is unannounced.

First stop is at the outer town limits and it's for fuel. At the gas station, as the cars finish fueling and pull away, we appropriate the pumps until the Club is using every pump at the station. Each pump is joined to a Prospect doing the actual fueling. Brothers pull through almost chaotically. Bikes are everywhere, lining up, fueling and then leaving loud and fast! The pumps are never cleared until the last Bike goes through, then our women square the bill. The owner is enjoying a nice, clear, quiet day when suddenly hundreds of Bikers invade his station. He's not sure what to think. For sure, fear tugs at his emotions. It's loud and frightful to him. There are always horror stories about Outlaw Bike Clubs destroying small towns. Then as fast as they arrived, they're gone! Now by comparison, the clear, quiet day is more noticeable than ever. Nothing left but some discharged oil droplets around the pumps, a story for all to hear, and a quick $500 in sales. When it's all said and done, the owner of the station hopes to see us again. It really was exciting and very prosperous.

Pumping gas is a terrible job for Prospects. Some of these paint jobs are pure artwork and cost a fortune. Many are Club Colors. I already have a busted lip from wearing my Colors in the Cadillac. All I need do to make it two busted lips is spill a single drop of gasoline on the wrong Brother's tank! God I hate this, how fucking nerve-racking!

After the Brothers fuel, they very sporadically pull onto the road where a few other Brothers are directing traffic. The Bikers are directed to turn onto a side street where they rev their motors and shoot down a long, narrow road to the cemetery. In all, there are probably three hundred and fifty motorcycles. It's hard for me to keep my adrenaline down; they're all running straight drag pipes and flying Colors. "Fuckin' A!"

I'm one of the last to arrive at the cemetery. All the Brothers are gathered around Rudy's grave. I'm handed a spray bottle, toothbrush, and small towel and told to clean Rudy's headstone. As I kneel down to begin cleaning, another Prospect, already kneeling and cleaning, looks up at me. We make eye contact and both stare emotionlessly for a few seconds. It's Prospect Brock! Locked in a stare down, I finally turn my eyes downward to Rudy's headstone, breaking contact. As we both meticulously clean, I deliberately maneuver myself so that Brock can see my new Bottom Rocker. He knows I'm showing off. He rebuts by pretending to crack his back; still on his knees, he straightens his back and crosses his arms, then twists his body from side to side, giving out a fake moan of relief. In his side-to-side positioning, I'm offered a plain view of both his Bottom Rocker and his Center Patch. Big fucking deal!

Suddenly, I fuck up! At that very moment, my pistol falls from its shoulder holster, landing directly on Rudy's headstone! Ker plunk!

"Pick it up!" angrily growls one of the Brothers gathered there. I quickly retrieve my gun and return it securely to its holster. "Now give me twenty-five!" The Brother loudly orders! After completing the twenty-five push-ups, I stand and double-check my gun, closely examining the shoulder holster. Once satisfied everything is okay, I look around and see I'm still receiving dirty looks from all the other Brothers until I pan my point of view back to Brock, who is proudly displaying a shit-eating grin on his ugly mug. That dumb Mother Fucker!

After the episode with my fallen gun and Rudy's headstone is cleaned, a Biker's ritual hated by law enforcement begins. First, the Prospects make sure all Brothers gathered have a beer, a newly opened beer. Then everyone closes in to form a tight circle around Rudy's grave, all 350 to 400 Brothers.

The President of Rudy's Chapter raises his beer in a toast-like fashion and says, "Here's to Rudy."

Next everyone raises their beer and loudly repeats "Here's to Rudy" followed by guzzling their beer, crushing the cans, and throwing the empties to the ground. Seconds later, all three or four hundred Brothers take out their pistols and repeatedly fire into the air until every gun is empty! It really is cool! Yeah, the cops, now only a quarter mile away leaning against their cruisers watching, hate it, but don't know what to do. After all, nobody gets hurt, and there are hundreds of heavily armed hard-core one percent Bikers, so they grin and bear it!

Now we all ride into the small town of Rudy's birthplace. A small town, yes, but there is no shortage of bars. Main Street is lined with our Harleys on both sides of the road—there's nothing but Harleys and bars. The security vans are now parked at either end of Main Street, still occupied by Brothers with guns. For hours, my job is to Run and Fetch, not Step and Fetch, beers for the Brothers while trying to stay on top of all their head games, and believe me they do have head games!

As a prospect, I must learn and remember what all Brothers drink, so when ordered to bring a beer, I'm sure to bring the correct flavor. In addition, what brand of cigarettes they smoke. Fucking up and bringing the wrong consumable can produce a painful consequence. A good trick is to have many Marlboros and Kools; this sort of covers both ends of the spectrum. Some Brothers smoke weird cigarettes so it's best to have a pack or two around for them. Common cigarettes can be had at almost any cigarette machine, but not so much the weird ones. Another problem for prospects is a Brother has the right to take your money and any cigarettes you may be carrying around, and they usually will. Therefore, you have to find a hiding place, not far, but secure so when asked for a cigarette you can run and get it, then quickly return. Be gone too long and a punch in the snoot may occur, especially after they're drunk. Brothers know prospects have goodies stashed. Their game is to try to find out where and take the mother load. Then you're screwed, because you no longer have cigs to pass out. They will team up. They'll follow you, and worst is if a drunk Brother asks, "Where did you get the cigarette?" You don't ever want to be caught in a lie. It's just about impossible to survive this without help. I have many Club Mamas helping me! They hand me cigarettes, they hold my money, not to mention tipping me off on things I can do for Brothers to make myself look good. I love them all.

After three or four loud, rowdy hours spent in the bars, all three hundred and fifty plus Harleys start and leave the small town at the same time. It is truly a sight to see, three hundred and fifty Harley Davidson's all being kick started at the same time, then lining up on Main Street to leave. There are many citizens watching, along with many cops!

The first Harleys pull down Main Street and begin lining up two abreast at the stop sign on the far end of town. The line grows longer and longer as Main Street is being back filled by Club Members on Harleys revving their motors and flying their Colors! When the line of Bikers fills the entire length of Main Street, the column is given the signal to go. There are still hundreds of bikes parked and lining each side of the road. One by one, they pull out from either side and join the long column as it leaves! The entire process of starting our Harleys and leaving this small town takes upward twenty minutes. Now the town is once again vacant and quiet.

We all ride slowly and deliberately to Rudy's house where his wife and two kids live. It's a small town but Rudy's Ol' lady lives in a large suburban-type neighborhood, newly developed with plenty of heavily weeded, empty lots scattered throughout. We surround the house with bikes and tents; bedrolls are everywhere. There are Bikers sleeping on Harleys parked up and down the narrow road and circular turnaround in front of Rudy's place, a cul-de-sac. Oh yeah, the security vans are now parked at the entrance of this dead-end road!

My sponsor wants ice water as soon as he wakes up, so I have some stashed via a Club Mama. As I said, you'll want to make friends with these women because prospecting is a million times easier with their help. I don't think it's a conscious effort for Club women to befriend prospects. I think they feel sorry for us. Maybe all women are born mothers. They see us suffer as prospects and feel a need to help. Patch Holders know it goes on but turn a blind eye; after all, they themselves received the same kind of help as Prospects. When a man does get his Top Rocker, he most certainly doesn't forget the women that helped it become possible. So once in the Club, protecting and respecting them follows. It's true, American women do play a key role in all walks of life, but often behind the scenes. In the Club, these girls are the most beautiful of all. There have been Brothers known to abuse women. But never another Brother's Ol' lady though, because they're "Property Of," and that's a good way to get Rat-Packed. Being Rat-Packed is when all Brothers present—ten, twenty, or more—turn and attack a fellow Brother, punching and kicking till he's near dead. You never fuck with another Brother's Ol' lady! Never! But most Mamas are former Ol' ladies or perhaps soon to be Ol' ladies. Nobody wants to see them bothered. There are no real Club rules protecting these girls, but if one is hassled, it's generally resolved quickly. They are recognized as a valuable resource and must be protected as such.

Speaking of women, here's a quick story for ya. It's about what the Club once did to a woman. You decide if this was cruel, or funny, or both. It happened during a Club National Run. There were so many hundreds of Brothers it would be impossible to say how many for sure. It was a three-day event. This girl showed up. She was very pretty, but not very smart. I guess one could say she did have a lot of heart, though, because a group of Brothers convinced her she could prospect for our Club. If she succeeded, then she would be a Full Patch Member. If she did not, however, then all she would lose was the Prospect Patch they were dangling in front of her. Well, she anxiously agreed and was given both a Prospect Patch and a Sponsor. Now remember, a Prospect must do whatever they're told by any member, so take a guess what she did for the next three days. At one point she vomited, and out came nearly a quart of pure semen! Yuck! At the end of the National Run, she was told the Club decided against her, and they took back the Prospect Patch! To this day, she still tells people she once prospected for our Club. Like I say, you decide. But remember, Bikers will be Bikers! Anyhow, back to the Graveyard Run!

I prospect into the night. I'm so fucking tired.

Around midnight I'm asked by a drunk Brother, "Who's your Sponsor?"

I reply, "Hillbilly."

He says, "He's a good man." Then he asks, "Do you know where he is?"

Without hesitation, I point to exactly where my Sponsor is bedded down and say, "He's right there."

The Brother says, "Good job, Prospect!" He then leans closer toward me and in a quieter tone, almost whispering, says, "I have a mission for you, follow me." I was led to a small group of Brothers standing in the shadows created by a streetlight that was being blocked by an old shed. As I approached and my eyes began to adjust, I could see this situation looked bad. I mean these guys are scary! I figured they were drunk and horny to fuck with someone, me! I cautiously entered into the circle. One Brother asked if I had a gun.

I nodded my head, and said, "Yes, a .45 automatic."

He then pointed past an open field full of high weeds to a parked car sitting anonymously with its lights out and asked for my acknowledgment, "Do you see that car?" Pausing briefly, I leaned slightly forward, squinted my eyes, and focused on a lone car sitting at the end of a dark, vacant street.

I said, "Yes, I do." From the looks of this situation, I could see no good was gonna come from it. He told me to belly crawl through the empty field and find out who and what it was. This could be serious. It could be cops or maybe orchestrated by the Club to fuck with me. Could it be a test? Worst of all, assassins! Man, I had better get it right.

As I began to crouch for my long crawl through the high weeds, a Brother handed me a .38 caliber revolver and said, "For sure this will give you five good shots." Revolvers don't jam; they're good back up. As trained, I checked the pistol to be sure it was in fact loaded and then stuffed it into my boot.

I begin belly crawling a tenth of a mile per hour, my brain is running ten thousand miles per hour. If it's an assassin, I could end up a hero. All I have to do is stop him. Of course, that may require killing him. However, if that happens, this could be the big one for me. I may even get my Top Rocker, yeah! The flip side to that coin is not so rosy however. What if it is a Hit squad and I don't stop it in time? I could be blamed. Or cops, how would I know? I do know this, if I report back bad info and there are negative consequences because of it, I'm fucked! What would be perfect is, just before an assassin fires a gun, I stand and save the day. That's got hero written all over it. My mind will not stop! What if, what if, what if. I try to stay focused on the reality of my situation. This is as real as any Military Grunt crawling through grass in actual wartime. The problem is, if I fight the enemy and win, instead of receiving a medal, I could go to jail for Murder!

I crawl, stop and listen, then crawl again. My Sponsor, Hillbilly, right now is my biggest hero because I am using a trick he taught me. A trick I thought I'd never need. I crawl, then stop and listen to the 'Crickets.' I close my eyes and concentrate on the chirping of every single cricket as far as I can hear. I want to be sure there is nobody else in this field. The crickets, as Hillbilly described them, are little detectors. But instead of a siren going off to warn of any trespassers, they do the opposite; they go quiet, simply stop chirping! After the person has passed, they resume chirping. One can lay with eyes closed and develop a mental image of any path an enemy has chosen simply by listening to the beautiful sounds created by these wonderful insects. I am being so quiet and moving so carefully, I'm actually crawling past some crickets without disturbing their song. What a cover!

I've been crawling now for over an hour and the car is closer than ever. It's a black two-door sedan. I can easily see two men in the car. It's weird because one is in the front driver's seat and the other is sitting in the backseat directly behind him. That right there tells me something's wrong. I can hear them whispering but can't make out what they are saying. For sure, the guy in the back is holding either a short rifle or what the cops call a Big Ear. That's a tubular-shaped listening device. Shit! Now I know this is no joke. It's the Real McCoy! These guys are either cops or assassins. I must get closer and figure it out. Whoever it is, I'm sure they have no idea I'm here. I no longer need the crickets; however, I haven't shed the possibility of someone else being in the weeds! Nevertheless, I now give the car top priority. I can see the windows on the passenger side of the car are up and the windows on the driver's side are down. I have to know what's happening here. If the dude in the back points the device he holds at my Club and it's a gun, not a Big Ear, then a Brother could die. I must not let that happen. This completely sucks! The mosquitoes are terrible; the little bastards are wildly feasting on me. Without response, I allow them to freely suck my blood. Not really a gift, it's just I most certainly can't smack one at this point in time.

It's funny because as I crawled through the grass being bitten by mosquitoes, I wondered how many soldiers during actual wartime ever experienced the same agony over a life-or-death situation. My situation may or may not be life or death, but I would be foolish to view it in any other perspective.

Well, here it is, the moment of truth. The dude in the backseat has raised and is now pointing whatever it is he holds out the window toward Rudy's house! Well, that's it. I can't fuck around any longer, I must react! I stand and rapidly approach the car. I don't run but I'm walking extremely fast at sort of an angle, more or less forty-five degrees between the passenger headlight and door. With their heads turned toward the party, I'm out of view—this is a good thing. I have my .45 automatic in my right hand, held down and concealed behind my right leg; it is locked 'n' loaded. I am almost to the car and still don't know any more about what's happening inside of it then I did an hour ago. And I still don't have a plan. I'm going on total instincts.

When I get to the car, I immediately open the passenger door as fast as possible! I was so close to these stupid fucks they didn't expect me. Getting to the car seemed so simple, I was thinking it's a setup. There may be more people in the weeds guarding these monkeys, but I stay focused on the car.

I pull the door open, lean my head and shoulders in, and loudly ask, "What's happenin', gentlemen?" First thing, I try to get a look at what the fuck head is holding in the backseat. These two jump from the combination of fear and surprise. There is no dome light. The guy in the back quickly puts whatever it is he's holding down between his feet and the back of the front seat. God, I wish I could see better! I hold no reservations about killing these two. If they do anything weird, I'm prepared to start blasting! How ironic, here I stand alone, my life is in danger and there are over three hundred Brothers a half mile away! Oh well, the Club is fond of saying "It's not the Patch that makes the man. It's the man that makes the Patch!" At that very second the driver starts the car's engine, throws it into gear, and goes like hell! The car's burning rubber and throwing loose gravel dramatically. It does a screaming one hundred and eighty degree fishtail and disappears at an enormous rate of speed down the dark, narrow road without the aid of headlights! When this happened I had to make a choice, either shoot these bums or let them go. Reluctantly, I chose the latter. I jumped backward, almost falling, and let the car pull away without shooting. The loose gravel thrown from the rear tires pelts my face. It stings and begs me for a retaliatory potshot, but I refrain. I stand alone in the dark, vacant street, now deathly quiet for a few seconds, analyzing what just happened. I let out an exasperated sigh of relief, turn, and make my way back through the high weeds to the party. I keep my gun at the ready; the crickets have not completely convinced me the field is free from danger.

Although I'm still psyched up, I can feel I'm going down for the count. I've had at best four hours of sleep in nearly thirty-six hours. I've been prospecting my ass off for at least half of those hours, and now this "mission of love" I've been sent on. It has taxed my nerves, and I'm not sniveling, just being honest about it! To be completely honest, I'm ready to get on my bike, ride to the nearest hotel, and sleep for a month. Fuck the Club, I'd rather sleep now and pay for it later!

CHAPTER FOUR

SOMEONE IS GONNA DIE!

After running-off the two would-be assassins, I slowly and cautiously make my way back through the high grass to our camp. I'm nervously thinking, what if I had shot and killed those two men? Killing them is not what's bothering me; it's getting away with murder that has me concerned. As a prospect, how can the Club trust me? I have no history of having proved myself in any way, so if I get caught by the police and charged with murder, how can the Club feel confident I won't turn State's Evidence on them, saying I was ordered to do it? And there has been no shortage of cops and helicopters watching throughout this entire Graveyard Run. The Club can't just leave a couple of bodies in a parked car only a half mile from their camp. So they could easily have buried me along with those two dudes in the car, covering up any loose ends along with our bodies. Would they do that to me? Who knows? One thing for sure, the Club would never harm a Brother in any way and will protect one to the ends of time. However, I'm not a Brother, only a prospect, and they're going to protect themselves first. So right now I'm feeling sort of jilted. What a Trick Bag that could have been; I'm ordered to kill for my Club, and out of love and loyalty I do, but then, to safely cover up the murder, maybe I'll be killed for doing it. "Fuck that!"

I am glad this has happened because I never thought about the risk I am taking by killing someone for my Club! And there's a very real possibility that I will kill someone for my Club. The risks I'm taking as far as the police go are obvious, but as far as the Club killing me to protect themselves against any possibility of me turning State's Evidence must be considered. I can't really blame them for something like that, even if it's me they're killing. They must not take any chances; they must protect themselves at all costs. So how do I get out of that Trick Bag?

I dwell on the problem for quite some time as I slowly make my way back. And here is the answer: If I had killed those two men in the car tonight, without a backup plan, I may have returned to our Club's encampment immediately following the murders. Big mistake, because now the Club would be directly implicated. Now that I've thought about it, and if anything like this ever happens again, after shooting the two, I would immediately lay the bodies down inside the car and drive it away, never returning to my Club's encampment. My Club would know I killed them both, so I would get credit for that and also for being smart enough not to involve them and for taking the bodies far away by myself. Done right, I would hold 100 percent responsibility for the two murders, exonerating my Club from any wrongdoing. Hence, there would be no reason to kill me for legal protection, only reward me for Takin' Care of Business. I'd drive them to a deserted place where I could burn the entire car with the bodies in it, destroying the forensics. Then quietly and anonymously make my way home, even if that took days. Once home, I would let the Club come to me. I would not go to them. Once the Club understood I had not only killed defending it, but also disposed of the bodies, along with removing the Club from any liability, my status as a prospect would be greatly improved! Hell, I may even have received my Center Patch! . . . "Ya gotta be smart!"

When I get back to the shed, there's nearly fifty Brothers, guns drawn, standing there waiting to find out what just happened. After I tell the story, I was led into Rudy's garage which was decorated more like a rec room than a garage. There were several newer lounge chairs and a very expensive kitchen table with four chairs sitting on top of a beautiful Persian rug. Hillbilly greeted me at the door; he directed me to sit at the table. He reached into a refrigerator and handed me an ice-cold beer. I drank that sucker in one steady pour straight down my throat followed by a smacking of my lips. Ahhhh! That may have been the fastest I've ever guzzled a beer. I nod at Hillbilly and give him a "Thank You." Oooops! I just spoke to Hillbilly! Fuck! After all the shit I've been through, now I'll get my ass kicked for sure. He could see I was tweaking.

With a gentle smile, he said, "Its okay, Prospect, you've earned the right to speak to me."

Oh fuck! I sat back in the chair and gave a generous sigh of relief, followed by a smile, then asked him, "Now that I can talk to you, may I ask for another beer?" As the words were leaving my mouth, this big motherfucker was reaching into the refrigerator and grabbing me another beer. Wow, you know I am really starting to love this guy. With one hand in a single motion, he opened the beer with his index finger while sitting it down in front of me.

Then with a half-smile said, "Don't get too used to it, Prospect! You still have a long way to go!" He grabbed himself a beer and sat down across the table from me. At this point other than him and me, the room was empty. He took out a large bag of cocaine and, with a razor, chopped and formed two lines. After completing the task, he leaned back in his chair, locked his fingers together behind his head, and said, "There you go, Prospect, knock yourself out." I wasted no time snorting both lines, then wiping the leftover crumbs with my finger before licking it. Again, I thanked him. He told me to relax and stay here, that he had to go get someone. As he was leaving, he turned and said, "Drink up! Have another beer!"

At this point, I didn't feel like a prospect, nor did I feel like a Full Patch Member either, but I felt secure in the belief that I was a part of this Club, more so than ever now. I guess brotherhood was beginning to trickle down to me. I was thinking if this is how good I can feel as a prospect, then to be a member would be unimaginable. The entire 'Motorcycle Club' concept has now drawn me in closer than I ever thought possible.

It didn't take Hillbilly long to return. When he did, it was with ten Presidents all from Chapters on this Graveyard Run. Wow, I snapped to attention! I gotta admit, I was nervous. Any one of these men could give the order and have me killed in a heartbeat! Not that they would, and I was never concerned about any negativity. It's just that being around men with such power is intimidating, and I am just a prospect! I figured they wanted to hear about the car incident, and I was right. They all came in and introduced themselves. Some I knew, others I knew of, and some I had never heard of. A popular question was "Did I see any tattoos?" That's when I started believing tattoos are a bad thing. Although artful, they are also unique only to the owner, making the mark a perfect brand for not only enemies but also the cops to identify! I'm thinking as cool as they are, I'll probably never wear one. I told them I couldn't even say for sure if the dude in the backseat had a gun or not.

"I kinda think it was, but who knows?" We talked a long time. Many Brothers stepped into the garage, listened for a few minutes, and then stepped back out. I know I satisfied every single Brother that what I did was exceptional. By the way, the Brother that gave me the .38 revolver was sitting there. He is the President of a very large Chapter I never knew existed. I pretended I knew who he was as I wiped my fingerprints off his revolver before returning it to him. We never leave our prints on someone else's gun. I had to pretend I knew who he was because Club members get really pissed off when a prospect forgets their name or doesn't know who they are. Right now things are going my way and I'm not going to fuck it up with something stupid like that. As the meeting was ending, one by one every single President gave me a hug and a handshake.

They all said, "Good job, Prospect!" When it was completely over, Hillbilly handed me another beer and chopped a couple more lines of coke for me.

He then said, "In all my years in the Clubs, I never knew anybody that got two Days Off in a row! But Prospect, all the Presidents said for me to give you a Day Off!"

I couldn't fucking believe it. Prospects never get a Day Off during a Club function. I'm on a Run and partying as a Top Rocker, a "Full Patched Member!" It's so fucking cool; Hillbilly and I are drinking together again.

We partied as Brothers while moving through the Club's camp. He was genuinely acting proud of me. He even introduced me as his Bro a couple of times. "Here's my Bro, Clutch." Wow! However, the icing on the cake was when Hillbilly yelled for a prospect to bring us two more beers and Prospect Brock showed up with them! I was drunk; the only thing keeping me upright was the cocaine. When I saw Brock, I saw red! I'm a member tonight; I have the power over him—big time! Brock handed Hillbilly both beers, ignoring me—Total Disrespect! Then he turned and shuffled off.

I immediately bellowed out, "Prospect Brock! Front and center!" He quickly returned. When realizing I was the one that yelled for him, he gave me a dirty look, which only fueled my anger! I was getting ready to tune'em-up when Hillbilly stopped my escalating anger simply by giving me an unapproving glare. I retreated from the situation by calmly asking Brock for a cigarette. He complied and once again shuffled off. Prospects are supposed to light the cigarettes they hand to a Brother, but he did not. I let it go because Hillbilly and Brock both know I don't even smoke.

Hillbilly knew I was done for the night and headed for trouble if allowed to continue.

Like a true Brother he led me to my Harley and said, "Prospect, do us both a favor, sleep. Your Day Off is gonna last until we get home, so sleep now. You ride with me tomorrow." I was sawing logs in five minutes.

I awoke with the sun to the sound of Harleys idling near and far, revving their motors and running full bore in the distance. There are Brothers everywhere, some asleep, some waking, stretching, many have ridden into town. They have left for breakfast in packs of ten and twenty, maybe more, maybe less. Some packs are coming back from breakfast as they pass other packs headed for breakfast. Little weaves toward the oncoming pack usually happens along with a One-Finger Salute as they pass one another. They are all flying Colors!

Fuck! It's alive and happening right now, already this morning. What I am saying is, there is an energy created by this many Brothers that's an indescribable experience. It's so fucking cool. All we do that's wrong can be justified by this moment. I'm sorry, but this is my Club and today I'm acting as a Full Patch Member.

There's a bunch of Brothers standing around what's left of last night's bonfire, mostly smoldering coals now. A few log ends that never burnt, left from longer logs that were carelessly introduced to the fire late last night near 'Drunkenstine Thirty' have been kicked back into the coals and are struggling to light. It's from those that early morning hot dogs are being cooked and distributed by Prospect Brock! Ha ha ha! He's been up all fucking night prospecting! He looks terribly burned-out, dirty, tired, and miserable. He has black smudge marks on his face from tending the fire. His hands are black . . . . Yee-Ha! I feel like a new man, lots of sleep and I still have the rest of the Day Off! Fuckin' cool! Fuckin' cool! Fuckin' cool! Thing is, I have to get next to Hillbilly because most of these Top Rockers have no idea I'm one of them for the day.

First things first though, I must permit Prospect Brock to cook me a couple of dogs. Yeah. Not a burnt dog, or needless to say, an undercooked dog, but I am worthy and deserving as an acting Full Patch Member of a perfect hot dog! And I am sure he's just the one to act on this request. I may need special condiments however, haven't decided yet, perhaps chopped onions or maybe even sour kraut. How about a nice chilidog? Basically, anything Brock can't produce? That should rattle his cage!

I stretch my arms high into the sky then expel a deep breath, mark my mug with an extremely pleased little smirk, and approach the fire pit. I can't believe Brothers are still drinking beer, but what's even harder to believe is they all look sober as judges. Well, at least the judges I've stood in front of. For sure, one must be able to hold his liquor in this Club. No Sloppiness Allowed! Every now and then, a Brother does get sloppy drunk, but he will always have plenty of babysitters.

Just as I was ready to place my order with Brock, a strong hand slapped down on my shoulder. Smack! I turned sharply, only to calm when I see its Hillbilly.

"Good morning, Clutch," he says clear and loud. Before I can reply, Hillbilly shouts out to the general crowd of Brothers, "Prospect Clutch has the Day Off. Please Bros, make sure everyone is aware."

"Thank you, Hillbilly. Can I get you anything? A hot dog, a beer?" I said, then looked directly at Brock who was now visibly showing signs of dismay over Hillbilly's announcement, and continued, "I'm sure Prospect Brock will be happy to serve us each a couple of perfectly cooked hot dogs." Hillbilly grins. He knows I'm horny to fuck with Brock.

"Tell ya what, Clutch, you get us each a couple of those perfectly cooked dogs and I'll get us a couple of ice-cold beers." Hillbilly said, then gave me an ornery wink.

I turned directly to Brock and sternly ordered, "You heard the man, Prospect! I need four perfectly cooked hot dogs!" God, that was better than sex!

About the time Brock finishes the hot dogs, Hillbilly returns with the beers. Brock attempts to hand all the dogs to Hillbilly. Truth is, that punk was never gonna hand any to me. Originally, I was only going to fuck with his head a little, but that pissed me off! Driven by anger, and void of any reasonable thought process, I walked about fifteen feet away and picked up a half full can of beer left over from last night. I turned and headed straight for Brock. My intentions were to throw the beer in his face, can and all. I was working on pure emotion, not a trace of intellect.

I knew Hillbilly was there and watching me, but what I didn't realize, he was with Brock's Sponsor, Crazy George, and he was also watching! Understand, at a large meet such as this, a prospect's Sponsor will tend to mother—well, father—his prospect to a certain degree. Even though I had the Day Off and was acting as a Full Patch Member, to this guy I was still a prospect and only a Bottom Rocker prospect at that! Brock has both his Bottom Rocker and his Center Patch, and even more so than that, Brock is his prospect, and that's who he is going to protect!

I stopped to figure out the situation, still holding that nasty half-empty can of beer. Once again, Hillbilly came to my dumb-ass rescue.

He slowly approached me and, with the smile I've been learning to love, said, "Clutch, I'll trade you an ice-cold beer for that old stale one you're holding." Fuck, this guy is becoming my best friend, as well as my Brother. And to think at one time I was plotting his murder! I understood he was trying to defuse a potential problem but I continued to hold the Silver Brock Bullet. So Hillbilly said in a much sterner voice, "Drop the fucking beer, Prospect!" Well, this put a damper on my fun! Nothing I can do about it. It seems Hillbilly is one-step ahead of everything I do or everything I'm thinking of doing. I don't suppose it's an accident. Hillbilly once belonged to the same Chapter as Brock's Sponsor and neither of those two want me Fuckin' with Brock too much. So once again, I pull the reins back on my Fuck-with-Brock Campaign. Well, I do have all day to resume that campaign.

The word is the entire Club will ride out together at noon sharp. We will pretty much do the opposite of how we came. Stop and refuel first, then one huge column of bikes running two abreast in tight formation, followed by armed vans, will roll down the highway. One by one, the column will grow shorter as we lose Chapters to exit ramps, until finally one last Harley pulls into my long driveway, delivering me to my place of rest.

I bullshit with Hillbilly for a while then he says in a perked-up tone, "Pack your gear, Clutch, you and I are going for a ride!" I got my shit together and we fired up our scooters then left together.

It was the first time I rode with him alone. We were riding side by side, two abreast, like Brothers. It was so fucking cool, his bike is beautiful. It has a 1963 Panhead lower end and a 1968 Shovelhead top end. This is an excellent way to go because the Pan top end doesn't oil as well as the Shovelhead top end and the Pan's lower end is excellent. The early Shovel lowers had some problems. And It is a Stroker, which refers to the motor. It's called that because the length of the piston's stroke has been modified to a greater up-and-down distance, giving the bike more torque, more horsepower. How he did it was pretty tricky. He used S&S eighty cubic inch flywheels, rebored their crank pin taper to accept the larger, original Harley seventy-four cubic inch crank pin. Now, with the original Harley crank pin, he returned the Harley connecting rods and pistons. The cylinder jugs required a thick shim to raise the entire top end so it can accept the longer stroke. In short, he converted his seventy-four inch Harley by modifying eighty-inch flywheels to an eighty-six-inch Stroker. In other words, Hillbilly has a Hot Rod Harley. Oh yeah, and that's exactly how it sounds; Strokers sound excellent! And Bikers are obsessed by the way Harleys sound!

So as not to put all my attention towards his motor, the bike is a beautiful Candy Apple red, with lots of chrome and to offset that, almost every nut and the head of almost every bolt has been fourteen karat gold plated. The Club's name is painted along both sides of the gas tank and the Club's Center Patch is painted on the top of the tank. He's running a rigid frame, bumpy but beautiful. Check this out, in the center of his sissy bar is an original chrome-plated Nazi bayonet. It's a parade dress issued knife with two swastikas cast into either side of its handle. It appears to be strictly ornamental, but in true Hillbilly fashion, with the proper know how, it can be removed in seconds and ready for combat. Oh yeah, this would-be piece of motorcycle artwork can be used on any unsuspecting foe in a heartbeat.

This guy has all kinds of tricks up his sleeve. He has switched the throttle twist grip from the right side of his handlebars to the left side and swapped the clutch lever with the brake lever. He said it wasn't hard for him to adjust to it because his first bike, "His First Born," was an old Indian Police Special and came from the factory that way. It was created for Police Departments so that the bike could be accelerated while the rider fires his pistol. Most men are right-handed. Hillbilly adopted the idea from Indian for that exact same reason. He also says, as a bonus, if anyone tried to steal his masterpiece, they would suffer great difficulty riding it. Think if a person was in a hurry to escape in a car they had just stolen but the gas pedal had been switched with the brake pedal!

He told me the left-handed throttle once saved his ass from a van that tried to pull up beside him on an expressway. The van, he said, had a hot rod motor and took him by surprise. As it got nearer, an enemy with a twelve-gauge pump shotgun that hung from the passenger window began throwing lead! Well, as I said, Hillbilly's scooter is no slow poke itself. He was in the right lane, and there was a car in front of him. He poured on the gas and began to pass the car on the right. He pulled his 9mm from his shoulder holster. What Hillbilly didn't know was the car in front was playing an active role in his attempted murder. Hillbilly fired over his left shoulder into the van as the van fired back! Several shots were traded. At the very second his bike was gonna blow past the front window of the car he was overtaking, he saw the passenger preparing to shoot a handgun at him. Hillbilly said he locked his rear brake and put the tire into a skid. His bike slid left towards the car, almost hitting it. This put him behind the passenger just enough to take a shot.

He laughed and said, "No shit man, worst shot I ever made! I missed the dude completely! No problem though, coz I hit the driver directly in the head!" The car lost control. He said at first it swerved right. He figured he might be crushed between it and the four-foot concrete wall that borders the lanes. Then luckily, it swerved back left and flipped over directly in front of the van, causing it to crash also. Hillbilly sped away into the night!

I'm telling ya, this guy is no Rudiepoot. Hillbilly typically carries three Buck knives. A very long straight edge model #119 strapped to his belt and then tucked into his right back pocket. His leather jacket covers the handle, making the knife extremely difficult to detect. He has two locking blade Bucks, models #110 strapped to his belt on each side of his hips, one for each hand I guess. He's carrying a Charter Arms snub-nose .38 in his boot, and a model #39 Smith and Wesson 9mm auto in a shoulder holster. Not to mention, he's six foot nine and 325 pounds of pure muscle, built like a rock! And he is an expert in martial arts. Hillbilly is very quiet and calculating. Also, I hear he makes a lousy enemy—easy for me to believe that. However, at this point in time, I can see he makes a great Brother too.

We rode back to the graveyard. With Hillbilly in the lead, I follow as we slowly maneuver our bikes respectfully around the graves that surround Rudy. We shut our machines off, put down their kickstands, dismount, then quietly sit cross-legged, Indian style, on either side of Rudy's grave. The sun was about an hour and a half into the sky and still a big beautiful orange ball. I could already feel the humidity rising along with the temperature. Hillbilly lit up a joint and then slowly puffed it two or three times before passing it to me.

As he exhaled the smoke, he nodded his head downward as if to use it to point to Rudy's grave and said, "I helped Rudy build his first bike. He and I did Boot Camp together, that's where we met. I lost track of him for a while after we shipped to Vietnam. I can still remember the excitement in the first letter I received from him describing his first confirmed kill! We hadn't been In-Country a month! That little fucker ended up with thirteen confirmed kills in all. Had it not been for him gettin' hit, he'd probably still be in Nam! He loved it, me too for that matter, all we needed was our Harleys and neither of us would ever have left!" He chuckled. Hillbilly spoke a little more about Rudy, always looking down at his grave as if he were talking to himself and Rudy, more so than I. Suddenly he looked me directly in the eyes, more seriously than I've ever seen from him and said, "Don't turn and look now, but on the far side of the cemetery sits a car. Is that the two dudes you saw last night?" I turned slowly, my eyes hunting until I could gain a clear view. It was not the same car, but there were two men sitting in it, one in the driver's seat and the other directly behind him in the backseat.

"Fuck! Who are these guys?" I don't scare easily, but when I saw that car, a cold chill came over me, almost paralyzing. I got the weirdest feeling that 'Someone is gonna die!'

CHAPTER FIVE

THEY KILLED HILLBILLY!

This bright, clear morning is promising a delightful day ahead, but that will only be true weather wise! That car sitting only a half mile away is promising Death, and my heart feels like unless something changes, soon there will be others joining Rudy in a cold, dark grave!

The car I belly crawled to was an older two-door black sedan. The car here at the cemetery is a late model, dark colored four door. It's too far away for me to recognize the men inside of it, but I'll bet if it's not the same two, they're somehow involved with the two I confronted last night. One way or the other, no good is gonna come from this situation.

Once again, Hillbilly asked, "Well, Clutch, is that the car you saw last night?"

"It's not the same car, but maybe the same two dudes! I don't think they're cops, and if they're not, then what I saw last night was a rifle, not a Big Ear!" I said. Hillbilly has long, thick red hair and a full red beard. Often, when deep in thought, he grabs the beard hairs from his lower lip with his tongue and upper teeth, then pulls them into his mouth and slowly chews them while he contemplates. This is what he began doing and this is how I knew he viewed this situation as very serious. Funny, because I'm not a small guy by any means, but Hillbilly has such a strong presence, he's so powerful, towering, and confident, I almost feel like a child that feels safe when Dad's around. Now that he's obviously shaken by this turn of events, I'm getting really worried.

"Okay, here is what we'll do. We'll ride out of the cemetery together, but when we get to the main road, Clutch, you go left and I'll go right. Then tear ass back to Main Street! I'll meet you at JJ's."

We started our bikes, maneuvered around the graves, again, slowly and respectfully, then down the long winding drive that led us out of the cemetery. We stopped at the large stone archway entrance long enough to look each other in the eyes, then nod and ride out in opposite directions. When we entered the main road, we both poured on the throttle. I pushed my bike as hard as it would run. I spoke earlier about riding fast as sometimes being a defensive maneuver; well, I was definitely in the defense mode, about a 100 miles per hour worth! Anyhow, I poured on the throttle near 110 miles per hour before locking up my rear tire and sliding into a right hand turn, then entering onto the road that takes me into town! After the turn, I have a nice clear view over my shoulder to see if I'm being followed. Doesn't look that way, but I still go like hell for two reasons. First, I don't want to be followed, and second, because I Love It! I slow down and turn onto Main Street, where once again the street is lined with our Club's Harleys and the bars are packed with our Club's Brothers!

J J's is near the center of town between two other bars. Guess what? Hillbilly is already standing in the bar's foyer. I pull up and carefully do a horseshoe-type maneuver, then back my bike to the curb beside Hillbilly's machine. My adrenaline is pumping, what a rush! I love riding 100 miles per hour to escape Death! If there's a pun there, it's not intended.

I approached Hillbilly. I did not know how to read his face, with him, one never does!

"What, did ya take the scenic route?" he said with a slight chuckle and a wink, then in a more serious tone asked, "Have any problems, Clutch?"

I said, "Nope! Musta been a False Alarm!" We entered the bar; it was standing room only, nothing but Brothers! A prospect I'd never seen before brought us each a beer. I introduced myself, and then thanked him. Hillbilly and I stepped outside to drink our beer in a less-crowded environment and discuss what we should do about the two dudes in the car.

We stood outside the bar and talked for about ten minutes; a cop cruising very slowly down Main Street stopped directly in front of the bar and yelled for us to come to him. I handed Hillbilly my beer and told him I'll go see what he wants. I approached the cruiser and knelt down on one knee so the cop and I were at eye level.

I asked in a very polite manner, "What can I do for ya, Officer?" He told me beer was not permitted outside the bar, but due to the overcrowded conditions he will not enforce it, providing we all keep a low profile on any alcohol consumed outside. As I was talking to him, I heard a voice come over his police radio. It was a female dispatcher responding to an earlier question, I presumed.

She said, "I think it has something to do with the Biker who was killed a year ago." I'm sure the question asked was about our Club and why we were there. The cop I was talking with knew what I had just heard. He gave me a look as if to ask, "Well, is that what this is all about?"

I said nothing, but as I stood, I respectfully patted his shoulder and said, "Okay, thanks." I rejoined Hillbilly. "Everything's cool, he just wants us to keep the beers down," I said.

Hillbilly gave an understanding nod and said, "With all the money we're spending in this town, that cop would be on the town's shit list if he ran us off!" I laughed while nodding my head yes in agreement. "Clutch, I called the Goons. We're going back to the cemetery to find out who those guys are. You stay by my side, and back me up, okay?" Hillbilly said.

I said, "Of course I'll back you up, man! Hillbilly, I'm still on a Day Off, right?"

Hillbilly replied, "Yep."

"Hillbilly, I know I'm just a prospect and not supposed to say this, but I see you as my Brother. I would take a bullet for you and I'll give one for you!" I said in a very emotionally broken voice! That Big Mother Fucker gave me a hug. God, I felt like a bear had me. While still in Hillbilly's embrace, he pulled back just far enough for us to be face-to-face. He stared at me for a few seconds, then grabbed each side of my head and kissed me on the lips!

Again, he pulled back slightly and while still holding my head said, "I hope you make Top Rocker!" He then gave me a gentle shove away from himself as he released me.

"You can bet your life I'll make it!" I said.

"How about if I bet your life instead?" He rebutted with a slight chuckle and a wink. He then turned away from me to talk with a Brother that had just walked up extremely fast.

Hillbilly said that he had summoned the Goons. The Goons, now they are a major part of this Club that I have not spoken of, and here's how they work. Every Chapter dedicates two of their most capable members as Goons. When they are all added together as a functioning entity, they comprise 'The Goon Squad.' These are the toughest, meanest, most deadly guys we have. Each Chapter has a reserve fund used exclusively for the mobility and functionality of the Goon Squad. They are our Hit Force, affectionately referred to as "Have Gun, Will Travel." Example: if there is trouble anywhere in the United States or abroad that warrants Pay Back, you can bet the Goons will come. Say a Brother is heavy-duty abused or perhaps murdered by another Club, or a citizen for that matter, then the Goons will probably be called. They will fly in, two at a time, booking hotel rooms on all sides of town. The Club will send as many as needed. They will quietly gather intelligence about the person or persons they are pursuing and establish the best method for Takin' Care of Business. Once a plan has been formulated, they will act, quickly and decisively. There is little defense against this form of attack. If the Goon Squad targets you, you might as well Kill Yourself.

To my knowledge, I have never met a Goon, but from what I understand, they are never very far away and always lurking in the shadows. Hillbilly gave them a call, so it will be interesting to see what happens. All I know is I may finally get to see a Goon, or better yet, meet one! Hillbilly and the Goons must know something about the dudes in the car. For that matter, maybe I'm the only one that doesn't. I'm starting to believe they may be a Hit Squad sent by the club we're at war with. I no longer entertain the idea of them being cops. Our Club will not fuck with a cop for doing his job as long as he does it with respect for our Patch and without abuse to a Brother. We have inside snitches everywhere. I'm thinking our Club found out about an ambush and Hillbilly is playing a key role in foiling it. That means I'm involved, Big Time!

Hillbilly and the Brother talked together very quietly with their backs to me for a few minutes when suddenly a high-dollar car pulled up and four very large Biker types climbed out and joined their conversation. I'd never seen any of them before.

I guess I was paying too much attention to their circle because one of the Dudes angrily leaned toward me and hatefully shouted, "Wat Da Fuck you looking at?" I offered no response, just retreated to my bike and sat quietly, head down, waiting for Hillbilly. When the six finished talking, it reminded me of a football team quick breaking from a play huddle. They all went separate ways, very fast, very serious, and very matter of fact.

Hillbilly came to me and said, "You ain't gonna get your Top Rocker, but if things go the way I think they will, you may receive your Center Patch!"

"Holy Fuck! Hillbilly, just point me in the right direction and tell me what to do," I said.

"Get on your bike, follow me!" he said. By the time we were starting our scooters, almost every Brother on Main Street began emptying out of the bars and heading toward their bikes. Harleys began firing up by the hundreds with small packs of Brothers leaving in groups of five and ten, fast and loud! The street almost instantly came alive with Harleys screaming in all directions! It was absolute craziness! Like furious hornets pouring angrily from their nest, it was evident our Club was On the Attack! There were even bikes flying down the sidewalk! With all the confusion, it was hard for me to stay with Hillbilly. Boy, I wouldn't want to be on the business end of this crowd. I don't know what the plan is but I do know there is one. Hillbilly would not be doing this without a plan. He sure got the Brothers mobilized fast. The Club is set up that way for emergency response in any situation. They take security very seriously. It's like the military in that respect. There's a chain of command that when called upon can expedite many Club members, ready for war, in a very short amount of time. These guys are Ready, Willing, and Able.

Hillbilly and I turned off Main Street; he pulled his bike to the side of the road and signaled me to pull alongside of him so we could talk. Brothers on Harleys are screaming past. I pulled beside Hillbilly and stopped. We're both standing, legs spread, straddling our Harleys, one hand on the throttle, fingers on the brake lever and the other hand on the clutch lever, leaning toward one another so we can hear to talk over the loud thunder created from all the Harleys.

Hillbilly was practically yelling. "Clutch," he said, "one of our vans left for the cemetery fifteen minutes ago. It's gonna block the entrance at the stone archway so nobody gets in or out! If our friends are still there, we'll have them trapped! About fifty Brothers are gonna ride around the van and cruise the cemetery looking for those punks. The rest of the Bros are gonna cruise the town looking for them. You and I will ride to the backside of the cemetery, there's a way out there, and it's possible they will try to use it to escape. Clutch, I think I know who it is and where they are. I want you to pull over where I show you and wait for me. I need you to cover my ass Clutch, this could get serious!" There was sweat pouring down his face and veins were popping out of his huge neck as he yelled to me. Bikes are still screaming past as Hillbilly and I pull away.

This is crazy mass hysteria! I'm thinking that's exactly the way the Club wants it though, just in case we have to Smoke Someone it will be easier to hide the murder this way. The police will know it came from our Club but won't be able to finger any one individual Brother from all the confusion. About this time, a very low-flying State Police helicopter roars past at treetop level! Vroom!

I follow Hillbilly down some back streets, then along a narrow winding road that runs parallel to a very wide creek, which leads us to the backside of the cemetery. We are about one mile outside the cemetery and there's only open field between us and it. There are no Brothers here at all. I can barely see some slowly cruising the graveyard on Harleys, but Hillbilly and I are isolated from all the activity. He signals me to stop and wait at an old footbridge that crosses the creek. I don't know why but I was wondering whether or not my Harley could make it across that bridge. He rides to an old abandoned barn about one hundred yards from where I'm sitting. My bike is now shut off. This place is very quiet, there's an eerie calm. The sound of my Harley crackling as it cools grabs my attention, it's somewhat hypnotic. I see Hillbilly shut off his bike and walk to a small door on this side of the barn, half-falling from its hinges. He crouches and enters the barn, reaching for his pistol as he does. At that very second I saw the white flash from a gun muzzle inside the darkened barn followed by a thunderous crack! Hillbilly falls backward through the old wooden door, tearing it from the remaining hinges! He buckles to the ground, twisting and coming to rest in the fetal position! Oh my God, Hillbilly has been shot!

I flipped out! I began kick starting my bike so frantically I forgot to turn the key to the start position! After a few kicks, when my bike wouldn't start, I threw it down and ran as fast as possible towards Hillbilly. Suddenly a pick-up truck came crashing out of the barn! It busted through the barn's side like an explosion, splintering wood everywhere and almost running over Hillbilly. As it pulled past him, the driver extended a handgun out of the window and began firing rounds into Hillbilly! I pulled my pistol and fired the entire clip into the truck, attempting to detour this asshole from shooting any more bullets into my Sponsor! The truck blasted past Hillbilly, then focused its attention on me! It turned slightly and came straight toward me. With no place to run and an empty clip, I clawed frantically at the inside pocket of my leather jacket trying to retrieve a spare full clip! The truck kept accelerating toward me, wildly bouncing front to back over the open field. I finally got my shit together enough to get a new clip from my leather jacket. I reloaded my .45 and started pounding rounds into the truck's windshield until it finally gave a surrendering turn away from me, and escaped down a dirt access road! At this point, I continued my run toward Hillbilly!

When I got to him, he was making gurgling sounds and blood was coming out of my sponsor everywhere!

"They killed Hillbilly!" I screamed. About that time, he moaned and slowly rolled over and opened his eyes. I fell to my knees and gently lifted his head onto my lap. I shed tears, many tears, as much from anger as from hurt.

Hillbilly rallied enough to ask, "Did ya get'em?"

I said, "No, sorry! Are you all right, Hillbilly?" I shouted.

He coughed a few times then quietly answered, "Fuck no, I'm not all right!" His mouth slowly filled with blood. The last words Hillbilly said to me was "Clutch, never forget, a man is only as good as the strength of his surrounding enemies." He then very peacefully closed his eyes and grinned while letting out what seemed to be an endless breath of air.

At that very second a police helicopter flew up fast and low, almost at treetop level, and began to hover. It had flashing red and blue beacons same as a police cruiser. A voice came out of its loudspeakers telling me to throw down my gun and lie on the ground. At the risk of being shot by the police, I refused to comply. I will not move away from Hillbilly and I will not disarm until I know he's safe! I can see police cars screaming toward me far in the distance. Brothers on Harleys are gathering at the edge of the cemetery, blocked by the creek, many have dismounted from their bikes and are wading across. Within minutes, Brothers surround me! A Brother named Ice Man takes my pistol and tucks it into the swell of his back. More and more Brothers arrive; some have crossed the creek on Harleys! Just as the first police car slides up, I stand and remove my colors. I know that is the one sure way the police in the helicopter can identify me. As I walk away from Hillbilly, I see Prospect Brock standing there and give him a fake hug.

As I do, I pass my Colors to him and say, "Hide my Rag, Brock, I don't want the helicopter cop to ID me from it." He concealed my Colors by placing them under his arm while walking away from me. More and more cops show up. A Chapter President yells for an ambulance. As the number of cops increase dramatically, I slowly and anonymously mix into the crowd of Brothers, which is now numbering near fifty! I do not want to talk to any cops as a witness!

An ambulance finally arrives, sirens blaring! The paramedics, with the aid of many Brothers, lift Hillbilly onto a gurney and wheel him to the backside of the ambulance. However, just before he was loaded into the vehicle, a group of six cops showed up and ordered all the Brothers away from the ambulance. The cops had come for one reason only, a picture! They all gathered so Hillbilly would be between them and the camera, in the foreground of the picture. They lined up shoulder-to-shoulder close along the side of the gurney, and posed with guns drawn! Some held their handguns into the air and others crossed their chests with their pistols. Then there were two cops with shotguns resting off their hips pointed outward, each gun in an opposite direction, one on either end of the gurney, parenthesizing the picture! It was as if Hillbilly was a big game animal like a zebra, just bagged on a safari! They all wanted in on this photo opportunity! I freaked out!

"Mother Fuckers!" I shouted as I ran toward this crew of cops! An extremely large Brother, Ice Man, came from behind me and cupped my mouth with his hand while restraining my person with the other!

He whispered, "Clutch, take it easy! The cops probably want to talk to you anyhow! Take Billy's Panhead and Get the Fuck out of Here! Right now, Clutch, that's an order!" He pointed past all the Brothers to a beautiful blue bike sitting alone, far from the others. I really didn't care what he had to say. I just about pushed him away to continue my attack, but several other Brothers quickly moved in on the cops! One Brother smacked the camera from the detective's hand, knocking it to the ground, and then kicked it away! By this time, Brothers were pouring in by the hundreds! The cops decided to give up their Photo Shoot and dispersed. Hillbilly was slid into the ambulance and ferried to a nearby hospital, followed by at least a hundred Bikers! I decided to take Ice Man's advice; I jumped on Billy's motorcycle and hauled ass out of Dodge, away from the crime scene.

I'm so fucking freaked out right now; I don't know what to do. I ride out of town and into the rural countryside. I find a nice single-lane dirt road that cuts through a wooded area; it's extremely isolated. I ride down it a few miles and then shut off the bike. While still sitting on the Harley, I bowed my head, and for the first time in my life, I prayed. I simply asked God to save Hillbilly. I did not attempt to make any deals with God, by saying 'if he did, then I would' . . . . because I knew that God knows as soon as I find the punks that shot Hillbilly I am going to feast on the pain I intended to administer to them before their death! I raise my head looking around at the beautiful woods and say aloud, "What to do now?" Most of all I want to see Hillbilly, maybe he's alive? However, if the cops recognize me, for sure I'll be arrested; they'll find something to charge me with! I could try to find the punks that shot him and then introduce them to Hillbilly's Prospect! On the other hand, maybe I should head back to Main Street? Fuck! I hate this! I continue to sit on that deserted road for hours trying to figure out what to do, often praying. Finally, after three hours, I decided to head back to Rudy's house.

I really do not have a clue as to where I am though, since I've never been to this town or this part of the state before. I took off on this bike fast; my only concern was getting away from the cops, so I never paid attention to which way I was going! Here is my situation: I was just in a shoot-out, my sponsor is probably dead, which makes me a key witness to the murder. I'm covered in his blood, I'm riding a Brother's motorcycle and don't know his legal name or address, only what Chapter he's from, the cops are probably looking for me, and I'm lost! Double Fuck! Oh yeah, and if I meet up with the Bad Guys, I no longer have a gun to defend myself! What's worse, I trusted Prospect Brock with my Colors! I swear if he fucks with my Colors, I'll kill him! I'm in no mood for any of his half-ass games!

Well, I can't stay here any longer, so I kick start this Harley; it fires up immediately. As I pull onto the main road, guess who? My buddy, Mr. Helicopter, is flying extremely low and very slowly, obviously looking for something or someone—maybe me! Still sheltered under the canopy created by all the trees, I'm not sure if he saw me or not.

"Fuck it!" I hit the road and go like hell. Boy, I'll tell ya, after all the shit I've been through, the wind in my face comes as a blessing! It sure feels good to be riding. Hillbilly often referred to riding his Harley as Two-Wheeled Therapy. At this point, I know exactly what he means. It's late afternoon and the sun has fallen deep enough into the horizon that I can easily gauge the western sky. I figure I must go east to get back to Rudy's. His house is on the south end of town, so I maneuver in that direction, hoping to avoid riding directly through town. A good plan and it works well. I make it back to Rudy's place without incident, no cops, no helicopters, and no bad guys!

As I pull down Rudy's dead-end street, I see our armed vans have been joined by several other vans, not surprising after what just happened. Rudy's place is swarming with Brothers, and none of them look very happy. There are also swarms of police cruisers lining up and down the road.

Cops are standing together in large groups talking, their radios blaring out coded messages, "Roger, his ten twenty is South Maple Street, possible five-oh-two." Whatever the fuck that means? Without any problem, I ride past the cops, my head down low, and wheel into Rudy's drive.

A Brother signals me to park the bike behind Rudy's house, out of sight from the police. I shut off the Harley, put down the kickstand, but as I lean the bike onto its kickstand and dismount, the Brother blindsides me with a hard right, a sucker punch to the head! Blam! The punch staggers me into the bike, knocking it and me to the ground. I fall into the bike, its red hot pipes burning painfully into my leg. While I'm down the Brother begins kicking my ribs. But even through all this abuse, my adrenaline lifted me onto my feet while the Brother was violently throwing punches to my head. Once on my feet, I reacted, Fuck the Club rules that address Prospects hitting Brothers. With a single punch, I knocked that Mother Fucker off his feet, a perfect one-punch Knockout! Down he went, and he fell hard! At this point, several other Brothers grabbed and dragged me into the garage, beating me all the while! I was beaten unconscious!

When I awoke, I found my hands had been handcuffed behind my back, and I was duct-taped to a chair. Ironically, the same chair I sat in a day earlier while being congratulated by Hillbilly as he chopped me two lines of cocaine! I was totally restrained in that chair, the garage filled with Brothers. The Club's National President, Bones, stood in front of me while putting on a pair of leather police motorcycle gloves. These gloves are made with lead powder sewn into the knuckles, so that when a fist is formed they become rock hard and add a few ounces to each fist! I had already been beaten badly, but it was obvious there was more to come!

Bones said to me, "You fucked up!" Then followed his statement with a right punch to my face. Blam! He hit me so fucking hard I went unconscious again for another couple of minutes. He paced back and forth in front of me impatiently awaiting my return to consciousness. I woke up and slowly rolled my head toward him.

I locked my eyes directly on his and said, "Fuck You!" Blam! Another right to the head followed by a hard left to the chin; this punch loosened a few of my teeth. My eyes were swelling shut from the beating; it was becoming increasingly difficult to see. Bones leaned down close to me; he put his left hand on my forehead and then with his thumb opened my swollen eyelid wide.

He said, "Can you see this?" He was now holding a large knife. He said, "I'm gonna cut-off your dick!"

I screamed back and asked, "Why? I have done nothing wrong!"

At that very second, a Brother standing close by threw a beer directly into my face and fired back, saying, "You're a fucking liar! You helped kill Hillbilly, then threw your Colors at Brock, and quit the Club!" The beer stung my eye terribly but the pain was overruled by the ridiculous accusations this Brother had just made! Bones zeroed in for yet another punch. Pow!

"All I ever wanted was to be a part of this Club, a Brother! I have done nothing wrong!" I screamed.

Suddenly the garage door flew opened and a large Brother entered saying, "Hillbilly is still alive! Doctors say that tough Son of a Bitch may pull through!"

Bones turned to me and said, "You can bet your life that you and I will continue this discussion!" The entire room emptied fast.

I love Hillbilly. I would never want him to die, and I was in terrible fear that he had, but now I have a completely selfish reason for wanting him alive. He is the only one that can clear my name! I will not quit this Club; they will have to kill me first! That's kind of my Ace in the Hole; that I'd rather die than quit! The only thing I care about is the Club, the same Club that has just falsely accused me of betraying my Sponsor while pounding the piss out of my face! I need to figure a way to see Hillbilly. I wonder where my bike is. What happened to my Colors? Boy, I'll tell ya, as far as the Club is concerned, I went from Hero to Piece Of Shit fast!

I fell into a deep sleep or maybe it was a state of unconsciousness. Either way, I had the most pleasant dreams. They were all about Nikkei. I mainly dreamed she and I were having sex. The Brothers in the garage must have thought I was one crazy son of a bitch, all beat-up, out cold, handcuffed and taped to that chair, head cocked to one side, and smiling! I was smiling until rudely awakened by an ice-cold beer thrown in my face. Splash!

"Get up, Clutch, party's over. We're gonna take you for a little ride!" A Brother said sarcastically. He used a large knife to cut me free from the chair. But when cutting the duct tape from my ankle, he carelessly cut a huge gash into my leg! He looked up at me and, while laughing, sarcastically said, "Oops, sorry about that! Yep, that's a good one, I better put some tape over it, wouldn't want you bleeding all over the Club's new van on your last ride home!" He then wrapped my leg with some of the tape he peeled from the chair. With my hands cuffed behind my back, blindfolded and tape around my head covering my mouth, I was led out of the garage to one of the vans now parked behind it, out of sight from all the police gathered along the roadside in front of the house. I figured the Club was going to take me for a Long Walk off a Short Pier! I thought about trying to escape, maybe making a run toward the police. But that's not my style, survival is however, and given any opportunity I'll seize the moment, at any cost! Faced with the proposal of perhaps having to kill a Brother in order to survive, threw me into more or less a state of meditation. I was calm and surrendered to the situation! Mellowed, I was thinking hard on what to do. I want to live, but if I hurt a Brother in order to do so, indubitably the Club will hunt me down and kill me anyhow. I was loaded into the van and off we went; four Brothers and me.

After we had driven for about an hour or so, one of the Brothers broke the silence when he asked me, "Are you a religious man?" He pulled the tape from my mouth, waiting for my response.

I answered, "I don't know, I prayed earlier today, for the first time ever." He asked, "What did you pray about?" I said, "For my Sponsor to live."

He shook his head in agreement, then said, "Well, he's alive, but you better say a prayer for yourself, because you ain't gonna be very much longer!" The van continued to roll on through the night.

I was fighting to stay awake, but every now and then, I would doze off. Every single time I did, it was followed by an extremely pleasant dream. Always short and sweet and always about Nikkei. I think it was a defensive move by my brain, incorporated to protect me from the reality of the situation, sort of like denial. In other words, while awake all I could concentrate on is what method they were going to use to kill me. Drowning, shooting or suffocation, which one and how painful will it be? This is the way it goes: The Brothers will take me to a location where it's safe to commit the murder. After everything is set up, an additional vehicle will come bringing a prospect, who will not know what's going on or why he's there until he's handed a gun and told to shoot me, to be the trigger man, to do the actual murder. If he refuses, they'll shoot him along with me. If he complies, he just committed murder, and now the Club knows that prospect can't possibly be a cop. Oh well, at the beginning they tell all prospects they must commit a felony in order to enter the Club!

Finally, the van turned onto a long, bumpy drive and eventually came to rest. Well, I guess this is it.

The side doors opened and a Brother hatefully shouted, "Let's go, Clutch, get out, now!" I had no idea where I was. I did, however, figure this was it, that it was the end for me. Probably they're going to shoot me in the head. I stepped out of the van and was led into a field. A Brother removed the handcuffs and told me to get on my knees. I reluctantly did so. I could hear two Brothers whispering, and then the van doors shut, the van started and drove off. I did not know if anyone was there or not. I just stayed quietly in the kneeling position. After about a half an hour or so, my legs were asleep and going numb. I finally spoke.

"Is anyone there?" I said. There was no answer. I asked again several more times, but never received an answer. Finally I stood, my legs wobbling. I struggled with the tape wrapped around my head, arms, and legs, until setting myself free. I tore off the blindfold and was shocked to find I was standing in the field that surrounds the front section of my house! I can't believe it. I'm home! "Fuckin' A!"

That's when I fell to the ground, this time in the sitting position. The entire weekend hit me all at once. The shoot-out, the beating, belly crawling to a car with assassins, Hillbilly being shot. I'm no punk, but my hands began to tremble! I'll admit a tear or two may have fallen from my chin. I figured this to be an appropriate time to say one more prayer. "Thank you, God, for bringing me home!" I rose, walked to the side door, and entered my house; it had that familiar smell, guaranteeing I was home! After washing up and eating, I climbed into bed and slept for thirteen hours straight! And that was my weekend Graveyard Run!

CHAPTER SIX

TURNED OBSESSION

If life can be compared to a deck of cards, then after this weekend's Graveyard Run, my deck has just been reshuffled! It is still the same deck, but will never be in the same order; it has been changed forever.

I quietly lay in bed following my thirteen-hour sleep fest, staring at the ceiling; every part of my body aches! I really do not have any ambition to get out of bed; I only want to lay here and reflect, to try to figure out what it is I want. Before the Graveyard Run, I never had any doubts about what I wanted, all I ever knew was the Club and that's exactly what I wanted. Now I'm not sure what has happened. Am I still a prospect? Do I still own a Harley? What's happened to Hillbilly? Does the Club think I'm the reason he was shot? Does Brock have anything to do with this? Speaking of Brock, right now, this very second, I'm calling his Ol' lady, Nikkei; she's really what I want.

The thought of connecting with Nikkei has pumped me full of ambitious energy. I spring from my bed and run to the living room phone then dial Nikkei's telephone number. As her number rings, I've convinced myself she'll never answer.

I say aloud, "Come on, Nikkei, pick up the phone!" Her phone will only ring so many times before an answering machine picks up. I find myself pacing and, with each ring, hoping that's not the last one.

Finally, she answers, "Hello." Oh my God, her soft voice is sweet music to my ears. Again, she says, "Helloooo."

I reply, "Nikkei my love."

"Clutch, is this you?" she asked.

"It is, I'm calling because I want you to come over here. I need to see you in the worst way," I said.

There is a very long silence and then she asks, "Is everything okay, Clutch? Is something wrong? You sound funny, like something's wrong."

I reply, "No, nothing is wrong. I just had what was probably the weirdest couple of days of my life! I need female company, your company Nikkei." To my relief, Nikkei agrees to come over in one hour.

I hang up the phone, jump to my feet, and start cleaning the house. After a quick clean job, I focus on myself; into the shower I go. After showering, I even change the sheets on my bed, just in case! An hour comes and goes but still no sign of Nikkei. That's okay, because one hour in 'Nikkei Time' equals two hours 'Atomic Time.' Finally, she shows up!

Nikkei never knocks; she just loudly says, "Knock, Knock" as she opens your door and enters. And here she is, as beautiful as you've ever seen; she's smiling from ear to ear, her tight blue jeans accentuating her luscious ass. She's wearing a skimpy halter top, showing off her sexy tan belly and slender hips. Her long dark hair and beautiful dark eyes drive me nuts.

Suddenly her lovely wide smile turns down, and in a demanding voice she asks, "What happened to your face, Clutch?"

I answer, "Oh, I got a little beat-up, no big deal."

She lightly chuckles and says, "You usually do the beating up, but it looks like this time you met your match!" I approach and hug her tightly until she pulls away laughing, then says, "Let me guess, you're beat-up . . . . and horny?"

I reply, "I'm beat-up, yes, I'm horny, yes, but even more than that, I'm in love!"

Once again, she laughs but then stops suddenly and very seriously asks, "In love with who Clutch?"

I put my arms around her pretty neck and then lean down, looking directly into her eyes and say, "With you!"

She pauses for a long time and then once again that Little Shit begins to laugh and says, "Wow, you must really be horny!"

I say to her, "I'm serious! I'm in love with you, Nikkei!"

She stares into my eyes for a long time, then takes my hand, and leads me into my bedroom. She sits at the edge of the bed.

With her hand flattened, she pats the bed directly beside herself and says, "Clutch, sit here." I sit beside her. She turns to me and takes hold of my hands, and says, "I love you too, Clutch, I always have!" With the tips of her thumbs, she gently rubs my hands in a circular motion. She continues, "What about the Motorcycle Club? Do you really think loving me is enough? You know your first love is the Club. I do love you, very much, but as far as commitment goes, neither one of us is ready for that."

She stands and slowly walks to the bedroom door; with one hand on the edge of the open door, she supports herself while she one by one removes her high-heeled stiletto shoes. Next, she closes the door and presses her back tightly against it and then slowly removes her pants and then her top. She comes to me. With her hands open, she slowly pushes my chest until I am flat on my back, my feet still touching the floor. She continues her advance, climbing on top of me. Her knees are on both sides of my hips, her feet are crossed inward locking the inside of my legs. Her hands openly lie flat on the bed, one on each side of my head. She arches her back as I rub her firm little ass. Her hair falls downward, surrounding my face. She slowly licks my neck starting at my Adam's apple, up and around my chin to my lips. With her tongue, she opens my mouth and begins kissing me. She rubs her vagina on my crotch as she reaches down and unfastens my pants. Then she stands and carefully pulls off my pants, one leg at a time. Like a soft song coming to a screeching halt across the record on which it plays, the mood is suddenly broken!

With one hand, she raises my leg, with the other she points to the knife slice near my ankle and screams, "What the fuck is this, Clutch!" After my morning shower, I had made a miserable attempt at patching up my wound, but it was too deep for the few Band-Aids I used, so it never stopped bleeding!

I say, "Nikkei, it's just a small cut, now come back here." as I reach for her.

She jumps backward, out of my reach, hands on her hips and yells, "Small cut my ass! You need stitches!"

I rebut, "Nikkei, for the first time in my life I'm gonna have sex with you, the woman of my dreams! Do you really think I'm gonna give that up and go to the hospital for a few measly stitches? Come on, Nikkei, please, I'm ready to explode over here!" Her hands still on her hips, elbows out, she cocks her head to one side and then the other while looking at my leg, exploring the situation.

Then she relaxes her arms, and in a quieter, calmer, more normal tone, says, "Okay, first I'll fix your leg, and then I'll fix your dick!"

I fall back on the bed, put both hands over my face, and say, "You, my love, are UnFuckin' Believable!"

Then Nikkei does just as she promised; first she takes care of my leg wound, then back on top of me and takes care of my dick! I have never had sex this good in all my life. She is on top, slow fucking, unselfishly doing all the work. She knows exactly when I am ready to orgasm, and in an extremely sexy voice, she asks, "Where do you want to cum, in my pussy or in my mouth?" I couldn't believe she said that! She is not just giving me permission to cum, but is asking where I prefer to do it! It is all I can do not to explode the second she asks! However, I struggle to hang on long enough to answer. She has such a beautiful sexy mouth, such luscious lips, I can't resist.

I have to say, "In your mouth would be nice." She looks directly into my eyes for a few seconds then smiles, and then goes down on me. Well, you can guess the rest! She doesn't stop there though, and neither do I! After about five minutes of that, I roll her onto her back. Now it's her turn! Kneeling on all fours, I start at her knees. One at a time I slowly lick my way up her leg to her beautiful muff, pausing there for a few slow licks up and down and then continue up her tan belly all the way to her lovely breasts. I give each breast equal attention and then begin my descent back down, still slowly licking and sucking. Once the cycle is complete, I stop at her pretty muff and, with my warm, moist tongue, explore her eager vagina. I tease her for quite some time before she gently maneuvers my head exactly where she wants it with both her hands as she raises her hips and slowly wiggles me into position! Once there, Nikkei relaxes her hips and lets out a long, pleasurable moan. My flickering tongue offers a relentless pace for a long time, until finally she gives a long surrendering quiver and then stiffens her entire body as she lets out one of the sexiest moans I've ever heard! She stops me by gently pushing my head away. I rest my lips on her silky tan leg as she quivers and lightly gives an occasional jolt. Her hands have retired on top of my head and face. I turn slightly and pull her finger into my mouth, then gently chew as we both lay still, she is in total ecstasy. After a few minutes, she runs her hands through my hair hooking her fingertips behind my ears and gives a soft pull, signaling me to move upward. I slowly move up on her, stopping once to have another taste of her firm breast and then for the first time in my life, I mount Nikkei and we fuck for hours. At times, I pound fast and hard but then fall back into a slow but steady thrust. She scratches my back and leans her head backward, screaming out in pleasure as she has yet another orgasm. We fuck in every position imaginable; we even hit the Missionary Position a few more times. Finally, when neither one of us can move anymore, we stop! We lay there, sweaty, naked, and laughing. Laughing because she said I made her sore.

I rebut, "You made me sore too!" as I lift my dick and proudly display the blisters.

I just never knew sex could be like this. Now I understand why some refer to it as Making Love. That's exactly what we did, Made Love. How shallow sex has been for me before Nikkei! Now after this experience with her, and last weekend's experience with the Club, on the Graveyard Run, I am confused! I don't ever want to leave her side! Not even for the Club! Thing is, in a lot of ways Nikkei is the Club; after all, she was raised by it! Well, if I play my cards right, maybe I can have both?

Nikkei and I lay on the bed together for hours, her head on my chest, her leg wrapped around mine. With her index finger, she plays with my stomach hair, slowly making little circular swirls. In my entire life, I have never felt this content. Neither of us speak; we just lay there contemplating each other and how our lives have been changed by this. Once again, my life's deck of cards has been reshuffled.

Nikkei and I grew up together; we go back as far as I can remember, and even further than that! As a little boy, I always had a crush on her. I would always guard and protect her in a physical sense, and she would always guard and protect me in an emotional sense. Our relationship was mutually perfect that way; we each offered what the other needed. But as I grew older, that crush turned into a powerful love. I never realized how madly in love I was with her until she began with Brock. Seeing her with him would push me into a jealous rage. Although I always held it inside and never showed that rage to anybody, there were times I'd find myself pacing around my house, ready to explode after seeing her with him. But this is the first time she and I have gone this far together sexually. In the past, we fooled around a little, kissing and such, but we never had sex before today. This is the first time we've ever Made Love.

Nikkei and I pretty much spend the entire day in bed together, sleeping, eating and watching television, and of course, Makin' Love. Nikkei said she is going to spend the night. I have an iron gate at the end of my drive and at dusk, I walk down my long driveway to close and lock the gate. I have a twelve-gauge pump shotgun, an Ithaca model #37 PD slung over my shoulder. As I'm locking the gate, I notice a black two-door sedan parked on the roadside just over the hill. It looks exactly like the car I belly crawled to a couple of nights ago. "Fuck!" It could be the same dudes that shot Hillbilly. On the other hand, it may be the club we're at war with, maybe they're one of the same! It could be cops, or maybe it's my Club coming back for Round 2! Then again, it may not be any of the above; cars do break down! Well, I don't believe in coincidences. Two black sedans in three days doesn't seem right to me, so just to play it safe, I drive my old tractor down and park it sideways at the gate, barricading the drive. I have a security light, a camera, and an intercom at the gate also. I have four Pit Bulls that when released freely roam the farm. I feel safe when they're out. I return to my house and check all my guns; I have loaded guns hidden throughout my house, in case of an emergency, I'm never too far from an equalizer! Okay the house is secured, the gates locked, dogs are out, and my guns are loaded. Time to get back in bed with Nikkei! She and I wrap up, arms and legs woven together tighter than a bird's nest! I never realized how madly in love I was with her. I mean, she's all I want. We both drift off to sleep, I sleep straight through the night without ever waking, and I never do that! Honest to God, it was the best night's sleep I've ever had!

I awoke to the pleasant smell of coffee and bacon. I open my eyes and no Nikkei. As I look to see if the bedroom door is open, my beauty enters the room carrying a breakfast tray and sporting a lovely smile.

"Mornin', Clutch," she says. I sit up and she packs pillows behind my back to support me upright while I eat. Nikkei is wearing an unbuttoned dress shirt of mine, complimented by a nice little pair of tight panties. As I eat, she curls up at my feet, her legs together, bent at the knees. Her elbow is on the bed, her hand supporting her head, cupped around her ear, hair draped through her fingers. She's so sexy; she is making it hard for me to concentrate on my breakfast. First things first; this is the only time in my life I've been served Breakfast in Bed. And I know, I'll never be served breakfast in bed by a prettier woman than her! I gotta admit, I got it made! I could get used to this very easily. After getting busy with breakfast, I get busy with Nikkei. Once again, we do a three-hour Fuck Marathon. I swear I just can't get enough of her. Again, after we Make Love; we cuddle, laugh and talk for hours. Nikkei tells me I fuck like a Champion.

I say, "It's only because of you, dear. I never have before with anyone else! You bring it out of me!" She looks at me and in an almost childlike, very innocent way, her face lights up with a huge, very pleased smile. Her smile goes from ear to ear as she looks directly in my eyes and she holds it for a very long time. It drives me nuts when she does that, it's so honest! She is right though. I'm having at least two, sometimes even three orgasms every time we Make Love. That last one was somewhat difficult to achieve because I have blisters from yesterday and this morning hasn't helped any. But if it's true, if I do fuck like a champion, then Nikkei is the reason why. I've never spent as much time getting my partner off as I do her; we are perfectly matched. As a matter of fact, we both fuck like Champions; but only with each other.

Nikkei gives me a kiss and asks, "What's next, Clutch?"

"What do you mean, Nikkei?" I asked.

She continues, "Between you and I? What's next?"

I lean close to her and say, "I want more, Nikkei. I don't think I can go on without you. Most certainly I wouldn't want to!"

Nikkei and I were both raised by the Club, with strong Club upbringing, strong Club honor, and Club morals. The one thing we were both taught is "A person is only as good as their word." You never break your word to one of your own. She and I both know if we can get each other to agree on a relationship and fortify that commitment with our word, then the promise has been written in stone.

She says, "I love you, Clutch, and I worry for you. I mean look at yourself, all beat-up, your eye swollen shut, a stab wound to your leg, your teeth loose from fighting! If we go on, I must have your word that you won't kill yourself in some sort of fight or a bike wreck or something stupid like that! I must also have your word that I will be the only woman in your life, not so much as a single blow-job from one of the Club Mamas! Last, I need your word that other than when you're taking care of Club business, you'll spend all your time with me. I go with you on all Club runs, all Club parties, we even go to the bars together." I unwrap from her, roll onto my back, and stare up at the ceiling, deep in thought. After a minute or two, I roll back onto my side, facing her and speak my piece.

I say, "Okay, Nikkei, I will give you my word on all you asked, but you must give me your word that you will never see Brock again and that you will stay by my side, with or without the Club in my life. And you will always stay loyal to me as long as we're together, which at this point I hope is for the rest of our lives. One thing, Nikkei, as long as I'm prospecting, you know I must do whatever is asked by any Brother. If I'm asked to be with another woman, for whatever the reason, I must, but other than that, I give you my word I'll never play you for a fool by fucking around." Now Nikkei rolls onto her back and stares up at the ceiling. Entranced, deep in thought, she lightly chews on her index fingernail.

After a couple of minutes she sits up and crosses her legs, Indian style, extends her right hand outward and says, "Deal, I give you my word!"

Then I sit up directly in front of her, and extend my hand and say, "Deal, I give my word also!" We clasp hands and do a single handshake, once up and once down.

It may seem as if we just entered into a business agreement. In a way, we did, but to Bikers, it is as if we just got married! Now we both lay back on the bed, looking up at the ceiling, both chewing our index fingernails, once again engrossed in thought; this lasts for five minutes or so, total silence. Then we turn to each other, and at the exact same time, we say, "Let's move in together!"

She grins and says, "Ditto," then squeezes my nose twice. "Honk-Honk." That's a game we played with each other when we were very young. To be honest, I had completely forgotten about it. We both start laughing.

Then I say, "You move in here, we can start moving ya today! Nikkei, this place is yours to do with as you please, move furniture around, bring more furniture, throw out furniture, paint, and do whatever you want." Now we rejoin our body's entanglement, legs and arms wrapped up like pretzels. Once again, at the exact same time we both say "I love ya," only this time I am quicker to say 'Ditto,' as I pinch her nose two times! "Honk-Honk." We both laugh. I get very serious and have a sentimental moment when saying, "Ya know why you never have to worry about me fucking around? Because I'm having the best sex of my life with the most beautiful woman on the planet! Why would I ever want to stray from that? You got me, girl! I'm hopelessly hooked!"

And there it is again; I provoked that innocent little girl's smile, a genuine smile, aimed directly at me. It goes from ear to ear and lasts a long time as she stares directly into my eyes. I think that smile is the reason I originally fell in love with Nikkei, at the ripe old age of five years old!

Nikkei says we're going to meet with her mother in two hours for lunch. She's been on the phone with her for the last half hour, talking about us as if we just got married! The plan is, after lunch we all head back to their house and use her mom's trailer to move some of Nikkei's stuff back here. Nikkei still lives with her mother and always has. Her mother is a very nice person, older yes, but extremely beautiful, not beat-up looking at all. She calls herself an 'Old Biker Broad.' She is smart, very witty, and very charming. She loves the idea of Nikkei and me getting together. Her name is Sam and she and my mother were best friends right up until my mother's sudden death. Nikkei finally gets off the phone with Sam and immediately dials her girlfriend's number! Again, she says, "We're moving in together," sounding as if we're newlyweds or something. In the next hour, she makes half a dozen different calls telling all her girlfriends that her and me are officially an item now. I definitely get the impression this comes as no surprise to any one of them—hmm—but why are they not asking about Brock? Oh well, who cares!

It's one o'clock in the afternoon when Nikkei and I pull into a small family-owned restaurant named Ma's Place to have lunch as planned. Nikkei is driving her car and I'm in the passenger seat. I don't know what's going on with me and the Club, but as a prospect I am only allowed to ride my bike, no driving cars, so I figure I'll play it safe! I open and hold the door for Nikkei as we enter the diner. I notice her mother sitting alone in a back booth.

As we approach, she stands and practically runs to me, throwing her arms out. She jumps into my arms and hugs me tightly!

Almost shouting she says, "Congratulations, Clutch, I've been waiting for you two to get together for so long, and now it's finally happened! I only wish your mother were here to see it! We used to watch you two playing together and always agreed that it was only a matter of time before you would marry!"

"We're not married, Mom!" Nikkei disgustedly said.

"Maybe not yet, but you will, it's meant to be!" Sam cheerfully rebuts.

We all sit at a booth and order lunch; the food here is great! After we finish eating, I order an after-dinner bottle of wine. I love listening to Sam tell stories about her and my mother. The stories are of them young and adventurous, true American women! She talks proudly of Nikkei's father and my father growing up together. It's easy to believe these stories are about the best time in Sam's life. And a very good time to be a Biker in our Club!

Well, it's been said, "Wine is a truth serum," and now I have met my moment of truth. I rise from the booth and then reposition Nikkei's legs so that she is sitting at the end of the seat, facing outward. As I return her feet to the floor, I kneel down on one knee, all in a single motion. She and Sam both look extremely bewildered about my behavior. They are looking at each other, shrugging their shoulders in confusion.

I say, "I have something to ask Nikkei, and I'm honored that you're here Sam, to witness what it is I have to say." I reach up and gently turn Nikkei's cheek, positioning her eyes to mine and continue, "Nikkei, I do and have always loved you my entire life. Although we have given each other our word, I want to take it one step further." I reach into my shirt pocket and place an engagement ring on her finger, then say, "Please, Nikkei, do me the honor of accepting my hand in marriage."

Nikkei gasps deeply and says, "Oh my God!" She finishes placing the ring securely onto her finger, then raises her hand almost to the tip of her nose, and carefully examines it. After a few seconds, she jumps from her seat directly to me. I stand as she bolts into my arms, tightly wrapping both her arms and legs around me. I stagger backward, unprepared for her sudden advance. She hugs me so tightly for so long I feel like I can't breathe.

I finally ask, "Well, is that a yes?"

"Of course it is!" she eagerly answers! Now Sam stands and joins Nikkei in her embrace of me; they are both crying.

The few people in this tiny restaurant all stand and clap as Sam announces our engagement. "Please congratulate Nikkei and Clutch, they just got engaged!" After the excitement, we settle back into our booth. Nikkei has her arm tightly around my neck as she looks at her engagement ring; she is practically choking me! Suddenly her mother says, "Oh my God! Clutch, is that your mother's engagement ring?"

I nod my head as I answer, "Yes, I've been saving it for Nikkei ever since Mom died. Understand, I always knew I would ask Nikkei to marry me some day!" Now Nikkei turns in the booth so that we are face-to-face. She climbs to her knees, then straddles her legs on both sides of me, wraps her arms around my neck, squeezing harder than one could ever imagine a little thing like her could.

She kisses my neck then softly whispers in my ear, "Thank you Clutch, I swear, I give myself to you!" Once again, we settle back in our booth, but this time Sam orders a bottle of champagne and we toast and toast. Sam tells us this is the happiest day of all the days of her entire life.

We leave the restaurant together; Nikkei and I follow Sam to her house. We never get a single thing moved all day! Sam is on the phone with everyone she knows, calling and announcing the engagement. She is already planning our wedding. I can't believe it; she's working on the guest list!

"Okay, we'll have the entire Club and all its affiliates. We'll cater in the food and drinks. No, cancel that! We'll cook an entire cow! Yeah, and instead of walking to the altar, you two will ride up on your Harley!" she said.

Nikkei interrupts, "Mom, please! Do I have any say-so in my own wedding?"

Sam replies, "Of course you do, dear, just not as much as me. I can't wait to be a grandma! If it's a boy we'll name him Kaden. If it's a girl, for sure she'll be Kylee. Come over here, Clutch, and give me another hug!" I give Sam a big hug. She says, "You know I used to change your diapers?" She looks at Nikkei and continues, "If Clutch is half as big now as he was then, you'll be walking bowlegged!" She laughs.

Nikkei replies, "I'm already walking bowlegged!" They both laugh.

I hate to keep saying it, but I've never been this happy in all my life. Nikkei's mother has always been like a mother to me—well, at least a strong aunt. To see her and Nikkei this happy tells me it really was meant to be, Nikkei and me that is! Those two keep arguing over who gets the phone next. Between the two of them, I'm sure the entire world knows Nikkei and me are engaged to be married. Hmmm . . . . I wonder how long it will take Brock to find out. That piece of shit told the Club I threw my Colors at him and quit. Well, to be honest about it, right now I'll gladly give up the Club for Nikkei. I always thought I'd have both her and the Club, but nothing is going to take me away from her. Nothing! I have a 'Turned Obsession' from the Club to Nikkei. I couldn't imagine how anyone could be any more in love than I am with her. I guess in that respect I should be thanking Brock, because it took seeing her with him to make me realize how I felt about her! I can't describe it; I'd see them together and my soul would go into a jealous rage. Well, that's over now and we're together. I am going to make her happy. I'll never break my word. I will do whatever she wants because I know Nikkei is very unselfish and she only wants what's best for the two of us.

Chapter Seven

PROPERITY OF CLUTCH

Having Nikkei here and making plans for marriage has hurled my mind deep into thoughts about our future. It has also confused me in many different ways about where she and our relationship will be if I ever do become a Full Patch Member of our Club. I could never allow the two of them to conflict on any serious level. If they did, as far as the Club is concerned, it must come first. If I ever put Nikkei ahead of it, for sure I'd suffer greatly and maybe even have my Patch Pulled. Nikkei, on the other hand, may go along with being second to the Club for a while, providing it was never over any serious issues, but eventually something would have to give. I could risk losing her love by not putting her first in my life. However, that's a million miles away right now, and perhaps not even a real possibility. The Club has beaten me and taken my bike and my Colors so I doubt very much if they even want me back. I must invest myself in the moment. Nikkei is here now and the Club is not, so she is who I will concentrate on. I must also concentrate on my job and the skills I'm learning in my trade so I can always make a good living and support Nikkei. Working hard, supporting a marriage, and making a good living may not sound like the goals set by a Hard-Core Biker, but I must follow my heart, and right now, this is how my heart is directing me. At this point in my life, my ambitions are only motivated by the concept of living with and marrying Nikkei, and my job makes that possible.

I do have a good job, and I am going to school to learn a good trade, but I've taken a couple of days off from both of them, and tomorrow it's time for me to get back to the grind. Through my father's Social Security benefits, I have been able to attend machinist school and am now working as an apprentice machinist. I work as many hours as possible at the factory, then attend school part-time to complete my four-year apprenticeship program. It's cool because right now there is such a strong demand for skilled machinists. If you can find the On Button on any machine, you'll be hired. That's perfect for me because I'm only a few years into the trade and not as skilled as the company would normally hire. Due to prospecting, my attendance has been less than perfect. Of course, I'm not sure how good it would be anyhow. The company tends to put up with these shortcomings because of the lack of skilled machinists. Also, I am very good at what I do for the little experience I have. I do mathematics excellent; my trig is better than most of the journeyman machinists in the shop. Even some of the older master machinists will come to me for help with trigonometry problems. As a machinist, I work hand in hand with mechanical engineers. I get along great with all of them. Many say I'm cheating the world by not becoming a mechanical engineer myself, but that will never happen, too much schooling, and I hate schooling. However, many different times engineers have come to me for help in solving mechanical problems. I don't have their education, but my mind works better than many of theirs when it comes to putting things together and making them work. In our factory, the engineers have nicknamed me 'The Inventor.'

My involvement in the machine tool trade has made me very popular in the Outlaw Motorcycle Club I ride with. I have been asked to machine many different custom motorcycle parts. The Club always pays me for my efforts. In fact, while I was attending machinist school full-time, I had quite the little business going and for most part, I still do! From cutting down extended forks, to balancing fly wheels, I do almost any machining asked. Due to my lack of experience, anytime I am approached with a project too complicated for my limited ability, I simply ask my shop instructor, Rudy, how to machine it; he is a master machinist. Rudy is an old biker and, for the most part, a cool dude. It is easy for me to believe during a younger period in his life he was involved with a bike club, but I don't know which one or how deep he was into it. I always slip him a twenty or better for any extra-curricular activity! He sees Brothers coming in and out of the shop, carrying bike parts and wearing Colors. He knows what's happening! Once I fucked up a Brother's bike part, I simply machined it wrong! Oh my god, Rudy freaked out!

He said, "Those guys are gonna kill you!" I reminded him, the part was made wrong under his direction. The truth is, it was no big deal; I had to replace it at my cost, but the Brother understood. I seized the opportunity to play with Rudy's head for a few days though, only in fun of course.

I asked him, "Does your insurance here at the school cover broken legs?" It was all in fun, but I kept it going as long as possible.

I spoke earlier about stealing Harleys; well, here is what we do. We use a horse trailer to steal and move stolen bikes to a suitable place where they can be stripped, usually a U-Store-It locker that has been rented in a false name. The stripping process never takes long. Depending on its year, a Harley only has two sets of serial numbers, one set stamped on its frame, the other on the lower motor case. If not reworked properly, these motor numbers can be a real problem. The police do what is called an acid test, where they swab muriatic acid directly onto the motor numbers. If the original set of numbers have been ground off and restamped with fictitious numbers, the acid will draw to the surface of the aluminum case an impression of the original numbers. We call them Ghost Numbers because after an acid bath, they will slowly appear in a wavy, light gray image, difficult to see, and they have definitely come back to haunt you. This happens because there is an impression left deep in the aluminum casting from the shocking blow created when the numbers are stamped, like a ripple effect. It is in fact, the imprinted molecular memory. Impossible to hide simply by grinding off the original numbers, and an instant trip to the "Crowbar Motel" and the machine confiscated! See how tricky the cops can be? The problem is solved by giving the numbered motorcycle case to me. I will take it to my machine shop school and machine the entire set of original numbers out, all the way through the case! They are 100 percent gone forever! We call that Doin' an Exorcism. Next, heliarc weld the through hole created by the machining process to its original appearance and then a little hand benching, followed by sand blasting the case. It's now ready for restamping. The same thing is done to the frame; however, it is much easier. The Club has an original set of Harley Davidson number stamps.

These stamps have a couple of different style characters, unique only to Harley Davidson, and for sure renumbering the bike is pointless without them. The fictitious numbers are selected by a series of techniques the Club has found to insure a clear title. After this process is complete, the bike is ours. There is no shortage of Brothers in our Club with two and some with even three different Harleys all numbered the same and licensed under one title. It's not a problem as long as the bikes are never together. My shop instructor, Rudy, knows when I'm doing illegal work, but turns a blind eye; and like I said, I take care of him. For a project as illegal as this, I always give him at least a hundred-dollar handshake on my way out. I always pay him according to what it is I do. Most of the other students are mainly attending the school to receive their VA benefits. They are Vietnam Vets and have good factory jobs; they have no desire to learn the machine tool trade. Their time at the school is spent mainly playing poker and drinking. The students that are there to learn, when sober, are working on shop projects like making hammers and small punches and such. None have any idea what I'm up to.

Aside from an "After Market Harley Parts Manufacturer," I've also become a great gunsmith. Only one problem, most of the gun parts I machine fall into the illegal ordinance category; I've made many parts to convert semi-autos into full autos. The civilian model M16 is a Colt model AR-15; it is the Club's weapon of choice. Any AR-15's with serial numbers less than nine thousand are extremely simple to convert to full auto. They require no machining to the lower receiver and will accept the auto sear I machine perfectly; when converted all AR-15's function reliably and are very dependable, a wonderful weapon indeed. The beauty of it is, after I'm done with the weapon, it is still perfectly legal until the auto sear I've made is installed; the weapon can be converted to full auto, selective fire, in seconds. We call that 'Rock 'n' Roll' and it can be returned to semi auto in seconds also; we call that 'Waltz.' Another Club favorite is sound suppressors, silencers. I've machined many of them and custom fit each one to many different guns.

Through my apprenticeship at work, I must attend ten hours a week at machinist school. While I'm there, I'm usually working for the Club, building Harley parts and gunsmithing. I even come in on my own time and use the shop; Rudy is always adequately compensated. Some Brothers have invited him to Club parties, but he always respectfully declines. At sixty years old, he retired from that sort of behavior many moons ago.

Well, here it is, five o'clock Wednesday morning, and I am rudely awakened by my alarm going off. Beep beep beep! I immediately sit up and still half asleep, I almost blast it with my .45 auto. "Shit! It's five in the morning and a work day!"

Nikkei has packed me a wonderful lunch and has laid out my work clothes—God, I love her! I slowly get out of bed, stagger to the bathroom, and ritualistically perform the three S's. After that, and feeling more alive, I quietly creep back into the bedroom to finish dressing. The moon is shining a beam of light around the edge of the window blind. The soft blue light has landed directly on Nikkei's exposed leg and ass. After I climbed out of bed, she adopted my pillow and straddled her leg over it. I stop and stare at this thing of beauty for a moment, and that is enough to give me a hard-on. Damn it! The last thing I need is to leave for work with a woody. Shit! I can't help it! I go to the living room phone and call in late for work. Then return to the bedroom, undress, fall to my knees, and begin kissing Nikkei's gorgeous ass. She very slowly rolls onto her back while generously spreading her legs, giving me a new vantage point in which I can receive her beautiful muff.

She runs her hands through my hair while letting out a soft moan. "Mmmmmm!" I give her head until she shakes; she then surrenders by pulling my head up to hers. I slowly penetrate my fiancée and fuck her until there is no doubt in my mind that she is 100 percent satisfied. I submit to the feeling and allow myself to reach orgasm. I then collapse and cuddle for five minutes or so before redressing. I lean over the bed and give my sleeping beauty a kiss good-bye then leave for work. As I am leaving she smiles and softly says, "Have a nice day, Clutch."

I work in a large defense plant; it's a huge union shop. Attendance wise, as long as I stay within the company's guidelines and the Union contract, I never have any problems, but I do play it right to the line. I do a good job and they are starved for good machinists, so I get away with a lot. I enter the plant and go to my department where my foreman greets me.

He says, "Hello, stranger." I just nod my head while forcing out a quick half smile. I talk to him for a few minutes and receive my day's assignment. I go to my machine and then get busy. Here at work I tend to keep to myself. I eat my lunch at my machine away from the crowd while reading the morning newspaper. However, today I am visited by Heavy; he's a Brother that works in a different, nearby department. He's not in my Chapter, but I know him well, and we get along great! When we talk, he treats me respectfully, more as a man and a friend, than as a prospect. In fact, it was through the strings he pulled that I was hired here into the apprenticeship program. He is six feet tall and has extremely wide shoulders; he wears a number 52 shirt size! Heavy has reddish-colored hair and a reddish-colored handlebar mustache and goatee to match; he kind of looks somewhat like a younger redheaded version of Colonel Sanders (the Kentucky Fried Chicken Dude), but his body is geometrically shaped like a giant rectangle. He is strong as an ox. His hair is very long; it falls to the middle of his back and is always in a ponytail with three bands equally spaced binding it together. Heavy smiles a lot; he can usually be seen laughing.

"Hello, Heavy," I say as he sits down beside me.

"Hello, Clutch, how's your head?" he asks in reference to my battle scars left over from the Graveyard Run.

"I'm okay; a little confused on wat da fuck is goin' on though! How's Hillbilly, have you heard anything?" I anxiously questioned.

"He's bad! His wounds are improving but he's still in a coma, Clutch," he answered very emotionally.

"Listen to me, Heavy, I did nothing wrong. I followed exactly what Hillbilly told me to do, and I had nothing to do with him being shot. There was no way I could have prevented it. Brock is a fucking liar; I asked him to hold my rag because I figured that is how the cops could ID me. Is that wrong?" I asked.

Heavy answered, "I believe you, Clutch, but of all people, why would you hand your Colors to that piece of shit?"

I drop my head in shame and slowly shake it back and forth, then say, "I don't know. I freaked out over Hillbilly, I guess." I look up at Heavy and ask, "Where's my bike?"

"I don't know. I hear it's still up north. Bones has your Colors, I do know that. He said you're on hold until he talks to Hillbilly," he said.

I ask, "And if Hillbilly dies?"

Now Heavy drops his head and shakes it back and forth for a few seconds, then stands and says, "If Hillbilly dies . . . . then you're probably out!" He pats my shoulder and says, "We better get back to work. The buzzer has already gone off. I'll be talking with ya, Clutch." Then he slowly walks away. I go back to running my machine, but I am not very productive. My mind is on the Club and where I stand with it, not here at work. Finally, the last buzzer that ends my day goes off and I practically run out of the plant and to my truck.

I pull down my long driveway; my heart is pounding over the thought of seeing Nikkei. I swear, I feel like a lovesick high school kid. I park my truck, run to the house, and fling open the door. I am bowled over by what I see and smell. My love has set a beautiful kitchen table and has prepared an entire meal! She is wearing a French maid's outfit and is lighting two table candles as I enter the room.

She turns to me and says, "Welcome home, sweetheart, now go wash. You'll find I've laid out a new pair of pajamas for you. Hurry now, supper will be ready soon." She leans forward and gives me a peck on the cheek.

After dinner, Nikkei says she has a surprise for me and taunts me with it for a long time. I continuously ask to see it but she keeps stalling. Finally, Nikkei takes my hand and tells me to close my eyes. She leads me to the living room chair and says, "Keep your eyes closed, no peeking. Now sit down, Clutch." I comply. Nikkei pulls her panties down and swivels her right hip toward me then says, "Okay, open your eyes!" I open my eyes to find I'm staring directly at her butt! There is a large gauze Band-Aid covering the dimple of her ass check.

"What is that?" I demand. She slowly removes the gauze, exposing a new tattoo! It reads, "Property of Clutch."

She giggles and says, "Remember the swap meet? Years ago, you wrote it with a felt marking pen. Well, sweetheart, this one won't wash off!" I couldn't believe it, what a woman! What a gift! I stand and give my woman an endless hug. After a long minute, she struggles loose from my embrace and says, "Aren't you gonna kiss my tattoo? It's very sore!"

I answer, "I'd love to" as I kneel and gently kiss the tattoo on her ass. Nikkei loves to have me kiss her ass; it's a symbolic gesture to her.

I guess all my life, as far back as I can remember, Nikkei would say, "Once you realize how special I am, you'll fall deeply in love with me, and then, you'll be kissin' my ass wherever we go!" Then she would stick her ass out toward me and give it a smack! Well, she was right. I have found out how special she is, and I have fallen deeply in love with her. As for kissing her ass, it happens with great frequency. I'm always kneeling and kissing her butt. She loves it when I do; she lets out a pleased little smirk! It's easy for me to believe she's thinking, 'I knew someday I'd have this guy kissing my ass!' Well, she's right again! As far as I'm concerned, that tattoo is the best gift Nikkei could have given me.

I help her clean the dinner table; we load the dishwasher and put away the leftover food and I take out the garbage. I stand on my porch for a few minutes enjoying the evening air; the weather is perfect, I love spring. Nikkei and I plop down in front of the television and cuddle for an hour before retiring to our bed.

Currently, any time I come in or out of my drive, I chain and lock the gate. As I said, I have a camera and an intercom down there. Well, just as Nikkei and I are climbing into bed, I hear a Harley through the intercom pulling up to the gate. "Fuck! Now what?"

I jump up and look carefully at the camera's monitor and see Fingers climbing off his bike. I push the talk button and tell him to wait until I secure the dogs. I put my pants on; give Nikkei a kiss, and say, "I won't be long. I'll just drive down there, that's easier than locking up the dogs." I tuck my .45 into the swell of my back, grab my pump shotgun, and climb into Nikkei's car, then drive down to the gate. I love Fingers and I respect him, but as a Full Patch Member he must do whatever the Club wants, whether he likes it or not. I'm hoping for good news, any good news will do, especially where Hillbilly is concerned, but I'm going to approach this situation cautiously. Fingers and I go way back. He's been in the Club as long as I can remember; he's one of the Brothers that helped raise me. My entire life, I do not remember him so much as raising his voice to me in anger. I truly love him, I think of Fingers as I do my own Brother. I hope to God he hasn't been sent here to fuck with me. I don't think I'm capable of raising a single hand in violence against him, even if it's in self-defense! I will, however, kill anybody that bothers Nikkei! I know he loves her too, so I'm not worried about that. Today at work, I talked to Heavy, but received little information about my situation with the Club. Perhaps Fingers can shed some light on it.

I very cautiously pull to the gate. I see Fingers' chopper, but do not see him. I stop the car and immediately jump out, then walk away from it. If someone is going to fuck with me, I surely don't want to be sitting in a car for it. It's near dark, and my security light has begun flickering in an attempt to light. I still do not see Fingers, and I do not want to shout, drawing attention to where I stand. I quietly step into the wooded area that borders the front of my property and crouch down. My shotgun is in the car, but I do have my .45 at the ready, one in the chamber, hammer back, safety on. I love .45's!

Suddenly, from the other side of the driveway but this side of the gate, Fingers appears. He has been in the woods also!

I quietly say, "Fingers, what the fuck are you doing?"

He answers with a slight chuckle, "Taking a piss, you Tweak-Head!"

In a half-joking tone I ask, "Did you come to smoke the Peace Pipe, or did you come to Smoke Me?"

He laughs again, this time louder and says, "You really are a Tweak-Head! Now show your mug, Prospect!" As I said, I could never hurt this man, so if he has come to do me harm, then so be it! I walk up and give him a hug. He kisses my forehead and says, "Good to see you, man! Looks like Bones did a number on your face?"

"Yeah, I'm all right. I just don't know what the fuck is going on?" I said.

Fingers puts his arm around me and leads me about fifty feet into the darkened woods. Then we sit on a fallen log and talk. He tells me he didn't have any of the answers I was looking for but that he believes my story. He also says he loves me and that I should just hang tough until we straighten this mess out. That I am safe as far as the Club is concerned, and not to worry, that our Chapter is not going to allow anybody to fuck with me until Hillbilly wakes up and tells his story. We talk for an hour or better. Our conversation becomes more relaxed; he does some reminiscing about me and my antics as a small boy. Finally, Fingers reaches into the inside pocket of his leather jacket and pulls out a small jewelry box. In the small wooden box is a pair of diamond earrings.

He hands them to me and says, "Give these to Nikkei and tell her I said Congratulations on her engagement."

I couldn't believe it. I ask, "How do you know her and I got engaged?" He just laughs as he walks to his scooter. He gives me a nod; kick starts his bike, and then rides off. Wow, I believe everything he told me. That guy is not only like a brother to me, but like a father also; I do love him. I feel so much better now, maybe everything is gonna be okay.

I hurry back to the house to give Nikkei her gift. These earrings look terribly expensive! I'm sure they are; with Fingers, there's never any shortage of cash. I give Nikkei her gift; she is excited as hell. She wants to know how Fingers knew we were engaged. I tell her that as many phone calls as she and her mother made, everyone is sure to know.

I turn out the bedroom light, climb into bed, and say, "Well, now that we're both awake, how about a good night fuck?"

She replies with an energetic, "Okay."

After Nikkei and I Make Love passionately for an hour or so, we retreat to our favorite cuddle position, nose to nose, legs and arms wrapped tight. We silently lay there, exhausted from the sexual wrestling match that makes us one. A few minutes into the cuddle, I begin to tell Nikkei about the weekend Graveyard Run, my Bottom Rocker, and Hillbilly. She just lays there listening. Nikkei never asks about Club business or Club Goings-On. She knows and understands the environment. There is a bond that is understood between all of us, and one never has to tell the whole story. But this time I do, I tell the whole story. Nikkei just lies there listening until I get to the van ride home; I become pretty emotional during my explanation of that Would-Be last ride. I sit up on the edge of the bed and tell Nikkei how there was never any doubt in my mind they were going to kill me. And that she was all I could think of. Nikkei knows I'm no punk; however, I never want to show any weakness to her. But I did. I begin to cry a little, never very much, but tears do roll down my cheeks for a while. She scoots close and hugs me. My head against her breast, she rocks me back and forth while pulling her hand through my hair.

With her hand under my chin, Nikkei gently lifts my head so we are making eye contact and says, "Brock called and told me what happened to Hillbilly. He said you were partly to blame. And that you threw your Colors at him and quit!"

I respond with a loud, angry question, "Nikkei, do you believe that?"

She returns a fast answer, "Of course not! I don't believe anything Brock says, especially when it's about you!" I stand, not completely angered, but my heart is racing. I walk into the kitchen and grab a beer from the refrigerator, then step outside to drink it on the porch. All I can think about is beating Brock to death. I empty the beer and return to Nikkei now sitting up in bed, back propped by pillows and smoking a cigarette.

I say, "Nikkei, I'm staying away from the Club until Hillbilly wakes up. Maybe longer now that I have you. I love Hillbilly, I would have done nothing to hurt him, so fuck the Club! I was going to see him the following day after I got home from the Graveyard Run, but that's when you and I hooked up. I'm sure Hillbilly will understand!" Nikkei stands, puts out her cigarette, and gives me a hug. She tells me she is and will always be mine, with or without the Club and that is her word.

She says, "Now come lay down Clutch, tomorrow is a work day." We get back in bed. She kisses me and says, "Heavy called me also. He was not so much pumping me for info but assuring me that he is on your side, and is behind the scenes helping!" I immediately sit back up. She reaches up and pulls me back down to my pillow, then covers my shoulder with our soft comforter.

I ask, "Why would he call you to say that?"

Nikkei replies in a sweet voice, "He called to congratulate me on our engagement, Clutch, that's all. He asked me if Brock has been a problem. I told him that Brock had called and what he said about Hillbilly being shot, and you throwing your Colors and quitting! That's when Heavy more or less told me everything is gonna to be okay, so relax and sleep now, Clutch, coz everything is gonna be okay. Always remember, sweetheart, no matter what happens, no matter how bad things get, we still have each other!" She gives me a kiss and says, "Nite."

Heavy is a good friend, much older, and like Fingers has been in the Club, coming and going in and out of my life as long as I can remember. Although I'm only a prospect, I see him as my brother/ father. Through the years he has helped me in many different ways. I know he wants me in the Club, but that doesn't prevent him from being the Club's Eye while I'm at work. He belongs to Hillbilly's old Chapter, down on the far side of the city, where Nikkei grew up. That's the Chapter she's from; the same Chapter Brock is prospecting for! Heavy was always telling Hillbilly what was going on with me and work. That would suck because there're times I could have taken a day off from work and not told Hillbilly. This would have given me an entire day off, without having to work or prospect. But now with Hillbilly in the hospital and the problem I have with Bones and the Club, working with Heavy every day could be more of a problem than ever. He's always been on my side though, and I'm sure he knows I didn't betray Hillbilly and quit the Club, so I think I may be able to use him to my advantage. I can send messages to the Club through him. Messages that will help clear my name while exposing Brock as a lying piece of shit. However, Heavy can be tricky. He is no dummy. He is, in fact, 110 percent for the Club and 'By the Book!' All the way, 'By the Book!' Every Club rule must be followed to the letter. He is extremely strict and extremely disciplined! As a Vietnam combat veteran, this guy is still as military as hell. Even before I was prospecting, he would have me doing push-ups whenever I did something stupid. But as I said, like Fingers, I could never raise a hand in violence against him, not even in self-defense! And I will try to use him to my advantage. After all, I have done nothing wrong, and I have nothing to hide. Well, tomorrow will come early and I'll be back at work soon enough, so maybe I'll be able to talk to Heavy some more.

Beep Beep Beep! "Fuck!" Five o'clock in the morning. Work Day and I am moving slowly, very slowly. The good news is, I didn't almost blast my alarm clock this morning. Yesterday, Nikkei yelled at me for threatening the clock.

She said, "Clutch, it's only doing its job! So grow up and get up!" I know that Little Shit is right, so I quit picking on the alarm clock. But this early in the morning, I do want to pick on something! One of my morning chores is tending to the dogs. After I battle with locking up and feeding my four Pitt Bulls, my morning need to pick on something is usually out of my system. I normally give my dogs free range over my property at night. Then kennel them by day. However, now that Nikkei is here, I have been keeping them chained at night and all day. I have a system in which I chain them to steel stakes I've cemented deep into the ground that surround three sides of my house. I've purposely cut their chains long enough so the dogs cannot touch one another, but only by less than one foot; it should be impossible for anybody to pass through the dog barrier. I have them tied nose to nose so that three sides of my house are impenetrable as long as the dogs are alive! Because this breed is so unpredictable and dangerous, I keep them away from Nikkei at all times. I do all their food and water. She can move freely in and out from the side of the house that faces our long driveway. Anyhow, once I feed and water these mutts, all my hostilities are pretty much humbled. I shower, and just as before, Nikkei has laid out my work clothes and packed my lunch. Plenty of food, many treats, and she put in lots of love also!

Chapter Eight

SWEET REVENGE

Driving to work isn't too bad, but I must hit the expressway and drive into the outside of the big city. It's about a forty-five minute commute. If I take a few side streets, a kind of slight detour, I can drive past my Chapter's Clubhouse, and this is what I do this morning. As I slowly cruise past I see Heavy's chopper sitting on the front porch and several other Harleys parked along the front of the house. This can mean many different things, but probably Heavy spent the night there. Maybe he was partying too hard to leave sober. Maybe he hooked up with a sweet young thing. Who knows? Just as my truck is about to pass out of view, Prospect Brock walks from around the corner of the house. We make eye contact, he stops dead in his tracks, and so do I! I can't help myself; I slam my truck into park and jump out! I run as fast as I can straight to that punk. Just as I reach him, he pulls a revolver from his shoulder holster. That doesn't stop me at all; I knock the gun out of his hand and into the air, causing it to go off. Bang! It lands in the yard safely away. I punch him so hard it knocks out all his front teeth. Down he goes. I began kicking the fuck out of his face, one after the other, as hard as I can kick! And I'm wearing steel-toed work boots. For a very long time I kick and punch him in an attempt to kill this Mother Fucker! I want to beat him to death! Suddenly, Heavy appears from the Clubhouse door. He too is wielding a pistol. He is obviously responding to the gun blast Brock fired when I initially hit him. Heavy is being followed by several other Brothers, all toting guns. My truck never went into park. It slowly crept to the roadside and is now anchored against

109

the curb. After seeing all the Brothers coming at me, I walk, not run, to my truck. As I am getting in, I shout for all to hear, "Tell that piece-of-shit Brock this is not over!" Then I speed off, climbing up and over the curb before centering my truck back on the road and burning my tires.

"Sweet revenge!" But not sweet enough by any means. I'm not done with Brock. I'm so revved, so psyched up I feel drunk! I'm having trouble keeping my truck under a hundred miles per hour and between the ditches. "Holy Fuck!" I say aloud, as I regain my composure and begin to calm, I begin thinking about what just happened. "Shit, this could get serious!" But my situation had already been serious, so "Fuck it!" All I know is I feel much better! I knocked all his front teeth out! And here is my defense: he took my Colors, and that is a killing offense! "So piss-on'em!" But I better watch my ass for a while, until this one blows over. And hopefully, it does blow over!

I pull into work and deliberately park in an assigned area; it is reserved for the corporate Big Shots. I do this to throw Heavy off. Then into the plant I go. My shirt is torn and I have a few scratches on my face, neck, and chest. I guess one could see it as if I was just in a fight, but who would be thinking that way this early in the morning? I get my assignment and go to my machine.

Beating Brock has put me in an excellent mood; I can't keep the smile off my face! Things are going great for me at work today. I'm machining an actuator for a magnesium helicopter generator. It must be completed As Soon As Possible; it's going to a Paris Air Show. I finish this part in record time and in excellent quality. The company is very pleased with my performance. At lunch break I go to Heavy's department and ask about him. I am told he is not at work today, that he called in a personal holiday. Hmmm, what's that all about, I wonder?

Well anyhow, my day ends, and on the way home I decide to cruise past the Clubhouse one more time. Is there any wisdom in this thinking? Absolutely not! But I do it anyhow. To my surprise, as I drive past the Clubhouse it looks almost deserted. But that's kind of how it goes, one day it will appear empty, but on the next, it could have hundreds of scooters in front of it. Oh well, I head home, but not before I throw my empty beer bottle into the front yard, followed by the middle finger. I should probably be careful, because fucking with the Club is like fucking with a sleeping giant, but I do it anyhow. "Fuck 'em!"

My return home is a carbon copy of yesterday's arrival from work. Nikkei has a beautiful table set with a lovely dinner to go on top of it. Once again, she is wearing her French maid outfit. Hence, once again making it extremely hard to concentrate on eating—well, eating dinner that is! Nikkei, however, is very interested in how I received these scratches if all I did was go to and from work. I sidestep the issue by ironically telling her, "I got them while beating up Brock!" That's such a bizarre answer she just shakes her head in disgust. She obviously thinks I'm joking, right up until a gang of Harleys pull up to my gate! "Holy shit!" This could be a real problem. At least fifteen to twenty bikes are at the gate. I view the camera's monitor and see most of the Brothers are from my Chapter. Well, that's good news. I see Heavy is with them. And guess who? Prospect Brock! And his sponsor, Crazy George, along with a few other Brothers from that Chapter. It's obvious they're not here for a social visit.

Well, it must be time for me to pay the fiddler, I guess. I'm not worried for Nikkei. I know all these guys love her and would never allow harm to come to her. I give her a kiss and assure her everything is all right. Then head down to the gate. I leave my .45 and my 12 gauge at the house, so I am defenseless in that respect. I would never shoot at a Brother anyhow! But I do figure I'm in for an ass beating. Remember I explained a Rat-Packin'? Well, I'm preparing for that!

As I walk down my long drive, I feel like a death row inmate on his last walk to the electric chair, marching to his doom. Even if I get Rat-Packed, it would be worth it to have pounded Brock's teeth out of his head. Maybe they are going to give poor Ol' Brock a second chance at me. If I can only be so lucky. I get to the gate and the Vice President of my Chapter tells me to follow him. Fuck, I hate this shit! He leads me back into the woods and we both sit on the same fallen log that Fingers and I sat on a day earlier. His name is Crusher, and he has earned that name!

Crusher says, "Clutch, I like you, I can remember you as a snot-nosed punk, fetchin' beer at parties for us, right here on this farm! When you wanted to prospect, I'm the one you approached, asking if I thought it was a good time for you to prospect. I told you then, as far as being easy, there is no good time, no matter who you are. Although your problem with Bones is unique, it's no harder for you to prospect than it's been for any of us! Clutch, we've come to give you a Rat-Packin'! Listen to me, don't quit, take your licks, shake it off, and get back to prospecting."

I throw my head up and ask, "Am I still a Prospect?"

Crusher nods his head yes and says, "You always have been. We gotta work out this thing between you and Brock. It must stop now! Also, Hillbilly has been asking for you!"

I jump up and emotionally ask, "Hillbilly is awake?"

Crusher smiles at me and says, "Yeah, he and Bones have had a long talk. After we're done here, you go and see your Sponsor."

Listening carefully to his direction, I nod my head in agreement, then ask, "Is Prospect Brock gonna be part of the Rat-Pack?"

Crusher sternly says, "Absolutely not! He is not in the Club. He is only a prospect, Prospect!"

I nervously say, "Well, let's get it over with! Do me a favor though, don't do it in front of the camera. I wouldn't want Nikkei to see!"

"Okay, Clutch, let's get it done!" Crusher said.

We walk back to the group of Brothers now gathered in a circle. As I approach them Crusher blindsides me with a hard right to the head! I stagger into the middle of the circle and it begins! One punch after the next, by all Brothers present. I put my fists up in the Praying Mantis position, trying to protect my head, but it is pointless. That does little to help, too many fists coming at me to block! Finally I fall to the ground only to be repeatedly kicked until once again I'm beaten unconscious by my own Club. The Club I love.

When I awake, all the Brothers are gone. I slowly sit up, covered in blood. I try to stand but I stagger and fall into the Iron Gate. It is then I see my Harley and, above it, my Colors hanging over the camera lens. Wow, I don't fucking believe it, my Colors! My bike! "I got my Colors back!" I stagger to my Colors then begin carefully viewing every inch of the cloth. I wipe the blood off my face with my Colors then put them on! As I do, I find a decorative pin, pinned on the upper right pocket of my Rag. I look at this mysterious object; I have never seen it before. "What the fuck is it? Who put it there?" It is a flat round pin about one half inch in diameter and has a solid gold swastika beautifully embossed in its center. I don't understand, but someone put it there, so I'm going to leave it. God, it feels good to know I am back in the Club and once again wearing my Colors! I climb onto my Harley and examine it carefully; it's in perfect condition! I unlock the gate and pull through, then relock it. I slowly cruise to the house, all the while spitting blood through my swelling, smiling, lips!

I climb off my bike and stagger to the side of the house, then clean myself with the garden hose before seeing Nikkei. When I enter the house, I find Nikkei at the door waiting. She takes one look at me and totally flips out. She begins screaming and 'Mother Fucking' the Club for what they have done to me! I do my best to calm her, but she is too pissed off! Madder than I've ever seen her before.

She tries to clean me up, but I say, "No, there's not enough time. We have to go to the hospital and see Hillbilly!"

She stops suddenly and asks, "Hillbilly is awake?"

I smile and say, "He sure the fuck is! Now let's go announce our engagement to him!"

After Hillbilly was shot, he was taken to a small hospital by ambulance where he was stabilized, then flown to a large hospital in the city, about an hour from here. Now that I'm prospecting again, I will have to ride my bike to see him. Remember, while prospecting, your only means of transportation can be your bike. That's okay, the weather is great and I love to ride. So Nikkei puts on her leathers as I do mine, we fire up my Harley and head for the city to see Hillbilly. But first I release my dogs so they have free range while I'm gone. Nikkei looks so good in a black leather jacket and chaps! I really have to fight with my dick to stay down. I'm not sure of the wisdom behind it, but I put my Colors on, and fly them all the way to the hospital. Nikkei has never seen my Bottom Rocker, nor has she ever ridden on this Harley of mine, so this is a very special ride for both of us, her on the back of my Harley and me flying my Colors. The excitement is almost but not quite enough to take my mind away from the pain I'm feeling in my ribs from being kicked during my Rat-Pack. Also, my head is splitting from all the punches I took. How could anybody box for a living? It sucks because at least if I earned the headache honestly, you know Self-Induced, I wouldn't feel so shortchanged. Nikkei is still plenty pissed off over the beating I took. I know this ride is exciting for her also, but like my pain, her anger is not completely diminished just by the excitement of the ride. I have given Nikkei my .45 to carry for me. It's an Old Biker Trick. If there is trouble, whoever the person causing it, will focus all their attention on me. With my pistol, and being ignored, Nikkei can and will get the jump on them. This is why you'll almost always see a one percent Biker with his Ol' Lady. Our women are as dangerous as they are beautiful!

We pull up to the visitors' parking lot at the hospital. There are bikes everywhere! I know they're our Club's because the bikes I don't recognize are parked alongside those I do. I park my bike beside the others, and then Nikkei and I dismount. As we head into the hospital, we're both surprised by Prospect Brock. He is walking from around the outside corner of the building. Nikkei and I are holding hands as we bump into him; all three of us stop and stare at one another for a long, uncomfortable moment. Brock's eyes are vacillating back and forth to mine then Nikkei's, and finally down to our interlocked hands! It's obvious to me Brock is here functioning as a prospect, guarding the bikes. He's wearing his Colors. His face is fucked up. Mine too for that matter, but he is missing his front teeth and has stitches on both sides of his eyebrows along with a large white gauze Band-Aid wrapped around his forehead, like a bandana. He looks like one of those old time pictures of a civil war soldier with the white gauze wrapped around his head. It's almost comical, but I refrain from laughing. I know I hurt him bad, but he looks much worse than I expected. I guess I must have been madder than I thought. I hold my Mug and he does the same. We cannot have any problem here tonight. Besides, I feel pretty good about the beating I already gave him. So no bad looks are exchanged; we just nod and continue into the hospital.

As Nikkei and I walk away from Brock, she gives a quick over-the-shoulder glance at him, then back to me and says, "What happened to him?"

I laugh and offer a simple, one-word explanation, "Me!" She doesn't know what to think!

Man, there are Brothers everywhere! Looks like they're pulling heavy-duty security here at the hospital, protecting Hillbilly. Good! This kind of security will only be done by Full Patch Holders; prospects are not to be trusted with a Brother's life!

It's easy for me to find Hillbilly's room. I just follow the trail of Brothers! To my surprise, I am being very well received by all of them. Many congratulations are given in behalf of Nikkei's and my engagement. Most are directed to her, but that's okay; it's helping to calm her anger toward the Club. She may only be 110 pounds, but make no mistake, that's 110 pounds of pure TNT!

As we enter Hillbilly's room, we come face-to-face with Bones, who is just leaving. He stops directly in front of me, blocking my way. He leans close; we are practically nose-to-nose. There is total silence in the room now. I don't know what to think. Bones is not a very large man, but he has a very strong presence. He has jet-black hair with a well-trimmed black beard. He has that 'Movie Star' look, every hair in perfect place. His eyes are unbelievable though, they will pierce deep into your soul, fishing out any fear or insecurities; he uses them to dissect your thoughts.

He stares at me for a moment then in his deep voice, he softly says, "Prospect, I see you got the pin I sent you" as he points to the swastika pinned to my rag, then continues, "Wear it proud, Prospect. It was a gift to me from your Sponsor. He gave it to me the day I received my Top Rocker! And now it is a gift from me to you!"

I said, "Thank you, Bones, it will never come off my rag, and when I die, I will be buried with it still pinned to my Colors!"

He pats my shoulder as he walks past me, and says "Good. I will be seeing you Clutch!"

Wow, what a rush!

I lean down and whisper to Nikkei, "Do you know who that was?"

She nods her pretty head and says, "Oh Yeah!"

Nikkei and I sit quietly while Hillbilly talks with all the Brothers gathered in his room. He really doesn't look too bad, considering he was shot seven times!

After a long while, Hillbilly turns to Nikkei and says, "I hear you're engaged?"

Nikkei gives him a huge smile while raising her hand to show the engagement ring and answers, "Finally. I was beginning to think Clutch was never gonna ask me!"

Hillbilly chuckles and says, "Come over here, let me look."

Nikkei stands and walks to his bedside, then leans down and gives him a hug followed by a kiss and says, "The world wouldn't be as good without you in it, Hillbilly." A slight tear rolls from her eye.

Hillbilly replies, "I ain't going anywhere soon, sweetie. I'm gonna play hard to get for the next thirty years or so! You can take that to the bank! Now let me see that ring." Nikkei laughs as she wipes a tear from her eye with her index finger and reaches her hand out to Hillbilly. He carefully examines the ring before giving me an approving nod, along with a nice smile and says, "Good job, Prospect!" He then turns his attention back to Nikkei and says, "Do me a favor, sweetheart, keep Clutch out of trouble while I'm in the hospital, will ya please?"

Nikkei smiles and replies, "I will try, but sometimes it's not such an easy job!"

Hillbilly says with a devious grin, "Well, darling, anytime you need help, you give me a call!" Then they both begin laughing; I also laugh, but it is easy to see my laugh is fake. Last thing I need is Nikkei teaming up with my Sponsor!

Hillbilly looks directly at me and says, "You and Nikkei go home now, it's late and you gotta work. Before you go, pull that curtain back and look at what's on the wall. Clutch, both of you come back to see me. I'm eager to see Nikkei again when I have more time to spend with her, and you and I must have a long talk." He writes down on a piece of paper the date and time, Saturday at 7:00 p.m., and then shows it to me before tearing it into small pieces. This way if the cops are listening, they will not be able to prepare for our visit. It is understood, he and I are being watched very closely now. The cops figure we know who shot him and we will be plotting revenge. BET, Biker Enforcement Team, has undoubtedly put most their resources on this shooting. They will be doing all they can to prosecute, not prevent any vengeance killings.

Hillbilly then turns to Nikkei and says, "Sweetheart, could you excuse us for just a minute or so?"

Nikkei smiles and replies, "Of course, Hillbilly." then leaves the room. I go to the dividing curtain and slid it back, exposing the wall behind it. On that wall was pinned a Center Patch! I walk to it for a closer look. It is beautiful, a nice, new, clean Center Patch!

Hillbilly says, "Don't touch it, Prospect!"

I turn and say, "I don't understand?" The room is still filled with Brothers, but all are silent now.

Then Hillbilly very seriously says, "That, Clutch, belongs to you! You were gonna receive it tonight, but after you fucked up with Brock at the Clubhouse, it goes to the wall!"

That's a Club tradition. When a Patch is Pulled from a Brother, it will be pinned to a wall. It is a form of disgrace. That one I knew, but it looks like if a prospect is in-line for a Patch, then fucks up before receiving it, it goes on the wall also. It's a head game!

I didn't know what to say, so I turn to leave, but before I exit I say to all the Brothers present, "Well, it looks like I'll just have to try harder, and I will! Good night, Hillbilly, I'll see ya when I see ya!"

As Nikkei and I are leaving, she says, "Is everything okay, Clutch?"

I answer, "It is Nikkei, it really is!" We climb on my motorcycle, and as we are pulling away, Nikkei turns and looks behind us to see Prospect Brock standing in an empty field beside the hospital. He has his hands on his hips, head down, and perambulating in a moping, depressed manner. He's here to guard the bikes, and I'm sure he didn't even see us leave!

Nikkei says, "What happened to Brock's Center Patch?"

"What?" I ask and then turn sharply to look. To my surprise, Brock is only wearing a Bottom Rocker. "Oh Shit! His Center Patch has been Pulled!"

Like I said, when a Patch has been Pulled, it will be pinned to a wall. This means both Brock and me have our Center Patches pinned to our Sponsors' wall.

Crusher said he wants the feud between Brock and I to end, but how is this possible? Even if I wanted to Kiss and Make Up, Brock would not. Let's have a look: His Center Patch has been Pulled. No doubt over me. His front teeth are gone, over me. And his Ol' lady is gone, over me! Oh, how he must hate me! That's his problem; he's no longer a threat to me. My intentions now are to focus on Nikkei and the Club. I want my Top Rocker ASAP!

Nikkei and I pull down our long drive; it's late for a work night. I lock the gate behind us and park my scooter on the porch. Nikkei goes in the house and prepares for bed while I chain the dogs. Riding with both Nikkei's arms wrapped tightly around me and her lips pressed against my neck is very provocative. Right now I'm trying not to consider her sexually because I'm tired, beat-up, and in dire need of sleep before work tomorrow. I go into the house and have a nice hot shower. My ribs hurt so bad it's all I can do to wash. I don't want to ask Nikkei to help. The last thing I need is her bathing me! That's got 'Hard-On' written all over it! After showering, I creep into bed, then reach up and turn off the lamp that sits on my nightstand. Click! The room is very dark now. Nikkei rolls over and wraps around me, her head touching mine.

With her mouth, she slowly chews and licks my ear, occasionally lightly blowing into it. Well, there it goes 'Up-Para scope!' It's impossible to be around a woman as beautiful as Nikkei and not spend every waking hour Making Love! And with Nikkei, there is no such thing as a Quickie!

Beep Beep Beep! "Fuck! Five AM. again!" I promised Nikkei I wouldn't shoot my alarm clock, but how tempting it is at this hour! Oh well, out of bed I climb. I do the three S's and then tend to my dogs. Although Nikkei and I were up late Makin' Love she still has found time to pack my lunch and lay out my work clothes—God, I love her! I give my sweetheart a good-bye kiss.

She smiles and says, "Have a nice day, Clutch, I love you!"

I reply, "I love you too, Nikkei." I'm a prospect again, so I must ride my bike to work, well, everywhere I go for that matter. Today that sucks because it's raining hard. Oh well, Fuck it, I gotta go to work. Riding in the rain sucks worse because I have no windshield and I'm feeling the Next-Day pains from the Rat-Packing I took. I wrap extra clothes in a plastic garbage bag and bungee cord them to my handrail, along with my lunch. I make it to work okay. I'm wet, cold and miserable, but such is life.

I enter the plant and go directly to the washroom to put on dry clothes!

While I'm changing, a voice whispers from behind me. "If you quit the Club, Prospect, you'll never have to ride in the rain!" I slowly turn to see Heavy standing there smirking.

So I retort, "But I love riding in the rain!" We both laugh.

Then Heavy gives me a serious look and says, "Clutch, you look like you just fought a death match with Satan himself and lost!"

I tell him, "And that's exactly how I feel!" Once again we both laugh.

Then I give him a more serious look, but still joking around, and say, "I didn't feel you pulling any punches last night during my Rat-Packin'!"

Heavy laughs and says, "Come On, Clutch, I was wearing boxing gloves, you fuckin' Sissy!"

I look at him while rubbing my jaw and say, "Yeah Right!" Again, we both start laughing.

He extends his hand for a handshake and says, "Welcome back, Bro!"

I shake his hand then say, "Thanks, Heavy! It's good to be back!" We hug and then walk together through the shop to our departments.

As we walk Heavy asks, "Did you see Hillbilly?"

I answer, "Yeah."

Heavy continues, "He looks pretty damn good for what he went through!"

I say, "I know, he's one tough Mother Fucker! Heavy, I can't tell ya how happy I am he's alive and that he's my Sponsor!" Heavy pats my back and continues on to his department, leaving me at mine.

My, my, how fast things change . . . and right now, I feel good. Can you imagine me saying that? I hadn't healed from the Graveyard Run when Bones pounded the fuck out of my head, then my chapter came to my house and I was Rat-Packed! Now every rib in my body hurts and I have cuts and bruises all over my body, yet I feel good. That's because I'm starting to see my dream of having both Nikkei and the Club come true.

Today is Friday. I promised Nikkei we would go out tonight, maybe hit some bars. Problem is, I don't want to be seen by any Brothers while I'm out partying, because that's not what Prospects are supposed to be doing. I told Nikkei we'll ride to a small town about two hours from home. It's as far away from the Club as I can get in two hours. The town has a junior college, and the bars there are wild. The plan is, she and I will sneak out about 6:00 p.m. I do not have to see Hillbilly until tomorrow night, so I got my ass covered there.

The last buzzer just blew, ending my workday. I go to the washroom to pick up the wet clothes I rode to work in and bump into Heavy.

He says, "Hi, Clutch, are you going to the city to see Hillbilly?"

I answer, "No, he told me not to come until tomorrow."

Heavy thinks about what I just said for a few seconds then replies, "So let me guess, you and Nikkei are planning to sneak off tonight and do some partying all by yourselves, far away from the Club?"

Wow, I told you this guy is sharp!

I say, "No, even with boxing gloves, you hurt me too much to be thinking about any of that. I think I'll stay home tonight and lick my wounds!"

Heavy laughs and says, "Yeah right! And I got some good land in Florida I'll sell ya cheap. Listen carefully to me, Prospect, don't fuck-up tonight! I don't want any phone calls. You hear what I'm saying?"

I pause for a long moment then say, "I do, Heavy, and you're right, maybe I really will stay home and lick my wounds!"

Heavy gives me a smile and says, "Okay, good, I'll be seeing ya then, Clutch. Oh, hey, since you're gonna be home tonight, you probably don't mind if I give you a call? Just to say hello, you understand?" He throws his head back as he lets out a long, devious laugh and then walks off. Who knows if he'll call or not? Either way, I had better stay home.

It quit raining, and needless to say, my ride home is much more pleasant than my ride to work this morning. As I cruise home, I'm thinking about what Heavy said. Problem is, Nikkei has her heart set on going out tonight. If I'm gonna have both her and the Club, I must learn to juggle them both. Well, balance them both I think is a better way of saying it. However, this would be a good night to go out because, come tomorrow, who knows what Hillbilly has planned for me?

I unlock the gate and pull down my long drive, still not sure if I should go out tonight or not. I park my bike on the porch and enter my house. Nikkei runs and jumps into my arms! With her legs bent at the knees and feet off the floor, she hugs my neck and kisses me frantically. "What the fuck is this all about, Nikkei?" I ask.

She answers, "I'm just happy to see you, Clutch, that's all! Did you get wet riding to work this morning?"

I reply, "Yes, very wet! Heavy saw me in the washroom changing this morning and reminded me if I quit the Club, I will never have to ride in the rain again."

Nikkei laughs and says, "I love Heavy, he's funny!"

I say, "He also sounded worried about you and me going out tonight."

Nikkei stops suddenly and in a concerned voice asks, "How did he know we were going out? And what's he worried about?"

I answer, "Well, he just figured we would. You know how smart he is, and I don't know why he is worried. He just has a bad vibe I guess."

Nikkei very disappointedly says, "Maybe we should stay home then?"

I reply, "I know. I want to get you out of the house for a while but Heavy kinda freaked me out! With all the shit that's gone down lately and the war, staying home may be a good idea."

Nikkei looks down to the floor and rubs her chin for a minute, then jumps up and down like a little kid and says, "Okay, it's final. We'll stay home, veg out on pizza, watch TV, and fuck like champions all night long!"

How can I not love this woman who has not a selfish bone in her body? Most women would be raising hell to go out.

I get serious and ask, "Are you sure, Nikkei?"

She answers, "As long as we are together, we'll have fun, that I'm sure of, so let's begin the party right now!" She sits a bottle of wine on the table in front of me and begins pulling pizza ingredients from the cupboard and refrigerator.

I grab and give her a tight hug and then say, "Thanks, Nikkei, I love you! Hey, does this mean you'll put on the French maid outfit?"

She squares up to me, puts her chest out, and jokingly says in a deep voice, "Clutch, do you want to eat or fuck?"

I laugh and say, "Fuck, then eat, then fuck, then watch TV, then fuck, then eat again and then finally we'll fuck again!" She laughs and goes back to scrounging through the cupboard.

As she does, she whispers under her breath, "Sounds good to me!"

Nikkei and I do just what we said. We stay home and eat pizza, fuck, watch TV, fuck, eat again, and then fuck again, proving that we do not have to go out to have a good time. Like Nikkei says, 'All we need is to be together, and anywhere will do!'

CHAPTER NINE

TIGHT BOND

After talking to Heavy yesterday at work and yielding to his advice to stay home last night, and having such a good time with Nikkei eating pizza, watching TV, and Makin' Love, I'm happy as hell I did not go out. As Outlaw Bikers, we learn to follow our Vibes or Gut Feelings and live off our instincts. It was obvious to me Heavy had a 'Bad Vibe' over Nikkei and I going out on the town. Who knows what may have happened?

Nikkei and I get up late the following day and spend it lounging in front of the television. Nikkei's mom, Sam, stops for a visit.

She always brings a bag of food for us, saying, "I wouldn't want you two love birds to starve! You both must keep your energy high so you can make me a Grandchild!" She has also brought some old pictures of my mom and dad and her and her husband, Nikkei's dad. We all sit on the couch together for hours looking through the pictures, laughing and talking; it really is enjoyable! I love Sam very much!

It's getting toward night fall and I must start thinking about going to see Hillbilly. My Sponsor told me to be at the hospital tonight at 7:00 p.m. He also invited Nikkei. It's getting late so we must get ready and leave. Again Nikkei and I will ride my bike to the city, again she'll be wearing her black leather jacket and chaps, and I'll be flying my Colors. Nikkei's mom is spending the weekend at our house, so I don't unchain the dogs before I leave. Nikkei and I give her a hug, fire up the Harley, and ride off. I do, however, close and lock the gate behind me. Sam has been to the city twice to see Hillbilly since he awoke from his coma. She has sent a small apple pie she baked for him; Nikkei is holding it as we fly down the highway. Boy, I have many things to tell Hillbilly. I already explained to Nikkei she will have to wait outside his room while he and I talk. She understands and after saying hello to Hillbilly, Nikkei and a couple of her girlfriends have planned to walk to a small biker bar around the corner from the hospital. The bar will no doubt be full of Brothers, so as Clubwomen, these three will be safe, and I won't have to worry about them.

We arrive at the hospital and go directly to Hillbilly's room. Nikkei secretly passes my .45 to me. She gives Hillbilly the apple pie, then a hug and kiss before leaving for the biker bar. All the Brothers gathered in the room leave; Hillbilly and I are alone now. Before we begin, I check to make sure the phone is unplugged, even hung up, the cops can listen through it. With all the activity in and out of the room, it's a given BET is on the hospital's switchboard playing cop games with the phones. As I lean down, I find the entire cord has been yanked from the wall. I hold the destroyed phone cord to my face, cross my eyes, and chuckle.

Hillbilly just gives me a shrug and says, "They just don't make them like they used to!" He turns the TV volume up loud and I sit beside him and lean over, so he and I can whisper to one another.

I begin by kissing Hillbilly's forehead and saying, "I'm glad you made it, Bro! I'm allowed to call you Bro coz I'm still on my Day Off, remember?"

Hillbilly chuckles and says, "I heard you had quite the ordeal! Bones tells me he tuned you up pretty good! Understand, Clutch, after I was shot, Brock seized the moment! Everyone was freaking out and looking for someone to hurt. Brock saw that as an opportunity to fuck you over with his wild accusations and then he made his story believable by having possession of your Colors. When Bones and the rest of the Brothers saw that, they wanted you gone. Brock figured that is exactly what would happen. He thought I was dead, and you'd be next, or at least Rat-Packed and Eighty-Six'ed from the Club! Hell, he had even put a bid in for your bike! What he did not understand is, the Club was not going to do anything until they talked to me first. However, because I was not feeling very sociable, having seven bullet holes in me and such, they put you on hold until I recovered from my traumatic coma. Anyway, when I told Bones the truth, he about shit himself. I swear, he had tears in his eyes over what happened to you! Then, when he found out you disrespected the

Club by going to the Clubhouse and tuning up Brock, he called and told Crusher not to do anything about it until he came and talked to you personally, but you had already been Rat-Packed! Hearing that, he got so mad he pulled the hospital phone out of the wall and then threw it. Your Colors and bike were already down here along with your Center Patch. Oh, by the way, I guess Ice Man has your pistol. Bones said he'll get it for you as soon as Ice Man gets out of jail. Anyhow, just between you and I, Clutch, your Center Patch will not be pinned to the wall very long. It's more of a formality! I see you got the swastika Bones pinned to your rag."

I graciously answer, "Yes, I love it! But as a prospect I'm not allowed to have any pins on my Colors."

Hillbilly is quick to respond, "Clutch, that pin is a gift from our National Pres! Never take it off your rag, ever! While you're prospecting, if any Brother tries to take it from you, let them know it was a gift from me to Bones when he got his Top Rocker, before I was even in this Club! That was before I ever even considered Patching Over. Bones gave it to you and said 'Never Remove It.' So never remove it! Anyhow, I hear you put it on Brock good! The reason you were Rat-Packed is not coz you tuned up Brock, but because you went to the Clubhouse to do it! Total disrespect, Clutch! What the fuck were you thinking?"

I reply, "Hillbilly, all I was doing was cruising past the Clubhouse when I saw him. I did not go there looking for Brock, or any trouble for that matter! I hadn't been around, so I thought I'd drive past on my way to work and have a look. But when I saw him, I lost all control!"

Hillbilly says, "You're lucky you didn't get yourself shot!"

I timidly answer, "I know!"

Then Hillbilly says with a smile, "Well, Brock got Rat-Packed also! And his Center Patch Pulled! One more fuck up from him, and he's out! Anyhow, you and Nikkei are engaged, huh?"

I answer, "Yeah, I love her 100 percent, Hillbilly, and that's what I want to say to you. I can no longer put the Club first in my life. I must put her first. I not saying I want to quit, but how can I give the Club 110 percent when all I do is think of her?"

With his tongue and upper teeth, Hillbilly pulls some of his beard hair into his mouth and begins chewing. He turns his head away from me, staring directly at the heart monitor.

A long time passes before he turns back and says, "Clutch, make no mistake about it. The Club demands 110 percent from all its members! But you're not the only one in love with his Ol' lady. We encourage a strong bond between a Brother and his woman. We give all Brothers space for that and accept their Ol' ladies into the Club, you know that! What's really bothering you Clutch?"

I get up and anxiously pace around the room for a minute or two, then sit back down and say, "The Club is all I ever wanted; it's all I ever knew. There was never any doubt in my mind as to me wanting to join. I haven't told you, but after Bones punched me out, the Club gave me a ride home in one of our vans. On this trip, the four Brothers riding along told and convinced me I was gonna to be killed. How do I defend myself against my own Club? I can't kill a Brother, even if it's to save myself! That's my problem; I love the Club more than I love myself, so if killing me is what they wanted, then so be it! However, one thing I did find out on that ride home is; I would kill a Brother to protect Nikkei! So maybe I love her more than I love the Club? I ask you Hillbilly, what's the answer? Coz on that long ride home, all I could think about was Nikkei. I kept passing out, and every time I did, I would dream about her. I swear, I'm no punk, Hillbilly, and given a chance, I'll prove it! But right now I'm thinkin'; I love her more than I love life itself!"

Hillbilly says, "You say you're no punk and given a chance you'll prove it, well, as far as I'm concerned, you've been given a chance, and you did prove it!"
Wow, what a rush!

We both just sit there in silence for a long time until finally I say, "Ya know, Hillbilly, my whole life I have always seen the future as me having Nikkei and the Club having me. I give you my word, whatever it takes, I will work it out so I can have both!"

He gives me a huge smile, and I lean over and hug him the best I can. I lean back onto one elbow and Hillbilly says, "Good! Good job, Prospect, now, listen to me very carefully. I know who shot me and you and I are gonna Take Care of Business. When you leave here tonight, take your Center Patch with ya. This is a new phase in your prospecting, Clutch. Everything up to now has been child's play. Now it's gonna get serious. Are you with me, Clutch?"

I stand and smile from ear to ear and repeat a phrase Hillbilly is fond of saying; it comes from a TV weekly, Beretta.

I answer, "Yes I am, and 'You Can Take That to The Bank!'"

He smiles and says, "Okay, go home and play house with Nikkei! In a few days, a man will visit you from Down South. You do not know him, but do exactly as he says, okay?"

I look him directly in the eyes and answer, "Of course I will!"

I then approach Hillbilly and give him another hug, followed by a kiss on the forehead! After that, I practically run to my Center Patch and remove it from the wall. Then as quietly as I can, I yell, "Fuckin' A!" Hillbilly laughs hard as I walk out of his hospital room, staring at my Center Patch.

I ride my bike to the bar where Nikkei is partying with her friends. This place is packed with Brothers. I did not trust putting my new Center Patch in my pocket in case it may blow out or something weird like that, so I rode here with it held tightly between my teeth!

As I back my bike to the curb alongside the others, a couple Brothers standing outside the bar smoking a joint call to me, "Come over here, Prospect! What's that in your mouth?"

I dismount from my Harley.

As I walk to them, I take my Center Patch from my mouth and say, "It's my Center Patch. Hillbilly just gave it to me!"

One of the Brothers says, "Well then, you must have a Day Off also! Come on, Clutch, let me buy you a beer!"

He puts his arm around my neck and leads me into the bar. We approach the bar and he orders us a beer. He then walks to the jukebox, reaches behind it, and turns the volume down very low. When he does, most the Brothers in the bar stop talking and look at him. He points toward me and yells, "Look Bros, Clutch got his Center Patch tonight! He has the Day Off!"

He then turns the music back up; Jimi Hendrix is playing 'All along the Watchtower.' He offers me a toast; as Bikers, we tap the necks of our beer bottles together and nod. One by one, Brothers keep coming up and congratulating me; they all bring beer! As I learned from prospecting, I mostly dump it out. Oh sure, I'd love to succumb to an alcohol buzz, but I must ride home with Nikkei in a few hours and I'd like to do that somewhat sober. Also, even though it's a Day Off for me and I may act as a Full Patch Member, I really want to watch what I say and do. Especially after all the Bullshit I've been through with Brock! It's Saturday night and everyone is happy because Hillbilly is recovering nicely. But we must not get Sloppy because we are at war. There is a Club van parked directly outside the bar, and you can bet it holds a couple of Brothers with AR-15's, pump shotguns, and plenty of ammo! So I rev-up my Party Motor, but not to Full Throttle.

I keep finding myself surrounded by Brothers wanting to hear the story about Hillbilly's shooting. The Brothers here are mostly from Chapters that surround this huge city, and for the most part, I know them all. They have all been to parties on my farm over the years. A few ask me about Brock, but I'm sure most the Brothers here have already heard I knocked out his front teeth, and about the Rat-Packing I received for doing it! They're all on my side; they all say they would have done the same thing. And the beer just keeps coming, one after the other.

Nikkei is getting drunk. Everyone is buying her congratulation shots and glasses of Champagne; she's loving it and having a ball. Well, it looks like she got her night out after all. She gets horny as hell when she drinks, so she's hugging and kissing all over me and her two girlfriends. Nikkei is not going to share me, but she likes to pretend by flirting around with the idea of a threesome. One of her girlfriends is a Club Ol' lady, so she's definitely off-limits anyhow. The other is a Club Hang-around, a very beautiful brunette. She's the one Nikkei is giving most of her attention to. I really don't care one way or the other, right now it just doesn't sound all that appealing to me. I love Nikkei and she's all I need. Also, I think a threesome with her and her girlfriend would be awkward. Nikkei and me are Old-Fashioned that way. She is possessive and jealous, so while drunk, it may seem like fun to her, but come tomorrow me and her girlfriend may both end up Dead! Especially if Nikkei thinks her girlfriend and I enjoyed each other a little too much!

The ride home is fun. Nikkei can't keep her hands off my Crank! The entire ride, every car I pass gets a bird's-eye view of both Nikkei's arms reached around me and playing with my dick.

We get home and are greeted at the door by Nikkei's mom, Sam. She asks, "How's Hillbilly?" Before I can answer, Nikkei grabs my hand and pulls me into the bedroom.

As she does, she tells her mother, "Sorry, Mom, can't talk, got something to show Clutch!"

I say, "Nikkei, how rude!" She just giggles then shuts and locks the bedroom door behind us. I think by now you all know what happens next! And happens!! And happens again!!!

The following day Nikkei is hung over. That's okay; she needed a night out on the town. I arose early and prepared a huge breakfast for both her and Sam, and served them both in bed. Nikkei spends most of the day on the couch, nursing her hangover. I spend most of the morning looking at old pictures with Sam. They are pictures of my mom and dad and Sam's husband, Nikkei's dad. My favorite is a picture of my dad's and Nikkei's dad's Harleys parked front to front. Their front wheels are facing each other three feet apart. It's a posed picture. Nikkei and I are standing in between the two front tires holding hands. It's Easter, she's in a nice, new white dress, and I'm wearing a little boy's suit and tie. We are only two and three years old. Behind each bike stand my mom and dad and Nikkei's mom and dad. Both our fathers are wearing their colors! How cool is that? A Biker's Family Portrait!

All day long, I've been pestering Nikkei to get up and sew my Center Patch on my Rag. Finally, around noon, she does it, but only after Sam threatens to do it first!

Sam says, "It won't be the first one I sewed on!" I must admit, it's one of my most treasured moments, having the woman of my love sew the Patch of my love, on the Colors of my love! You watch, I'm going to have both, Nikkei and the Club!

Sunday has come and gone; it was very pleasant spending it with Nikkei and her mother. As I said, Sam is like a mother to me. I'm at work now and things are not going so well. Our company has just announced we lost a major weapons system to a competitor, which means layoffs are possible. Our business is referred to as 'feast or famine.' At lunch, Heavy comes to my machine and talks about it for a few minutes.

As he's getting ready to leave, he says, "After work, you come with me, okay? Meet me at the south guard gate. You got it, Clutch? Don't be late!" He is very specific and very serious; I know something is up, something involving Club Business.

My workday ends, and as planned, I meet Heavy at the south guard gate. He tells me, "Get in my car, we're going for a little ride. It shouldn't take long."

We drive to a small bar not far from the plant. The two of us sit in a far corner of the dark bar; I stand and walk to the bar, then order us each a beer. As I'm waiting for our beer, the back door opens. The bar is dark; bright sunlight bursts through the doorway around the figure of a very large man. It's difficult to see. He enters the bar, followed by two others. The three of them give the appearance of Tough Biker Types. I'm hoping this isn't trouble; we are At War. They all belly up to the bar. I'm given my beers and quickly return to the table where Heavy is sitting. He and I talk for a few minutes when suddenly the large Biker Type stands, beer in hand, and approaches our table. This guy is as large as Hillbilly! I don't know what to think or do. This guy is huge and I don't have a gun. I look at Heavy, but he doesn't seem alarmed. So I sit back and patiently wait to see what this guy wants, all the while trying to read Heavy's face for trouble. He comes to our table, pulls out a chair, turns it around backwards and then sits down. The other two that came in with this guy are now turned on their bar stools, elbows on the bar behind them, and watching us closely. Once again, I look at Heavy and try to read his response, but he doesn't budge, he never says a word, he doesn't smile or frown. I don't know what to think!

Finally Heavy says, "Dealer, meet Clutch, Clutch, meet Dealer." Oh cool, Heavy knows this guy, so I relax. We both tap the necks of our beer bottles together as we nod. What I don't know is, I was just introduced to the man that is going to lead me into the most deadly part of my life! Blood, death, and destruction—an Angel of Death; we will share a 'Tight Bond' and soon he will prove to be my closest friend and Brother!

Heavy says, "I'll leave you two alone," as he joins the other two Bikers still sitting and watching from the bar. He gives them both a biker-type hug, then all three sit and turn facing the back bar, quietly talking and sipping beer.

Dealer says to me, "I hear good things about you, Clutch. I've been told you are a good man. Well, I'm gonna find out if it's true or not. If and when you get your Top Rocker, you'll find out who and what I am. Until then, you are on a need-to-know basis with me, understand?" I nod my head in agreement, and he continues. "Your sponsor told you I was coming. Well, I'm here. Unless there's a problem, I will be staying at your house off and on for a few weeks. Is that a problem?"

I reply, "No problem."

Again he continues, "What about your ol' lady? Will she have any problem with it?"

Once again I reply, "Nope, she's a good woman and will do anything I say."

Dealer stands and says, "Okay then, it's settled. I'll be out there tonight, but I'll call first."

He turns and joins the others at the bar, they all stand to leave but not before Dealer and Heavy hug. After the three leave, Heavy rejoins me at the small table.

He says, "Okay, Clutch, I'll take you back to your bike. Let's go!" On the way back to the shop, Heavy asks, "I hear Dealer is gonna stay at your place for a few days?"

I answer, "Yeah, what do you know about this, Heavy?"

He angrily snaps back, "I know it ain't none of my business! So shut da fuck up, Prospect! I only asked coz I haven't seen Dealer for a long time and he told me to stop out at your place for a beer, that he will be there for a few days!" He was yelling.

"Sorry, Heavy, I didn't mean to be Loose-Lipped. I just wondered what was going on, that's all!" I apologetically said.

Heavy calmed a bit, but still says loudly, "It's like this, Clutch, Dealer will tell you as he sees fit, and that is that!"

Heavy drops me off at the plant; I climb on my bike and head home. I can't help thinking about my meeting with Dealer. Man, he looks like he could snap a man's neck in a second! That's one scary dude. I mean him and Hillbilly look as if they came out of the same mold. As I ride home, I continue to wonder about Dealer and his connection with Hillbilly and the Club. I'll bet he's a Brother, he almost has to be, but Hillbilly never came straight out and told me that, so who knows? These guys are always so fucking Top Secret about everything! I suppose that's the way one becomes after being in an Outlaw Bike Club though. I'm that way also, but never as much as the members. Well, I'll just have to learn. It's called Survival; never tell the whole story, not to anyone. Hillbilly often says your own worst enemy follows you around everywhere you go; there's no escaping it because it's your mouth. So always, keep it shut. The jails are full of prisoners that Got Away With It, but opened their Big Mouth after the fact and that's what convicted them!

I get home okay, park my bike on the porch, and Nikkei greets me at the door. She is sporting a warm smile and offers me a kiss by standing on her tiptoes, head out, lips puckered. I give her a long hug and kiss.

She asks, "Work late today?"

I answer, "No, Club business."

Oh boy, that shut her right up. She won't ask any more questions now that I said that.

I say, "Nikkei, I hope it's okay with you, but a Biker named Dealer is gonna stay here for a few weeks, okay?"

She replies, "Whatever you say, Clutch."

"Sweetheart, this is for the Club, but anything that conflicts between you and me, will be settled by me siding with you. I put you first over the Club, and that's it! My goal is to juggle the two of you in perfect concert, but if push comes to shove, I go with you!" I sternly said.

She never says anything, just comes to me with a soft kiss and a tight hug.

The phone rings and its Dealer; he says he's on his way over and he will be here at eight o'clock sharp. I give him directions and tell him I'll meet him at my iron gate.

About a quarter to eight, I walk down to the gate. I'm carrying my 12-gauge pump, and my .45 is tucked into the swell of my back. I unlock and open the gate. Exactly eight o'clock and four Harleys followed closely by a van pull into my drive. They don't stop. They are moving fast and loud as they pull past me and head to the house. I close and lock the gate, then double-time it back to the house. Wow, these guys are Serious. I still don't know who they are, but I'm pretty sure they're Brothers. At least that's what I think.

I get back to the house and there's six dudes standing around the four Harleys. I walk up to Dealer and say, "Hello, Dealer, what do you need me to do?"

He says, "Do you want a beer? I know I do!" He looks over at one of the men standing in a tight huddle and orders, "Prospect, get me and Clutch a beer!" The dude immediately runs to the van, opens a large cooler, and returns with two ice-cold beers. He opens the first and hands it to Dealer, then opens the second and hands it to me.

I say, "Thank you." The prospect then runs and fetches the other guys standing there a beer each. We all stand in a circle around the bikes and drink beer.

Dealer says, "Oh, by the way, everyone, this is Clutch. Clutch, meet Rocky, Skull, Billy, Big Bob, and that's Prospect Petie." I nod at each one as he introduces them, but never say a word.

I still do not know for sure if any of these guys are Club members, but who else can they be? For sure, Rocky and Big Bob are the two that were with Dealer at the small bar where we met. Rocky is not a very large man. He is a soft-spoken, mild-mannered type of person. In his relaxing voice, he says to me "Nice place you have here," as he turns his head and pans over my farm. He then asks, "Is that your '65 Pan?" As he points to my motorcycle, all the others turn and look. It's easy for some to gauge the year of my bike because it's the last year of the Panhead and the first year of the electric start. So if you see a Panhead with an electric start, it's a 1965.

I answer, "Yes it is."

"Let's have a look." He says as he walks towards my Harley. I follow him, and am followed by the others. We all gather around my bike. I receive many compliments from them. I explain the bike is a retired Police Special and that explains the paint job's theme of Brothers on Harleys, being chased by cops in cars. I tell them a Brother in my Chapter, Buttons, did the paint job, he's the artist. As soon as I said the name Buttons, Big Bob and Skull sharply turn and look at each other. I don't know what provoked this response, but I did see something there. Prospect Petie is keeping busy running for beer and lighting cigarettes. I can see he hates it.

Skull is looking at the Electra Glide emblem on the front fender of my bike and asks, "This is an Electra Glide? I thought all late-model Panheads were Duo-Glides?"

Rocky, who obviously knows enough about my bike's vintage to gauge its year from a distance, looks at Skull and cheerfully says, "Here's how it went, the last year of the Knucklehead was 1947, the first year of the Panhead was 1948, but basically the only difference between the two bikes were their motors. The first Panheads were Panhead motors on Knucklehead chassis. In 1949, Harley changed the front-end from a Springer, which the Knuckleheads always had, to a hydraulic telescoping oil-filled tube type front-end, just like this one right here." He points his finger straight down at my bike's front-end and continues. "And that hydraulic front-end gave birth to the Hydra-Glide! But the bike still had the Knucklehead's rigid frame! Then in 1958 Harley changed the frame to a swing arm frame. Now the bike had hydraulic shocks in the rear as well as the front, so with the two suspensions, the Dou-Glide was born. Then in 1965 the Panhead went to a twelve-volt electrical system with an electric start, and . . . . ta-da, the Electra Glide was born!"

Big Bob and Skull look at each other, pleased with Rocky's expertise on the History of our beloved Harley Davidson Company. Then they turn back to me and ask if they can have a look around the farm. I reply, "Of course you can, make yourselves at home, Mi Casa Es Su Casa." I sure hope these are Club members I'm being so gracious with. They mosey down to the old barn to begin their exploration. They slowly walk away, leaning toward each other and quietly whispering back and forth. Their black leather jackets emit a dual shine. Their chain wallets, Buck knives, and black leather gloves are typical Biker attire worn by men sworn to our lifestyle. These two are quiet and reserved; they are confident, alert, and show they hold a high command of any situation. They have the look of men that don't scare easily, or maybe not at all!

I can see there's little about Harley Davidsons that anyone can tell Rocky that he doesn't already know. He politely asks, "Clutch, will you fire up your bike? I'd like to hear it."

I smile and reply, "I'd love to. How would you like me to start it, the Kicker or the Button?" I only asked that because it's so fucking cool to have both.

Rocky knows I'm just fooling around; he laughs and says, "Your choice, Bro!" I stop suddenly and briefly give him a blank stare, because the term Bro is reserved for Brothers only. That doesn't mean a prospect can't be called Bro; it just means that it doesn't happen very often. But I still don't know if this guy is even in my Club, and if not, that would explain him using the term.

I decide to use the Button to start my bike; it starts instantly. I allow it to idle for a few seconds, then rev the motor loudly. After a few seconds of that, I once again return it to an idle, looking at Rocky for his approval; his face is aglow with a huge smile extending from ear to ear.

Bikers are obsessed by the sound of a Harley Davidson! And although Harley Davidson's have a sound unique only to Harley Davidson, many Harley's have an individual sound unique only to themselves. This happens because their owners have put on different pipes or a different carburetor. Or maybe the bike has been tuned differently; it may be running a different cam. However, the trained ear of a true Biker, as he listens to a Harley ride by, can analyze its owner's skill of working on the bike by the uniqueness of its sound. So if a Harley screaming past sounds very good to the trained ear of a true Biker, he instantly stops whatever he's doing while the sound of the passing bike reaches its clearest and loudest point, then as it fades, the Biker will smile and say, "That bike sounds good! That Mother Fucker did a nice job on that one!" He displays a calm, genuine smile from the joy the sound has brought him. The passing bike's owner, although anonymous, has been analyzed as a worthy Biker and is rewarded by the compliment. But sometimes a Harley roaring past will not sound so good. In fact, it sounds so bad to the trained ear that after analyzing its owner, a true Biker only wants to beat the shit out of him!

Well, it's obvious to me, with the huge smile now generating from Rocky's face, I passed the test. "This Fuckin' Harley Does Sound Good!"

I push the Kill Switch, stopping my machine, and look over at the four Harleys these guys rode in on. I ask Dealer which one he belongs to? They all rode in so fast and loud that through the excitement I really don't know for sure what bike Dealer was on. He points to what I think is the nicest one of the bunch, and the bike I thought he was on. We walk to it and Dealer puts his hands on his hips, lustfully staring at his machine. With a large sigh, he says, "Yep, it's my Firstborn!" Meaning, the first bike he built. He continues with a large smile, "Been riding this scooter since high school. Of course it didn't look like this then!" He chuckles and then proudly says, "I was given this Putt by my father, who bought it new in 1947. I grew up looking at it and helping my dad wrench on it. It was a crashed basket case when I got it, though. It took me a long time to get it up and running, and I wrecked it the very first time I rode it! At eighteen years old, I didn't even have a driver's license or a seat for that matter! I was sitting on a bunch of towels I rolled up. Some Old Cunt pulled directly out in front of me and I T-boned her! I ended up with a spoke skewered completely through my foot! No license, no insurance, no seat. On the day I got this bike running, I rode it. I wasn't gonna wait over a few small technicalities like that! This is my third frame, and the one I think I'll stick with." He squats down and then with great affection, gently runs his fingertips down the length of his bike.

This bike has had its 1947 Knucklehead motor Blue Printed, which means the entire motor has been dismantled and all dimensions on every moving part machined back to their original factory specifications, all at the low limit of their tolerances. After Blue Printing, a motor is better than it was when it originally came new from the factory. That motor sits on a beautiful custom ridged frame made by 'Experts' out on the West Coast. Dealer is running a fast back teardrop gas tank. He sits on a small, custom-made, by-his-design solo seat, with a Pinnie Pad directly behind him, secured to the rear fender. The front end is an old military Wide Glide totally rebuilt and completely chromed. He's running custom risers with Broom Stick handlebars. The frame has a soft rake that fits perfectly into that front-end. The machine has a streamlined drag bike look. It's painted an orange color with yellow flames. And here's the kicker, in the center of the gas tank is a large Death Head beautifully air brushed over a raised 3D molded image of the skull and cross bones. The Death Head has a unique color theme that accents its profile and contrasts the rest of the bike perfectly. This bike is of showroom quality.

I'm not sure if the Death Head molded and painted on his tank is representative of the small Death Head Patch some Brothers wear on their Colors or not. But it looks the same, and I don't believe in coincidence.

Dealer stands and slowly withdraws his attention from his bike, then turns to me and asks, "Clutch, is your Ol' lady around? I'd like to meet her."

I answer, "Of course, I'll fetch her for ya."

I go into the house and find Nikkei. I tell her, "I think these guys are Brothers, but I'm not a 100 percent sure, so keep that in mind. Anyhow, the dude staying here, Dealer, wants to meet you." She comes outside; I can see her beauty stuns all that are here.

I say, "Dealer, meet Nikkei."

He steps up to her and says, "I heard Clutch had a pretty woman, but I didn't know you could rival a Goddess!" as he reaches for her hand and kisses it, total respect!

Nikkei turns her head down and begins to blush. She looks up and gives Dealer a quick glance and says, "Thank you, Dealer." Then she returns her head downward and continues to blush. It was easy to see she is blushing, we all do! Dealer releases her hand and introduces the others; thank God he did because I couldn't remember any of their names!

He then turns to Nikkei and says, "I talked to Clutch about it, but I wanted to clear it with you also. Is it okay if I stay out here off and on for a few weeks?"

Nikkei replies, "Of course it is. I already cleaned the spare bedroom for ya."

Dealer thanked her then told Prospect Petie to unload his stuff from the van and put it in the spare bedroom. Nikkei smiles and says to Prospect Petie, "Come on, I'll show you his room."

After Dealer's gear is unloaded, the others say their proper good-byes, climb on their Harleys, and leave, followed closely by the van.

After I return from the iron gate, Nikkei, Dealer, and I sit at the kitchen table and talk for a few hours before retiring to bed. Nikkei comes right out and asks Dealer, "Where are you from, Dealer?" He tells her the name of his Chapter, far south of here. She smiles and says, "I'll bet the weather is a lot nicer down there than up here." It was just small talk. She is not pumping him for information; she's too smart for that. But I am greatly relieved because that is the first real confirmation I have had that Dealer is a member of our Club, a Brother. What a relief! Nikkei looks at me and says, "We better get to bed, Clutch, five a.m. will be coming sooner than you want!" She then turns to Dealer and says, "Dealer, make yourself at home. If you want to shower, help yourself. There's food in the fridge and new bedding in your room."

Dealer says, "Okay, Nikkei, thank you very much!" I hand him a key to the gate and one to my truck, then welcome him to take full liberties with both.

I say, "Goodnight, I'll see ya around four o'clock tomorrow afternoon."

Dealer stands and gives me a Biker hug, then says, "Good night, Clutch, good night, Nikkei, again thanks!" We all three retire.

Once again I rise with the sun. Well actually, I beat that sucker by an hour. I begin my morning chores, but as I go out to feed and water the dogs, I find Dealer is already awake and sitting on the porch swing beside our Harleys. He's s enjoying a morning cup of coffee. I quietly say, "Good morning, Dealer, have you been up all night or are you just an early riser?"

He never answers my question, just smiles and says, "I heard you getting up so I poured a cup of coffee for ya." With his head, he nods to a cup of coffee sitting on the porch windowsill. I embrace the steaming cup of hot coffee. Gripping both hands tightly around the warm cup, I pull it close to my chest and lean toward the warmth it provides my face and neck. With my legs stretched outward, I sit sidesaddle on my Harley and sip this wonderful nectar. Dealer makes great coffee. Mmm! I explain my morning chores, but mostly my method for chaining the dogs nose to nose so three sides of my house are well protected. I could see Dealer likes that system and rewards it with a smile. He tells me he and I are going to take care of some business soon, but first he has a mission for me. He hands me a key and tells me to go to a specific storage locker and pick up a package. He gives me an address and tells me to deliver that package to a man called String Bean. He says, "Clutch, you drive your truck today, okay?" I agree, then finish my chores, kiss Nikkei good-bye, and leave for work.

On my way to work I am thinking about what Dealer had told me. I wonder what's in that package and if he really is an early riser or had been on the porch deliberately just to talk to me.

While at work, I definitely get the impression Heavy is avoiding me. I approach him many times, but I don't think he's interested in anything I have to say. He finally tells me he is really busy today and doesn't have time to talk. I think I may have freaked him out yesterday when I asked about Dealer and why he is here. I'm also getting the impression Dealer is a 'Heavyweight' and deeply involved in the Dark Side of our Club. And whatever it is Dealer and Hillbilly have planned for me, for sure Heavy doesn't want to know anything about it.

When my work day ends, I drive straight to the storage locker. When I get there, I circle the entire complex checking for anything suspicious. Everything looks cool, so I drive to the unit Dealer delegated. I'm a little nervous; I know this package must be illegal. I retrieve it from the locker; it's about the size of a shoe box and completely wrapped in gray duct tape. I put it under my seat and drive to the address Dealer gave me where I'm supposed to drop it off.

When I arrive at this rundown, city-type junkyard, an extremely dirty man comes out of a small building and asks if I am Clutch. He then introduces himself as String Bean. It is easy to understand why he was given that name; he is about six feet six inches tall and at best 150 pounds, wet! He has the appearance of a grubby Grease Monkey. You know, one that spends so much time working on cars that he never has any time to bathe. I give him the package and leave.

Dealer is not here when I get home. I give Nikkei a kiss and head for the shower. As I shower, Nikkei comes in and sits on the toilet lid to talk to me. She tells me earlier today she saw Dealer coming from the shower with no more than a towel wrapped around his waist. She says, "Clutch, he has a tattoo that covers his entire back!" She tells me the tattoo is the three piece patch, top rocker center patch, and bottom rocker, from the same club Hillbilly Patched Over from. But on his left shoulder is a tattoo of our Club Colors, our three piece patch, and on his right pectoral, he has the Death Head tattoo. Wow, he also must have Patched Over from Hillbilly's old Club. Uh-oh, that means Dealer is Special Forces. I knew there was more to this guy than meets the eye.

Nikkei and I eat, and then lounge around for a few hours before going to bed. She does not want to fuck tonight; she only wants to give me head. Sometimes that's how she is, and that's exactly what she does. She gives me a perfect Blow Job!

Today is my day off from work, so Nikkei and I sleep in late. We get out of bed and go to Ma's Place for brunch. After we eat, we swing by the Harley Shop and pick up some parts I ordered a few weeks ago. As I'm leaving, I see four members from the club we're at war with; they are all flying Colors. I turn my back so they don't notice me, then get in Nikkei's car and tell her to make haste and leave.

We get home and Nikkei sits on the porch swing reading a book while I put the parts on my bike. I'm changing my tranny sprocket from a twenty-four-tooth to a twenty-five-tooth sprocket. The bike will not be as fast Out of the Hole, but my Top-End speed will be increased at a lower RPM.

I hear a bike coming down my drive and figure it must be Dealer because he's the only one with a key to the gate. Nikkei stands and looks down the drive. She says, "Here comes Dealer! I love his bike!"

He pulls up, shuts off his scooter, then asks, "Nikkei, can I borrow Clutch for a few hours?"

Nikkei says, "Yes, and while you're gone, I'll go to the store and buy some groceries. Dealer, do you like blueberry pancakes?"

He takes a hundred dollar bill from his chain wallet, and as he extends it to her, says, "Yes, I love blueberry pancakes! Since I'm gonna be around for a few weeks, let me give ya some dough for grub."

Nikkei takes the bill and says, "Thanks. Is there anything in particular you want, Dealer?"

He answers, "Nope, anything y'all eat is fine with me. Thank-ya, Nikkei."

Dealer has a bit of a Southern drawl and tends to present himself not just as a Biker, but also as a sophisticated 'Southern Gentleman' type. He's very polite to women, always opening the door for them, and saying "Please" and "Thank you, Ma'am." Nikkei says she love the way he talks with that Southern accent.

Nikkei goes back in the house; she's getting her purse to leave for the grocery store. Dealer turns to me and quietly says, "We'll take your truck, Prospect. You drive, and bring your gun!" We climb into my truck and leave. I open the gate and pull through; I leave it open for Nikkei who will be leaving shortly. Dealer gives me a concerned look and asks, "You're not locking it?"

I answer, "No, Nikkei is on her way out."

Dealer sternly replies, "Then let's wait for her."

I say, "Okay."

As we wait, Dealer asks to see my gun. I hand him my pistol, a .45 ACP, 1911 Government model, stamped 'U.S. Army.' The same model being carried by our soldiers in Vietnam right now as we speak. He gives it a close examination; it is obvious he is no stranger to that weapon. About ten minutes pass before my

Carefree Beauty pulls through; she blows me a kiss and toots the horn as she passes. Beep beep! I close and lock the gate, then return to the truck.

After carefully wiping his fingerprints off my gun, Dealer hands it back to me and says, "Nice, it's in good shape. Maybe someday I'll teach ya how to make it Rock 'n' Roll!"

I give him a surprised look and ask, "You can make a .45 go full auto?"

He never answers, just smiles!

I have no idea where we're going or why. After a half hour of driving and many back streets, Dealer finally directs me to pull into the small parking lot of an old abandoned service station. It's very 1950ish! We get out of my truck; he directs me to follow him to a side door. As we walk to the door, Dealer takes two pairs of rubber surgical gloves from his back pocket. He hands me a pair and says, "Put these on, Clutch."

Dealer unlocks the door and we both enter. He turns around and locks the door from the inside, then hands me the key. He says, "Do not lose this. You'll need it soon!" I give him a reassuring nod and put it on my key chain, then follow him through a maze of rooms. He lifts up a small trap door, exposing an old rickety wooden staircase that leads into total darkness, and says, "You first!" He reaches to the wall and flips on a light that illuminates this small dungeon like basement. Shit, this place is spooky! I get the feeling this would be a very good place to be murdered.

I climb down the steep stairs into a small room. I see the duct taped box I got from the storage locker is sitting on an old wooden workbench. Dealer climbs down the tight steps and hands me a tubular device. He says, "Ever seen one of these before?" I examine it carefully, and then shake my head no. He grabs it back and places it on the workbench. He then reaches into his coat pocket and hands me an electronic device and says, "How about one of these?" Once again, I admit to having no knowledge about this device.

I shake my head, crack a smile, and jokingly say, "It looks like a bomb component."

He says, "You're right."

The smile quickly leaves my face!

He turns and very seriously looks directly into my eyes and says, "You must do everything exactly as I tell you—exactly!" He is holding the device in his right hand and repeatedly pointing it at me as he talks, like a schoolteacher holding a chalk board pointer during a lecture. He specifically says, "If you fuck up on this in any way, you can possibly blow the two of us into very small pieces, okay?"

I nervously say, "Yeah, Sure!" I gotta admit, I'm a little uneasy about all of this.

Dealer slowly cuts open the box that sits on the workbench. When he opens it, all I can see is coffee. Surprised, I ask, "Dealer, the box is filled with ground coffee?" He never answers. He carefully fishes deep into the box and pulls out a long, skinny plastic-wrapped blue tube and then two more.

He hands me one and ask for my approval, "Whata ya think, Clutch?" I examine it carefully; it reminds me of a long, skinny sausage tube with its ends crimped and held by aluminum clips. It has 'DUPONT' written in large white letters down its length. I slowly rotate it and read the smaller print beneath the manufacture's name Dupont; it reads, '1 lb. Explosive, Composition #4, 60% extra.' We have three pounds of C4, Plastic Explosives, enough to rattle somebody's world! Dealer and I work on three different bombs, with three different detonators, obviously built for three different attacks. One has a mechanical detonator Dealer makes from a mouse trap. He has cut the bottom out of a chrome Sportster gas tank; we put one half of the first tube into the tank. He rigs up a small radio safety switch with a few batteries and an electronic bypass. This bomb cannot be activated until that switch is turned on via a remote control. The other two bombs have radio detonators. They have to be detonated by a transmitter held by someone nearby monitoring their target. The second bomb has one pound of C4, and the third, a pound and a half. Because of the threat of an outside radio wave coming from a Citizen's Band or a Police Band radio accidentally detonating the bomb, the switch has three stages. The transmitter must be pressed simultaneously three times in a row—1, 2, 3—to activate it, then Ka-Boom! Dealer is very specific about this; he says, "These bombs must only be detonated at their intended targets! I will not tolerate a mistake!"

We now have three bombs. The plan is I set off two of them at two different times. The first is a booby trap. It's planted inside the chrome gas tank; it has the pressure release switch Dealer made from a mouse trap fastened to the bottom of it. This bomb will go off as soon as the gas tank is lifted. It also has the safety switch I must activate by pressing the transmitter three times; this is so we don't blow up a curious woman or kid! The second bomb is much larger, a full pound of C4, and is to be planted beneath the wooden porch of the same house where the gas tank is set. I will detonate that bomb after the gas tank bomb explodes and Bikers gather on the porch to see what happened. A day before my bombs go off, Dealer will plant the third and by far the most powerful; it's one and a half pounds of C4. He will put it in the car of the President to the Chapter of the club we're at war with. After my two bombs explode, he will follow that car in the hope the dude picks up other members. Dealer figures they will drive to the country to find a safe place to talk about what happened. Dealer has had many of our Club members following and watching these targets. All the homework has been done. They have a place picked out for me to sit and watch so I can activate the first and then explode the second bomb when it will do the most damage. This is going to happen in two days, that's a Sunday, like the attack on Pearl Harbor. Early Sunday morning, after everyone has been out all night partying and are hung over!

I have two radio transmitters. One will activate the bomb in the gas tank, and the other will detonate the bomb under the porch. Dealer has made it clear, "No Fuck-ups! Unless it's a Biker picking up that tank, do not activate it! No Women! No Kids!" He tells me, if I blow up a kid with the first bomb, I might as well blow myself up with the second.

Dealer by far has the toughest job between the two of us. He not only has to plant the bomb but then follow this guy around before detonating it. There is another Brother that's going to help him, but I don't know who he is, nor will I ever for that matter. I have two Brothers working with me also, but do not know who they are either. The plan is to go to my position, then cover them as they set the bombs and leave. Then I just sit and wait until sunrise. This probably won't happen until late morning.

Dealer describes to me the place where I'll sit and watch, then detonate the bombs. It reminds me of the Kennedy assassination, where Oswald was in the third-story Book Depository. I too am going to be on the third story, only this is not a Book Depository, it is a Church! It will be full of people and I should have no problem coming and going without being noticed. The church is far enough away from the blast site so no innocent people will be hurt. The bombs will be set at a house behind the church. It's across the street and there's an empty lot on both sides of it. All the people coming and going will be at the front of the church, out of harm's way. Dealer has had a Brother or two there for weeks, watching this environment. Everything seems simple enough; I'm not nervous in the least, and I have absolutely no misgivings about any of this. That Club fucked with us, and now it's time for Payback!

CHAPTER TEN

NOMAD

Well, here it is. I'm driving to the city where the bombing will take place. It's about a six-hour drive. I'm dressed in nice 'Sunday-Go-To-Meetin' Clothes and driving a high-dollar rental car, wearing gloves of course. Dealer says the more expensive the car you're driving, the less chance of being stopped by the police. The car has been rented under a false name with false identification. The church I'm going to is having a midnight service followed by coffee and an all-night prayer meeting. I pull into its huge parking lot and park the car. I count the rows so I know exactly where I parked. I had Nikkei cut my hair, and I'm clean shaven. I wear not a single tattoo. Like a virgin, I've been saving myself for a tattoo of our Club Colors and the beloved one percent. With short hair and clean shaven, nicely dressed and no tattoos, nobody is going to see me as a Biker. I'm the Cognito Kid. Personally, I kind of like being dressed this way. I feel out of sight, like a spy. And now this experience is changing my entire outlook on tattoos. I may never wear one.

I enter the church through a basement door. I do not want to talk to anyone, but I can't appear rude either. Dealer told me to be extra careful and avoid any "Church People" because they always want to shake your hand and talk. Dealer had given me a detailed layout of this church to memorize so I know exactly where to go. It works perfectly; I'm in a three-story bell tower. To gain access I had to go through a locked maintenance door. Dealer provided me with the key. I settle in and hunker down for my long wait. Its dark, about eight o'clock in the evening, but I can see the target house fine from here. With just my pistol, there is no way I will be able to back up the Brothers setting the bombs. That part of the plan is null and void. I'm hoping that is the only thing I've been misled on. Dealer has given me some speed, but I'm reluctant to take any. I can't allow myself to fall asleep, but I want to have a clear head also.

Hours go by but they seem like days. Right now I'll say the waiting is by far the hardest part of this job. It's after midnight, three o'clock in the morning, to be exact. There has been a lot of activity at my target house—Bikers coming and going, loud music, and lots of yelling. Two Bikers even got into a fist fight. Very entertaining I must say. Around midnight, a drunken Biker staggered from the house and fired a pistol into the air. As long as the cops stay away, let them Party-Hardy; it will only make this job easier. The bombs will not be set until just before daybreak, so the harder they party, the harder they'll sleep.

Its five o'clock, and I'm still just sitting here! This is terrible; I have so much built-up energy, I feel like I could run around the world five times. I have a new respect for patience; it's just as tough as anything else, right up there with prospecting. In other words, I'd rather run the Marshmallow Race than sit here and do nothing for nine hours! I'd like to drift off and think of something pleasant to pass the time, but I must stay focused on my mission. The house has been quiet now for the last hour or two and the sun should be making a personal appearance in the next hour or two, max.

It is now six o'clock, and the house is totally quiet, just like we planned. I see a van turn the corner and slowly cruise past; it's one of ours! I can't see what's happening, but for sure everything is quiet and looks good.

The sun is coming up now. The van cruised through a while ago and I've never seen it since. I hope they did what they were supposed to do. It's still too dark to see, but soon I will be able to.

Another half hour passes and I can just barely make out an object in the front yard. As the sky lightens, I can definitely see it's the chrome gas tank. Cool, they pulled it off. Now it's up to me! I guess I never really thought this would happen. I always felt something would go wrong, preventing me from pushing the button, but even as it becomes more of a reality, I remain calm. I can plainly see the gas tank, but I can only assume the bomb under the porch is there.

The day breaking, making visible the Sportster tank, has been my biggest excitement so far. Now several more hours have passed and once again I'm bored out of my mind. I have, however, been hearing more and more activity in and around the church. Then suddenly the church bells begin ringing. Ding ding ding! I jump a mile high! We planned this for a Sunday morning and knew the bells would go off. I brought ear plugs not only for the explosions, but the bells also. I fight frantically to extricate them from my pocket and insert them into my ears. I finally succeed. Ahh, that's much better. Dealer told me if this thing hasn't happened yet, then it probably will soon after the bells go off. He said, "Think of the bells like an early morning rooster, bringing the party-ridden Bikers to life!"

I get on my knees and watch the house very carefully through a series of small openings in the brick work, placed there by design. The openings have a checkerboard pattern and are absolutely perfect for this attack. Suddenly the house door opens and out walks a Biker. He goes to the edge of the porch and pisses, then returns into the house without ever noticing the gas tank! "Fuck!" Next, a car pulls up and a Biker gets out and walks directly to the tank. I prematurely activate the bomb. Click! Click! Click! He looks at it for a few seconds then walks into the house, never touching it. "Shit!" Now the bomb is activated! Anybody touching the tank will detonate it, even a passerby! A few seconds later the same Biker comes back out of the house with two others and points to the tank. All three approach it; they form a circle around it and discuss its presence. A few other Bikers come out and stand on the porch looking; they talk back and forth to each other. Finally one of them kicks it with his foot. Ka-Boom!

The explosion is so intense it knocks the windows out of this church! My head is knocked back from the blast. I can see all three Bikers have been blown back and are now lying on the ground, but I'm too far to make an assessment of their damage. It's weird because a huge smoke ring maybe thirty feet in diameter rose above the blast sight. I've never seen anything like this before, so maybe that's common. A few minutes after the blast, I see one Biker trying to get up. He's yelling for help; one of his legs is obviously gone. I think he's the one that detonated the bomb by kicking it. All the windows in the house have been blown out and the door is hanging half off its hinges. A woman sticks her head out but is pulled back by a Biker. He knocks the door the rest of the way off its hinges and comes out onto the porch, and then another and another; they all have guns! Two Bikers go to the dude that's yelling for help; they carry him back to the porch and lay him down; now a fourth comes out of the house. There are two Bikers in the front yard trying to help the two remaining Bikers that were blown up and three on the porch, plus the one lying down. Well, that's good enough for me! I point the radio transmitter toward the house and say, "This one's for Hillbilly!" Then push the button three times fast. Ka-Boom! This blast is much more intense than the first. There are pieces of debris at least fifty feet high. It blows the entire porch away, taking with it a large portion of the house. The two dudes standing in the front yard have been blown to the road; I figure it got them too. Well, I'd love to hang around and enjoy the fun, but I really must be leaving now. As instructed by Dealer, I smash the two radio transmitters with the heel of my boot into very small pieces. Then pile them safely on the cement floor and with a can of lighter fluid light them on fire.

I make it to the car without incident, then head home. I've never done anything like this before. On the way here I was wondering how I'd feel afterward. Well, I'm completely calm and relaxed. In fact, I really feel pretty good about what just happened. I'm exhilarated, and my senses are high. I actually feel quite powerful. Not invincible, but I feel like anybody that gets in my way is doomed. But the truth is, I couldn't have done this without Dealer. I must get closer to him and find out all he knows. I suppose it's like being in the army, where attacks such as this are a team effort. After you blow someone up, you as an individual feel pretty tough, but to really be invincible you must be tough as a Team. But for sure, my Life's Deck of Cards has once again been Reshuffled.

I make it home safely. It's pretty weird because whenever I've been away from Nikkei for any length of time, she is all I think about, especially when I'm this close to the house. But as I unlock the gate, my mind is on Dealer. I feel a strong pull toward him, like a craving to learn more about killing. I really have a strong desire to learn everything I can about bomb making. I must be careful; I'm really digging this too much. I hope he's safe and everything is going as planned.

I'm met at the door by Nikkei; she gives me a long tight hug and says, "Welcome home." We talk briefly, then she pulls me to the shower where I'm bathed and dried by her, then led to the bedroom where we make love. This session did not happen with the same intense rhythm we normally share. I just returned from blowing up a bunch of Bikers and sex is not really on my mind. I hope Nikkei didn't notice, but the guy she just fucked is not the same one she's been fucking.

After the bedroom, Nikkei and I sprawl on the couch and pig out on frozen pizza. We lay on our backs with our heads at opposite ends of the couch. Our legs are gently intertwined and woven one around the other; the coffee table is pulled close so the pizza can be easily reached.

The six o'clock news comes on and Nikkei asks me to change the channel; we seldom ever watch the news. I insist we leave it on; Nikkei loves to read and retreats to her book as I watch the news. The newscaster announces the breaking news: "Two huge explosions have devastated a Motorcycle Gang's Clubhouse. Several are dead, many hospitalized." The news station airs a taped report from the crime scene. They announce, "No citizens were injured; only minor damage to a nearby church and neighboring houses." I'm thinking that's good news. After the broadcast, the news anchor announces a third explosion, a car bombing, possibly four dead; details are sketchy, more at eleven. I had leaned toward the TV as I watched the segment. When it ended, I sat back and grabbed another slice of pizza. I take a bite and look at Nikkei; she is dead silent. She is chewing her index fingernail and staring directly at me. She's wondering if this is where I've been for the last day and if this is why Dealer was here. Nikkei loves the Club, but this is the part of it she hates the most and can live without.

I try to relax her suspicions by grabbing her toe and pretending to bite it. She pulls away and continues to chew her nail and stare. Finally she stands, and as she stomps to the bedroom says, "Remember, Clutch, you gave me your word you won't die in a bike crash or be killed in a fight!" She turns sharply and enters the bedroom, slamming the door behind her.

"What the fuck is your problem?" I softly say. "You know we're not Boy Scouts!" I deliberately say it softer so she can't hear. I stand

and go to the bedroom, but as I pass Dealer's room, I see it has been cleaned and all his gear is gone. I open our bedroom door and ask Nikkei, "Where's Dealer's stuff?" She is laying on the bed reading.

About the time I'm going to ask the same question again, she looks up from her book and answers in a confused tone, "Dealer left yesterday, shortly after you. You didn't know? Didn't he tell you?"

I tried to act as if he did and say, "He told me he may or may not leave."

That is pure bullshit! Dealer never said anything about leaving here.

Nikkei answers, "Oh yeah, he cleaned his room, gave me a hug and thanked me, then left. He invited us down to his place. He said come anytime."

I nod and say, "That's cool . . . . sounds like fun! Maybe this summer we'll ride down there?"

She's still pissed off, so I jump on the bed beside her and kiss her stomach, trying to calm her down. She pushes me away and angrily says, "Stop it, Clutch!" I climb on all fours and act like a rabid dog, growling and biting at her belly. She begins kicking and squirming, then finally breaks into a hard laugh. I sit up on my knees and get serious.

"Nikkei," I say, "I'm not going anywhere. I love you and I'm a man of my word!"

She gives me a very serious stare and then says, "Promise?"

I answer, "Yep, I do!"

She tries to give me that little girl's smile, but I can see it has been stolen by the news report and isn't genuine.

She sits up and gives me a hug, then says, "You'll also be breaking your word if you go to prison!"

Nikkei loves the Club and was raised by it, but war, and all it insinuates, is new to her. To watch a news report showing our Club's retribution on another; the power, and all the death has freaked her out. And to think I may be directly involved and the attack may have been orchestrated from her home is a lot to accept. She's never been close to that part of our Club; in fact, that level of violence is new to our Club. I'm sure she is evaluating the violence and the possibility of the war escalating and what that means to us and our relationship. Although her Life's Deck of Cards has not been Reshuffled, her Deck has been cut!

I have given much consideration to the possibility of the cops investigating me over this; I'm no doubt their prime suspect. I have already established an alibi; I have a credit card receipt signed by me for Sunday morning breakfast at a restaurant in this town. It logs the time and date of my meal within one hour of the explosions, making it impossible for me to have been six hours away. Also, I have the waitress that will say I was there eating with Nikkei; she remembers because she remembers Nikkei's engagement ring. And then I have Nikkei; she will say anything that helps me. Of course, I'm hoping it doesn't go that far.

It's starting to get late and I must get up at five for work tomorrow. Nikkei and I lay together in bed, but it's the first time we don't cuddle! We quietly lay back to back, both deep in thought. She's worried about our future, and I'm thinking about Dealer and when we'll meet again.

At five o'clock, I get out of bed, do my chores, and leave for work on my Harley. Nikkei never awakens! At work Heavy is still avoiding me like the plague. "Fuck 'em!" I'm sure he wants to see how things go after what just happened. In other words, am I Hot or Not? Hot is what we call it when you're under investigation by the cops. I guess it's said because you're on their Hot Sheet. Anyhow, I can take a hint, so I quit trying to talk to him.

Work ends and I go home only to find Nikkei is gone! I search the house, but no Nikkei and no note. "What the fuck is this all about?" I'm sure my phone is tapped so I ride to a phone booth and begin calling around looking for her. Nobody has a clue; I tell them all to call the pay phone if they hear anything. What really has me freaked out is her car is still in our driveway along with my truck! I'm getting nervous; this is not like her. I have called everyone and nobody knows anything. I have everybody I called looking also. My bike is parked beside the phone booth. I walk to it, put my hand on the handlebar then my forehead on my hand, and just stand there, head down, worried sick. Suddenly the pay phone rings. I run to it and answer. "Hello."

It's Nikkei. She says, "Clutch, it's me, I'm home. Come home now, I must talk to you!"

I ask, "Nikkei, what happened? Are you all right?"

She answers, "I'm fine, now come home!" Then hangs up the phone.

I immediately fire up my Harley and head home. It's late in the day and cold; the roads are slick from a light rain we had earlier. I value my riding skills but push this Harley much harder than these road conditions allow. As I approach a side street a car pulls out directly in front of me. To avoid hitting it and instead of laying my bike down, I ride between it and an oncoming car. Vroom! My bike is doing seventy miles per hour as I squeeze between two passing cars. Wow! What a rush! That doesn't slow me down in the least. I must see Nikkei and find out if there is a problem.

I pull into my driveway and the gate is open. That's not good; we always lock it. I pull past and leave it open. I park my bike on the drive about halfway to the house and cautiously walk to a window and look in. I have my pistol drawn and its Locked 'N' Loaded. I sneak around the house, looking through every window, carefully studying the inside of my house. Finally I see Nikkei; she is sitting on the couch. Her legs are bent at the knees, her feet are on the couch up against her butt, her arms are wrapped tightly around her legs, her head is turned sideways, and her cheek is resting on her knee caps. She doesn't know I'm here; I watch for a while then tap on the window. She looks up and sees me, then waves me in.

I come in the house with my gun drawn. I enter the living room and sit beside Nikkei; I'm still suspiciously looking around the room, not yet convinced everything is cool.

Nikkei raises her pretty head and says, "I had an interesting day. I spent it downtown at the federal building. It would seem the FBI is very interested in our relationship and your relationship with the Club. And they're very interested in Dealer!"

"Nikkei, what did you tell them?!" I demand.

She sits up and angrily fires back at me, "Give me a break, Clutch! I never said a fucking word other than I want a lawyer! What the fuck is going on, Clutch?!"

I say, "Nikkei, they're shaking the tree to see what falls out, that's all! We can't talk here or in any vehicle, so let's go for a ride. Come on, sweetie, everything is cool. We'll go have a drink at Papa-Dadieo's."

She struggles out a half smile and says, "Sure, okay, I'll get ready." Nikkei gets up and puts on her leathers. I love seeing her dressed in black leather.

Nikkei hugs me tightly as we ride to Papa-Dadieo's, her cheek pressed against my back. When we arrive, I find the bar to be surprisingly empty. Nikkei and I sit quietly in a back booth softly discussing what the police talked to her about. They asked her about me and my involvement with the Club. They wanted to know if she and I are legally married. I figure the reason behind that question is to understand if she can testify against me or not. But their main interest was in Dealer; they had his legal name and many pictures of him. She's pretty upset, but I do a good job of calming her.

Nikkei is streetwise, but I reiterate the rules, "Never talk on the phone, in any vehicle, or to anybody about anything, Amen!"

We talk for two hours before I stand and fetch us another beer; we figure one more then we are homeward bound. As I'm waiting for the bartender to get the beers, the backdoor bursts open and in pour fifteen to twenty Indians! They live about forty-five minutes from here on a reservation. They always come here in a small caravan of pick-up trucks, three in the front seat, four or five riding in the bed. Bumper to bumper, blowing their horns, waving their arms, and yelling; they're a rowdy bunch. Nikkei and I know all of them; they are our friends. They are also friends with our Club. We all get along great; I've told them they remind me of a Bike Club, without bikes! And they say, our Motorcycle Club reminds them of an Indian tribe, without Indians. Personally, I see the similarity in both.

These Indians, guys and gals, are high energy. From the time they hit the bar until the time they leave, there's never a dull moment. A couple of the girls are sitting with Nikkei, loudly laughing and carrying on. I'm at the bar drinking with a very large Indian named Thorpy. I've been out to the Res killing deer with him before; he's cool as hell. This bar went from Dead to Rowdy as Hell as soon as they arrived. Nikkei and I stay an hour longer than we planned; we say our proper good-byes, and just as we are ready to leave, fifteen to twenty Harleys pull up to the bar. The front door opens and in walks mine and Nikkei's two Chapters! And they are also Rowdy as Hell! I really didn't want to prospect tonight, but it's going to be hard to get out of it now.

Crusher walks up and stands between Thorpy and me, then put his arms around both of us, with one knee bent and leaning hard into our shoulders. It is easy to see he is feeling no pain! He says, "Hello, Thorpy, hello, Prospect." He then turns back to Thorpy and says, "Ready for round 2, Engine Man?" Thorpy delivers his answer by nodding his head yes and grunting. Each of these men is near six feet six inches, and both are well over three hundred pounds, making them an even match for the up and coming competition. Crusher, still looking at Thorpy, says, "Let's do four." Once again Thorpy answers with only a strong grunt yes.

They each order four pitchers of beer; these are not the full-sized glass pitchers, rather the smaller plastic one-quart pitchers! They stand shoulder to shoulder facing the bar, hands locked tight behind their backs. The entire bar, both Brothers and Indians, stop what they are doing and crowd around to watch and cheer for their comrade. I give the start signal by saying, "Ready, Set, Go!" Then loudly slapping my hand down on the bar. They bend over and pick up a pitcher of beer with their teeth, then tilt their heads back and begin chugging the beer, hands still locked behind their backs. Obviously the race is to see who can drink all four pitchers of beer the fastest. The entire bar goes crazy cheering these two on, the Indians cheering for Thorpy and the Brothers cheering for Crusher. Total hysteria! Like I said, our Club gets along great with these Indians, so no matter what the outcome of the chugging contest, it's all in fun—I hope! They're running neck to neck through the first pitcher. At the exact same time they lean forward and slam the first empty down, then pick up the second full pitcher, again with their teeth, tilt their heads back and continue chugging. The bottom of the pitcher slowly goes upward until they finish that one, then they are going for the third. This bar is going absolutely wild! There're Indians and Brothers standing on bar tables to receive a better view. The third pitcher is finished and they're still neck to neck. At this point the entire bar is loudly stomping their feet in rhythm to their chant, "Drink, Drink, Drink!" Suddenly, Crusher stops, the pitcher still clamped fast in his jaws. His eyes are tearing badly; he bows forward and sets the half-empty pitcher of beer on the bar. Knowing Crusher would never quit willingly, Thorpy is still chugging but he has, however, slowed down his pace and is carefully watching Crusher to evaluate why he set his beer down. Like a scene taken directly from the movie Exorcist, Crusher opens his mouth and pukes a four-inch diameter stream of pure beer foam with such force it goes across the bar and hits the potato chip rack secured above the back bar!

The force of the beer foam vomit knocks most the small chip bags off the rack. The stream of foam lasts for maybe five or six seconds and is approximately four feet long. It's cool as hell! Worthy of the Guinness Book of World Records!

The entire bar begins screaming and laughing even louder. In this competition the winner dumps the remaining beer over the loser's head. Trust me when I say, "Not many outsiders to our Club can get away with pouring a half-drunk pitcher of beer over our Vice Pres's head! Not without coming face-to-face with death!" But as I said, these Indians and our Club share much respect and friendship. Crusher takes his defeat like the man that he is, and as Thorpy slowly pours the beer on his head, Crusher kneels down a little, throws his head back, and begins drinking it. An approving act giving acceptance to his loss. When Thorpy initially began pouring beer over Crusher, all the Indians victoriously cheered louder, applauding the win. The Brothers, however, did not see it that way; they viewed it as if the Indians were emphasizing the loss. They all stopped to watch Crusher's reaction; all Crusher would have had to do is smack the pitcher away from his head and all Hell would have broken loose. These Indians are tough as nails, and so are we, so I'm glad that's not what happened. When Crusher started lapping up the beer being poured on him, the tension was immediately broken, and all the Brothers rejoined the festive howling. That was a victory in itself. When the beer was done being poured, Crusher and Thorpy turned and gave each other a respectful hug, which ended any doubt that we are not friends. Crusher took his defeat graciously, calming Club egos and fortifying our friendship with the Indians. Indeed, he is a true Leader and a Valiant Warrior.

The poor bartender, she had to clean up the entire mess! But Crusher tipped her well, as we all did, and the puke wasn't really puke. It was beer foam, so how bad can that be? Of course, I wouldn't have wanted to clean it, and luckily, as a prospect, I didn't have to.

I slow my drinking way down after the Brothers show up. Even though I was not given a Day Off, I'm being treated as if I had. I light some cigarettes and fetch some beers, but all in all, it is a fun night for both Nikkei and me. We stay until closing time then all ride out together—straight to my house! A long column of Harleys followed by three pick-up trucks full of Indians. Yep, we bought tons of Beer-To-Go, and went directly to Prospect Clutch's Pad. We drink until the sun comes up. I have Brothers and Indians sleeping everywhere. I even have one sleeping in the bathtub! At five o'clock in the morning, when I'm normally getting up, I am going to bed. Needless to say, I call off work sick!

About nine o'clock, I'm awakened by loud yelling. "What the fuck is that!" It sounds like someone is in a fight or something.

I grab my gun, and as I'm putting on my pants, Nikkei sits up, still half-asleep, and confused she asks, "What the hell is going on, Clutch?" as she wipes sleepy-dust from her eyes.

I answer, "Don't know, sounds like Whirly's havin' a go with somebody!" Whirly is only a few years older than me, and he is a Firecracker. He's been known to jump on and beat the shit out of people for absolutely no reason other than he didn't like the way they looked. He's not short and stocky, more medium height and stocky. And he loves to fight. I run out of my bedroom and see half a dozen Brothers on the porch, yelling at a couple of detectives and two uniformed cops. There's a bunch of Indians standing back, obviously there as backup; they're ready for action!

Crusher runs up to me and says, "Clutch, go back in your room, that's an order!" I immediately turn and go back to my bedroom.

The yelling and screaming continues for five or ten more minutes. Finally, through my bedroom window, I can see all the cops walking down my driveway leaving, followed by who else, but Whirly! He's marching directly behind them like a Nazi Soldier, Goose-Stepping, keeping his legs straight at the knees, and raising his feet to shoulder height with each step. That crazy fucker, I had to laugh! It's impossible not to like him.

Whirly is 100 percent A Character. He is always doing something crazy that makes everybody laugh. But unlike a comedian that's making a conscious effort to be funny, Whirly is not trying; it just happens that way. Whenever Brothers are assembled and telling funny stories, Whirly and many of his past antics generally monopolize their conversation. He has blond hair and deep, piercing blue eyes; he's definitely of the Aryan Race. He's not a huge man like Hillbilly, or Dealer for that matter, but not a small one either. He's about six feet two or six feet three and probably around 230-240 pounds; he is extremely strong, well built with little body fat. One thing for sure though, Whirly has giant, muscular legs. That's right. When dressed in shorts, the rest of his body doesn't even look proportional to his legs! "Those suckers are huge!" And when it comes to fighting, he uses them perfectly! Whirly's Frog Legs are not his only offensive weapon though; he also has Head Butting down to a science. I don't think I would be exaggerating to say he has probably knocked out over thirty men in his lifetime with a single head butt! He rides an old restored 1947 eighty-cubic-inch Flathead Harley, and it fits his personality perfectly. Because that bike originally came with a sidecar, its transmission has a factory-installed reverse gear, pretty common back then. Amazingly enough, even after ten or fifteen beers, Whirly can ride the bike Backward. Not far, but at a party he can usually be seen shooting across an open field backward, screaming, "Yeee-Haa" and kicking his heels inward, as if spurring a horse. It's so fucking funny to watch him do that. He's even been known to sit on the gas tank backward, lean back, and grab the handlebars while riding the bike in reverse. Like I said, "His personality fits that bike perfectly!"

I go back to the living room where most are gathered. The excitement of being visited by the cops has the entire house full of Brothers and Indians awake now. Many have cracked open beers; all are grumbling for grub. After the cops have for sure gone and their reason for being here heavily discussed, the decision is made; we'll all ride to "Ma's Place" for breakfast.

Nikkei declines to go; she says, "I'm gonna stay here, sweetheart, clean up the mess." I give her a kiss good-bye.

As I am preparing to start my Hog, Crusher leans over and quietly says, "After breakfast, you and I must have a long talk!" I just nod my head yes, confirming my acknowledgment. No doubt he wants to talk about the cops that were just at my house wanting to talk to me.

This is fun, twenty Harleys running straight drag pipes, cruising through this small town, flying our Colors, followed by a caravan of Indians in pick-up trucks. We get plenty of looks from the citizens. Some wave, some stare blankly, others utter obscenities, under their breath of course! The streets here are of old cobblestones; it is very cold and they become extremely slippery when cold. But we still ride two abreast in tight formation. If you want to ride with my Club, you better be an excellent Bike Rider!

We wheel into Ma's Place and pile into the restaurant. It's midmorning Tuesday and the place is empty, but they know us here and are happy for the business.

We're acting like school kids, throwing toast like Frisbees at each other, flipping food with our spoons; most are having a beer with their eggs and bacon . . . . yum!

For the mess we make, the restaurant is tipped very well. After eating we all return to my place. It's a little before noon now and has warmed considerably. The plan is we'll build a bonfire, then drink and eat the day away. Problem is, there's nothing to eat! So Whirly and Buttons come up with the brainy idea to steal the neighbor's goat and cook him; amazingly enough, everybody thinks this is a good idea and commends the two for thinking of it. Yeah, whenever Whirly and Buttons hook up, look out. Think of it as Satan babysitting Hitler! Only I'm not sure who's who in that mix.

Off go Whirly, Buttons, and two Indians in my pick-up truck driving around the countryside looking for a critter to snatch for our evening meal. Personally, I hope they don't come back with the neighbor's goat. Although he's a farmer, I think that goat is more or less a family pet!

Wood has been gathered, and the bonfire is burning quite well. Some Brothers are pulling logs from the woods with their Harleys; they did have my old tractor out hauling logs, but it's now stuck in the farm pond, steaming! Oooops!

Crusher tells me to follow him; we walk deep into the woods far away from all the activity. He tells me he knows exactly what happened last Sunday between me and Dealer. I never say a word, I just listen. He coaches me on the up-and-coming questioning I'm going to receive from the Feds. Right now BET is hard at work looking for a lead. Crusher tells me if worse comes to worst and I'm charged with a crime, I'll be bailed out and given the Club's attorney. This is a gift because prospects are never bailed out of jail by the Club. But that rule has only applied to much lesser charges. If I would be charged, it would be the first time a prospect was charged with such a serious crime as blowing up a Clubhouse and killing four Bikers. Let's face it, that has Life in Prison written all over it. Crusher tells me I did a good job, and the Club is going to keep me under the radar for a while until things blow over. I ask him about Dealer.

He proudly says, "Dealer is fine, and everything is cool where he's concerned. He did ask me to thank you for the hospitality though." I told Crusher that Dealer invited Nikkei and me down to his Chapter for a visit.

Crusher answers me with a somewhat confused look, "Dealer does not have a Chapter. He's a Nomad!"

A 'Nomad' is a member of our Club that does not belong to a Chapter. He pays his dues directly to the Club's Mother Chapter. A Nomad can float around from Chapter to Chapter as he pleases, like a Loner, but he's a Loner with a Patch! I'm not sure I completely understand it, but one thing for sure, I have a strong bond with Dealer that can never be broken, and I will see him as soon as I can. I ask Crusher who else in our Club knows what I did Sunday.

He answers "Don't you worry about who knows what. You just worry about me sitting here with an empty beer, Prospect!" Crusher laughs as I run to the cooler to fetch him another beer, ending that conversation. I could get away with running slower for the beer, but just to make myself look better, I sprint as hard as I can.

The party is going well; it's about three thirty in the afternoon when a long column of Harleys pull down my driveway. There's near forty bikes. It's a very impressive sight. They're all flying Colors. As exciting as it is for me to see and hear all the Harleys coming down my drive, the excitement is overruled by the concept that I now have to prospect that much more. You know, run for beers, light cigarettes, do push-ups, how I hate it! They park their bikes in one big clump with all the other Harleys. I hope there are a few prospects with them. I'm still too far away to see who all is there, and I'm not very anxious to walk over and look because they'll put me to work, prospecting.

Now there are basically two groups of Bikers. The smaller group is at the fire with the Indians, and the larger of the two are dismounting from their bikes and walking toward the fire. I'm still off in the distance with Crusher.

Finally he stands and says, "Come on, Clutch, party's over; time for you to go to work!" All the Harleys that just pulled in were being followed by a van. Its side doors open and out climbs Prospect Brock carrying a large beer cooler. He struggles with it all the way to the fire; he sets it down and starts passing out beer. Heavy is in the pack of Bikers that just arrived. He walks up to Crusher and me and gives Crusher a hug.

He then turns to me and says, "We left Prospect George at the gate. He's pulling security down there."

I say, "That's fine, Heavy. Do you need a beer?" He answers "Of course I do, Prospect!"

I run as fast as I can to the cooler. Brock does not see me. As he lifts the cooler's lid, I reach in and grab a beer before he realizes it is me, and then say, "Thanks, Prospect!" I turn and run back to Heavy, open the beer, hand it to him, and ask, "Anything else?"

He says, "Nope, I'm good. Why weren't you at work today, Prospect?"

I answer, "Coz I got run over by a beer truck!" He and Crusher both laugh.

Then Crusher says, "I know the feeling! That same truck ran me over also, and Thorpy was driving it!"

When he said that I had a flashback of him puking pure beer foam across the bar and knocking the potato chip bags off their rack! I put my head down and laugh.

Heavy points his head toward the drive and curiously says, "What da hell is this?"

Crusher and I turn sharply to see Whirly returning from the would-be hunt. He's blowing the horn as he leans from the truck's window, yelling, "Dinner is here!" He drives to the bonfire. All the Brothers gather around the bed of the truck. They are all laughing and howling; it is obvious there is some kind of animal in there. In a very excited tone Crusher says, "Come on; let's go see what that crazy Fucker has!" We double-time to my truck and look in the bed, only to find a small Donkey!

Whirly climbs into the bed of the truck; he proudly stands tall, high above his quarry, one foot perched on top of his kill, hands on his hips. His face is radiating the look of a triumphant big game hunter who just bagged a trophy buck. He boldly pans his view over my farm as if surveying the Kalahari. He turns to me and says with high command in his confident voice, "Prospect, take this critter over there, then gut and skin it. Let's get this sucker cooking, I'm starving!" He points to an area we have set up for just such activities.

This farm is set up for these kinds of Club parties; it's been going on here as long as I can remember. I think these Bikers think of this place as more theirs than mine.

We have a strong steel tube secured between two tree limbs with a winch fastened to its center for hoisting up animals and gutting them, usually pigs. I drive my truck under it and hoist the beast up, then gut and skin it. One thing is for sure, donkeys stink! Over by the bonfire is a bricked-in fire pit with a stainless steel spit hooked up to an electric rotisserie. Once secured, the animal is slowly turned over heat controlled by coals shoveled from the bonfire then raked evenly beneath it. We have a large paint brush attached to a broom handle used for basting the beast. It's a good system proven through many years of feeding hungry Bikers. Done right, this donkey may not taste all that bad, but after smelling it, I have my doubts.

I transport the donkey to the cooking pit beside the bonfire, then with the help of Prospect Brock, skewer it and hook up the turning apparatus. After that, Brock is assigned cooking detail. The way it's been going is, I'm prospecting yes, but nowhere near as hard as Brock. That is deliberately being engineered by the Club. Brock's Center Patch is on his Sponsor's wall. My Center Patch is on my back! He's in a period of disgrace, and I'm in a period of favor.

After the Sunday bombings, our Club wants to show its presence, and this is pretty much what this gathering is all about. Harleys are pulling in and out of here like crazy; our Patch is being flown all over town. I just received a report of a police cruiser sitting alongside the road just past my driveway; he's obviously monitoring the activity at the gate. The Feds want to bring me in for questioning; it's possible that's what the cop is doing there.

It's obvious to me that this party is going to go all night long, so I ask Nikkei to call me off work again tomorrow.

These Brothers are going nuts. They're shooting guns in the air; they're wrestling with each other, and racing their Harleys across the open fields. Some are dragging Prospects behind their Harleys with long ropes. One can easily see this is a victory party. But Sunday's bombing was a battle won, not the war. And what I'm too young to understand is, the club we're at war with will never wave the white flag. That's the real problem; neither club will! Therefore, neither club will ever win. It will always be Tit for Tat. But right now, we're having a victory party, and I can see most Brothers here know I had something big to do with it. I'm not the guest of honor, but I'm not prospecting very hard either.

Heavy approaches me and says, "I have a message for you from Hillbilly. He says for you to lay low for a few weeks, do not go to the hospital. He said enjoy the time off, you earned it!" Heavy pats my shoulder and continues, "You keep up the good work Prospect and you'll go far in my Club!"

I reply, "Thank you, Heavy. I'm gonna have my Top Rocker ASAP! There is nothing gonna stop me!"

He smiles and says, "I believe you, Clutch, but don't get ahead of yourself. You just now got your Center Patch, which means you've entered into a new phase of prospecting. Now more than ever you must be smart and keep your mouth shut. You must forget about all the bullshit with Brock. You must keep focused on staying alive and out of jail. This is when it gets serious."

CHAPTER ELEVEN

NO CHOICE

It's been three months since the Sunday bombings. I'm handcuffed to a chair, sitting in a police interaction room. I've been here all day long; they have run every game possible on me, but I'm not biting on any of it. I know I have the cops very frustrated and upset. I remember all the games the Club has run on me, and now I know why they did. Because of our lifestyle, one must be wise to these kinds of head games; the cops play them and so do our enemies. But unlike the games the Club plays on me, if I lose out on any one of these, I won't be doing push-ups; I'll be doing jail time. It's funny because the cops don't understand our Club at all. That's easy to see with the questions they ask and the silly games they play. Their worst game is to think I'll believe one of our Club members has turned State's Evidence on me, and all I have to do to save myself is give testimony against my Club, how ludicrous! Who the fuck do they think I am? The only words that have left my mouth since I've been picked up have been "Talk to my attorney! I have nothing to say!" I keep remembering a T-shirt Whirly wears that reads, 'You Have the Right to Remain Silent, So Shut the Fuck Up!' I never saw it with a double meaning imposed, until now.

BET, Biker Enforcement Team, is here; they are in the shadows though. They have not and will not ever introduce themselves as a member of BET. But I play it safe and assume as far as this Federal Building goes, they're all B.E.T. The Feds will hold me for seventy-two hours, three days; that's the longest they legally can without charging me with a crime. The truth is, nobody, not our rival club or the cops, were ready for the retaliatory strike we administered that Sunday morning. No one expected that level of violence. The cops are only assuming it was our Club that perpetrated the act. It's just like I told Nikkei, "They're only shaking the tree to see what falls out!"

I've been in a holding cell this entire time, isolated from the jail's general population. But today is my last day, and the cops put an informant in with me. What a joke. He came in yelling at the cops, calling them Pigs, and threatening their families. I've been watching for that. He keeps trying to talk to me; he wants to shake my hand. I tell him, "Over there on the wall is a phone, call someone that gives a fuck!" Here's the game this Monkey is playing; he is no doubt working for the cops to save his own ass from a crime he's been charged with, or he may even be a cop! I'm sure the plan is, if he can't get close enough to me for me to say something to him that can be taken out of context, then twisted and used against me, then the next phase of the plan will be to start a fight with me. This way the cops can trump up some charges and hold my ass in jail a little longer. Either way, I'm not going to take the bait; my Club has already advised me to watch for such cop games.

Finally, I'm released! Nikkei picks me up. The first thing she says to me is, "Hey, Clutch, what kind of birds can't fly?"

I disgustedly answer, "I don't know, Nikkei, what kind?"

She says, "Jail Birds!" And then she starts laughing her pretty little ass off. I do not enjoy that joke nearly as much as she. But that subtle abuse is a far cry better than staring at bars. She drives me straight to the VA Hospital where Hillbilly has been staying for his physical therapy. He's recovering perfectly and should be coming home soon. The VA is downtown here in the big city only a few blocks from the federal jail house where I've been locked down. Nikkei says Crusher told her to pick me up and bring me to the hospital.

We walk into Hillbilly's room; I see Crusher and his ol' lady, Brandy, are sitting there. Brandy and Nikkei go outside to smoke. Crusher unplugs the phone as I turn the volume up on the TV.

Hillbilly asks, "How did it go in there, Clutch?"

I answer, "Not bad. All I ever said was ask my attorney. Yeah, I was put in isolation, away from the general population; a snitch was sent in last night and wouldn't shut the fuck up! Other than that and having to eat their food, it was pretty much uneventful.

They got nothing. Hillbilly, do you realize, next week I will have been prospecting for one year?"

Hillbilly laughs and says "My, my, how time flies when you're having fun. Clutch, I'm getting out of the hospital in a few days. I want you to ride down here on your bike and we are all riding out of here together, Colors flying!" We all talk and laugh for a long time. As I was leaving, Hillbilly says, "Clutch, don't forget, it's not how long you prospect, it's how well you prospect!"

I ask Nikkei to drive past the Clubhouse on our way home. She says, "Clutch, if it's all right with you, I would really like to just go home and spend time together, alone!" Because I have no real reason to go to the Clubhouse, I say, "That's cool, Nikkei, we'll just go home then." It is obvious to me Nikkei is no longer as tuned into the Club as she once was. I was always concerned about balancing her and the Club so I could have both, but it looks like she must learn to balance me with the Club also. Only problem with that answer is, I'm not sure she wants to. Ever since the Sunday bombings, I can see her attitude toward the Club has been changing for the worse. I think she is afraid I'm going to end up in prison with my blood brother, Kebus. Well, it's settled then. I must really apply myself to reassuring Nikkei that things are okay. I do not want any tension in our relationship, especially if the tension is spawned from the Club. I never want to have to make a choice between her and it. Hillbilly won't be out of the hospital for a couple more days. I figure I'll use that time to mend our relationship. Lately sex hasn't been as vibrant as it was in the beginning, and I know it's not Nikkei's fault. I've been preoccupied with the war and the cops. It's easy for me to gauge the strength of our relationship through our sexual activities, like a barometer. It's just common sense, the sex is better when we're getting along better. That's not 100 percent accurate because there's been times Nikkei and I were fighting but stopped long enough to fuck, and when we finished, we picked up fighting where we left off.

As we get close to home I tell Nikkei, "Let's spend the weekend in bed together, fucking, eating, and watching TV. No Club, no Brothers, just you and me." She looks at me, and for the first time in a very long time, I see that little girl's smile. It goes from ear to ear as she looks me directly in the eyes; it lasts a long time.

As we pull into our drive, I ask Nikkei, "Why did you leave the gate open?"

She gives me a blank stare and answers, "I didn't, Clutch, I'm sure I locked it!"

Once again I ask, "Nikkei, are you 100 percent sure?"

She says, "Yes, Clutch, I'm 100 percent sure!"

I ask, "Did you bring your gun?" She gave me a worried look and shook her head no.

"Fuck!" I tell her to turn the car around and pull to the road. I say, "If there's any sign of trouble, split!" I quietly climb out of the car and carefully walk to the house.

I cut through the woods and come out on the back side of my house. My dogs are staring but they know it's me, none of them bark. I'm thinking about releasing them but sometimes that's not such an easy task. After all, they are Pit Bulls! It's weird because if anybody is around here my dogs should be going nuts. Unless they know them! What I really want is my shotgun and pistol. I crouch down and slowly walk to the back porch side of my house. Just as I began to step onto the small porch, a loud voice comes from behind me.

"Bang! You're dead!" I immediately turn to see Dealer standing there, smiling. I about Shit my pants!

"Dealer!" I loudly say. "How the fuck are ya?" Then I give him a tight hug; it is obvious I am thrilled to see him.

He smiles and says, "Hey, Clutch, trying to sneak up on me, A?"

I laugh and say, "I saw the gate open. I had no idea it was you. You scared the shit out of me, Dealer!"

We talk for a few minutes; I tell him in a roundabout way what happened at the Federal Building, but this close to the house, I want to be careful what I say. Who knows who's listening? He tells me not to worry about it, that we'll talk later.

I guess I never thought it was weird he shows up coincidently just as I'm getting out of jail from being the main suspect in the bombing he engineered. Especially when he's the one who always says, 'Don't ever believe in coincidences. They don't exist.'

This is the first time I've seen Dealer wearing his Colors. Nikkei said she saw he has a Death Head tattooed on his right pectoral, but now I see the small Death Head Patch sewn to his rag. Dealer asks, "Is it okay if I shack up here again for a few days?"

I answer, "Absolutely, Mi Casa Es Su Casa!"

His Harley is loaded with stuff; he has a bedroll, a small duffle bag, and some other stuff tied down all over his bike. It's obvious he's been on the road for quite some time! After all, he is a Nomad. I'm helping him untie and unload his gear when he asks, "So how's Nikkei doing?"

"Oh shit, Nikkei!" I said "I left her at the gate! I'll be right back."

I take off running down the drive. Dealer shakes his head, laughing. Needless to say, when I get to Nikkei and she finds out Dealer is here and going to be staying with us again, she's not happy at all.

She tells me, "I'll see ya later, Clutch!" Then drives off, burning the tires. So much for working on our relationship!

Nikkei has never done anything like this before, but I don't think there's too much of a problem here; besides, I'd rather see her leave for a while and cool off, than stay and be rude to Dealer. That's the one problem I need to avoid, having to either back up the Club or Nikkei while they're both present. Nikkei recognizes the problem, and that's probably why she left. Either way, I really need to work on our relationship.

I lock the gate and return to the house where Dealer is adjusting the rear chain on his second Harley. He has two beautiful-looking bikes. On this Harley, the front end is extended fourteen over and raked to match. And like his '47, He's running Broom Stick handlebars with some really groovy risers that put them in a perfect location to match the bike's style and his comfort. I think it looks beautiful, but personally, the front end is too much over stock for my liking. A front end that long has to affect the way the bike corners and I'm into total performance, especially in the corners.

He asks me, "Where's Nikkei?"

I shamefully answer, "Dunno, she got pissed off and left I guess." He never replies. I really want to be careful here. It's a touchy situation, and I don't want to gain a reputation in the Club for not being able to control my woman. Control is a big word, but one must keep up appearances. The truth is, Nikkei and I control each other through our love, not dominance. That might not sound like the image of a true Biker, but one must keep his Home Front sound, and whatever technique he uses is his own business.

"Clutch, follow me!" Dealer sternly says as he walks into the woods. Once deep in the woods, he turns and says, "Do ya think it's safe to talk here?"

I answer, "I don't think it's safe to talk anywhere, Dealer."

He says, "Why, don't you trust me?"

I quickly respond, "Of course I do, but maybe the cops are listening."

"Then how will you know what it is I have to say?" He asks.

"I don't know," I timidly answer as I shrug my shoulders.

Dealer says, "It's never 100 percent safe to talk business, but if you know a third party is not listening, and you can trust the person you're talking to with your life, then that's the best you can do. But if a Brother can never trust a Prospect 100 percent with his life, then how can I trust you with what it is I have to say?"

I think about what Dealer just asked for a long time then answer him, "You can trust me 100 percent with your life, Dealer, because even as a Prospect I am your Brother. Being a Prospect is only a formality. As I have not had a long history with you to prove my loyalty, I will never be able to prove it if you don't first offer me some trust."

Dealer looks at me for a while then leans close and quietly says, "I have a mission for you. Clutch, if I've gauged you correctly, then I figure this will be one of the most important missions of your life. And it's gonna begin right now!"

Knowing what my last mission with Dealer consisted of, who knows what death and destruction he has in-store for me this time?!

I say, "Whatever you need, Dealer, I will do!"

He says, "Good, I have a package for you to deliver." He told me what Chapter and the Brother's name to deliver it to. Shit, that's two states away! He reaches into his inside pocket and hands me a small package then says, "Don't get lost. This must be delivered by noon tomorrow. Clutch, do not give this package to anybody but him. I'll be here when you return." We talk for a couple more minutes and then Dealer more or less interrupts me by saying, "Good-bye, Prospect!" I thought it to be somewhat rude.

Fuck! I have 'No Choice' but to do as I'm told. I would at least like to see Nikkei before I go. Hopefully she doesn't think I left just to get even with her for leaving. I'm thinking this is a twelve to fourteen hour ride. Dealer wants me to drop this package off and pick-up another package, then return back here by this time tomorrow. That doesn't leave any time to dillydally. He also told me to fly my Colors there and back. "Why, I wonder?"

I grab some stuff, also my leather jacket, gloves, and my pistol, and then head out. I guess Nikkei is just going to have to understand.

Every chance I get, I give my bike full throttle. I must be careful though. I can't be stopped by the cops, but I have very little time to get this job done. The wind, however, does feels good. I love flying my Colors, but we are at war. So once again, I must be careful because some see them as Colors and others see them as targets. So I will not allow any cars to get close behind me. Like I say, speed is a defensive tactic.

I'm about six hours into my journey. I'm wondering what's in the package. If I'm stopped by the cops and searched, you can bet they'll be asking the same question. That being known, I must keep this bike near the speed limit. Man, I'm hungry.

Here I am at my destination. This is the first time I've ever been here. This Clubhouse is cool. At the driveway's entrance is a stone archway and written across it in huge letters is our Club's name! I push the intercom button and say, "I'm Prospect Clutch, here to see Joker." The gate electronically opens and I ride up to the Clubhouse where I'm met by a group of Brothers. I've never seen any of them before. They're all wearing Colors.

A Brother approaches me and says, "I'm Joker, you got something for me?" I look at his Colors; he has a "Pres Patch" above his left pocket and his name above his right pocket, and he is also wearing the Death Head Patch.

I say, "I do." Then I hand him the package.

After a very close examination, he smiles and says, "Good, good job, Prospect, now come in and have a cold beer." I would love a beer, but I must leave. No way can I refuse though, so I thank him and we all go into the Clubhouse.

The lower level of this house has been turned into a bar; it really is quite nice. Joker goes behind the bar and serves us all a beer. Behind the bar is an intercom system; he pushes a button then leans toward the unit and says, "Woman, come." Within a minute, a very beautiful brunette walks down the steps and enters the bar area. Joker says, "Do me a favor, woman. Cook Prospect Clutch a couple hamburgers!"

She looks at me then offers up a lovely smile and says, "I'd love to." Damn, is she ever sexy!

I talk with Joker and the other Brothers for a while, then this little beauty returns with two delicious burgers and hands them both to me. Our eyes lock for a long time.

She has beautiful eyes, and I say, "Thank you very much."

She smiles and in a very sexy voice says, "Anytime, Clutch."

I wolf down the burgers in record time and then thank Joker. I ask him if I can leave because I must be back sooner than I think possible.

He laughs and says, "Not before you do this." He then chops and forms two lines of crank on the bar top. I snort them both, and once again thank him. Joker hands me a small package, similar to the one I brought him, and says, "Only give this to Dealer and tell him I said hello."

Back on my bike and headed home, the burgers and the crank have given me a second wind. I must watch though because with the crank buzz, it's easy to push my bike well over the speed limit, and once again, I'm carrying a package that's no doubt illegal as hell.

I'm about an hour from home and wired as hell. Joker gave me a quarter gram of crank for the ride home, but I haven't dipped into it yet and probably won't being this close to home. I pull down my drive and see Dealer standing with Heavy, Buttons, and Whirly. Dealer looks at his watch, checking the time, then says, "Everything go okay, Clutch?"

I've performed this mission in record time and proudly answer, "Yep."

He says, "Good, coz I have another mission for you!"

I hand him the package Joker sent, then smile, and ask, "What can I do next?" After my long journey, I'm thinking this will be something easy I can do around here.

He says, "I have a telephone number for you to memorize then take to Bones."

Holy Shit! Bones! That's the Mother Chapter, and its ten hours north of here! I must get my shit together because this may be serious.

Our Club does this often, and this is the way it works. Dealer has taken a telephone number from a random telephone booth he selected earlier; he then gives that number to me to memorize. I will personally deliver it to Bones. In return, Bones will give me a date and time to memorize and I'll bring that back to Dealer. On that date and time Bones will call Dealer from a random phone booth he selects. Nothing is 100 percent safe, but it would be almost impossible for the Feds to listen because there's no way of knowing what phone booth Bones will use, what phone booth he will call, or when he'll make that call. Unless of course, I'm a snitch! That's what really bothers me. A Prospect is never trusted with a mission such as this; especially where the Club's National President is involved. These two guys could talk about anything, from the Sunday bombings to an up-and-coming bomb attack. Even though they talk in code and are always careful not to incriminate themselves, I doubt if they would trust me with that. So to say the least, I'm a little suspicious.

I don't even talk to Nikkei, I just leave. For the first hour I ride, I continuously rehearse the telephone number in my head. I don't dare forget it! And for sure I don't dare write it down. There can be no fucking up here; I must give Bones the correct number. Like a child singing the ABC's, I've put the telephone number to music and sing it hundreds and hundreds of times in my head.

When I left, I asked Dealer, "What about my Colors?" He answered, "Fly 'em!" I have a bad feeling something is wrong with this. I don't understand why I'm flying my Colors; we're at war, so flying my Colors while riding alone is dangerous. Also, a Prospect should never be trusted with delivering a telephone number to the National Pres. I wonder if I'm being set-up. Maybe they think I snitched while in jail. The lack of sleep and the crank will play games with your head, and that's what I'm contributing these thoughts to—I hope. Although it sure would be easy for my Club to shoot me from an overpass since they know where and when I'll be there. And I'm flying my Colors so our rival club will be blamed. For sure once I'm dead and gone, there can be no worries about me turning State's Evidence on Dealer and the Club for the Sunday Bombings.

Dealer put an almost impossible time limit on this job; he wants me back tomorrow morning. Well, I don't have a package this time so I run my Harley full bore. At best, all a cop will get is a speeding citation out of my Wired Ass. Of course, I'll have to dump my Crank into the wind. My bike is legal and so am I. The Club insists we keep all the little things clean—driver's license, registration, bench warrants. We're always being stopped by the cops; this way you don't have to worry about going to jail over something stupid like that.

I stop for fuel in a small town just north of mine. I'm familiar with this station; I know 'White Gas' can still be purchased here. Not many places have it anymore, but whenever I can, I run it in my bike. That shit burns hot! After filling my tank I use the restroom and do another line of Crank, then off I go, in more ways than one. Yeee-ha!

I get to the Mother Chapter's Clubhouse but Bones is not here. A Brother named Offal invites me in. He tells me Bones won't be back and to write down the telephone number and he'll give it to him. I have no tolerance from lack of sleep and loudly tell him, "Absolutely not!" Big mistake! After a hard punch to my gut, he tells me to give him the number or I'll be leaving with a broken nose. He said Bones asked him to get it from me, so it's okay, and for me not to be stupid. Fuck! I'm in no mood for this, so I say, "Okay, I will . . . . oh shit, I can't remember it."

He says, "Prospect, you better shit me a telephone number or else!" At this point he is waving a knife at me. I don't know what to do. If the Club needs this number, I should give it to him; it may be very important he gets it. But I was told not to give it to anyone except Bones himself. I don't say anything; I simply stare at the ground. This Brother slaps my face hard with his right hand, and then says, "Do you see this?" With the knife's tip he points to the Death Head Patch on his Colors. "Do you know what it means?" he said and then slaps me again with his other hand. I'm beginning to get pissed off.

I slightly raise my voice and say, "I have no fucking clue what that Patch stands for, and I cannot remember the telephone number!"

He slaps me again and shouts, "Why can't you remember the fuckin' number, Prospect!" He was yelling at the top of his lungs.

I yell back, saying, "Because I've been awake for two fuckin' days! That's why!" He sat down on a small couch there in the room and stared up at me for a solid minute without speaking a word.

Then with a reversed demeanor, he softly says, "Ahhh, you poor, poor boy. I'm so very sorry to hear that. Maybe I should lay you down in my bed, tuck you in, then read ya a bedtime story." He then jumps back on his feet and once again begins yelling. "You sniveling Maggot! I don't give a fuck when you did or did not sleep last! I want that fucking telephone number right fuckin' now!" I do remember the number, but there's no way he'll ever get it now! I'd rather drink gasoline and piss on a fire than give it to this moron.

Once again Offal's demeanor vacillates back to a soft, quiet tone. Like a Schizophrenic, he's giving me the 'Good guy, Bad guy' routine all by himself! He goes to the refrigerator and takes out two beers, opens them both, and hands one to me, then gently says, "Drink this, maybe it will help jog your memory." Although his tone was soft, he said the word memory very sarcastically. As I drink the beer, he turns the stereo on and plays soft elevator music. When I finish the beer, he hands me another and then dims the lights. He sits down and never speaks another word; he just sits there staring at me. This is weird.

I am having trouble staying awake; he has turned the heat up in the room. Why is this Brother doing this to me? None of this makes sense; maybe the Club is setting me up. I'll bet they think I snitched them off while in jail. If I pass out, they're probably going to duct tape me to this chair like they did before and then have Bones beat me to death. If I give Offal the number, maybe he'll let me leave and I don't have to worry about being set-up and beaten. One thing is for sure though. I can't allow myself to fall asleep.

Last time they thought I fucked up, when Hillbilly was shot, Hillbilly told me the Club was not going to do anything to me until they okayed it through him first. But he's okay now; so maybe he's the one that thinks I snitched. Maybe he's the one that's Setting me up. The Crank I've been snorting has my head all fucked up. Maybe everything is okay and I'm just tweakin' from the Crank, and this Brother is just an Asshole. He continues to sit in total silence and stare at me as I fight to stay awake.

I hear a pack of Harleys pull up and in walks Bones. "Hello, Prospect," he bellows out in his deep voice. I immediately sit up and look around; the Brother that's been fucking with me is gone. Where did he go? Wow, I feel like I'm in the Twilight Zone! I'm still holding my beer, I must have fallen asleep!

I stand and respectfully say, "Hello, Bones, I have a number for you."

He says, "Good, write it down on this." He hands me a small, pocket-sized notebook. I write the telephone number down and hand it back to him. He looks at the number then smiles. He flips through the notebook then stops at a page that he tears from the book. He scribbles down some numbers and hands it to me, saying, "Memorize this, Clutch." As I studied the time and date recorded on the torn page, he takes out a small bag of Crank and forms two lines on the table. He says, "Do this, Prospect!" I snort them both. He then says, "Now get us each a beer!"

I know I have to turn around and head back home with this time and date, but there's no way I can refuse a beer from the National Pres and ask to leave.

He lays out more Speed and I fetch us more beer. This goes on for the better part of three hours, then finally Bones says, "Clutch, you have a long ride in front of ya. Ya better shove-off!" He sticks a quarter gram of Crank in the top pocket of my rag and says, "Here, take this and the next time we meet, you'll be Born Again!" I'm not sure what he meant by that, but I thank him for the Speed!

Back on the road and feeling very high and very wired. Dealer is gonna have my head. I'm three hours behind schedule!

I finally get home and I'm met at the gate by Heavy; he's madder than a hornet. "Where the fuck you been, Prospect!" he yelled. And continues to yell, "Now give me twenty-five!" I get off my Harley and do twenty-five push-ups. I tell Heavy Bones talked to me for three hours and I couldn't leave. Still yelling, he shouts, "I don't want to hear any excuses! I don't want to hear any sniveling! When Dealer gets back, your ass is grass!"

I look surprised and ask, "He's not here?"

Heavy says, "No, he told me to get the info Bones gave you!"

I say, "Sorry, Heavy, Bones told me to give that information to Dealer, and him only!"

Heavy became even madder; he starts shaking and screams, "Don't fuck with me, Clutch. I'm in no mood. There's been some shit go down that I can't discuss. Now give me that information . . . . or else!" He's still yelling at the top of his lungs. I don't know what to do. If there has been some sort of emergency, Dealer may need me to give the time and date to Heavy. I trust Heavy, so maybe I should go ahead and give it to him.

I think about it a little longer then say, "I can't, Heavy. Dealer told me to get this info from Bones and Bones personally told me to only give it to Dealer. Sorry!"

He shakes his head back and forth for a minute, then says, "Okay then, Clutch, have it your way. You'll just have to follow me then!" He starts his bike and rides off hard. I start mine and follow.

Now where the hell are we going, I wonder. I follow Heavy into a gas station; he tells me to fill both bikes. Then he walks to the pay phone and makes a call.

When he returns from the phone, he says in a somewhat calmer voice, "Are you gonna give me that info now?"

I answer, "No, I can't, Heavy!"

He fires back at me, saying, "Remember that Rat-Packin' you got? Well, if I don't get that info, you're gonna get another one that will make the first look like a high school spankin'!" He glares at me for a minute, but I don't budge, so he says, "Okay, it's your funeral!" He starts his bike and once again takes off like a bat out of hell.

Man, I don't deserve to be Rat-Packed again. And I don't understand why Heavy is so mad. Maybe I should tell him?

We get on the expressway and ride for two hours. Then onto the turnpike, I have no idea where he's taking me but I hope Dealer is there. We ride for four more hours, only stopping for gas; every time we do Heavy uses the phone and I sneak in a line of Crank!

Finally we pull up to a bar named 'The Hotel'; no doubt it's called that because there are rooms for rent above the bar itself. It sure would be nice to crash in one of them for the night. Hopefully that's why we are here.

I follow Heavy into the bar. He orders us each a beer; we sit at a small table and he softly says, "Clutch, I have to have that info, so please, I'm asking you nicely, give it to me." He stares at me for a minute then raises his voice and demands, "Give me the fuckin' information, Prospect, that's an order!" I fall back in my chair not knowing what to do; I debate the Trick Bag I'm in and solve the problem by defaulting to what I've been taught, even by Heavy, and that is, when in doubt, follow the chain of command. Bones told me to only give this information to Dealer, so that's what I'm gonna do.

I look at Heavy and calmly say, "I won't, Heavy, I'm not playing games with you. It's just I know what Dealer is about, and I figure Bones must know also, and they were both very specific with my instructions and what I should do. They both told me to only give this info to Dealer. Sorry, I don't want to seem disrespectful, but I can't!"

Heavy glares at me for a moment then says, "You're a Dumb Motherfucker, Prospect!" He stands up, violently knocking over the chair he was sitting on, grabs his beer, then stomps up the steps that lead to the hotel rooms above the bar. That's the last time I see Heavy for the rest of the night!

I sit in the bar for a couple hours wondering what's going on with Heavy. I hear two Harleys pull up to the bar. The door opens and in walks Fingers and Whirly. They both look mad. Whirly walks up to me. As I stand, he angrily says, "Let's go, Clutch, right now!" I don't ask any questions; I just follow them both to our bikes. We ride back to the turnpike and continue on mile after mile, hour after hour. I swear I can't keep my eyes open; I keep falling asleep on my Harley! Every time I do my bike slows down considerably, signaling Fingers who blows his horn and wakes me up. I look around, refocus, and then throttle my bike. At one point Whirly has to ride up beside me and smack the back of my head to wake me up!

We stop for gas and Whirly gives me some Peanut Butter Crank. That shit will make your hair stand up! It worked; once again I'm awake, big time!

We ride through the night. The weather is perfect, nice and cool, and my Harley loves it. She's running like a Swiss Clock—well, like an American Harley. The sun is rising over my shoulder; it's casting a reflection across a huge beautiful blue lake. As tired as I am, this moment is worth it! The wind in my face, the beautiful sunrise, and flying my Colors while riding with two Brothers. It's cool as hell! My mind is wandering uncontrollably; this whole trip seems more like a dream, not an endless bike ride. What's really bad is I have no fucking clue where we are.

Finally we pull into a restaurant. We all three order coffee. Whirly says, "Clutch, Heavy says you won't give your Chapter the info Bones gave you, don't you trust us?"

I say, "I'm not trying to be an asshole. It's just Bones told me not to give it to anyone but Dealer."

Fingers very softly says, "But he's not here, Clutch, and he told us to get it from you, so tell us."

I say, "I can't, Fingers."

He and Whirly both stand and Whirly says in an irritated voice, "You stay here . . . . Prospect!" They both leave on their bikes.

"Wat da fuck is this Bullshit all about?"

About the time I was gonna curl up on the seat and sleep, I hear a Harley pull up and park beside mine. I figure its Fingers or Whirly coming back. The restaurant door opens and in walks Crusher. And he too is obviously pissed off. I just don't understand what's going on, why are our Chapter members all showing up one at a time like this? I'll bet there's been some sort of a problem. Maybe a Brother has been murdered. Maybe BET has busted some Brothers, like a raid or something. Maybe I'm being blamed.

He stomps directly to me and blurts out a loud demand, "I'm gonna make this as clear as I can so that even you can understand, Clutch. I need the information Bones gave you to give to Dealer! And that's an order!" I don't know what to do now. This is my Vice Pres, and this sure seems serious. Maybe I better tell him. Of course if I follow the chain of command, the info came from Bones and I was told by him that only Dealer gets it. So I better not say.

I tell Crusher as seriously as I can, "I really don't remember, Crusher. Maybe if I eat and sleep for a while I will."

He shouts back at me, "You're not gonna eat or sleep, Prospect! You're gonna come with me!" I follow him out to our bikes and off we go.

Once again we ride and ride and ride. I'm completely out of Crank now and going Down for the Count. I really don't remember the last time I slept; I do, however, know it's been days. We stop for gas and Crusher gives me some more Peanut Butter Crank. Back on the road and I am now considerably more awake, well at least my eyes are! They're the size of golf balls! Two huge bloody golf balls staring falsely into the wind! Finally I see the expressway home. I follow Crusher as we merge onto it. I feel so much better now, knowing exactly where we are. Maybe Crusher is taking me home. With each hour we ride and every road we take, my confidence builds that I'm homeward bound. Finally I'm convinced. I haven't slept in nearly four days, but I know my driveway when I see it.

I can't keep the smile off my face as we pull down my long drive, until we get to my house that is, when I see twenty-five Harleys sitting there. Now what the fuck is going on? As I climb off my bike, a huge crowd of Brothers approach me; they all look angry. This herd of Bikers is being led by Hillbilly! I jump off my bike and give him a huge smile, but he doesn't reciprocate; he looks madder than hell. Now what the fuck does he think I've done? All the Brothers gather and form a tight circle around me, shoulder to shoulder. There's Heavy, Whirly, Fingers, Buttons, Crusher, my entire Chapter, and more! It looks like a Rat-Pack to me; they probably think I snitched in jail. Well, this is it, they'll have to beat me to death because I did not snitch, so I'll never quit fighting, and I'll never quit the Club . . . Fuck 'em!

Hillbilly says in a very calm voice, "Hello, Prospect, you and I have a little problem."

I ask, "What is it, Hillbilly?"

He says, "You have some info from Bones, but you refuse to tell your Chapter. You say it's for Dealer, but he isn't even in your Chapter. He's a Nomad! We need to know, Clutch. I'm your sponsor so what's it gonna be?" I'm happy he hasn't accused me of snitching, but this still completely sucks!

I say, "Hillbilly, Bones, our National Pres, told me only to tell Dealer!"

Hillbilly locks his fingers, stretches his arms out forward, and cracks his knuckles, then in an ironically calm voice says, "Well then, maybe we'll just have to beat it out of ya!" I don't answer; I don't know what to say! Hillbilly says, "Listen to me, Clutch, after you take your beating, unless you want another one just like it, then you write the info down on this!" And he throws me a Top Rocker!

I catch it and don't even realize what it is I caught! Between the Crank, the lack of sleep, and this would-be Rat-Packin' I am preparing for, I'm totally confused. The Rocker is folded up; I open and stare at it for a long time. All the Brothers are totally silent now. I am trying to realize what just happened. I was standing here waiting for a beating when suddenly Hillbilly threw me a Top Rocker? "Wat Da Fuck?" And then suddenly it hits me. I just went through Hell Week, and now I'm in the Club! I'm now A Brother!

I begin yelling as loudly as I can, as do all the Brothers! It's like a dream come true. "I'm in, I'm finally in!" I put the Rocker between my teeth and hug Hillbilly as tightly as I can for as long as I can. And then Heavy and Crusher and Fingers, then Whirly, all my Brothers! I look over and see Dealer quietly standing there, arms out waiting for my hug. I hug him for all I am worth.

Again, I Have 'No Choice,' if I live to be a thousand years old, I will always consider this to be the happiest day of my life! I can't help how I feel!

CHAPTER TWELVE

ALABAMA TICK

It's April 29, 1975. I'm sitting with Dealer and Hillbilly, drinking coffee and watching Saigon fall on the morning news. As retired Special Forces men that served active combat in Nam, this is extremely tragic to both of them. I can see they both wish they were there. We all three sit quietly and watch as the American Embassy is being overran by NVA. Dealer and Hillbilly sit stunned. As Special Forces Men, they have each been in that exact same embassy, guarding diplomats and such. They sit shaking their heads in disgust, pinning the blame on Nixon first, Secretary of State Robert McNamara second and the media third!

It's been six months since I received my Top Rocker. I kind of went crazy for the first couple of weeks after receiving it. Everybody does, but that's behind me now. Hillbilly has made a 100 percent recovery, less the small belly button-looking, dimpled scars left from the seven bullets that tore through his body. He says he's gonna have them tattooed to look like eyeballs, the bullet hole being the pupil. Dealer and I have become very close, as have Hillbilly and I. We have been Taking Care of Club Business quite well together, with Precision Accuracy. The Club has been referring to us as The Three Musketeers, only we haven't been using Muskets—if ya know what I mean.

Receiving my Top Rocker has been like being Born Again; there has been so much indoctrination I haven't had much time to pursue exactly what the small Death Head Patch means. But today it's volunteered to me when Dealer throws a Death Head Patch onto the coffee table directly in front of me and asks, "Did ya ever figure out what this is?"

I pick it up and examine it closely, then say, "No, I figured when you and Hillbilly want me to know, you'll tell me." Dealer looks at Hillbilly and slowly gives an approving nod to my answer.

Then Hillbilly picks up where Dealer left off, saying, "Well, now we want you to know."

He then looks back at Dealer, who says as he points to the Death Head Patch on his Colors, "The Death Head Patch means that we are Goons."

Then Hillbilly speaks, "Only a Goon can wear this Patch, Clutch! We are a Club within the Club. So secret and so deadly that not even the Brothers fully understand this Patch. Every Chapter must have two Goons. When your blood brother, Kebus, lost his last appeal, our Chapter became short a Goon. Now we are asking you if you wish to sew it on your Rag."

I am totally shocked, speechless. I hold it up against my Colors at the approximate location it is worn and say, "I think it would look pretty good right there."

Dealer nods and says, "So do I!"

Then Hillbilly nods as he stands and extends his arms for a hug, saying, "Me too! Welcome aboard, Bro!" I stand and hug him and then Dealer.

We return to our seats; our focus is pulled back to the television, and the fall of Saigon. Dealer somberly says, "I would never say I'm glad my father is dead. I loved him too much to say that! But I will say I'm glad he's not here to see this! He loved this country and fought hard for it in two different wars. Now to see how badly this one has gone due to that Fuckin' Nixon, Dad is probably rolling over in his grave!"

Hillbilly and I just sit and respectfully listen.

Dealer emotionally points to a small patch on his Colors that has a Swastika embossed into it and proudly says, "This was my Pop's U.S. Army's regiment's Patch. He told me how much he loved it and how unhappy he was when the Army took it off their uniforms. He explained what the Swastika meant and told me the U.S. Government should never have allowed Hitler to deny them the right to wear the Swastika. He said that was a battle lost right there!"

Hillbilly listens intently. As a military man he has a strong connection here and values Dealer's knowledge and opinions toward the Swastika. I am totally surprised to hear Dealer suggest a Swastika had been worn on the U.S. Army's uniform, and not all that long ago.

With my curiosity aroused, I respectfully ask Dealer, "That Swastika Patch on your Colors was your Dad's, and he wore it on his Army uniform?"

Hillbilly is looking at me then turns his head to Dealer, intently awaiting his response.

Dealer stands and pours himself another cup of coffee then tops-off ours and knowledgeably says, "This was the Forty-fifth Infantry Division's Patch. The four legs of the Swastika represent the four states it comprised—New Mexico, Arizona, Colorado, and Utah. If you look at a map, you'll find the borders of those four states form a Swastika. They wore it all through Europe during the First World War. Make no mistake, many American men died fighting for our freedom while wearing this Swastika Patch. Like the people from our southern states being told the Stars-n-Bars should not be flown, this Infantry Division was not very happy when they were told to take it off their uniform. I think Pop said it was around 1939. Because of Hitler the U.S. Army changed it to a Thunderbird! The Forty-fifth ID were proud American Soldiers. If not for guys like that fighting for our country, its possible guys like us would not exist! There are many Governments that would gun us down in the streets for wearing Colors and organizing this Club. That's why to protect ourselves; we must first protect the Constitution of the United States, even if it means fighting our own government! The truth is, nobody knows where the Swastika originated, but we do know it's as old as mankind, and has nothing to do with Adolph Hitler, other than that moron adopted it for the few years he was in power! It's been found on pottery dating back for thousands of years. It can be seen on stone walls inside caves, carved by Cave People. The early Christians endorsed the symbol as one from God, and who knows, maybe it was. After all, it's as old as mankind. There has never been any one single location where this beautiful cross originated; rather, it's been found in nearly every civilization all over the world throughout history. It usually comes in the form of a Good Luck charm, or a peace symbol . . . After Hitler, there's a little irony for ya! But I won't let that Asshole or his fucked-up Nazi Party stop me from wearing a Swastika. That's the right my Father fought hard for, The Right to

Freedom of Expression! Our very own American Indians use it as a peace symbol and for religious reasons. I'd like to see the U.S. Government try and tell them it's wrong!" Dealer stomps his foot down hard on the floor.

Damn! Dealer sure got emotional over that one. He's now pacing around the living room.

Then Hillbilly speaks his piece on that subject. "I too wear the Swastika on my Colors and have one tattooed on my arm, but my reasons don't go as deep as Dealer's. I guess I wear a swastika in defiance to our government. They say they don't like Outlaw Motorcycle Clubs, well I say, Fuck You, you created us! But I do know the Broken Cross is thousands of years old. I first started wearing it out of respect for the members of the Club Dealer and I Patched Over from. Nearly all those guys wore Swastikas. They told me it was an Aryan thing. Well, I've found out it is an Aryan thing, but it's not exclusive to that by any means. If someone thinks it is unique to Aryans, or to Hitler, then they're disconnected from the truth! We have many different races of men in our Club, and out of respect to them, this Broken Cross cannot be considered in total regard to only the Aryan race. I'd rather consign it to total rebellion against the U.S. government for fucking with the Constitution!"

Hillbilly calms for a moment, then looks at the TV and raises his cup of coffee, doing a toast to Dealer's Dad. "Here's to your Pop, Dealer. I know he was a good man, a good soldier, and a strong American. That Fuckin' Nixon should be shot! Look how dumb the general American public is. They celebrate Nixon's trip to China and reward him for opening the door to that country, but let me warn you now, Brothers, you think we've lost a lot of manufacturing jobs to Japan, just wait and see what happens when China is done with us. There won't be anything left! And Nixon can be blamed for starting it. To be a Super Power we must have powerful factories and powerful farms, just ask Tricky Dick how that's gonna play out now that China is here. End-Day Bible Prophecy says from the East will march a 200-million-man army. Sounds like China to me!"

Well, the fall of Saigon has obviously stirred my Brothers' emotions, and for good reason. They fought hard, risked their lives, and killed many for our country in that war. Now it's just been pissed away, leaving nothing more than the Lie it was Built Upon. "Fuck You, Richard Nixon, may you rot in Hell!"

Trying to calm the situation, and knowing how Hillbilly and Dealer both love to mentor me, I change the subject to something I've been meaning to ask anyhow. "Hillbilly," I say, "Why do some Vietnam Vets call the Gooks we're fighting Charlie?" I curiously ask, hoping this new venue will distract my Brother's anger and help expedite a mellower mood.

Hillbilly sets back with his head down, staring into his cup of coffee for a long moment, obviously steering his emotions away from Nixon and the fall of Saigon. The morning news has upset these two soldiers, and their anger is high, like a car speeding down the highway at one hundred miles per hour. With such momentum, it won't stop easily.

Finally he turns to me with the smile I was trying to provoke and answers, "It's taken from the phonetic alphabet: Alfa, Bravo, Charlie, Delta, Echo, ect, ect. We are fighting the Viet Cong, and we have abbreviated their name to VC, but while on the radio, a Radio Operator would never use just the two letters, V. C. They always use the phonetic alphabet, so a Radio Operator would phonetically say, "Victor, Charlie," whenever communicating the letters VC. But then we abbreviated that also, and now the Viet Cong are just Charlie, get it?" He concludes by saying, "It's an Army thing!" Then Hillbilly nods his head one time, winks and smiles.

I ask many more questions, most of them off the subject, but all of them designed to calm my Brothers' emotions and turn them away from the trauma created by the morning news. These two have given much to me, and I must give back whenever possible. They both know I'm trying to draw their focus away from the fall of Saigon, but do not resist. They'd rather retreat from their anger than allow it to ruin their day!

Back at home hours later, Nikkei sits reading a book as I sew the Death Head Patch on my Rag. She has no idea what it means, but she does understand it comes shrouded in mystery.

Her and my relationship has fallen dramatically, not from lack of love, or lack of sex for that matter. But I have not been able to balance her and the Club in proportions equal to her liking. The Club has come first in every aspect of my life, and I plan on staying in the Club for the rest of my life. Now she understandably wonders what the future holds for us. I do want to give Nikkei more time. I figure now that I have my Top Rocker and as things settle down from the excitement of receiving it, maybe I can.

Tonight is our Chapter's weekly Church Meeting. I can't wait to walk in with this Death Head Patch. We are also holding elections for a new Chapter President, now that it has become obvious that my older brother, Kebus, will be spending the rest of his life in prison. It's funny because the Feds tried to cut a deal with him. They said they would drop all charges (all the phony charges), if he helped them investigate our Club so they can build a case on Racketeering and Organized Crime, 'The RICO Act.' As he laughed, he said, "Eat Shit and Die, Pig!" Kebus is Top Shelf.

I ride my bike to the Clubhouse, flying my Colors of course. Our Chapter has grown considerably. We now have sixteen members. Although Dealer is a Nomad, he has been spending most of his time up here with our Chapter. He's been staying at Hillbilly's house and will no doubt be attending our Church tonight. There are times Church Meetings get pretty loud. We try to bleed out any bad blood between our members during these meetings. If there is a problem between two Brothers, Church is the time to solve it.

This Club is a democracy. We vote on everything. Any issues that will affect any of us as individuals, as a Chapter, or especially the Club as a whole, are voted on. Each Chapter votes for all their Officers—Pres, Vice Pres, Sergeant at Arms, and Treasurer; we vote them in, and if need be, we vote them out. Also, the same with our National President; the entire Club, all Chapters, will vote on him. There have been many complaints over the years that we're too much of a democracy, and so busy voting, it's hard to get anything done.

The Secretary Treasurer goes over Club dues, who owes, who doesn't owe. He goes over any loans made to Brothers. We charge interest on the money, but unlike a bank, as long as the interest is paid up, we will extend the loan indefinitely. If the loan was for bail money consisting of an arrest while Taking Care of Club Business, we don't consider it a loan at all and there is no interest. The Sergeant at Arms reviews any Hang-Arounds that may be potential prospects. He goes over security and any lack of it. Then we do a Roll Call for any fallen Brothers followed by a toast in their honor. Now it's time to vote for a new Pres. It's starts by Crusher, our Vice President, asking for any nominees. Hillbilly begins by standing and walking over to me and then placing his hand on my shoulder and saying, "I nominate Clutch!"

Holy Fuck! Boy did that ever come as a surprise to me. I was thinking of nominating him!

Then Crusher says, "I second that! Are there any other nominees?" One by one, every single Brother stands and nominates me until it becomes obvious that it would be pointless to vote.

Crusher says, "Well then, so be it. Clutch is now officially our new Chapter President!"

Then all Brothers stand and clap. One by one, they all walk past and hug me, followed by their congratulations!

When I get home Nikkei asks, "Well, did the Club elect a new Chapter President?"

I give her a hug, then smile as I hand her my new Pres Patch and say, "The Club voted me in, unanimously!" She smiles and gives me a congratulatory hug, but I can see she isn't sure what that means to our already declining relationship.

She forces out a worried smile anyhow and says, "Well then, I guess congratulations are in order!"

The next day at work Heavy approaches me with a congratulatory hug and says, "I heard you were voted in as Pres last night, unanimously. Congratulations Clutch!"

I say, "Thank you, Heavy."

I want to tell him I have a Death Head Patch also, but figure I'll wait until he sees it on my rag. That way we never have to openly discuss it.

Then Heavy says, "Here's some news for ya. We gave Brock his Top Rocker!"

I immediately snap to attention and sternly question, "How in the fuck could that happen?"

Heavy says, "Calm down, Clutch! How do ya think? Read the morning paper!"

At lunch break I sit and anxiously flip through the morning paper to the 'City and Region' section. I read about an unsolved murder; 'Killed execution style,' 'Suspected gang related.' I know this guy! He is a member of the club we are at war with. This is the guy I was stalking, the one I was trying to set up through Cindy and Nancy. Brock must have whacked this dude then received his

Top Rocker for doing it. He only got his Center Patch back a few months ago, so that's the only explanation.

There is a circle here. After Nikkei and I got together, I quit fucking Nancy and Cindy. Nancy is the one I had watching Cindy. Cindy is the girl that had been to the murdered guy's house and the one I was going to use to set him up. It looks like Brock beat me to it. After Nikkei dumped Brock, he started running around with both Nancy and Cindy and must have picked up where I left off. I knew there was an opportunity for a free Rocker there. This guy drank hard and would pass out all over town. Just like in the wilds, there is a 'Selective Order' among the Biker community. It's Darwinism, and nature has a way of weeding out the Dumb and the Weak!

Brock is a conniving Son of a Bitch, so I guess I shouldn't be surprised he saw the opportunity and capitalized on it. Well, that's bad news for me. I was so hoping Brock would never wear my Patch. After I got my Top Rocker, Brock still only wore a Bottom Rocker; his Center Patch was still pinned to his Sponsor's, Crazy George's, wall. I was told by Bones himself, even though I had the power over Brock, not to kick him too hard. I worried then that Brock might make it in, having support like that.

Even though Brock got in, he never finished prospecting and there are some Brothers that resent that. They feel he still has a lot to prove. Many members feel the Club's rule that Brock got in on shouldn't exist, that if a Prospect kills for the club, it should be part of prospecting, not a free ticket to a Top Rocker!

It's June 6, the invasion of Normandy's anniversary, D-Day. I'm talking with Hillbilly; he has a mission for me. Our Club has many Hang-Offs. We pretty much use every one of them for anything that will benefit our organization. There is one named Rocky; he's been hanging around since the early days. All Prospects are former Hang-Arounds or Hang-Offs, but Rocky is much too crazy to ever be allowed to prospect. We are all crazy, but like Hillbilly says, "One must learn to take the Crazy out of Craziness and replace it with Method," and there is no method to Rocky's craziness; he's just one crazy son of a bitch.

Example, once when very high on Crank, for three days he put every cigarette he smoked out on his forehead! Yep, he would sit there, light up a cig, and when it reached its end, he would pound it out on his forehead. When I saw him days later, he had a huge scab in the middle of his forehead, one about the size of a Styrofoam coffee cup lid.

Astounded, I asked, "How many cigarettes did you put out on your head, Rocky?"

He boldly answered, "I don't know, about three days' worth!"

And to me, that's crazy—without method!

Rocky is a Vietnam Vet; he got really freaked-out over there. I don't know what he saw or did, but whatever it was, it fucked his head up Big Time. Although he was as crazy as they come before Vietnam, afterward, he became a Loose Cannon. Rocky has one of the strangest collections of anybody I know. In fact, it's the strangest collection I've ever heard of. Some people collect guns, some collect coins, others collect stamps, but not Rocky—he collects Suicide Notes! And he has many. He worked at the Army Morgue in Vietnam and was able to accrue the bulk of his collection there, but even now, he watches the newspaper, and when he sees a suicide, he'll try and get in touch with the surviving family members and offer big money for the suicide note if one was left. How weird is that?

Rocky is going to jail soon, for a very long time. He kicked down a man's front door over a drug deal gone bad, and while inside the house screaming, he shot and killed the dude's Parrot. That's right, the guy had a high-dollar Talking Parrot, and just to prove he meant business, Rocky blew it into little pieces with a .44 magnum. He racked up all kinds of felony charges over that episode. Because the cops want him so badly for big-time drug dealing, the judge is going to give him the maximum sentence on all counts. My mission is, before Rocky goes to prison, my Club wants me to try and talk him into killing a member of the club we're at war with. The guy's name is Blues. Rocky has killed for us in the past, but this guy is tough as nails and a worthy adversary. Hillbilly heard Blues owes Rocky a large amount of money for two kilos of Cocaine Rocky fronted him. When Blues found out Rocky was headed for prison, he refused to pay. Well, Rocky is not one that takes being Punked lightly. In fact, he's as dangerous as he is Crazy. Hillbilly wants me to Stir the Pot a little and try to get Rocky mad enough to kill Blues. It shouldn't be too tough. Rocky is a stick of dynamite. All I need to do is find the fuse and light it.

I think it's a great idea and opportunity, one we must capitalize on immediately. So I eagerly accept the mission, and I'm now on my way to find Rocky and begin 'Stirring the Pot.' I stop for gas at a 7-Eleven just up the road from his house when he pulls in screeching the tires of his hot rod Camero. He slides up to me, gets out of his car, slams the door, and stomps directly to the gas pump where I'm filling my bike's tank. The rest of this situation plays out like a scripted Hollywood movie. "Really quite Un-fuckin'-believable!"

First off, Rocky is yelling insanely. I try to calm him but have little success. One thing for sure though, the dude working in this Seven-Eleven is a cop, planted here specifically to keep an eye on Rocky because of his deep involvement in drugs and also a few murders along the way. I warn Rocky about the dude inside, now eagerly watching our every move, but Rocky doesn't budge; all he wants to do is scream. Like I said, There's no method to his Madness. Rocky opens his long coat and flashes a Thompson submachine gun for me to see. Again, like I said, the dude I'm going to try to have Rocky kill is named Blues, and guess what, Rocky is on his way to kill Blues! Problem is, I know the employee in the Seven-Eleven is a planted cop, and Rocky is gonna blow it if he doesn't quit being so emotional and ostentatious with that Machine gun. Hell, we may both go to jail. He yells, "Blues is gonna be Hamburger when I'm done with 'em!" Then he opens his trunk and shows me two hand grenades. We call them Pineapples. The planted cop doesn't see the Thompson or the Pineapples, but I know he's listening.

For my safety and defense I say, "Rocky, I'm telling you to go home and relax, and not to harm anyone. Please, Rocky, don't do anything you'll regret!"

The truth is, I want Rocky to kill Blues. I just don't want to be charged with giving him the order to do it or to be charged as an accessory. So now, instead of trying to talk him into killing Blues, I'm trying to talk him out of killing Blues. The exact opposite of why I'm here. This completely sucks! But honestly, I don't put too much effort in trying to stop him; I just want it on record I tried.

Well, it doesn't matter what I say to Rocky. He has his mind made up and that is that. He drives straight to Blues' house, and at a high rate of speed, he drives his car straight through the front of the house! The Camaro smashes through the living room and into the kitchen, killing one Biker. Rocky staggers out of his damaged, steaming car surrounded by a smoky cloud of falling debris and opens up with the submachine gun, killing two more Bikers. Blues runs down a long hallway and locks himself in the bathroom. As he's trying to escape through a small window, Rocky pulls the pin on a hand Grenade and slides it to the bathroom door. He is so out of his mind crazy he not only blows up Blues, but gets himself also! Blues died instantly, but Rocky is in the hospital now in critical condition, surrounded by cops.

Hillbilly comes to me the following day, chuckling, and asks, "Clutch, what the fuck did you say to Rocky, you persuasive Mother Fucker?"

I was supposed to try and talk Rocky into killing Blues, but we were thinking probably with a high-powered rifle from a quarter mile away or something like that. But this was Too Much even for guys like us. "That crazy Son of a Bitch!"

"How would you like to have him mad at cha?"

It's the first day of August and the temperature has been punishing. Today is the fourth day in a row of record-breaking highs. It doesn't bother Nikkei at all; she's been lying out tanning most of the time, running back and forth to the shower. I'm on my knees rubbing oil on her sexy tan body when two Harleys pull down my drive. It's Dealer and Hillbilly; they're flying their Colors and being followed closely behind by a van. At the risk of being redundant, let me repeat myself. The van is used for protection, so while on the road, nobody can get close to the bikes. Not without taking a barrage from the van that is! We do use cars when necessary, but all our vans have been armor plated, and a van has plenty of room for the passenger to stand and shoot.

I go over and give them both a hug, then nod to the prospect driving the van. Hillbilly says, "Clutch, we may have some business to take care of. Brock has come up with a plan we are calling Trojan Horse." Hillbilly explains the plan to me. The club we're at war with still has a Chapter in our city, and they run a junkyard on the outskirts of town. Many clubs are involved in the junkyard business; it's an excellent way to move stolen cars and bikes, and dispose of bodies. By the way, rumor has it, that's what happened to James Hoffa. He was put in the trunk of a car, crushed and cubed, then sent to the smelter where he swam in a bubbling vat of molten steel. Anyhow, Brock knows a girl who will tell that Chapter she knows where a Harley sits that can be stolen easily. He's sure they will take it to that junkyard to be stripped, probably with the help of two or three of their members. Hillbilly says, "What we need to do is fill the bike with explosives that will trigger as the bike is being stripped!"

I say, "Sounds good, have any Goons checked into it?"

Dealer says, "Yes, I have, everything is just as Brock says. We need you to do an exorcism on the motor numbers to the Trojan Horse Bike. I'll give you the new numbers to be restamped. And when we put the bike back together, we'll put it back together full of C4!"

I smile and ask, "That was Brock's idea?"

Hillbilly laughs and says, "You, Clutch, more than anybody, should never underestimate his ability to scheme!"

I nod my head yes while laughing and say, "You're right!"

Dealer goes to the van and takes out a Panhead lower number case. He hands it to me then asks, "Think ya can have it done in a few days?"

I reply, "Yes, I know I can."

He says, "Don't use Harley stamps, because after you renumber it, I want you to destroy the stamps you use. We don't want any signatures for the cops to read. No loose ends, if ya know what I mean. We only need numbers on the bike to make it look good. By the time they figure out the numbers are bogus and not Harley Davidson's, it will be too late. You'll like this, Clutch. The numbers I'm givin' ya to restamp on the bike are registered to that club's National President!"

I laugh hard and say, "Nice touch!"

Dealer and Hillbilly leave along with the van and I return to Nikkei. She gives me the cold shoulder. I know the problem; she worries whenever she sees me with Dealer and Hillbilly, quietly talking alone. She figures we're planning on Takin' Care Of Business.

Well, it's October; several months have passed since Brock's Trojan Horse. The weather has been perfect! My relationship with Nikkei, however, has not been! It's been like a rollercoaster, not so much up and down, but a hundred miles per hour around hairpin curves, scary as hell. As the President, I'm always with the Club in one form or the other. When I do come home, like the roller coaster, I'm doing a hundred miles per hour. You know, eat, into the shower, fuck, sleep, then up early, and leave for work. I'm like a traveling salesman who's never home, but worse, because of the Club, Nikkei has to worry about where I am and what I'm doing! In addition, I don't have any answers for her, at least any that will offer comfort.

Brock's Trojan Horse plan worked like a Swiss Clock—well, like an American Clock. You know the kind of American-made clock that is wired to a detonator! I gotta hand it to him; it worked perfectly. Now he's a fucking hero; he's digging himself into the Club tighter than an 'Alabama Tick!'

Brock is not only a master at scheming but also a master at politics! Rumor has it he may be the next President of that Chapter. Make no mistake, him and me hug each other when other Brothers are around. We have the Club convinced we've forgotten our differences, but either one of us would love to see the other fall. I know he's a piece of shit, but Brock is a master at politics. So every time I think he's going to revel himself for what he really is, he somehow turns it around and comes out smelling like a rose.

Mid-December, and my heart is as cold as the outdoors over the news I just received. Brock was voted in as Chapter Pres last night! Dealer and I are at Papa Dadieo's drinking, Hillbilly is supposed to be here soon. I bluntly tell Dealer I think Brock being Pres is a big mistake. I'm not very good at politics. I guess I'm too truthful, but that is one thing Hillbilly, Dealer, and me have in common. We're all truthful. We can see into each other's hearts, and we know when one is truly happy or sad. We play no games with one another, just total honesty, trust, and love. That's what Brotherhood is! It's being so tuned into your Brother you know what he's thinking and what he's going to say even before he says it. I guess I really wouldn't care so much about Brock, but I know in my heart he holds a vendetta for me! Not to mention, our personalities simply clash, and they clash hard! The truth is, I don't even see him as a Biker. He doesn't know that much about Harleys, and personally, I don't think he rides worth a shit! Now that may sound petty to some, but I only think he's here because of the criminal aspect of the Club and all the backing he receives from it, minus the Biker side! And the Biker side is the side with the Brotherhood, and Brotherhood is what holds the Club together. Hence, if I'm right about Brock, then him being here will only weaken our Club! Especially now that he's Pres!

Hillbilly finally shows up. There are many other Brothers in the bar, but Hillbilly, Dealer, and me are sitting by ourselves. Because we three wear the Death Head Patch, the other Brothers here give us our space. They figure because we're all three sitting together, we're talking business!

Dealer tells Hillbilly that I don't like the idea of Brock being Pres of that Chapter. Hearing this, Hillbilly leans back in his chair and begins chewing his beard. We are all quiet. Dealer and I sit looking at Hillbilly, awaiting his response.

Finally, Hillbilly bellies back up to the table; he looks straight into my eyes, serious as hell, and says, "Why?"

Trying to find an accurate response I stutter out my answer, "I-I-I'm not sure. I . . . I don't trust his heart. I'm not saying he's only out for himself, but I do not believe he's a true Biker that understands Brotherhood. I can't really put my finger on it, Hillbilly, but it's more than just a personality clash between him and me."

Once again Hillbilly leans back in his chair and begins chewing his beard.

He looks at Dealer and asks, "What do you have to say about this?"

Dealer looks down for a few seconds at a beer cap he's been playing with, then looks up at me and says, "I agree with Clutch!"

Then Hillbilly says, "Me too. We must trust our Gut Feelings, but we have to be careful here. The last thing we need is bad blood between our two Chapters. But let's all keep our eyes open and our ears to the ground for a while. And Clutch, you be smart, because you and Brock do have clashing personalities, so don't let your personalities clash!"

Dealer and I both laugh, and I say, "Okay, well said, Hillbilly!"

Its early spring 1976, and I have met every Goon in the Club. Like Dealer said, we really are a Club within the Club. In fact, I must continually remind myself there's a Club outside the Goon Squad. I think it's only natural though, to want to click together with the guys you share your deepest secrets with. Brock's old Sponsor, Crazy George, is also a Goon. He and Hillbilly are very close. I know whenever we're out partying together he's analyzing me against Brock, trying to figure out who to believe. For that reason, I've never said a word to him about Brock that wasn't positive, because I know he's watching for me to try and discredit Brock.

Today we are riding our bikes deep into a National Forest to discuss a new outline for the total manufacturing and distribution of Crank, Methamphetamine. To date, different Chapters have been 'Cooking' it; we have a couple of chemists working for us, and we have all been selling, but it's now become obvious the money potential here is endless. We have a couple of college boys in our Club that have very successfully laundered drug money into legitimate businesses. It was through them that we have also incorporated our Club and have legally registered our name and the Club's Center Patch as a Trademark. Now it cannot be used by anyone without our written consent!

There are about twenty-five motorcycles, two vans, and a few cars following us. This National Park is a place I'm very familiar with. This forest butts up against the Indian Reservation that we're friends with. I love this place, the forest and the lakes. I've spent much of my free time out here. Today we have come to spend the entire day cooking, fishing, drinking beer, and relaxing with our ol' ladies, but most of all, setting up a master plan for our drug business.

There is a small picnic area; we pretty much take it over. We pull all the picnic tables together and set up camp. All our bikes are parked close by the tables. Our women are cooking burgers and our two vans are at the small access road that leads to this picnic site. There are two Brothers in each van armed with AR-15's and 12-gauge pump shotguns pulling security. There are also a couple of Brothers and a few prospects fanned out deep in the forest, covering our Flank. At mid-afternoon all the Brothers gather at the tables, and our women distance themselves so we can talk business. This group of Brothers is mainly comprised of Presidents and Goons! We've come here so we can talk business safely, out of reach from the long arm of the law. We all feel it's never 100 percent safe to talk, so we have a ghetto blaster set up and blaring. Also we talk quietly with our heads down and in code.

We name different squads to handle the cooking of Meth, distribution and then security. The Goon squad has always been used for Takin' Care Of Business when someone fucks with us, but now for the most part, we are gonna be the muscle end of our drug business. We still set up additional security for guarding cook sites and such, but the Goons will be doing all the heavy stuff.

Brock comes up with an ingenious idea for 'Numbering' the entire structure so we can easily track how much Crank is available and where our enterprise sits without any outsiders knowing what the Numbers represent; it really is smart. You know, I could almost start liking him for that idea alone; the problem is, I like hating him more than I like liking him. That goes against our Club's code of Brotherhood, but I'm afraid if I allow myself to begin liking Brock, I'll fall prey to his insidious, lying, manipulative ways, and end up blind to his narcissistic agenda.

One thing Bones has made perfectly clear; and that is 'Buffers,' that's the theme of the day!

He says, "We must have Buffers at every level of this enterprise. We must keep our hands clean. No member of this Club will ever actually touch a single gram of meth unless it's for Personal Use. And all Buffers must be cleared through the Goon Squad; any problems, remember, all Buffers are disposable!"

We all ride home feeling pretty good about what we're about to do. The goal is to stretch our enterprise across the entire Club and then use our profits to invest in legitimate businesses. We are setting up our own legal security force. It's Brothers without felonies that can be licensed to carry and conceal guns. Our Club has been doing muscle work for organized crime families, and we have learned much about the way they operate. Bones wants us to pick up a few of their traits and incorporate them into our Club's behavior with business.

We get home and Nikkei and I for the first time in a long time, fuck like champions. It's weird, because I live with her and see her every single day and sleep with her every single night of my life, yet I still miss her terribly.

Although I must work tomorrow, I cannot fall asleep. Nikkei, however, has had no problem in that area and consequently is sleeping like a log. I'm going over in my head a new system that Brock came up with. This one is for security, and just like the 'Number' system he invented for monitoring our drug business, this idea also proves to me he's much smarter than I once thought, or at least that's what I think.

The idea he introduced is a security technique for each Chapter. He named it "Call." It will mainly be used on the weekends. Each member of the Chapter will take a turn staying home either on a

Friday or Saturday night and monitoring his phone. It starts at six
o'clock in the evening and continues through the rest of the night
until six o'clock in the morning. Every Friday and Saturday night
each member of the Chapter must call in and report where he is
and leave a number so he can be reached there. If a Brother moves
to another location, he must first call-in and say where he's going,
then call when he arrives and give a number there. The Brother on
'Call' will keep a running log of where everybody in his Chapter is;
this way, if there is trouble, the entire Chapter can be summonsed.
All the nearby Chapters also exchange the name and number of
the Brothers on Call. That way if needed, more than one Chapter
can be called for backup. Whenever we're at a bar, there's always a
Club woman sitting beside the bar phone. All she has to do is Drop
a Dime, dial one number, the Call number, and within minutes,
the entire Chapter is on their way. One set-back; anyone listening
to our phone calls will also know where everyone is. Obviously, if a
Brother is Takin' Care Of Business then he will not call-in, or will
call-in with false info on his whereabouts. So in that respect we can
use Call to send misinformation to the cops when needed.

Every Brother in our Club has a homemade 'Resistance Meter'
hooked-up to his phone. A telephone works on DC, Direct
Current, and each and every individual phone will pull the same
resistance when lifted from its receiver. The homemade Radio
Shack resistance meters will monitor the resistance it takes for two
telephones to operate. If a third party, the Cops, plug in a phone
tap, the telephone connection will instantly pull more resistance,
and the meter's pointer will register it; it will "Red Line." Now we
know a third party is on the line. We simply say, "Someone just
came to the door . . . . I gotta go!" And hang up. The cops know
we have them, but that doesn't stop them from trying to bug our
phone lines. To be perfectly legal, unless a Grand Jury has given
the okay, a conversation can only be taped as long as one person
participating in that conversation is aware of the recording device.
There cannot be a third party unaware to the other two taping
the conversation. But how often do you think the cops go by that
rule? They could never use it in court for that reason, but they will
definitely use it to advance their intelligence.

I get up late and go to work. At lunch I'm visited by Heavy; he tells
me late last night our adversary club kidnapped a Brother, Smack,

from his Chapter. I always figured Smack would get it; he's much too loose for war. He was in Nam but never saw combat; he was in the "Rear with the Gear." Anyhow, after beating and torturing him, his kidnapers put him inside a fifty-five-gallon drum. The drum was sealed and placed in the back of a pick-up truck. They were driving along the expressway on their way to give Smack a "long walk off a short pier." The cops pulled the truck over for having a flickering taillight. Can you fucking believe it! The cops heard Smack thumping around inside the drum and began asking questions. When they opened the drum, Smack popped out like a Jack-In-The-Box! He told the cops everything. The two dudes driving the truck are Full Patch Members of the club we're at war with, but instead of going to a Stone Quarry to drown Smack, they ended up going to jail. Rumor has it from one of our Downtown Snitches, Smack has agreed to turn State's Evidence on the two Bikers driving the truck. Our Club is at war with them, but we don't snitch. All Smack would have had to do was tell the cops he was only playing games with those two guys; the cops wouldn't have believed him and taken all three in to be questioned, making his escape good. If Smack does turn State's Evidence on those two Bikers, then he can no longer be in our Club. We will Rat-Pack him, then take his bike, his guns, his money, his woman, and lastly, his Colors!

Chapter Thirteen

DOES DEATH COME IN THREES?

I slam my porch door so fucking hard it breaks the glass out of it, kick start my Harley, and rev the motor loudly as I back it off my porch! Nikkei is at the door, yelling. She shouts to me, "Remember, Clutch, you gave me your word you wouldn't die or go to prison!" I completely ignore her as I fly down my driveway. I don't even relock the gate as I pull through; I just hit the road and give it hell. I'm passing cars on the left, the right; I even ride down the sidewalk to avoid a traffic build up at an intersection.

Fifteen minutes ago, I was sprawled out on the couch with Nikkei, quietly watching TV when the phone rang. I answered to Hillbilly. He said, "Bad news, dude. Fingers was shot and killed an hour ago. Meet me at the Clubhouse." He then hung up. We do very little talking on the phone so that's all I know. I just can't believe Fingers is dead. As far back as I can remember there's always been Fingers; he's been like a father to me. I love him as much as I love anybody. I hit the expressway and I'm doing a hundred miles per hour plus. I'm watching for a possible ambush. Without knowing what happened to Fingers, I can only assume it was a Hit from the club we're at war with, and I may as well figure they'll be watching for our Chapter to gather at our Clubhouse for a meeting to figure out what happened and what to do about it. So it would be easy for them to calculate I'll be on this road at this time!

"Bring It On, Mother Fuckers!" I shout into the wind. After hearing Fingers is dead, I'm ready to kill. Nothing takes the pain out of losing a Brother faster than choking the life away from the man that caused his death!

I continue to ride a hundred miles per hour plus, passing cars on the right if need be. I even squeeze between two cars driving abreast, my mirrors almost hitting theirs. I don't give a fuck. I love Fingers and now he's gone, taking a large part of me with him!

I have about five more miles to ride before I need to exit the expressway. I can see two Harleys riding side by side just ahead. As I grow closer I can see their flying our Club Colors. It's Heavy and Whirly, guaranteed they too have heard the bad news and are headed to the Clubhouse. I down shift my bike and pour on the throttle until I join them. Heavy turns his head and sees it's me and then gives the thumbs up sign. We exit the expressway, and as we sit at a traffic light, two more Bikers pull up and join us. It's Bones and a Goon from his Chapter named Offal; they're being followed closely by a van. Our small caravan of Bikers pulls into the Clubhouse, already filled with many very unhappy Club members.

The road in front of our Clubhouse is lined with Harleys. There are Club vans parked at either end of the street and one parked across the street directly in front of the Clubhouse; all three are obviously holding Brothers with guns. There are small groups of Brothers standing throughout the property quietly talking. More and more Harleys carrying Brothers roll in and I can hear many more coming in the distance.

Hillbilly approaches me with a hug. I say, "Hello Bro, what happened to Fingers?!"

He put his head down, slowly shaking it back and forth, and then says, "His Ol' lady shot him five times! She emptied her revolver into him!"

I angrily shout, "What da fuck for?!" Hillbilly bows to my rage, raising both his hands up before answering.

"I don't know exactly what happened! The way I understand, he was at the bar making time with a barroom hussy when his Ol' lady came in screaming. He threw her out, but she came back. This happened several times and finally she left. When he got home and walked through the door, she opened up on'em without warning. He went down but managed to get off a few rounds, hitting her in the gut. They both lay there and bled to death. The neighbor heard the shots and called the cops. But by the time they arrived it was too late."

I think about it for a few seconds then ask, "Where's his Colors and his bike?"

Hillbilly says, "We have his bike. I found out he was wearing his Colors. I figure they're at the hospital with his personal belongings."

I say, "Okay, send Buttons and Whirly over to his mother's house, tell 'em to take flowers and offer our condolences. Then tell 'em to take her to the hospital and get his Colors. Hillbilly, have them do it right now! We need to know if the hospital or the cops have his Colors. If the cops have 'em, that means you and I may have to get them back ASAP so Fingers can be buried in 'em!"

Hillbilly gives me a hug and says, "Okay, Bro, I'll take care of it." He turns and walks into the Clubhouse.

As Chapter Pres, I must stick around the Clubhouse and stay on top of things. But right now I feel like being alone, so I give Bones a hug and tell him I must split for a while. I climb on my Harley and off I go; I jump on the expressway and just ride. I'm not going any place in particular; I'm just riding and flying my Colors. Like Hillbilly says, "It's Two-Wheeled therapy!" After a few hours I stop in a small bar, it's a redneck-looking joint. I've been here before, but only once, and a long time ago. When I walk in, I can feel all eyes on me; this place is full of would-be tough guys.

I belly up to the bar and order a beer. There is a long, large mirror behind the back bar. Through it I see two dudes at the pool table giving me the eye. Like I said, my Colors are seen as a target to some. I didn't come to fight; all I want to do is drink my beer in peace. My mind is on Fingers, not those two 'Rudiepoots' playing pool, but with the mood I'm in, it won't take much to make me Dance!

I'm not sitting at the bar, rather standing at it, with one foot on the brass rail that runs the length of the bar just above floor level, and leaned over with my elbows resting on the cigarette scarred bar top. A man enters the bar and pulls up a bar stool directly beside me. He looks at me and nods with a smile, then says, "Howdy." I don't reply. He looks all right so I nod back. He's wearing a cowboy hat and boots; he tells me he's a long-distance truck driver. He finishes his beer and on his way out, hands me an entire bundle of writing pens bound together with a single rubber band. They are promotional pens that have the company's name on them for which he works.

It's a very large national trucking firm that we have all heard of. He says, "Here ya go, partner, pass 'em out to your friends."

I thank him with a nod as he leaves.

About one hour and three beers later, one of the dudes playing pool leans on the bar beside me and orders two more beers. As he waits he looks at the bundle of writing pens on the bar in front of me and loudly says, "How ironic; all those pens given to a dirty, greasy Biker that can't even spell his own name!" That was all it took. I gave him a karate chop directly in the throat. Wham! He grabs his neck with both hands and staggers backward, gasping for air. I square up to him and let go with a nice one-two combo into his chin and down he goes, Out Like a Light! Seeing this, his buddy immediately charges across the barroom, swinging a cue stick. I sidestep it, and then run his head directly into the jukebox, smashing its glass front. He falls to the floor, out cold. I'm not bragging, but the entire process of knocking both these maggots out only took eight seconds. Once again, the bar is mine.

The rule is, any time you fight in a strange bar, you leave before the cops come or the dudes you're fighting with come back with a gun. I know the rule, but I came to drink beer and haven't finished yet. So I turn back to the bar and continue drinking. I carefully watch through the Bar's Mirror as the two dudes slowly stand and stagger out of the bar. I order another beer and am reluctantly served. I drink it followed by another, and then leave; that took twenty minutes plus.

I no sooner ride off when the bar door opens; it is one of the dudes I punched out. He is carrying an old military 1903-A3, a .30-06 caliber. He slowly walks around the bar looking for me. He carefully checks the restrooms and then the kitchen. After a few minutes, he walks back outside then insanely fires five rounds into the side of the building, blowing out huge chunks of brick. He slowly and methodically paces around the parking lot for a while before leaving. This happens in broad daylight; the cops never do come.

The moral to that story is, Bikers are not the only Crazy ones. If those two had been hard-core Bikers, I would have gotten out of there as soon as I was done with them. I figured these two for harmless Rudiepoots and stayed for two more beers, ignoring the 'Leave Rule.' Had I stayed for yet another one, it's very possible that last beer could have been my last beer ever. A .30-06 round shows no mercy.

I ride back to the Clubhouse, then our entire Chapter and I ride out to Papa Dadieo's where we spend the rest of the night drinking in Fingers' honor. God, I miss him! He used to say, "If you're a one percenter, you'll probably die Suddenly . . . . Suspiciously . . . . and Untimely!"

It's early Sunday morning, Hillbilly and I are discussing what to do about Fingers' missing Colors. The hospital said he wasn't wearing Colors when he was brought in.

Through our connections Downtown we managed to find out that the first cop on the murder scene, knowing Fingers was dead, cut his Colors off and now has them in his home closet as a trophy. He's been bragging about having them all over the police station. This cop is young and has only been on the force for a year or so. He's extremely Gung Ho and out to save the world from all of us Rotten Bikers. A few months back he hit one of our Hang-Offs in the mouth with a Maglite, breaking out a few teeth.

Fingers will be buried in two days; that's how long we have to get his Colors back. This cop lives alone on the top floor of an apartment complex. Each building has eight units, four up and four down. One of the top end apartments is vacant now. The plan is, while the cop is working, I'll break into the empty apartment and climb into the attic, then crawl through the rafters to the cop's attic. I'll be able to drop down directly into this Pig's closet and get Fingers' Colors back!

We think about leaving a Calling Card, but we figure when he realizes the rag is gone and not being able to put a time on when it was taken, will be all the calling card we need. He'll freak!

Hillbilly finds out when this cop is going to be at work, and then drops me off at the apartment complex. Hillbilly is waiting for me in the cop's assigned parking space. This way if the cop should return home early and unannounced, he'll have to get past Hillbilly first, maybe not such an easy task! Taking our Colors is a killing offence! But we are going to leave this cop alive, provided we get Fingers' rag back. If he ever crosses our paths again however, it may not go so easy for him.

I go to the door of the empty apartment; it is blind to all the other apartments by its design. The corridor leading to the front door has a jog, making it invisible to the other apartments. All these units are built the same. I'm thinking to myself, if we ever decide to murder this guy, this would be the spot to do it! I've never been any good at picking locks, but as I grab the door handle to begin, the door swings open. I enter and cautiously go through the apartment to verify that it is in fact empty. Wow, someone fucked up and left the door unlocked. I'm thinking it's an omen sent by Fingers. I close and lock the door, then chain it.

I climb into the attic and down the long tunnel of trusses; it's hot up here! I remove the ply board lid covering the cop's attic way, gaining access into his apartment. Like a spider, I drop directly into his closet, and Bingo, there is Fingers' Colors. It couldn't be going more perfectly. I take hold of Fingers' Colors; they are soaked in his dried blood. This is terribly upsetting to me; it's a good thing that cop isn't here. I would probably ventilate his ribs after seeing my Brother's Colors in this condition! Before I climb back through the attic way, I figure I'll snoop around a little.

I open the cop's dresser drawer and find a bag of pot and some porno, along with Fingers' Buck Knife. "Mother Fuckin' Pig Thief!" echoes through my head. I know its Fingers' Buck knife because our Chapter had this model #110 custom made. It was engraved by an American Indian, a close friend of Fingers; this man is an artist at engraving. He put custom-made Buffalo Horn handles on the knife and engraved the Club's name and Center Patch into it. It's one of a kind, very beautiful, and very expensive. I put the knife in my back pocket and continue my search. I feel under the cop's pillow and find a pistol, so I figure what the fuck, and I take it also. I go back through the attic and out of the apartment complex. I nonchalantly remove the rubber gloves I'm wearing and calmly walk to Hillbilly's car and we drive off. He looks at me and asks, "Is everything cool?"

I hold up Fingers' Colors and answer, "Mission accomplished!"

I tell Hillbilly I have one of the cop's guns, and it would have to have his fingerprints all over it. I say, "Maybe we should leave it at a crime scene?"

He laughs and says, "That's a very good idea, Clutch!"

Today we bury Fingers. A Biker's funeral is whatever he requested, and it's usually a wake, followed by a long funeral procession. Fingers' last request was he wanted a Blow Job! You know how hard it is to find a girl that will do that to a dead guy? He couldn't have asked for something easy like flowers or to be cremated and then have his ashes sprinkled around a whorehouse. No, not Fingers. He wants one last BJ! I hope he forgives me because the female doing it is fat and ugly! On short notice, that's the best I can come up with!

As far as funerals go, Fingers' had a good one. There was a several-hundred-motorcycle procession. He was buried in his Colors with full honors, and oh yeah, he got the Blow Job he asked for! "I'll see ya Bro, RIP!"

A week after we buried Fingers we found out Smack, the Brother that was kidnapped, did in fact turn State's Evidence against the two Bikers that kidnapped him. Brock had him Rat-Packed and Eighty-Sixed from the Club! Oh well, ya gotta go by the rules. Bikers don't snitch! Personally, I always viewed Smack as a Slow Leak!

Heavy told me about Smack being booted from the Club. He said him and Brock got into a loud argument over Smack's bike. Brock wants it, but doesn't want to pay the Chapter a fair amount. The bike's probably worth three grand. Brock only wants to pay a third of that for it. Although Heavy has a legitimate bitch over the bike, there's friction between him and Brock anyhow. Brock knows Heavy and me are tight, and I figure he doesn't like Heavy for that reason. Fuck 'em!

Our drug business is booming. We've been cooking kilo after kilo, and the Tweak Heads are lining up for it. As Goons, every now and then Hillbilly and I have to collect on bad debts. One dude became a real problem. We had him working for us, but he never talked to a single Brother personally. It was always done through a middle man, a Buffer. When he found out our Club was behind the entire operation, he got scared and threatened to go to the police. He is one of those guys that do speed with a needle. That was perfect for us; Hillbilly and I gave him a lethal dose of pure meth. As he lay near our feet, convulsing from the overdose, we sat in his living room waiting for him to die while looking through a stack of Playboy magazines. We playfully held up Center Folds for each other to see while scoring the women from one through ten, then arguing about the numbers, "There's no way she's an eight! I'd only give her a five—tops!" When we were sure the guy was dead we quietly left! But on our way out, I opened his refrigerator and took out two beers.

As I handed Hillbilly one, I said, "He won't be needing it!"

Now that the Goon Squad is handling the dirty work for our drug business, it seems all we do is spend our time together hunting people, beating people, and when necessary, killing people. I worry we're drifting away from being Bikers and becoming more like Mobsters. It's not just Hillbilly and I; it seems the entire Club spends all its time riding around in high-dollar cars—Cadillacs, Mercedes—and counting their drug money. Nobody ever even rides their bikes very much anymore; some Brothers have motorcycles that don't even run. There's a Club National Run coming up soon, and it's a 'Mandatory.' Mandatory means every member must show his Mug; all Brothers must attend. Bones is madder than hell about the direction the Club is turning. He angrily announces, "This is a Mother Fucking Motorcycle Club! Any Brother that does not show up on the National Run this year riding a Harley Davidson will have his Patch Pulled and will be a Prospect again! No exceptions!" Boy, you should see all the Brothers scrambling to get their Harleys up and running after hearing that!

The difference between us and an organized crime family is Brotherhood. We love one another. In a crime family they do not; it is not uncommon for them to have power struggles and killings within their own organization. We would never do that; in fact, it's quite the opposite. We help and protect our Brothers. If a Mobster is arrested and facing a large prison sentence, it is not uncommon for his crime family to have him murdered for fear he'll turn State's Evidence on their organization in order to save himself. Even if that was not his plan, often the individual finds out a Hit has been put on him from his own family and that forces him into becoming a Federal Witness. Trust me when I say, many Mobsters have shot themselves in the foot simply by scaring a fellow Mob Buddy into the Witness Protection Program by trying to have him killed. That just doesn't happen with Bikers, and that's because of Brotherhood!

That's the problem I have with Brock; he would do better in the Mob because he doesn't understand Brotherhood. After Smack was Eighty-sixed from our Club, Brock ended up with all his property; his bike, his guns, even his Ol' lady, Weird Sally. Now he and Heavy have bad blood over the property he took and never paid the Chapter for. That's always been my problem with Brock; he's only out for himself. He's not a Biker, hence not a Brother. I told Heavy he should transfer to this Chapter and get away from

Dave Ebert

Brock. This got around to a few Brothers in his Chapter and now they're pissed-off at me. I feel a small feud brewing.

The biggest problem Heavy has with Brock is that Brock helped two of his friends come into our Club. Neither of them prospected very long or very hard. Heavy is not the only member of that Chapter upset about it. Many are calling those two, "The New Bros." Along with Heavy, there's a couple of Old-School Brothers that regret Brock ever becoming President. It's obvious to me; Brock is trying to push them out of the Club as well as Heavy.

Dealer and I are drinking at Papa Dadieo's when Hillbilly and Crazy George pull in. Crazy George is Brock's old Sponsor and one of the Goons in that Chapter. We all four sit at the bar for hours discussing Brock and the two dudes he brought into our Club. At one point Crazy George and I get into a short argument over it. I simply tell him I think it's wrong, and he only agrees with it because it's his Chapter and he doesn't know what to do about it. Like I said earlier, Crazy George is always watching me, analyzing whether or not I'm playing politics against Brock. All I know is, our two Chapters have a very strained relationship for the first time ever, and Brock's to blame. We all see it. Even Heavy says that all the Bullshit may cause him to retire!

Hillbilly and Crazy George are very close; I know it's only a matter of time before Crazy George will understand that my opinion of Brock is only motivated for the good of the Club. The one thing I have going for me is Crazy George himself. As a Goon, he and I are among the elite, and unlike the other members of Brock's Chapter, the Goons are on the outside looking in; far away from Brock's influence and talent for playing politics.

I stand and tell my Brothers good night. On my ride home I worry for the future of our Club if Brock and men like him are allowed to flourish in our tight Brotherhood; it will have to weaken our organization.

Heavy said because of Brock, he and two other older members of that Chapter are thinking of retiring. I never believed they would until all three of them stopped by my house and told me they announced their retirement last night at that Chapter's Church meeting. "Holy Fuck!" To me this is very serious, and I blame Brock completely. He's bringing in his own people and forcing out any Old-School members that may oppose the way he runs that Chapter.

In our Club, one can retire with honors after seven years. That may not seem like a long time, but those are seven years in the fast lane. To retire with honors means you can keep your Colors and wear them once a year on the Club's National Run. You can come back into the Club "Active" anytime during the first year following your retirement. After one year, you have to prospect again. Nobody is going to prospect again after seven years in the Club and retiring with honors, so I figure we have one year to talk Heavy and the other two Brothers into returning active. I doubt if any one of the three will as long as Brock is around. I hate that Mother Fucker! I see him as a cancer in my beloved Club.

The following day, Hillbilly, Dealer, Crazy George, and I are together and planning what we call a "Tune Job" that actually means A Beating. After we finalize the plan, I tell them Heavy announced his retirement. Crazy George missed his Chapter's church meeting, so this is the first he has heard about Heavy leaving. Crazy George and Heavy are very close; in fact, Heavy was a Goon in that Chapter with Crazy George for many years, so they obviously share many of their deepest secrets. Hillbilly and Dealer expressed dismay, but Crazy George was obviously shaken up over the news. He must know Heavy's decision was spawned from Brock's appointment as Chapter President. I steer clear of that subject, but do mention the loss of a great Brother. But I also kind of mention the politics of losing Heavy when I say, "Under Club bylaws, he can come back within the first year, so maybe he'll come back if it's to my Chapter?" That pretty much points the finger directly at Brock. And for the first time I can see in Crazy George's eyes, his suspicion is turning away from me and to that piece of shit, Brock.

Well, I'm going to make it my goal to stop Brock and get Heavy and the other two Brothers back. There's no doubt in my mind, if Brock will play politics to push the Old-School Bikers out, then he'll stop at nothing to get me out of the Club.

Well, I have the Goons. Although Crazy George is in that Chapter, he's a Goon first and will do what's best for the Club as a Whole. I must get him on my side. The technique I'm using is, 'No Technique.' Brock is playing games against me, and Crazy George is standing back, watching and analyzing, and a good way to beat someone that's playing games against you is simply, Don't Play! . . . . Let them beat themselves!

When our meeting ends, Dealer and Hillbilly are headed over to Papa Dadieo's. They ask me to ride along, but I tell them I promised Nikkei I'd be home for dinner. I jokingly say, "I haven't seen her in months." But the truth is, I really haven't! Well, I have, but not with any good quality time. Like I said, I'm in and out of her life at a hundred miles per hour!

Crazy George says he'll go if I go. Well, I can't turn that down! He and I need to become closer, so I agree, and all four of us ride to Papa Dadieo's, flying our Colors.

We hit the back roads; we are riding fast through the night, two abreast in a tight group. We are all pretty much dressed the same—our Colors over our black leather jackets, fingerless gloves, and tight blue jeans with pant legs rolled up, exposing our high-top black leather boots. Our tightly packed group of four may be small by number, but none of us are! At six feet and two inches and 215 pounds, I'm the runt of the litter! Crazy George is next at six feet and four inches and 250 pounds. Then there's Hillbilly and Dealer; they both tower near six feet and nine inches and weigh in at over 325 pounds! As our bikes thunder down the highway, it's exciting to me as a Goon to be riding with three other Goons. We are all carrying guns, and with our excellent ability to fight, it's easy to get the feeling of invincibility. Our Colors flap in the wind behind each of our backs as our exhaust pipes pound out a loud warning into the night: "We're Ready, Willing, and Able! So don't fuck with us!" Although we're not out Takin' Care of Business, our small, fast-moving Goon Squad still has that look of one single entity, the Angel of Death.

Walking through the door at the bar is exciting for me because all four of us are wearing the Death Head Patch. We are a Club within the Club. Crusher is at the bar and I see his ol' lady, Brandy, is sitting by the bar's pay phone. If there's any trouble, she's ready to make that 'Call,' and you can bet she has a pistol in her purse just in case anybody tries to stop her! The bar is full of Brothers. I party for a few hours then finally leave for home; I must spend some time with Nikkei.

I get home and everything looks normal. The gate is locked, dogs look fine, Nikkei's car is here, but when I enter the house there is no Nikkei. "What the fuck is this all about?" Maybe she got mad and left because I promised to be home for dinner hours ago. Maybe the cops came and took her again. If she got mad and left, then why is her car here?

It doesn't make sense the cops took her in again because things have been cooling off and the only thing she tells them is "Talk to my attorney!" So what's the point in questioning her? But then, where the fuck is she?

I snoop around the house and find her purse; she never leaves without taking that! There's a book she's been reading lying on the floor by the couch. I can see it has been carelessly thrown to the floor; it's resting in a Teepee fashion and between its hard covers, the pages are entangled, bent, and torn. Her coat and all her clothes are here; everything looks to be in place as if she's here, but she's not. I'm pretty drunk, so after several phone calls looking for her, I reluctantly go to bed, alone.

I get up early, I'm somewhat hung over. Once again I search through the house, still no Nikkei. I ride over to Hillbilly's house and tell him and Dealer about her being gone. I can see they figure everything is fine, that she either moved out or will be back soon.

I go back home and make more phone calls, but nobody knows anything. Night comes and once again I climb back into an empty bed; I must work tomorrow.

At five in the morning, the alarm goes off. I jump up and run through the house looking for Nikkei, but still no sign of her. I look in the drive and see her car is still sitting there.

At work I tell Heavy about Nikkei being gone; he offers more concern than did Dealer and Hillbilly, but he, too, thinks she moved out on me because of the Club.

It's now been a week since Nikkei disappeared. I'm sure there's a problem out of her control. I'm riding my bike to Brock's Chapter's Clubhouse. I received an emergency call from Crazy George about a half hour ago telling me to call Hillbilly and meet him at that Clubhouse, that Brock's Ol' lady has just been shot, and probably won't make it. Her name is Weird Sally. She stayed with Smack, but when he was Eighty-sixed from our Club, she moved in with Brock. She's more of a Club Mama than an Ol' lady!

I get to the Clubhouse and find Hillbilly and Crazy George standing in the road talking. They tell me Brock's at the hospital. I ask what happened; they say that Brock and Weird Sally were in for the night when someone knocked on their front door. When Sally opened it, a single gunshot from what appears to be a 12-gauge shotgun went off, giving her one in the gut. Brock saw a car speed off. We figure the blast was meant for him by our rival Club.

I'm madder than hell; I liked Sally. I tell Hillbilly and Crazy George, "We need to hit back hard. Let's give 'em both barrels!" I know this sounds bad, but I'm thinking; too bad it was Sally and not Brock!

I'm riding home from work on my Panhead when stopped by the Police. It's been two weeks since Sally was murdered and still no answers as to who did it. I've given no reason to be stopped by the police, but it's not that unusual for the cops to pull over a Biker and fuck with him. After he checks out my driver's license and bike registration, the cop asks me about Sally's murder. This throws my brain into high gear. Putting the ball back in his court; I give my formula answer, "I don't know, why do you ask?" He staggers around with that one for a few seconds, then brings up a few interesting points that more or less insinuate Brock may have been the one who shot Sally!

No doubt this street cop was sent by BET. That's a cop game, "Stirring the Pot" within our own Club, but the cops know we are not stupid and are extremely tight. What the cop told me makes sense though, and I begin to consider the possibility that Brock may be the one who shot Sally. If he did kill her, as far as his standing in the Club goes, nothing will change. I know that sounds bad, but you're allowed to shoot your Ol' lady. Not that Brothers go around shooting their Ol' ladies, but it wouldn't be considered a violation against the Club. But Weird Sally is a little different, because she's Heavy's daughter!

When Heavy was told his daughter was murdered by our rival Club, he came out of retirement with a vengeance! He wants Payback. There could be a big problem here; If Brock is the one who killed Sally and Heavy figures it out, there's nothing Heavy can do about it. The Club will back up Brock. If Heavy fucks with Brock, the entire Club will come after him because he turned on his Brother. After all, Brock is a member and a President, Sally was not—RIP.

I don't dare say anything to anyone about what the cop told me. But now that I've been thinking about it, I've been swayed to the belief that Brock did it. I'm not the schemer Brock is, so I'm not sure what would happen if I talked to Heavy about this. It may look as if I'm just trying to cause problems for Brock. Heavy and I did, however, do some talking at work the other day about Brock. He tells me Brock has been running his mouth against me over Nikkei's disappearance. It would seem he's been asking, "What good is a lovesick President that spends all his time looking for a woman that probably ran off with another man?" That one really rattled my cage, but I didn't volley back by telling him my suspicions about Brock being the one who killed his daughter, Sally. It's easy for me to see Heavy loved her and misses her terribly.

I am an excellent Brother to all my Club members and an excellent President to my Chapter. I do, however, spend mega amounts of time looking for Nikkei. After Weird Sally was murdered and we initially blamed our rival Club, I tossed around an idea; if they would kill Sally then maybe they kidnapped Nikkei. Now that I'm almost sure that Brock killed Sally, that idea no longer makes sense, but I'm sure something terrible has happened to her. She's been gone so long! We just buried Fingers, and then Weird Sally, God, I'm worried for Nikkei; 'Does death come in threes?'

One more time I bow my head in prayer, only this time I do make a deal with God. I tell him, if he'll bring Nikkei home to me, I'll do whatever it takes to make her happy—even if that means leaving the Club! I do, however, hold back from outright saying, "I'll quit the Club." I tell God, I don't think I should have to leave the Club, because in my mind a sin is only a sin if it's against my Brothers, and I don't sin against my Brothers. I'm not saying I live purely, but I am saying, "I live honest to my beliefs."

Chapter Fourteen

NIKKEI

The temperature is peaking into the upper eighties; humidity is high. Whirly and I are sailing down the highway, riding side by side and proudly flying our Colors. It's Friday night and we are headed to a bar on the far side of this huge city. Traffic is light, allowing our bikes to freely thunder down the road undisturbed. Like an artist's brush passing across the canvas; from front to back, the chrome on our machines brightly sparkles through the pale night as we pass under each streetlight. This is Brock's Chapter's territory. In fact, the bar we're headed to is controlled by that Chapter. The plan is we're going to meet Heavy there. Ever since his daughter's murder, he's been in very bad shape emotionally. I swear, I've never seen a man so fueled by anger and so hell-bent on vengeance. That's all he talks about—how much he misses his daughter and killing the person or persons who murdered her. Sometimes I feel guilty because I think I'm only listening with selfish intent, just so he'll be indebted to hear me talk about how much I miss Nikkei. Unfortunately, it's a common bond we both share.

Nikkei has been gone for over three weeks now, gone without a trace. The club we're at war with sent a message to me through one of their Hang-Offs. He said they had nothing to do with Nikkei's disappearance. Although we're at war and I do not like those guys, I know they're not punks. They didn't send this message because they're afraid of my retaliation, rather out of respect and to reiterate an Old Biker Rule: 'We don't fuck with families.' I believe them, and that only serves to confuse me even more on what could have happened to my beautiful fiancée.

Whirly and I pull into the bar. It is packed with Brothers; many of them are from Chapters up north. We walk in and a Brother from Brock's Chapter, one he recently brought into the Club, walks up to me and says, "If you're looking for your Ol' lady, she's not here!"

I loudly fire back, "What da fuck is that supposed to mean?!"

A half dozen Brothers standing close by stop what they are doing and focus on this potential problem. He is obviously drunk.

He says, "Well, I just figured because you spend all of your time looking for her, so that's what you must be doing here!"

Whirly immediately steps between us before a fight breaks out. He grabs my arm and says, "Come on, Clutch, let's find Heavy."

I never speak a word, just glare at this guy as hatefully as I possibly can while Whirly pulls me away.

I pan my eyes through the bar; our Club Colors are everywhere, along with black leather jackets and tattoos. The bar is dim and smoky; the jukebox is pounding out loud music from 'The Doors' "Been Down So Long."

We find Heavy and all three of us sit at a small table, drinking and talking. About an hour goes by then Crazy George comes over and sits with us. We make some small talk, I tell a couple of funny jokes, and then Crazy George asks what happened at the door when Whirly and I came in. I told him what 'New Bro' had said to me. Crazy George did not like that at all. In fact, I had to talk him down from going back over there and calling the Brother out!

Crazy George tells me he put a new motor on his Harley and invites me outside to have a look. When we get outside to his bike, I can see the new motor story was only a ploy to get me alone. He tells me he's starting to understand my feelings toward Brock and that he also is beginning to share the same feelings. He tells me to keep it to myself, but he believes Brock killed Sally. He also says that Brock has been trying to make me look bad because I'm spending so much time looking for Nikkei. He then says he talked to Dealer and Hillbilly about both issues and for me to keep my mouth shut until we figure out what to do about it. But for sure, don't say anything to Heavy. I tell him I also think Brock killed Sally and what the cop that stopped me said. I explain some of the details Brock gave about her murder that doesn't make sense. Then Crazy George says something that completely puts me on the War Path. It makes me totally crazy!

He began by leaning close to me and saying, "Clutch, I have something to tell you, but first you must give me your word you won't freak out!" This threw me a little, but I assure him I will not. Then he continues, "I think I know where Nikkei is!"

That was all he had to say. I broke my word; I freaked out! I step up close to him with my chest out.

"Where?!" I demand.

He retreats back one step, puts his hand flat against my chest, restraining my position, and says, "Calm yourself, Clutch! You have to listen to what I have to say. There's nothing we can do to help her right now, but if you freak out, you'll blow it and you may never see her again. Now shut the fuck up and listen to what I have to say!" I begin pacing in circles, hyperventilating. Finally I stop, bend over, and put my hands on my knees. I stay in this position for a long time, breathing heavily until I collect myself.

After I do, I stand and say, "Okay, I'm sorry. Go ahead, George, I'll be cool!"

Crazy George once again steps close to me and says, "Okay, are you sure you're cool?"

I anxiously say, "Yes! Please! Tell me what you know!"

He says, "Okay, now listen, I'm not sure about any of this. I could be 100 percent wrong, but I think Brock has Nikkei." I stand speechless, in total shock. If anybody other than a Goon would have said that, I would have had to laugh. But I know there must be something happening here or Crazy George would have never said it.

In total mood reversal, I look at George and ask, chuckling, "How'd ya come up with that one, George?"

He tells me what he knows and what he thinks and why he thinks it. It is now making more sense to me than ever before. He's absolutely right. Brock has kidnapped Nikkei, and she's still alive! The exhilaration of thinking Nikkei is still alive and I may find out where she's at, is shortly overruled by the anger that follows, thinking Brock has something to do with her disappearance. Is it possible that Nikkei was not taken by force though? That she voluntarily left me to go back with Brock? No way, I'll never believe that. But my heart is instantly invaded by suspicion. I will not, however, share these doubts with anyone.

George tells me Brock's father left him a small cabin on a large spread of land surrounded by swamp, and that's where he thinks

Nikkei is. He said Brock has been leaving overnight and taking food and different supplies, and that's why he believes Nikkei is still alive. Nobody knows where this place is, but George has told Hillbilly, Dealer, and many other Goons what he thinks. They are all trying to find out where this cabin is without Brock getting wise to them. If Brock finds out we suspect him, he'll move her for sure, or worse . . . . !

Crazy George puts his arm around me and very seriously asks, "Clutch, make no mistake. We must know, and you know better than anyone else. Do you think Nikkei has gone back to Brock of her own free will?"

I look him directly in the eyes and say, "I swear on my Patch, if she's with Brock, he took her by force!"

George replies, "Okay, Bro, that's all we need to know."

"George, I gotta go. I can't walk back in that bar right now without killing Brock," I said as calmly as possible.

Crazy George gives me a hug and says, "We'll take care of it Bro, you have my word. We are the Goon Squad, and we right all wrongs!"

I return his tight hug and say, "Do me a favor and square it with Heavy and Whirly that I left. Tell 'em I'll check 'em out tomorrow. Good-bye Bro, I love you 100 percent!"

It's after midnight and I leave alone, riding full bore through the dirty city streets, flying my Colors. The summer heat has brought out a large group of indigenous city dwellers, a large crowd of hippies. They stop what they're doing and stare as I loudly scream by. Like a lion growling in the darkened jungle, my bike is pounding out a thunderous beat against the tall city buildings, promoting me as a dangerous predator. A newspaper's page that litters the street is violently sucked into my bike's vortex, and is briefly pulled behind my machine and raised high into the air as I blow past. It then gently butterflies back to earth, my Panhead is throwing fire from its pipes as I ride out of sight.

I hit the expressway and cruise. The wind in my face always brings me home, home to a place that's relaxed, with a secure feeling, a feeling of having no past and no future, only the moment, my bike, and my Colors.

As I exit the expressway and enter the long curving road that leads me to that cool little town I live in, my thoughts go directly to Nikkei. Is it possible I'll see her again soon? Wow, my heart begins to race. The closer I get to my house, the more she consumes my mind. All I can think about is how much I miss her and how much I love her. I immediately put my thoughts on hold and then challenge myself. "Would I give up these Colors this very second to see Nikkei again?" For the first time in my life, it becomes obvious to me, I can't have both her and the Club. Because the Club demands 110 percent and I love her more than that. Wow, I made a deal with God. Looks like he's gonna keep up his end of it.

I get home and find the thought of possibly having Nikkei back keeps me from sleeping. This house is alive with her memory and her sweet smells. Once again, I 100 percent promise God that if he returns her to me, I will do anything he wants me to do. Only this time, I say it on my knees.

Early the next day I'm woken by the roaring sound of a single Harley echoing through my intercom. I turn and view the camera's monitor. It's Whirly down at the gate; he's looking directly into the camera and holding out his bottom lip for me to see. "Now what's that crazy fucker doing?!" I smile, press the intercom, and tell him, "I'll be right there."

I go down and unlock the gate to let him in. Now I see what he was trying to show me; it's a busted lip! He says, "Let's go have a nice cup of coffee, Bro, and I'll tell ya what happened last night after you left the bar!"

It's not all that unusual for Whirly to be fighting; in fact, it happens on a regular basis. Remember, this is the guy that's been known to hit people for no reason other than he didn't like the way they looked! Of course in his defense, the ones I've seen him hit for "No reason" looked like worms to me also. They just had that "Punch Me Face" look about them. As we return to the house, I can see there is something unique about this last fight he's been in though!

We sit at the kitchen table enjoying a nice cup of hot coffee and I ask, "Okay, Bro, what the fuck did you get into last night?"

He tells me one of the New Bros, which is what we're calling the two guys Brock brought into the Club, came to his table where him and Heavy were having an intense discussion about Weird Sally's murder and interrupted by sitting down. Whirly and Heavy stopped what they were saying and looked directly at this guy, hoping he would leave.

Of course, he did not, only loudly blurted out of his drunken mouth, "What, did your Pres have to leave to go look for his Bitch?!"

Whirly looks directly at me with his War Face and says, "That was it Clutch, Brother or not, I knocked him out with a nice one-two punch!"

Fighting among Brothers will happen occasionally, but it is seriously looked down on unless the fight resolves the problem; in other words, no grudges. Sometimes that's what it takes to wash away any bad blood. However, this fight was more or less between two Chapters, and that's very serious shit.

I ask Whirly, "You knocked him out?"

He loudly answers, "Fuckin'-A right I knocked that Motherfucker out! But I didn't stop there. The other New Bro Brock let in, Road Kill, got in my face. We argued a bit, and then he hit me!" He grabs his lower lip as proof, and then continues, "So I gave him a couple also! This guy is tough as nails, Clutch. I had to work overtime knocking him out. Brock's entire Chapter was gonna jump me but Heavy, Crazy George and all the Brothers from up north stopped it."

I think about it for a minute then say, "Fuck it, shit happens! But one thing for sure, our Chapter won't let anyone bother you over this, not even Bones. We'll talk to Hillbilly and let him know what happened. He'll talk to Crazy George and George will back us up. He's our inside man in Brock's Chapter, him and Heavy both. Hillbilly, Heavy, and Crazy George, all three have heavy-duty pull with Bones and the Mother Chapter. So Brock is outgunned in that respect and on his way out of our Club as far as I'm concerned!"

I stand up and say, "Whirly, there's shit about that Chapter and Brock going on that I can't talk about right now, but it's enough to make me want to go to war with them. All I need is the okay from Bones and we'll go Pull all their Patches!"

I tell Whirly to stand up. I approach him face-to-face, look directly into his eyes for a long time, and then give him a tight hug, and say, "Thanks for backing me up, I love ya, Bro. You are definitely 100 percent, one percent!"

Whirly and I are getting ready to ride over to Hillbilly's house when we hear him and Dealer at the gate. Dealer opens it and they both ride in. We meet them at the front porch; neither looks very happy. Fighting within the Club can be a very serious offence.

Hillbilly dismounts from his Harley, looks directly at Whirly then angrily asks, "What the Fuck happened last night, Whirly?!"

Just as Whirly begins to answer, two more Harleys come down my driveway. It's Crusher and Buttons.

Crusher climbs off his bike and walks directly to Whirly; he also angrily shouts, "What the fuck happened last night?!"

Because everyone knows Whirly loves to fight, they all assume he started this one.

Whirly begins to tell his story, but before he can finish, a half dozen more Harleys, one by one, pull down my long drive, all Brothers from this Chapter. These guys are revved up; they all want to go to war with Brock's Chapter. They're all madder than hell and going to back up their Brother Whirly to the end. These guys are Ready, Willing, and Able! I remind them we all wear the same Patch, but that doesn't calm their anger much. What they really want is Brock and his two New Bros out of our Club.

Although not an officer, Hillbilly is the one we all look up to for answers, wisdom, and advice, but this time he stands silent, as does Crusher and Dealer.

Buttons looks at me and says, "Well, you're the Pres, so what are we gonna do, Pres?"

I say, "There are some very serious allegations against Brock. If it happens there is truth in any of it, I will have a Sit-Down with Bones. We must keep our Club strong, so whatever Bones says we will abide by. Until then, let's all cool off and stay away from that Chapter for a while . . . . Oh yeah, if anybody fucks with Whirly over what happened, then back him to the death!" As I'm saying that, I put my arm around Whirly and give him a tight squeeze.

Whirly has a well-earned reputation for loving to fight! Probably because he's so good at it! But I can see how Brock can use his reputation to try and make this fight look like Whirly's fault.

By this time, our entire Chapter is at my house. They send a couple of Prospects up for beer and ice, and the party begins. Hillbilly pulls me to the side and tells me Crazy George told him and Dealer everything—how he feels about Brock, what he believes happened to Sally, and of course, Nikkei. He says, "Remember, you got the Goon Squad backing your ass!" and for me to be smart and keep my mouth shut. I thanked him with a hug.

I cannot describe to you how much it means to me having Brothers as beautiful as Hillbilly, Dealer, and Crazy George backing me up. I can go to my grave knowing I experienced true

Brotherhood during my life. I told God if he brings Nikkei back I'll do anything, but if leaving the Club is what God wants me to do, how can I ever walk away from Brothers like that? If I'm not careful, there is a tug-of-war here that could end up tearing my heart in half. How can I ever choose between Nikkei and the Club when I love them both more than I love life itself? There is little doubt in my mind; I want my woman back at any cost, but should I throw a disclaimer in there—at any cost, less the cost of my Club?

Another week has come and gone and still no sign of Nikkei. Dealer and Hillbilly have been sneaking off with Crazy George and I think they are making progress on finding her. When I get home from work tonight they all three said they'll be waiting at my house to talk to me. They must have something important to talk about. I hope its good news about Nikkei, but it's probably Club business.

I have never been a religious man, but since I've been praying for Nikkei's return, I've now found and understand faith. I figure, its God I'm dealing with, so it's only logical to have faith. Either you trust him or you don't; there's no in-between. God may not give us everything we want, but he will give us everything we need. And although I want Nikkei, most certainly, I need Nikkei. Therefore, I trust God will do as I ask; he most certainly has the power to do it. At any rate, for the first time since Nikkei disappeared, I feel confident she will be home soon.

As I cruise home from work, I try to figure out what it is my three Brothers have to say. It could be anything, from we must blow somebody up, to they have news about Nikkei. I pull in my drive and find I was right for trusting God and my Brothers. There is Nikkei standing with Hillbilly, Dealer, and Crazy George! Honestly, I start shaking. Before I run to her, I bow my head and say, "Thank you, God!" Then I bolt to my fiancée!

She extends her arms wide and receives me, I enter into her embrace lifting her feet high off the ground and tightly squeezing as I spin her in a circle. I'm kissing and whispering in her ear, "I love you, I missed you!" Dealer, Hillbilly, and Crazy George walk away, giving me time alone with Nikkei.

I can see she lost some weight, but for most part looks as good as she did the last time I saw her one month ago. Although she is responding to me with many hugs and kisses, it is not with the same intensity as I'm giving her. I figure she must still be in shock from whatever experience the last month has laid upon her.

After a long time of hugging, kissing, and touching her, Nikkei and I join my Brothers in the living room. We all sit and talk to Nikkei about her experiences.

She tells us it started a month ago when Brock came to the door. He knew I was at Papa Dadieo's. She said he had obviously been drinking heavily. He told her I had been in a serious bike crash and he was sent to pick her up and take her to me.

Brock used 'Call' to find out where I was. Here's the irony. 'Call' was his idea; now he's using it against his own Club!

Nikkei says she was so upset she didn't even grab her purse, just blindly left with Brock. "I figured something was wrong when he drove to the expressway," she said. "He was very drunk and looked to be potentially violent."

He kept telling her, "Everything is A-OK, so don't worry!"

She said he made her lay on the car seat so she couldn't see where they were going. He told her it was a precaution the Club uses whenever bringing anybody to the house they're headed to.

She told us, "I knew that was bullshit, but I was afraid if I refused he would become violent. And I still believed Clutch had been in a serious bike wreck so I wasn't thinking clearly. Also I didn't feel like arguing with Brock's drunk ass. I figured Brock had to have been sent to our house by someone special because he had a key to our gate!"

When she said that, Hillbilly and Dealer both stared expressionlessly at me. Nikkei continues, "After a couple of hours, we arrived at a small cabin. It was Brock's father's old place. We went in and Brock passed out on the floor."

Nikkei told us she couldn't find his car keys. She said she went outside and figured she'd walk to a phone. The cabin is in the middle of a huge swamp, it was midnight and there were many mosquitoes and spooky swamp noises, so she gave up on that plan. She said she snooped through the cabin, all the while stepping over Brock, but then finally gave up and fell asleep on the couch.

The next day when Brock woke, he realized what he had done during his drunken stupor. Fearing Club retribution, he continued his lie to Nikkei, telling her to stay at the cabin. He's going to leave for a short while, but not to worry, everything is okay. He told Nikkei he would return with Hillbilly to give her a ride to see me.

Nikkei knew that was all bullshit, but continued to play along, not realizing how far Brock was willing to go with this.

As soon as he left, Nikkei took off walking in the hopes of finding a phone. She still didn't realize she had been kidnapped and was going to be held prisoner. Brock didn't realize that either. This was not a calculated plan composed by him, but rather the aftermath of a drinking binge. In fact, he wasn't sure what to do. He wasn't going to kill her, but he knew if he brought her home, I would go nuts and he would be booted from the Club. He was buying time while trying to scheme his way out of this predicament.

Nikkei says, "I walked and walked, but its all swamp out there and there's not a single house anywhere, only a maze of small jeep trails!"

She said after walking for a half hour down the straight, narrow dirt road that leads from Brock's cabin, she saw a car flying down the road followed by a large contrail of dust. Her initial excitement was lost when she realized it was Brock.

His car came to a sliding halt as he leaned from the window and angrily demanded, "Get in the Fuckin' car, Nikkei!" She feared he might beat her. They drove back to the cabin where he flipped out over her leaving! His demeanor had changed to anger and violent behavior. Nikkei said this is when she began to realize how far Brock was willing to go. He was punching walls, throwing things, and at one point, he pulled his pistol and dry fired it into his own mouth! He began laughing insanely and told Nikkei the next bullet will be live and in her mouth!

She says, "Like a switch turning a light from off to on, he instantly and schizophrenically calmed!"

He explained that I was dead; he told her not to worry, because he still loved her and would take care of her.

He said, "Please, Nikkei, I want you to take me back!"

He said he was not going to hurt or rape her, but she would have to understand that he and only a very few others know where she is. That he was her only hope; that she could never leave the cabin without him.

He said, "Eventually you'll know Clutch was no good, and we two were meant for each other!"

In Brock's twisted psychotic mind, he figured in time Nikkei would fall back in love with him. Then he'd turn the story around and tell the Club she ran off on her own free will, dumping me and crawling back to him where she belongs. Sounds like a good plan, only one problem, she was never in love with him. She was only with him in the attempt of Kick-starting my love for her by making me jealous. She's not the first woman that's done something like that, but now it's backfired on her. By the end of their relationship, Nikkei didn't like Brock very much, but now she hates him. He doesn't care for her either; it's just he needs her to help him get out of this problem he's in.

After three hours or so, one of Brock's New Bros, Big Bart, shows up at the cabin. Nikkei has never seen him before and does not know he is a member of our Club. He's one of the two friends Brock let in. As she tells the story, none of us have any idea who it is she's talking about. That is another piece of the puzzle we must put together.

Big Bart worships Brock and believes any and all of what Brock tells him. And like Brock, I don't see him as a True Biker either. Brock and Big Bart go outside the small cabin and talk for a very long time. Brock lied to him also; he told Big Bart Nikkei was being sought by the Feds as a federal witness. If she was allowed to testify, many Brothers will go to jail. Brock said Nikkei is an excellent liar and would deny all of this, and that I am a lovesick, love-blind punk that believes anything Nikkei says. So he was ordered to bring her out here until the Club figures out what to do with her and me. He told Big Bart not to touch Nikkei sexually or abuse her in any way; he said do very little talking to her because she's very persuasive. He told Big Bart it was his job to guard Nikkei and he would be back and forth to relieve him from time to time. He very sternly demands that Big Bart never speaks to anybody about this, not even Bones. He convinced Big Bart that what he was doing was for the Club and he would be properly rewarded. Because Big Bart is a fat slob that doesn't work or have any family, this was a perfect job for him. All he needs to be happy is a television, lots of food and beer, and he can stay at the cabin forever. Like a Brainwashed cop, now that he's been told to guard Nikkei, he will guard her forever without question.

That's basically the story. Brock randomly went back and forth to the cabin a couple times a week checking on things, and he spent most all of every weekend there. He told his Chapter he had a dying mother he was caring for and that's the reason for so much absenteeism from the Club. Crazy George stopped buying into that story after a while and became suspicious as to what Brock was up to. He began thinking; perhaps Brock was working for the Feds? That's what eventually led Crazy George to Nikkei.

Big Bart never physically harmed Nikkei, but he mentally tortured her. He was always playing with guns and often pointed a pistol directly at her head, telling her it was time for her to go, and then dry firing the gun. Click! Nikkei told us he once actually fired a round inches from her head. Then he fell back laughing while telling her, "It will happen, you will be shot! You will never leave here alive, Snitch-Bitch!" Snitch-Bitch is the name Big Bart gave Nikkei, and that's the only way he would address her! It was as if Brock and Big Bart were playing the "Good Cop/Bad Cop" game on her. That's probably the truth, and it was probably composed by Brock to drive her closer to him. That Motherfucker!

Anytime Big Bart would leave the cabin, he would handcuff Nikkei to a chain he anchored to the floor. She would stay that way until he returned; also, that is how she slept every single night. And that is how my Brothers found her, alone and chained to the floor. Makes me wanna kill!

After two hours of sitting and listening to Nikkei tell her story, I had to be physically restrained by my Brothers not to go and kill Brock that very second. It's hard to understand how I can be so happy Nikkei is back and so insanely angered by Brock all at the same time. I'm angered to the point I think I would rather leave Nikkei after not seeing her in a month just to go and kill Brock, even if that took days! Well, one thing for sure, there is going to be a 'Sit-Down' with Bones.

CHAPTER FIFTEEN

KISS AND MAKE UP

After hearing Nikkei tell her story my three Brothers prepare to leave. I realize I must put my attention toward Nikkei, not Brock. I have plenty of time to take care of that piece of shit. He does have a genius for scheming though, and without Nikkei ever having been beaten or physically damaged in anyway; it's possible all he has to do is deny her story and say she came to him. Now it's her word against his! And he's a Brother and a President! By offering a different version and saying Nikkei willingly came to him of her own free will, maybe he can sidestep any Club retribution. He'll have to explain why he wasn't Brother enough to come forth and tell me he had her. But if he can turn this situation into a personal argument or debate between him and me, maybe he can cover up the truth. Well, I'm in no mood for debate; I want Revenge. I've killed people for a lot less than what Brock has done!

Crazy George believes Nikkei's story, but fears Bones and many Club members may not. Dealer hasn't completely made up his mind. He found her handcuffed and chained to the cabin floor, but thinks it's possible she did leave willingly with Brock at first, and there may never have been a lie told about me being in a bike crash. Also, Brock having a key to my iron gate doesn't make much sense to any of us. Dealer and I are the only two with a key to that gate . . . . other than Nikkei . . . ?! Hillbilly, believing Brock killed Weird Sally and now this, is thinking Brock has to go. But we can't run around killing Brothers. The problem is, there's a strong possibility through politics, lying, and scheming, Brock could get away with both crimes against our Club. Then who knows what he'll do next?

Dealer and Crazy George leave, they're going to meet up with Hillbilly at Papa Dadieo's in one hour. Hillbilly tells them he has some things to take care of first, but he'll see them there. Obviously, I'm staying home with Nikkei.

Dealer and Crazy George ride down my long driveway headed to the bar. Hillbilly sits quietly on his Harley until they're completely out of sight then turns to me and says, "Come close." I step up close to him; he hooks one arm around my neck and draws my forehead to his. With our heads downward, he softly says, "Brock has to go! You and I are gonna do it! Don't fuck up, Clutch. Brock probably doesn't even know Nikkei is back yet, so keep focused on her. You and I will be talking!" Hillbilly starts his beautiful bike and rides off. What he just said to me saves Brock's life, but only temporarily.

It's so nice having Nikkei home again, but she has changed, not necessarily for the better or worse, but for sure, she has changed. She is not the carefree, high-spirited little girl she once was. Her beauty still remains, but I know the Club is aging her prematurely; the war, the worry for my safety, my commitment to the Club more so than to her. And then there's her kidnapping; not knowing whether I was dead or alive, or worse, if Brock was planning to kill her. Seriously, how much of this can she take? This is not going to work unless I distance myself from the Club. It's obvious to me; her life's deck of cards has been violently reshuffled!

One of the largest punishments I've received through all of this is, Nikkei has lost that little girl's smile, and only God knows what part of her has been damaged for that smile to be a casualty. It's just no longer there, robbed by my lifestyle. Like a reflection in the mirror, I can see how this Biker lifestyle has changed her, and I can only figure it's happened to me also. I guess the difference is, I slowly evolved into the Club's environment, and she did not. Although she was always one of us, she was more or less standing on the outside looking in, never really seeing what we're capable of. When she and I hooked up, she stepped into our inner circle and was able to have a closer view at the violent side of our Club, and that scared her. She reevaluated our Club from rowdy Bikers to hard-core Outlaw Killers!

Nikkei is sitting at the kitchen table as I prepare her favorite meal, spaghetti. She is unusually quiet; our conversation only consists of her giving me single-word answers to most of my questions—yes, no, I don't know. When she does say more than that, it's done as briefly as possible as she stares off into the distance with an expressionless, blank look on her face. I desperately try to bring her back from wherever it is she's at, but I cannot!

After dinner, we cuddle on the couch and watch TV, but again, it's almost like being with a zombie. What happened to my little girl?! She told me she was not raped or physically abused, so what else could have done this to her?

As I lay on the couch with Nikkei, my mind turns to its jealous side. Here is a place I desperately try to avoid because it has caused so much damage to our relationship in the past. I get the most bizarre thoughts of Nikkei cheating on me and plotting against our relationship. Once all she did was hang up the phone as I entered the room. That was all it took for me to imagine there was another man in her life. Anyhow, I've tried to outgrow these insecurities, but now I find once again I'm struggling with many jealous ideas about Nikkei and Brock. Maybe she did go by choice? On the other hand, maybe he did trick her at first, but after a while, she fell in love with him? It's so crazy and unfair not to trust Nikkei; she is the victim here, yet I'm blaming her for it.

I suppose there have been many women abused, like a rape victim for example, that experienced the same thing and had their lives destroyed by it along the way. A woman is raped and then her husband and friends blame her for it! I'm not going to allow myself to be led down that same path by my jealous, insecure heart. It's just I will not allow myself to be played for a fool. Now I must calculate how far I'm willing to go to protect myself; far enough to lose her?

Even though Nikkei is lying beside me, she's not really here. I try to find a way to bring her home, but with every attempt, I fail. I made a deal with God, asking him to bring Nikkei home. He has kept up his end of that deal, Nikkei is here. But really only part way; now it's up to me to bring her the rest of the way home, and I think I can only do that by revising my lifestyle. So I have to make a decision, to keep my word to God and have Nikkei home completely. Or stay with the Club and continue in this lifestyle, and risk losing her completely.

Nikkei and I climb into bed together for the first time in a month. The entire time she was gone, I always felt like if I ever had her back, things would pick up exactly where we left off. That isn't the case; that period of my life is gone forever, and the passion we once shared most certainly was not shared here tonight. I practically had to beg her to have an orgasm, and Nikkei is usually multiple as hell, I mean one after the next. After we finish, she simply rolls over and stares at the wall!

I get up, walk out of the bedroom, return with a beer in hand, and then sit at the edge of the bed. I look at her and say, "Nikkei, I can't pretend to understand your problem, but whatever it is, please sweetheart, let me help you."

She looks up from her pillow and forces out a slight smile, followed by a bullshit explanation, "I have no problem, Clutch. I just want to lay here, okay?"

Wow, I don't need a truck to run me over; I know that was a nice way of telling me to "Fuck Off!"

I get up, finish my beer on the porch swing, then return to my bedroom and find Nikkei is sound asleep. This only fuels my growing anger. Trying to understand Nikkei's problem, I stand and stare at her for a long while, then lean down and kiss her forehead. I get dressed and leave on my Panhead for Papa Dadieo's. It's the first time I've seen Nikkei in a month, and I'm headed to the bar!

I cannot figure out the mood I'm in as I ride hard toward the bar, a hundred miles per hour plus. I'm leaning deep into the corners, rubbing my foot pegs and the heels of my U.S. Army issue boots on the pavement. I feel anger, not just toward Brock, but to Nikkei also. That has to be wrong, but I can't help how I feel. I have always followed my emotions over my intellect, but this time intellectually I know I should be fair with Nikkei and give her as much latitude as possible. But I can't help feeling she should have been able to escape from Brock's clutches, if she really wanted to.

My ride to the bar is specific. Although my Brothers gave me a brief description of how they found Nikkei at Brock's cabin and what was going on there when they did, I must have all the details. I must satisfy myself that Nikkei did all she could to escape from Brock.

I now have two different conflicts in my heart. One is between Nikkei and my Club. If I cannot have both, her and the Club, then which one do I turn my back on? Now a second conflict has been introduced into my heart, one that could possibly solve the first. If I find Nikkei did not do all she could to escape from Brock, then that tells me she has feelings for him. But the other side of that coin, and where my second conflict lies, is maybe she simply couldn't escape and it's my jealous heart inventing this conflict. In which case, I could lose her over nothing. If I find she betrayed me however, my first tug-of-war has ended; I'll go back to my Club 110 percent and will never have any regrets about getting rid of her. Then never again risk a relationship with any other woman, so I never have to deal with the heartache of being pulled away from my Club. That's almost the easy way out. The problem is, I trust and love Nikkei, and I want to believe her story, but I do not know how to not be jealous, and my jealousies have spawned these thoughts of betrayal.

So that's my mission for the night, to try and exonerate Nikkei from all doubt of betrayal. But if I do, then I'm back to my original conflict: who to choose, Nikkei or the Club? Maybe subconsciously I want Nikkei's betrayal, so my first conflict will end, along with me and Nikkei, and I can get on with my life in the Club. Also, I need my Brothers' opinions on these issues. I'm ready to share my feelings with them; that's what true Brotherhood is all about. Most of all, I just want their company.

When I get to the bar, I see sixty or seventy motorcycles parked there, all from our Club, our Affiliates, and our Hang-Offs. There are two police cruisers sitting on opposite sides of the road at either end of the bar, approximately one-quarter mile back away from it!

A retired member of our Club owns Papa Dadieo's. Although he's no longer Active, he is definitely Affiliated. The cops that sit and watch the bar are so fucking ignorant about us; they see this many Bikers and freak out. But this gathering wasn't planned. Sometimes it just happens this way; suddenly and without warning, there's a multitude of Brothers. The truth is, the cops really don't have anything to worry about. Whenever we have this many Brothers gathered, it's the worst time to fuck up; consequently, we're on our best behavior. As far as the war goes, our enemies would never hit us now. It would be like attacking a military outpost.

When it comes to making an arrest, the cops may get a straggler or two for minor infractions, maybe even a DWI, but for most part, on nights like this our Club is traveling in large packs. There is safety in numbers, and in the early to mid-seventies, the cops are not prepared for such strength and organization as our Club exudes. So when many are running in a tight pack of Harleys, the Cops generally allow them to pass without hassle.

When I pull up to the bar and see it's packed with Brothers, many from my Chapter, I receive an overwhelming feeling of exhilaration and excitement. This is what I need; I need to forget about Nikkei and find my place here with my Club. Well, at least that's what my brain is telling my heart. But as I pull into the parking lot, guess who? Brock is here. "Fuck!"

I wheel my scooter in and park it with all the other Harleys. My mind is briefly taken away from the anger of seeing Brock's bike simply by pausing for a moment to stare at all the beautiful Machines. Looking at all these lovely motorcycles makes my dick hard. Now back to Brock.

Just as I'm ready to pull the bar door open and enter, Whirly cruises in on his Flathead. He scopes out the situation by slowly riding past all the Harleys while surveying who belongs to them. He then rides up to me and shuts off his machine.

"Hello, Bro," I say as I lean down and give him a hug.

He turns and nods towards Brock's bike and angrily says, "What's he doing here?"

I know exactly what Brock is doing here. He knows Nikkei is gone from his cabin and he's here feeling out the situation. He has brought along his entire Chapter, no doubt for back-up. Of course, I'm sure that was never explained to any of them; they probably figure they're here to 'Kiss and Make Up' but Brock knows he can change that in a heartbeat with just a loud argument!

Whirly knows nothing about Brock killing Weird Sally or kidnapping Nikkei, and I keep it that way when answering him, "I don't know, just out partying I guess. Maybe his Chapter has come to kiss and make up."

Whirly angrily looks at me and says, "Well then, let's go in and find out!"

He starts his Harley. It fires up with a single kick, he then slowly rides past all the other bikes one more time, doing another head count before he parks it beside mine.

He and I enter the noisy bar and are met at the door by Hillbilly; he gently pushes us back outside to talk. We stand between three motorcycles backed up to a small area cornered by the bar's entrance and Hillbilly lights up a joint. He puffs it two or three times, then slowly hands it to Whirly. He raises his head and exhales a huge cloud of marijuana smoke into the calm summer air high above us; it seems to linger forever. He looks at me and says, "Clutch, why are you not at home with Nikkei?"

Whirly immediately snaps to attention, staring straight at me. The joint only inches from his mouth, he blurts out, "Nikkei's back?"

I look at him for a long, uncomfortable moment and say, "Yes and no!"

The joint still only inches away from his lips, he replies, "Talk to me, Bro!"

Whirly is still frozen, staring straight at me, when Hillbilly slowly reaches over and gently removes the joint from his hand, takes a puff, then returns it. Whirly never moves.

I say, "Nikkei is at my house sleeping as we speak, but she has changed 100 percent from the way she was before her disappearance."

Hillbilly now enters into the conversation by asking, "How so?"

I answer, "Ya know that Thousand-Yard stare many soldiers have after seeing so much shit in Nam?" Hillbilly slowly nods yes, as I continue. "Well, that's what she has!"

Once again, Hillbilly nods his head and gives out an understanding grunt, "Umm!"

Whirly puffs on the joint with a confused look and questions, "Where the fuck has she been, Clutch?"

I lean back against the bar wall and look at Hillbilly. We silently stare at each other for a long while. Whirly looks back and forth at each one of us, one and then the next.

Finally, he demands an answer. "What the fuck is going on here, Clutch, that you need Hillbilly's approval to answer my question?!"

Hillbilly shrugs his shoulders and says, "Okay, Clutch, we can't keep a secret from a Brother after he asks, so tell 'em what's goin' on!" Hillbilly takes the joint from Whirly, has another hit off the number, and passes it to me, then continues, "You two stay right here. I'll be back faster than you can say Ticonderoga!"—a phrase he often repeats. He then turns and goes back into the bar. Whirly's eyes follow him to the door, then turn sharply back to me.

I explain, "To be in this Club, you must first be a man. You must also know, understand, and believe in Brotherhood. God rewards the rich love we share by giving us each other."

Whirly intensely looks at me through his piercing, deep blue eyes, waiting for the punch line.

I continue, "But for our sins, he has given us Brock! Whirly, Brock is here tonight fishin'. He's fishin' for a reaction from me for a wrong he committed against our Club. He figures if he can get our two Chapters fighting, then it will help him cover up that wrong. I need you to swear on your Patch that you will not fight here tonight with any of that Chapter. That's exactly what he wants!"

Whirly puts his head down for a minute then raises it and once again looks me directly in the eyes and says, "Okay, I swear that I will not start a fight here tonight, but I also swear I will finish one if need be!"

I laugh and give him a hug then say, "I truly love you, Bro!"

Hillbilly returns with Dealer, Crazy George, and Heavy. They join us; we all six form a small circle.

Hillbilly lights another joint, looks straight at me, and asks, "Is Whirly cool?"

I answer, "I don't know, are you cool, Whirly?"

He pauses for a second, and then suddenly, as if a burst of energy went through his body, he immediately bends over forward, his head almost touching the ground, then quickly rises back up, and throws his hands high above his head. Then like a ballet dancer, he slowly spread his arms out and says laughingly, "Yes, I'm as peaceful as a tulip!" That crazy fucker!

All six of us party outside the bar while standing around the large herd of Harleys, talking about and admiring each one. We freely climb around and sit on many different scooters. It's okay for a Brother to sit on another Brother's bike uninvited, but I wouldn't advise doing it unless you are in our Club. There has been more than one broken jaw administered to people that took the liberty of touching a Brother's Bike without first gaining permission. It's not a good idea, and every now and then a citizen must be educated to our ways. For the next hour, we all climb around on scooters, drink cold beer, smoke dope, and just be Bikers.

Our small party ends abruptly when Brock walks out of the bar with one of his New Bros followed by a few younger members of that Chapter. They come over to us and join our party, but Whirly and I step back, cautious to their advance. Heavy and Crazy George assume Brock's up to no good and are carefully watching him. Hillbilly and

Dealer don't want any fighting between our Club members and are on their guard; they're both ready to defuse any potential problem well before it begins. With much tension and suspicion, no one is relaxed and partying anymore; we all just stand and look at each other, trying to figure out how this is all going to end.

Hillbilly is not just a warrior, but a diplomat also; he looks at Brock with a warm smile and very diplomatically says, "Hello, Brock," as he lights up yet another joint.

Brock returns the smile and replies, "Hello, Hillbilly," as he reaches for the joint Hillbilly is extending to him.

The mood remains tense, but after a few minutes, it became obvious Brock is not going to pull anything immediately. He's much too clever for that. Hillbilly steps up and gives Brock a warm handshake followed by a biker-type hug. When witnessing this, a cold chill climbs through my body. Hillbilly and I are going to murder Brock, yet Hillbilly has the strength to reassure him everything is okay by giving him a hug along with a loving handshake and smile, what power! Personally, I would like it better if we fought right up until the end. Fuck all the smiles! A diplomat I'm not!

Brock and his New Bro pretty much shake hands and hug everyone present except Whirly and me. Total disrespect, everyone here is aware of it, but we all let it go. The New Bro with Brock is the same one Whirly knocked out one week earlier; his Club name is Road Kill. He is a famous Kickboxer. But not famous like Cassius Clay, or someone like that—you know, someone the entire world has heard of. But famous in the kickboxing community and to anyone who follows the sport of kickboxing. He has fought many fights on television and toured the Orient for two years kickboxing. If I had to choose between him and the other New Bro, Big Bart, I'd have to pick him. He seems more like a Biker to me. I think his biggest problem is he can't see past Brock's bullshit. One thing for sure though, you can bet he hasn't forgotten Whirly knocked him out one short week ago. We're all watching him for retaliation.

Whirly and I slip into the bar and join the party; this place is wide open. When Bikers are partying like this, it's typical for one Brother to dump an entire pitcher of beer on another Brother's head. This happens with great frequency; consequently, the floor is flooded with nearly a half inch of beer; perfect for slipping and falling on your ass.

I'm very stoned; pot fucks me up, especially when I've been drinking. This place is standing room only. The owner of the bar, Papa, has hired a band for the night. They are crammed into a tight corner in a back room of the bar. Ol' ladies and Club mamas are wildly dancing together; most are wearing Club Property Patches.

Whirly and I push our way to the bar and are each handed an ice-cold pitcher of beer. Our Club will drink free all night long, and then tomorrow Papa will count the empty kegs and how many bottles of booze we went through and bill us accordingly. He figures his cost then doubles it, and that comes out to be about half off normal barroom prices for us.

There are two Brothers behind the bar, bartending, along with a couple prospects.

Just as I turn my back to the bar, one of the Brothers bartending leans across the bar and dumps an entire pitcher of beer on top of my head, then yells, "That one's on the house, Clutch!" At that very second, the front door bursts open and in rides a Brother on his Harley. He is being followed by another, and another, and another!

The way this bar is built, motorcycles can form an endless circle riding thru the front door, down along the front of the long bar then out the back door. They slowly circle around the outside of the building, then back through the front door and repeat the process. In all, there are near thirty Harleys circling through the bar. As they ride down the front of the bar, they are handed pitchers of cold beer to chug. The bar is going crazy. The band is pounding out "Bitch" by the The Rolling Stones.

After a long time, the Brothers stop the Merry-Go-Round of Harleys, but the last few through in single succession do a long, loud, burnout down the entire length of the bar. This bar has an old-type wooden floor. I swear, along the front of the bar the wood is no longer visible; it's nothing but rubber from all the years of burnouts. This place is 100 percent a Biker bar. The bar stools are made from old junk Harley parts welded together, handlebars, sissy bars, tanks, fenders, seats, etc, etc. Very artful and extremely sturdy. The tall ceiling above the bar has an old K-Model Sportster hoisted up and mounted to the wall. There is a long shelf lined with old original one-quart cans of Harley Davidson motor oil, and written above the collection in Old English Print are the words Mother's Milk. Old Harley pictures adorn the walls everywhere.

By this time Brock and his entire Chapter are inside the bar partying; most have given Whirly and I hugs. These are more than just greeting hugs; they are also "Kiss and Make up" hugs, and that's a good thing. I really do not have any hostilities toward any of these men. We are Brothers; we all got along great up until Brock became President of that Chapter. They're only doing what a Brother is supposed to do, and that's backing up their own. Of course, the problem with that explanation is, I am also one of their own. The difference is, I'm not from that Chapter. Our Club is structured somewhat as our country is structured, where the Club as a whole can be compared to the country as a whole, the "United States" of America, and each Chapter functions as an individual state. But unlike the United States between the years 1861 through 1865, there will be no Succession here, only Expulsion, if need be!

Well, what we all worried may take place, and what we all wanted to prevent, just began. Whirly bumped into Road Kill or vice versa, and now they are both squared off, toe to toe, nose to nose, and loudly arguing. Whirly gave me his word he would not start a fight, but right now Road Kill is dead in his face, big time. Whirly is not the type of man one can yell at for any length of time without provoking a response. Finally, Whirly head butts him hard and down he goes. All the Brothers begin yelling and arguing about who is at fault. Road Kill stands up; it's easy to see he is still stunned from the head butt. I approach Whirly, but before I can get there, Road Kill performs a flying Round House kick, landing it directly into the side of Whirly's head. This time Whirly goes down hard. Now I run to Whirly, but as I do this Motherfucker does another flying kick, this time landing it into my gut. He kicks me so hard I go down on my back, sliding three or four feet across the beer-soaked floor. The kick knocks the wind out of me; I just lay there gasping. Seeing this, Buttons charges across the bar, smashing a half-full pitcher of beer over Road Kill's head; he buckles to his knees, supporting himself upright with one hand flat on the floor while shaking his head back and forth. Two Brothers from Brock's Chapter jump on Buttons and the brawl begins. It seems the entire Club is involved—fists flying, legs kicking, wrestling on the floor in all the beer. The bar is now total pandemonium. Disgusted, Hillbilly and Heavy walk to a safe corner of the bar where several other nonparticipating Brothers are standing and saying "Fuck 'em, let 'em fight!"

Brock retreats to the same Neutral corner where Hillbilly, Heavy, and many other nonparticipants are standing and watching the mayhem. He expresses his dismay and tells Hillbilly this is exactly what he didn't want to happen, that he came here tonight hoping to Kiss and Make Up. That's Brock's genius for scheming. He sets up the situation, then Stirs the Pot just enough to get the fire lit, and after it's lit and burning, he walks away announcing his dismay. Like a dog that just crapped and is now covering dirt over it with his back legs in the hopes no one will Wind him from the smell. Unfortunately for Brock, Hillbilly sees straight through his deceitful games. This entire night has only fortified Hillbilly's resolve to murder Brock.

The drunken brawl doesn't last very long, but it was definitely between Brock's and my Chapter. Nobody was hurt, but there are plenty of busted lips and bloody noses. When it ends, Whirly and Road Kill quietly walk outside alone; they go into the woods behind the bar and continue their fight. These guys are both in the Heavyweight category. All Brothers present stay in the bar and let them fight it out. At one point they bump into the outside wall of the bar so hard it knocks a bar light down from the inside wall, smashing it into the floor. Finally, after five or ten minutes, they both appear from behind the bar and stand among all the Harleys talking. They talk and talk, sometime waving their arms and yelling! Then finally after a long time they do exactly what Brothers should do, they hug. With their arms tightly around each other's shoulders, they walk back into the bar. They are both badly beaten up. They make their way through the brawl's aftermath of broken chairs and overturned tables to the bar where they are each handed an ice-cold pitcher of beer. Still connected together by their arms around each other's shoulders, they stand there holding a pitcher of beer each. They toast to our Club's name, they toast to one another, and they toast to their battle wounds, which they both examine carefully while laughing.

After seeing what Whirly and Road Kill just did, I walk over to Hillbilly and say, "I'm impressed. There may be hope for Road Kill after all."

Hillbilly turns to me and smiles, then says, "I think you're right. All he needs is to be weaned from Brock, and that will happen as soon as you and me murder Brock." He gives me a wink.

As warm and loving as Hillbilly can be when you're his Brother, he is equally that cold and calculating when you're his enemy. Another cold chill runs through my body when I see Hillbilly smile over Brock's destiny!

This brawl hasn't ended here; there will be many questions asked by Bones and the Mother Chapter as to why? Two Chapters fighting must not continue. One thing for sure though, the entire Club will respect what just happened between Whirly and Road Kill. I mean that's the way it should be. If the only way to bleed out any bad blood is to fight, then so be it. Then Kiss and Make up! And these two have done it like true Bikers, Picture Perfect! They have done more than just Kiss and Make up however, because they were never tight to begin with. What they just did and what has just happened is, after the fight, a strong bond binding a powerful Brotherhood has begun to grow between the two of them; one that ends up being sealed to their backs with our Patch!

Well, in all the excitement, I never did have that chat with Hillbilly about Nikkei . . . .

CHAPTER SIXTEEN

ROAD TRIP

I ride home alone from Papa Dadieo's, leaving the bar well after its legal state closing time. The bar is still packed with Brothers and no doubt will be hours from now. Trying to quiet my Drag pipes, I pull my clutch in and back off the throttle, allowing my motor to almost idle. I want to coast past the cop that still sits down the road from the bar. A State Police cruiser has joined him; even though I'm half drunk and plenty stoned, I don't view them as a threat. Right now, my mind has swung its concerns back to Nikkei; the sun will be rising in a few hours and I've been gone from home all night long. That's not how I figured I would celebrate her homecoming, but I didn't leave last night to get away from her or to selfishly party with my Bros. I left last night to talk to Hillbilly, Dealer, or Crazy George and try to get all the details of how they found Nikkei. I must exonerate her in my mind from any possibility of having stayed with Brock willingly.

As I approach the cops, I have to release my clutch and give my bike some gas, the exact opposite of what I was trying to do. From all the beer and pot I consumed, I obviously gauged my speed incorrectly; at the speed I'm traveling now, I will only roll pass them at five or ten miles per hour. An unacceptable speed, and in my condition the slower I ride, the more I wobble my bike. Having to speed up sucks because I'm running two-inch straight drag pipes, loud as hell! And the more gas I give, the louder they become! Both cops are standing in front of the first cruiser talking in this muggy, early morning, soft summer heat. And "Heat" is exactly what I want to avoid. Not the summer heat, but the Heat that climbs out of those police cruisers. The last thing I need is a DWI. The cops could be waiting for this in the hopes that while arresting a single Biker, all the other Bikers will come to their Brother's aid, giving cause for many more arrests. They may have an entire army of cops on alert just around the corner.

I begin slowly accelerating my Harley, trying to keep it as quiet as possible as I ride past the cops, when the State Trooper steps out onto the road in front of me and raises his flattened hand, signaling me to stop. The other cop appears to be strategically maneuvering himself into a position so he'll end up directly behind me when my bike comes to a rest. Fuck! This sucks Big Time. I am a rolling violation. Although I'm not carrying a gun, I am however, over the legal Blood Alcohol Limit and stoned. I'm running illegal pipes and I have a knife with a locking blade, which was illegal in this state during the seventies. In addition, I have a gram of Crank in the pocket of my Colors . . . . Oops!

I stop my bike only inches from the State Trooper's feet without a single weave or wobble. Just as I suspected, the other cop steps directly behind me, out of view. This tall, muscularly built Trooper motions me to kill my engine by running his index finger horizontally across his throat. I know these guys already have a plan and know exactly what they're going to say and do, and I doubt if I'm going to enjoy that plan very much. I don't want to piss them off by not complying so I reluctantly push the kill switch on my handlebar, stopping the motor. What reasonable choice do I have?

The tall, beer-gutted Trooper walks up and stands beside me, then softly says, "Good Morning. I need to see your driver's license and bike registration, please."

Although his tone is professionally polite, I can see this guy is ready for action if need be. I don't say a word, just nod my head as I reach back and remove my chain wallet from my Levis.

He then asks the question I was so desperately hoping to avoid, "How much have you had to drink tonight?"

I wasn't going to give him the formula answer "Two," so I try a different approach. "Probably more than allowed to be operating this machine on a public highway, but I really don't have far to go . . . . Sir," I say as I hand him my driver's license and Bike registration.

The word Sir did not flow naturally from my sentence. It was accented louder and came out in a totally different tone, as if I really didn't mean it or was not familiar with using the word. Like all of a sudden I remembered the word existed, and at the very last second, inserted it onto the end of my sentence.

As he shines his flashlight to read my credentials, he scans across my chest, looking very close at my "Pres Patch" and then carefully studies my "Death Head Patch."

He says, "So if I give you a field sobriety test, you think you can pass it?"

I look him in the eyes and softly laugh, answering, "That depends on how generous you're feeling tonight!"

He humorlessly leans toward the cop standing behind me and hands him my license while asking if he'll run a check on me. This is exactly why we keep all our fines paid, so we don't end up in jail over some bullshit bench warrant issued from a speeding ticket or something stupid like that. He shines his flashlight on my motorcycle, viewing the beautiful paint job that depicts cop cruisers with beacons flashing, giving chase to Brothers on Harleys. I know he had to Dig It. He carefully studies the serial numbers on the neck of my bike frame and then pans his light onto my motor serial numbers, probably making sure they match. These State Police know what they're looking at. I'm not concerned because my bike has the original Harley serial numbers and a clear title with proper registration. At this point, my concerns lie on the gram of Crank in my pocket and my intoxication, and then my knife, and lastly, my illegal pipes.

The deputy returns from his cruiser where he has been checking me for warrants. He walks up to the State Trooper, and as he hands him my license, he says in a deep, clear, military-style, sergeant-like voice, "He's good, no warrants, and a very good driving record!"

I couldn't believe it. Just like a character from out of the movies, this big, beer-gutted Trooper hands me back my license. Then hooks both his thumbs inside his belt, one on either side of his protruding belly, and begins to rock back and forth on his boot heels while rolling his tongue around the inside of his mouth, contemplating the situation and debating what to do about it. Still very stoned, I almost laugh and struggle to look concerned about my predicament!

After a few minutes, the Trooper says, "Are you the boss over all those guys at the bar?"

This question returns me to the gravity of my situation, I carefully answer by asking, "Why would you ask that?"

He says, "I see you have Pres on your vest. I'm assuming that means President, so are you the President of that gang?"

I give him a long, sober, serious look and say, "Maybe."

He pauses for a moment, rolls his tongue around his mouth a few more times, then continues, "Well, I think you are, and I also think you have been drinking too much to ride this motorcycle, so here's what I'm willing to do. I will not charge you with DWI, but I will not let you ride this bike either. I will, however, allow you to push it back to the bar, but you must give me your word that you will order your gang to stay there until they're all sober enough to ride, and you too! If I catch you or any one of your gang on the road again tonight, I'll charge you with DWI! Now, is that fair and do we have a deal?"

Wow, I immediately reach up and shake his hand in agreement.

So that was it. With their beacons brightly flashing, piercing deep into the darkness of the night, and one cop car in front of me and one behind me, I push my bike back to the bar. It has to look like a parade as I slowly approach the bar sandwiched between two police cruisers with their cop lights flashing. One thing for sure, I refused to wear my colors as I embarrassingly pushed my Harley down the highway, so I drape them over my handlebars.

When our slow-moving caravan with such ostentatiously bright flashing beacons reach the bar, all the Brothers are standing outside watching and wondering, "Wat Da Fuck?" No doubt, we are a sight; better than going to jail though. I roll my bike in with all the other bikes, the cops shut off their beacons but continue to sit at the side of the road directly in front of the bar. As soon as I set my bike on its kickstand, Brothers immediately surround me. They all want to know Wat Da Fuck is going on.

I tell them the story. I can give an order to my Chapter not to leave the bar, but only suggest it to the members of the other Chapters. No Brother here is unreasonable to this situation; in fact, they all know that cop just gave me a break and respect him for that.

I tell all of them, "We need all the PR we can possibly get! I gave that cop my word we will all stay until we sober up. We need to send a message to them. We will always return the same respect that is offered to us. So please stay here until the sun comes up and you feel sober enough to ride. Or call an Ol' lady to come pick you up!"

Whirly, standing beside Road Kill, loudly laughs and bellows out, "I gotta admit, things are gettin' better when the cops are ordering us to stay in a bar! Yee-Ha!"

Road Kill laughs and gives him a pat on the back; all the other Brothers start laughing and cheering. They all go back into the bar, but as they do, most give a respectful wave or salute to the cops. Both cops, one by one, return the gesture to all. I think as they sit, they both feel a little 'Celebrity Status'. Like I said, "We need all the PR we can get."

I look at both cop cruisers sitting there and say to Hillbilly, "I can't stay here. I must get home to Nikkei!"

He sternly says, "Be smart Clutch, there are plenty of sober Prospects inside the bar, have one of them ride you home!"

I smile and say, "Thank you, Bro, you're absolutely right!"

I yell to Buttons, who is standing by the door and tell him to bring me a sober Prospect. He immediately goes into the bar and within minutes returns with a Prospect. I ask that Prospect if he is sober, if his bike is legal and did he have a valid driver's license and Registration. He tells me yes on all counts.

I Then say, "Okay, go over to that State Trooper's car and tell him you're going to ride me home. Show him your driver's license and ask him if he wants you to take a field sobriety test."

Without question, the Prospect did exactly as I ordered him to do. The cop never tested to see if he was drunk or not; he probably figured if he was, he wouldn't be talking to him. The Prospect returns to Hillbilly and me; I tell him to give me a ride home and guard my bike when he gets back.

I tell him, "Don't leave it alone, sit on it! If anything happens to my scooter, I'll cut off your dick with a rusty Buck Knife!"

Hillbilly laughs. That Prospect just found himself in a Trick Bag; it may seem like easy duty to sit on a motorcycle while guarding it, but when he gets back to the bar, all the drunken Brothers will be ordering him off my bike to fetch them beers and such. They'll be screaming at him for sitting down on the job. As a Prospect, he has to do as I tell him because I'm a President, but there are other presidents at the bar along with his Sponsor, not to mention many other drunk Brothers horny to fuck with a prospect. Boy, is he ever in for a long morning.

We pull out of the bar—me, a president, riding "Bitch" on the back of a Prospect's bike! What's worse, it's a Sportster! Nothing against Sportsters, but this one only has a Penie Pad for me to set on, and no sissy bar, so I have my arms wrapped around his waist, hanging on for dear life! Just to put a cherry on top the cake of my day, I rest my cheek against his back, only to entertain the police of course and to get a laugh from my one percent audience. As we pull away, the cops are both giggling, and the entire parking lot full of Brothers are laughing and cheering as loudly as possible at my comedy show. Once again, I will not wear my Colors.

Needless to say, it was a long ride home. I hope it's also needless to say, as soon as we were out of sight from the bar and I was finished entertaining the Brothers, I removed my cheek from the Prospect's back. Sportsters are very fast motorcycles, but I told the Prospect to keep this one under fifty miles per hour.

As I get closer to home, my thoughts grow closer to Nikkei; once again, my mind swings its concerns back to her and our relationship. I'm hoping she's been asleep all night long and won't realize I've been gone. When we get to my drive, I instruct the Prospect to drop me at the gate. I thank him for the ride home, but in the same breath remind him what I said about guarding my bike. By the way, Buck Knives don't rust. They are among the finest in the World. So that part of my threat is pure Bullshit. But that Prospect knows he better not push the issue, because he won't get off on a technicality such as that!

I creep down my long drive and quietly enter my house. All the lights in the house are still off with the exception of one small night light in the hallway, exactly the way I left them last night. The sun's early dawn has created a soft blue light that fills the house. I lightly step into the bedroom and see Nikkei is still sleeping. I quietly undress and sneak under the covers; just as I do, she rolls toward me and wraps around my body. Oh, wow, how nice it is to feel her in my bed again. I thank God and then out I go, fast asleep.

The next morning—well, late the same morning, I'm awakened suddenly by Nikkei jumping up and down on my bed. I sit up, confused, and ask, "What the hell are you doing, Nikkei?" I wipe the sleepy dust from my eyes. She is smiling, thank God!

She says, "I'm leaving, but this time I'm taking you with me!"

Still sitting up, I put one leg on the floor, then ask, "Nikkei my dear, what are you talking about?"

Smiling, she says, "Well, you told me you want to make me happy and will do it at any cost, so right now the cost of my happiness is one Road Trip!"

I struggle to stand, then make a staggering path directly to the coffee pot where I guzzle a quick cup of coffee followed by a refill, then return to the bedroom.

"Nikkei," I say, "let me get this straight. You want me to take you on a Road Trip? Where and for how long?"

Her smile breaks into a laugh as she returns jumping up and down on the bed, spinning in circles and shouting, "Anywhere! For as long as we can stay away! Days . . . . Weeks . . . . Months!"

I pull her down so she is sitting on the bed, instead of bouncing on it, and ask, "Are you serious? Do you really want us to take off? What about my job and the Chapter? After all I am the President!"

She becomes very serious, taking my hand and saying, "Clutch, I need this . . . . we need this. Please, Clutch, do this for me!"

I've said I tend to act on my emotions, not my intellect, and right now I feel happy because for the first time I see Nikkei happy.

So I look at her and, without any more debate, say, "Okay, we can be out of here today. I have to square it with work and talk to Crusher. Meanwhile you start packing!"

I walk to my closet and take out a box I had hidden on the top shelf out of her sight.

I hand it to her and say, "Here ya go, Nikkei, you wear this while we ride."

She opens the box to find a beautiful black leather vest with a Property Patch sewn across its back! The Top Rocker on these Colors we give our Ol' ladies reads "Property Of." They do not have a Center Patch and then the Bottom Rocker has our Club's name. Nikkei does not share the great exuberance that I showed when receiving my Patch, but that is like comparing apples to oranges. She knows what these Colors mean and knows how hard they are to come by, but I'm thinking she wants to distance herself from Club activities.

But she does stand and give me a tight hug, saying, "Thank you . . . . I will always treasure them, Clutch!"

I spoke of my jealous side. Well, that immediately kicks in and I wonder if Nikkei's lack of excitement is because the wrong man's name is over the front pocket of her vest. Instead of reading "Property of Clutch," maybe she would rather it say, "Property of Brock." I trifle back and forth with my jealous emotions for a while and then conclude by saying to myself, 'Fuck it, if that's what she wants, then no point in worrying about it. What's gonna happen will happen! It will all come out in the wash!' Angered, I turn sharply and exit my room. Nikkei cocks her head slightly and gives me a confused look.

Giving your Ol' lady a Property Patch should be a very special moment for the both of you, a time of celebration. Alcohol consumed, loud happy songs; maybe even get a BJ out of the deal. But this was more of a somber moment, almost depressing, and I end up feeling anger instead of joy. Once again, Brock has taken away something very dear to me.

I call work and take some vacation time. I also call Crusher, our Chapter's Vice Pres, and tell him I'm leaving on a Road Trip and for him to stop at my house as soon as possible so we can work out any details during my absence. Crusher only lives a few miles from me. He says, "I'll be right over!"

I go outside to examine my Harley. While I was sleeping some Brothers, sober Brothers, in Santa Clause-like fashion, rode around delivering Harleys to the houses of passed-out Members that left their bikes at the bar last night. Nikkei went down and opened the gate for them while I was sleeping; now she knows where I spent the night and why I slept so late. My bike's in perfect condition. I wonder if the same can be said about the Prospect I ordered to guard it. "Ha Ha Ha . . . . Poor Bastard!"

Crusher pulls down my drive; I meet him at my porch. He and I talk for a long time, working out any details or problems that may arise while I'm gone. He's a good man and a perfect Brother; he understands what it is Nikkei and I must do and graciously gives us our space. I thank him with a hug and he rides off. Well, that's it. I'll finish packing, and then turn a wrench or two on my Scooter, then we'll leave.

I'm changing the oil in my Harley when Dealer pulls down my drive; he's wearing his Colors and a huge smile. When I see him, I have to smile myself. He carries a strong energy, like an aura that offers up a powerful presence, one I love to be around. He dismounts from his Knucklehead and walks up to me and gives me a long, tight hug, then says, "Hello, Pres, I've been talking to Hillbilly and I'm thinking at your next Church Meeting I may ask to come over to your Chapter!"

This brought an enormous smile to my face.

I say, "Bro, that's great news. We would love to have ya! We need all the good men we can get!" I tell Dealer Nikkei and I are leaving for a few days, maybe longer, perhaps a week. He wants to know where and why. I tell him no place in particular. I'm just gonna get on my bike and ride. I say, "We need time together . . . ." But before I could finish what I was saying, he interrupts me by finishing what he thinks I'm going to say.

"Away from the Club?" he said.

I look at him and very seriously say, "I won't lie to you, Brother. You know that's true, and if I have a heavy heart about something, I will let you know what I'm feeling. You know that's true also. So here it is. I've tried to balance Nikkei and the Club and failed. I now believe it's time I must make a choice between her or our organization. Brother, this is not something new. I've been struggling with it for a long time. I love the Club and I love you and all my Brothers, but if my heart is not 110 percent with the Club, then I'll become a Slow Leak. And that's not what I'm about!"

In true Brother Fashion, Dealer gives me a hug and says, "Clutch, you will always be my Brother, with or without your patch!"

I don't want to sound like a Punk, but that brought tears to my eyes. I give Dealer another hug and he rides off. As he departs, we are both unaware that the next time we meet, our world will have been drastically changed forever.

Nikkei has packed light, as have I; we have stuff bungee corded and taped all over my bike. I've made arrangements with Dealer and Hillbilly to feed and water my dogs while I'm gone. Buttons said he'll probably stay at my house off and on to keep an eye on things also. Nikkei has asked her mother to stay as well. I put on my Colors, as does Nikkei, and off we go. Where my long driveway meets the road, I stop and ask Nikkei, "Which way, dear?" She thinks about it, then points left; I confirm my acknowledgment by turning left.

It is a beautiful day and has been all day long. Nikkei and I have been on my bike for seven hours straight. We only stopped for gas once, and we took a half hour to eat. Once before and once after that, Nikkei asked me to stop so she could "Wash her hands." For any Bikers that may be reading this, that is a nice way of saying "She Took a Piss." Yeah, I learned it watching TV.

We pull into a small hotel and book a room. Nikkei walks across the street and buys a bottle of wine and a large bag of steamed shrimp. We're calling that dinner. We shower, then eat, and climb under the covers together. We are each holding a glass of wine as we watch an old Three Stooges comedy, "Disorder in the Court." Nikkei and I both lay there laughing our asses off. We love the Stooges; we can watch them for hours. I don't care how many times I see the same episode, I always laugh.

Nikkei and I make love with much passion. I must say, that part of our relationship is getting back to the way it used to be. We're not quite there yet, but headed in the right direction.

The next day we share a nice breakfast then hit the road somewhat early, and ride, ride, ride! This is so fucking cool, not a worry in the world. I swear, I could live in this moment for eternity!

Chapter Seventeen

ROAD TRIP
'LOVE STINKS'

We pull down a long, lovely, secluded little one-lane road, well off the beaten path to have lunch. About a half mile off the dirt road is a small pond; I pull my bike up to its nature beach area and build a small fire. As Nikkei skinny-dips, I cook some marshmallows she had stashed in our duffle bag. I open a can of mustard sardines and put them with two apples we have. Ahhh . . . . yes, this is the life, marshmallows and wine followed by sardines, apples, and wine! That may not sound good to some, but try to look beyond the fine cuisine at my company. I have a beautiful brunette swimming naked and then a beautiful Harley, and draped over its handlebars, my beautiful Colors. That's all the company this man needs!

Nikkei comes out of the water and wraps up in a blanket, then sits down beside me near the fire. I roast marshmallows to feed her; she eats them as fast as I can cook them. We both enjoy a nice glass of merlot, then back in the water. We swim together for an hour or so before Nikkei climbs out of the pond and lies on our blanket; she signals me to come to her. I lay beside this beauty, and we make love under the hot summer sun, beside this beautiful pond surrounded by trees. We make love and sip wine for the rest of the day. Once again, I could spend eternity in this moment.

I've already made up my mind. I'll never have both Nikkei and the Club; too much conflict of interest there. But when we return from this trip, I will make a choice. The only thing that will stop me from giving myself to Nikkei is if I feel she did not do enough to break free from Brock. On this trip, I will very tactfully explore that possibility while exercising much caution toward the jealous side of my nature.

Nightfall is upon us now and we are still at the pond. I have a small tent; I call it my "Just in case" Tent. I ask Nikkei if she wants to stay here for the night and she says, "Yes, I would love to." So just in case it rains, I set up my tent and collect some firewood; we sit under the star-filled sky, enjoying the night air, alone with one another, accompanied by another bottle of red wine.

The morning has come too soon. I'm awakened by a skunk that has taken a deep interest in the empty can of sardines I carelessly left outside our tent. He has competition from another just like him. They have been loudly hissing at each other for a long time as they spar for the empty trophy, but nothing too violent yet, and I hope it stays that way. If either skunk shoots off his stink gland, for sure our tent and bike, not to mention Nikkei and me, will end up stinking obtrusively. As I lay carefully listening, I wonder; do skunks even spray each other, I mean, what's the point? They're both skunks. But if they do, at this range, Nikkei and I are in for deep trouble.

I nudge Nikkei and tell her we have to make a fast getaway because skunks are infiltrating our camp. We're both wrapped up in a single sleeping bag, partially unzipped. Still drowsy from sleep, she leans up on one elbow and whispers to me, "Are you serious?"

I quietly answer, "Yes, there are skunks outside, can't you smell them?"

At that very second, a huge skunk waddles into our small tent, rooting around. I quick aim my .45 right between his beady little skunk eyes. I figure one round will not only take care of business, but it will also make for a messy tent, so I'm reluctant to fire. Another problem is, I hate killing animals. I don't want sprayed, but to be honest, I'd rather take a chance on being sprayed than to outright kill him just because he has that capability. After all, we're in his territory now, he's not in ours!

I very quietly tell Nikkei not to move, but the skunk tries to climb on her anyhow. That was all it took; she freaks out! She tries to knock the varmint away, but it climbs right back on her.

I demand, "Nikkei, don't do that!"

She very emotionally yells, "Fuck you, Clutch, then get this motherfucker off me!"

I grab the empty wine bottle and try to push it out of the tent. It sharply snaps at the empty bottle a few times then turns and hisses while making his retreat, but just as it is leaving, that son of a bitch lifts its tail and squirts the inside of our tent! I do not know anything about skunks, but I don't believe it was a full blast. Nevertheless, it was enough to ruin our day. I feel jilted. I was being nice to that skunk, and that was totally uncalled-for. It was never in any danger from the wine bottle I was poking at it, and I had already laid down my gun. I don't think he did it out of fear or because he felt threatened; I think he did it out of spite. That little Prick! Fuck it now, I no longer have to worry about being sprayed, so I jump up, gun in hand, and with my feet, like a soccer ball, I maneuver that prick to the water's edge where I kick the bastard into the pond. I did it so fast it never had a chance to squirt me again. When I gave it the final 'field goal' type kick, it let out a loud moan as it flew through the air, landing in the deep water. It very poorly doggy paddled back to shore then hastily returned to the fern filled, misty woods. I kept the varmint in my gun sights the entire time. As he disappears into the woods, I turn and look for his rival! After all the excitement, he was also in retreat; Makin' Tracks for the woods, the empty sardine can hanging from the side of his mouth. "That greedy little Bastard!"

By this time, Nikkei is madder than hell. She bolts from the tent, comes directly to me and starts pounding on my chest with both fists. Finally, I grab both her wrists and hold them away from me, saying, "Stop it, Nikkei, I've done nothing wrong!"

She yells, "You're lying! You did do something wrong! You could have shot that skunk before it ever came near our tent! And we would not be stinking the way we do!"

I've smelled dead skunks on the road before and no doubt they stink, but to take a direct hit from one is without a doubt the worst violation my nose has ever experienced. I'm calling this explosive odor TNT, "Total Nostril Trauma."

I finally calm Nikkei down enough so that she stops wanting to hit me. She knows I won't hurt an animal without just cause, and that's why she's so mad; she figures shooting this varmint before he sprayed us, was just cause!

Early-morning fog slowly rises from the surface of this tiny pond. The sun has just begun to rise; it's blurry image struggles for recognition through the pond's steamy breath. In their deep voices, bullfrogs hidden in the thick reefs that surround the shoreline croak out an anonymous warning to each other of our invading presence. They openly discuss Nikkei and me as we stand waist deep and wash in the warm water. By comparison, the cold air that contrasts with the warm water forces us shoulder deep, maybe more; the warm water invites us to completely submerge and comfort our frozen noses and ears. We can see our breath. We diligently scrub as hard as we can with these tiny bars of complementary soap Nikkei appropriated from our last hotel, though the effort seems an exercise in futility; this odor is as stubborn as the cold air that lingers above the pond's surface.

Nikkei has offered her apologies for so angrily beating me on the chest. And I have graciously accepted them. In a concerned voice, she wants to know my opinion on the chances of the attacking skunk's return. As I scrub her tiny arm bravely lifted from the warm water and steaming in the cold air, I tell her it's highly doubtful. Besides, the water offers a safe refuge. But if he does return ready for combat, I promise to use my pistol and send him to the Happy Hunting Ground in Skunk Heaven.

I burn my tent and sleeping bag along with our Levi's and T-shirts. The only thing I don't burn from inside the tent is our Colors! An old Biker habit has protected them from the skunk's fury. Whenever I'm on a Club run, I always put my Colors inside and at the bottom of the sleeping bag, and that's where Nikkei and my Colors were during the brutal skunk attack.

We are now back on the road, and even at sixty miles per hour I can still smell the skunk. Nikkei riding directly behind me would have to be getting it worse. But our sense of humor has returned, and that's a good thing! For sure, one thing I found out is, no matter how long you stink like a skunk, you never get used to it! What's really cool is when Nikkei and I walk into a diner for a burger and a beer, and in no time flat, we empty out the entire place and have it all to ourselves. Being as I don't like crowds or the general public, that gives credence to an old American proverb, "Every cloud has a silver lining!"

After seeing how fast we cleared out the diner, Nikkei wants to have a little more fun with the way we smell. Two dudes just entered the bar area of this tiny diner; the bar is segregated from the dining room by a small corridor, but there is a clear view from one to the other. These two deliberately and obviously stare down the bar at Nikkei, total disrespect to me. The taller of the two motions Nikkei to come sit beside him by patting an empty bar stool and whipping his head to one side. Grrrrrr! These two look like they just walked out of the movie Deliverance. Nikkei looks at me, giggling.

I say, "I think those two like you, Nikkei. Maybe you ought to go say hi."

She says in an ornery voice, "The tall one is kinda cute. I love his bib overalls, straw hat, and the way both his teeth really brighten up his smile. Maybe I'll get lucky tonight?"

I ask her, "Why don't you go find out, dear?"

She stands and takes one last puff from her cig, then pounds it out in the ashtray. She gives me a smile and then heads for the two dudes now sitting at the bar with their backs to us.

Nikkei slowly approaches the bar; she puts on her sexy, hip-swinging, ass-wiggling walk. About halfway to them, she deliberately drops her pack of cigarettes. She loudly shouts out, "Oh shit!" They both turn and look. Nikkei slowly bends over to pick up the cigs, showing them her cleavage. Now that she has their full attention, she stands back upright and again steps toward them, smiling, but as she does, her cigarette lighter falls to the ground and slides under a table. This time, she first turns around before bending to retrieve the device, giving the two Hicks a long, wonderful view of her lovely ass. These guys are falling apart; they are obviously farmer-type young men with no manners or understanding of respect, total Hicks! For sure they obviously have never seen anything like Nikkei before, aggressive and beautiful. I swear their tongues and eyeballs are popping out of their heads. After picking up her lighter, she continues her sexy march directly to them. When she gets there she puts her arms around both of them and in an extremely sexy voice asks, "Could either one of you two handsome guys buy a lonely girl that's looking for a little fun an ice-cold beer?"

I swear it was one of the funniest things I ever saw. Once they got a whiff of her, their smiles instantly dropped off their faces, and they couldn't find the door fast enough. In their sudden, hasty departure, they left full beers, money, and a pack of cigarettes on the bar top!

Nikkei smiles and returns to me at our small table; I'm still laughing my ass off! She says, "See, Clutch, all you have to do is spray me with skunk juice and you'll never have to worry about me being with another man!" She chuckles and gives me a large smile.

We are pretty much done here. We've eaten, had a couple ice-cold beers, and oh yeah, stunk up the joint terribly and run off all the cliental. The manager is now glaring down the bar at us, so with my head, I motion to Nikkei, let's leave. We slowly walk out of the diner, arms around each other. Nikkei puts on her sexy walk just as we pass the manager and gives him a single wave good-bye. She throws up her hand and wiggles her fingers, then says, "Toodle-Doo," and smiles. This guy is grinding his teeth.

Back on the road hours later, I blow my horn as we cross another state line. We pull into a Rest area/Welcome center. This time, Nikkei and I both must "Wash our hands." Afterward, we agree to find the nearest hotel and sack out for the night.

We wheel into a small hotel named Dave's Place. One thing for sure, Dave is not big on cutting the grass; the shit is up to our knees. I pay for a room and we settle in for the night. As soon as nightfall comes, I push my Harley into the room, then Nikkei and I climb in bed. We still smell so bad; making love is almost an effort. Afterwards, I playfully sing a J. Geils song lyric, "Love Stinks . . . Yeah, Yeah!" as I dance naked around the room pretending to play the guitar!

The guy at the desk, smelling me as I paid for the room, gave me a fruit jar full of milk. He told me to wash with it and it would help reduce the skunk odor. Both Nikkei and I do so, but I'm not sure how much it helped.

The next day I get up feeling great. "I don't think we smell as bad today. What ya think, Nikkei?" I said.

Nikkei happily answers with a huge smile, "I think you're right, but Dave is gonna have to fumigate this room." I laugh in agreement.

I go back to the hotel office. It's part of this dude's house, and I bum another quart of milk.

I say with great enthusiasm, "I think the milk is working."

Nikkei and I once again shower and wash in milk. As she rubs milk on my body, my dick gets Hard!

"Hey, this is kinda kinky, a milk bath!" I said.

The truth is, the milk is not what was doing it for me; it was being in the shower with Nikkei that has my little Nazi ready for battle! We begin kissing passionately as the water pours over our heads. Nikkei climbs on me, wrapping her beautiful, long legs around my waist. With my hands spread wide I reach down and cradle her ass, supporting her ride. She takes hold of my swollen tool and guides it inside herself. I fuck her while standing in the shower for twenty minutes or so and then carry her to the bed where we continue for the rest of the day.

I've said our lovemaking sessions are a barometer to me; I can easily gauge the strength of our relationship by the intensity we share under the covers. I won't rate it at one through ten, but right now, I'm thinking she and I are a strong couple again.

The manager, well the owner I guess, knocks on the door and wants to know if we're leaving or staying another night. Well, that means it must be after 11:00 a.m., and I'm still wrapped up with Nikkei. I turn my head toward the door and loudly yell, "Leaving!"

Then Nikkei instantly yells back, "Staying!"

I turn to her and stare.

There's a long pause at the door, then he asks, "Well, what's it gonna be, leaving or staying?"

I sit up and loudly answer, "Staying," then in a softer voice, I say, "I guess."

Nikkei reaches her arms around my neck and smiles as she pulls me back to herself. And yet another moment is introduced, one I can spend eternity in.

Nikkei and I never really ever finish making love. We only pause long enough to rest, eat, sleep, work, and basically do whatever life throws at us day to day. But now that we are here, alone in a strange motel room, days away from our Motorcycle Club and any distractions that may follow it around; we're able to catch up on lost time. I think that was Nikkei's wisdom when engineering this trip. But we're both lying side by side now resting, sore from riding on the Harley and sore from riding on each other.

Right now I feel as bonded to Nikkei as I have ever felt. So I figure it's a good time to challenge myself to what has become my most sought after question. If Nikkei and I could stay this close forever, would I leave the Club, cementing our relationship to just each other, outside the demanding influences of the Club? The problem is, I still want both, her and the Club. How can I walk away from my Brothers? They have never done anything wrong to me, only offered love. I hate this shit, having to make a choice, but one thing is for sure, if I stay with my Club, I know I'll lose Nikkei. Not that she'll physically leave me. She won't do that, but she'll become a mental wreck; one that's aged before her time. I'm not prepared to trade her off that way; she doesn't deserve it. Like my Brothers, she also loves me. How can I watch her self-destruct when her only sin is me? Even my jealous side cannot invent enough faults and suspicions to trade her off to a life of mayhem.

It's around 4:00 p.m. and I walk up to the hotel office to pay the guy for another night. I use his phone and order a pizza. He said he was headed into town and would pick it up for me along with the bottle of wine I requested. I ask him to pick up two half gallons of milk also, one for me and one for him to even-out my milk debt. He laughs and agrees as I hand him a twenty-dollar bill.

The hotel room has no phone and no TV, hence no disturbances. So without distraction, Nikkei and I enjoy the pizza together. We also enjoy a bottle of wine together, and lastly, we enjoy each other together, all night long!

Chapter Eighteen

ROAD TRIP
'BULLETS 'N' BLUES'

The following day Nikkei and I pack up late. I spend near an hour bullshitting with the owner of this hotel. He's a pretty cool dude, if I had to pin a description on him it would have to be a hillbilly. But that's okay in my book; many of my Brothers are hillbillies, even Hillbilly! We were not flying our Colors when we arrived here, but he saw me wearing my Colors as I was packing up my Harley to leave and asked many questions about our Club. I don't mind at all. I'm proud of my Club and who I am. The questions were presented respectfully and without malice. He's just curious. He has seen our Patch around, and ever since the war we have become somewhat notorious. I tell him I enjoyed my stay, and I'll tell my Brothers back home, if ever in this neck of the woods and looking for a cool place to bed down, come to Dave's Place. By the way, there is no Dave. He said when he licensed his business at the County Courthouse, he did not have a name planned, and a name is required at that point in the process. Rushed by the long line impatiently standing behind him, he was told to step aside until he had a name. Not willing to go to the back of the line he had already waited an hour in, he looked at the clerk's nametag that read "Dave." He told the clerk, "Congratulations, you just invented a name for my hotel, Dave's Place!" I never did ask his real name.

Once again, I have wind in my face. Ahhhh . . . . It sure feels good. I love riding; it's truly what I'm about. I'm about Nikkei and the Club also, but the problem there is I'm confused about which one I love the most, and they both conflict. When it comes to riding, there is no conflict and I have no confusion; I simply love it! All my life I always felt I would someday have Nikkei and the Club would have me. And I would be riding my Harley with her on the back while flying Club Colors. Well, here I am, sailing down the highway, flying my Colors with Nikkei directly behind me flying her Property Patch. But it's nothing like I once fantasized. I never thought about the atrophy this lifestyle would cast upon her. The truth is, before I was in the Club, like Nikkei, I was extremely naive about what really goes on inside of it. As I slowly entered the organization, I slowly evolved into what it is, never looking back until I had to look back and see what it was doing to Nikkei. When I began this journey, I decided by the time I return home, I will have made a decision on either giving up the Club or Nikkei. Now that we're thinking of heading back home in a day or two, I must aggressively pursue my challenge of either one or the other.

After a couple hours of riding, Nikkei and I wheel into a noisy bar for lunch. The good news is, we hardly smell like skunk! As soon as I open the door and have a look at the clientele, I get a Very Bad Vibe! They're all wearing bandanas with the two colors that belong to the club we are at war with. It's obvious to me, that's not an accident. There are only a couple of bikes parked outside the bar and I did not realize this is definitely a big-time Biker bar. This could be bad.

All eyes are upon Nikkei and me as we belly up to the bar. The bartender is a very good-looking female with lots of tattoos, obviously a Biker Chick. She is also wearing a bandana around her forehead with the two colors that represent the club we are at war with. Nikkei and I are both wearing our Club Colors, her Property Patch, and my three-Patched vest. Nikkei is carrying my pistol in her purse, thank God!

I know this part of the country is that club's territory, but never gave it much consideration. My concerns have been on Nikkei and our relationship, not on Nikkei and her safety. Hopefully, I haven't fucked up by wearing my Colors in this Would-Be Hot Spot. I will, however, fight to the death to defend my Patch and Nikkei, even if that means killing somebody before a fight should ever happen!

Once I said an old Biker trick is to have your Ol'lady carry your gun. The problem here is the entire bar is filled with Bikers.

Assumedly, they are all wise to that trick and are watching Nikkei because of it. So right now my concern is, if there is any trouble, Nikkei maybe targeted first.

Most the men in this bar look to be Hang-Offs from our rival club. But there is one dude sitting at a corner booth that I'll bet my bike is a Full Patch Holder from that club. Just like a vampire, a Full Patch Holder always has an entourage of disciples following, protecting and of course, taking orders from him! They will do anything he demands, anything at all!

Well, I'm not gonna run. I won't back down, and if trouble starts, I won't quit. I will promise one thing however, if I take a beating, they will have to earn it. And if I should die, so be it. I never thought I'd live forever anyhow.

I order two beers and two shots; I ask for a glass, a salt shaker, and two slices of lemon. I fill the glass with beer, but as I do, I intentionally pretend to carelessly tip it over, spilling the entire beer across the bar top. The pretty bartender brings me and Nikkei a bunch of bar towels to mop up the spillage. In all the confusion, after the bar top is cleaned and dried, I end up with an extra towel. Nikkei and I do a toast, then lick salt from our fists and drink the shots of tequila, followed by the lemon slices. Everything looks perfectly normal over here, but what I've just accomplished is, I very nonchalantly acquired a towel, a very heavy shot glass and a salt shaker, and when combined, they can all be used as a deadly weapon! I carefully place the shot glass into the center of the towel, and then twist it several turns until it creates a Black Jack. Next, I fill my left hand with as much salt as I can hold. Nikkei knows exactly what I am up to; she is quite aware of our situation. I now have the homemade Black Jack concealed between my legs and being held by my knees pressed together. Both my hands are on the bar, one is filled with salt. Nikkei is carefully watching my every move for any type of signal; we both sit quietly sipping our beer. I figure we will finish our beers then leave; that way it doesn't appear I ran out of the bar like a punk.

About the time we are getting ready to leave, a tall Hang-Off approaches me; he walks up and stands close to my right side—bad choice. He is obviously here to fuck with me, but for his own self-defense, he should be standing to my left, between Nikkei and me. Oh well, live and learn!

I figured I'd never walk out of here easily. I turn slightly toward him and very politely say, "What can I do for ya?" This guy has a lot to consider here; he must watch I don't pull a knife or a gun on him. He must, while watching me, keep an eye on Nikkei so that she doesn't pull a knife or gun on him. Then, of course, if we should fight, he must watch at any time that Nikkei doesn't hand me a knife or a gun to be used on him. No doubt they have already checked outside and know I'm alone. Maybe, they have called for reinforcements.

This six and-a-half foot, 280-pound would-be tough guy grins and answers, "You can start by taking off your Colors. They offend me!"

That was all he had to say; there is no point in prolonging the inevitable. I reach down and grab the twisted towel hidden between my legs, and in a single motion, I stand and swing it backhanded at his face. He sharply leans backward and avoids it. When he does, he blinks his eyes! Perfect, this is what I needed. Like a cobra striking its prey, I fire back with my left hand, filling his eyes with salt just as they reopen. Once again, he steps backward, but this time cupping his eyes with both hands and letting out a loud painful yell! "AHHHH!" Now I come back around with the shot glass-filled towel. In a powerful downswing, I connect a violent blow directly on top of his forehead. That's a safe place to clobber someone if your intent is only to knock them out. In the side of the head, the temple, you can easily kill someone with a weapon such as this. He instantly falls to his knees. I step up to him and grab the back of his head, locking my fist tightly in his long hair and pull his face into my knee as I violently raise it up and forward. This kick finishes the job. There's no doubt in my mind, I broke his nose with my knee to his face. He goes down for the count. When he does, his head hammers the hard tile floor so hard I almost feel sorry for this unconscious piece of shit.

I immediately turn to see Nikkei. She has my gun drawn and is holding it in front of her face pointed upward; she is swinging her head back and forth, panning the bar for aggressors. She has my back covered, what a good woman, huh? Nobody else in the bar is aggressing toward us; they all just sit and watch. Still holding the homemade Black Jack in my right hand, I reach into my pocket and throw a ten-dollar bill on the bar, then tell the pretty bartender, "Keep the change!" Like Bonny and Clyde leaving a bank they just robbed, Nikkei and I walk shoulder to shoulder backward out of the bar, she with a gun held at the ready; me armed with a blood-stained towel and shot glass Black Jack!

Nikki is still holding my gun at the ready while I start my Harley. My Panhead starts with one kick; she mounts my bike while watching the door. As we pull out of the Biker bar, I turn to Nikkei and say, "That was fun!" We speed out of sight.

I gotta admit, Ol' Nikkei was right in there backing me up. She really is a good woman, streetwise as hell. Suddenly, as that thought goes through my head, my heart is instantly overwhelmed by suspicion. If she is so Fuck'in streetwise, then how in the hell did she ever allow herself to be kidnapped by Brock?! Angered by these thoughts, I pour the gas to my Harley, entering a series of curves at a hundred miles per hour plus! I just can't get that out of my head; I do not understand why she could not have figured out a way to escape from Brock's cabin in a month's period!

Nikkei figures my speed is prompted from the fight.

What I'm thinking is, maybe I do not have to make a decision by the end of this trip on whom to choose, her or the Club. Maybe I can have both after all; perhaps Nikkei can learn to adjust to the hardcore way of life I've brought her into. Even if she doesn't, I really don't have to quit my beloved organization; all I may have to do is just back off a bit. I don't need to be President, or a Goon for that matter! This would give me more time to spend with Nikkei. I still have another problem though, I made a deal with God. Hmm. I am a man of my word, and I have full intentions on holding up my end of the bargain. But I'm not even sure exactly what it is God wants me to do. If there is truth and love between me and my Brothers, then how can that be bad? I can see choosing between Nikkei or the Club cannot happen now, at least not on this trip. I must know for sure what it is God wants from me, and I don't think that's reneging on our deal, I hope. So in conclusion, if God really wants me out of the Club, then he must give me a sign.

For the first time during this trip, I'm homesick. That fight I was just in—well, the thumping I gave to that Rudiepoot, has gotten me revved up, and now I'm missing my Brothers. I feel like turning my scooter around and heading back home, back to my people. For whatever reason, pounding the piss out of that Hang-Off's face has made me homesick. Maybe I associate violence with my Club. Or maybe I associate winning with my Club. Maybe it's the protection all my Brothers give each other and how nice it would have been to have my entire Chapter with me as I walked into that Shit-Hole Dive Bar. Probably, all of the above; one-way or the other, right now I'm thinking the Club is where I belong. One thing for sure, I must watch my Brain doesn't twist things around in my favor, where I'm taking the easy way out. So at least as far as Nikkei and God are concerned, I must follow my heart.

Nikkei and I get a room for the night and through my strong suggestion, we decide to head home early tomorrow morning. This is a very nice hotel; it offers a dining area, pool, and sauna. Nikkei and I decide to take full advantage of all three.

Halfway through our dinner, and finally freed from our waiter who is satisfied we are comfortable and without need of him, Nikkei very seriously looks directly into my eyes, then out of the blue says, "Clutch, there was no way possible I could have gotten away from Brock!"

I kind of downplay the statement by returning a nonchalant response. "Sure, I know that, Nikkei, I believe ya!"

She continues to stare at me for a long time then says, "No, you don't, Clutch. I can feel your doubts about my loyalty! Clutch, I know how you are. If you're not 100 percent sure about me, you'll end up hating me over this, and that's not fair. I'm the victim here!"

I look at her for a long time; she has tears in her eyes. Half of me believes her, the other half doesn't; half of me wants her, the other half wants the Club. Total conflict! My brain is telling me, 'She's the one that's pulling me away from my Brothers and I should hate her for it!' My heart, on the other hand, is telling me, 'She's an innocent victim, one I love, pulled into a terrible situation by me, the one she loves!'

I ask Nikkei in a very calm, specific voice, almost like a cop interrogating a suspect, "The entire time Brock had you, you never had sex with him?"

Boy, my words came out wrong on that one!

She angrily snaps back, "Fuck no! And Fuck-You for asking that!"

Tears are now flowing much harder. An older couple dining a few tables away, hearing Nikkei's loud vulgarities turn and stare at us. I angrily stare back, forcing their eyes into retreat; Nosey Old Fuckers!

Then I turn back to Nikkei, and in a sweet voice, I apologize, "I'm sorry, Nikkei, what I meant to say was, were you raped?"

Still angered, she says, "Yes, I was raped, but not like that! I was raped by being kidnapped and humiliated! I was raped by being chained to a floor every fucking night! I was repeatedly raped by having a gun pointed and dry fired point-blank at my head. My heart was raped every time I was told the man I love, you, was dead, and if I don't cooperate I'm next! Now that I'm free from all of that and back with you, it would seem I'm gonna be continually raped by your suspicions! So Fuck You! Fuck Brock! And Fuck that moron he had guarding me!"

She tries to stand and leave, but I stop her by jumping up and offering a tight hug and another apology.

Wow, I didn't mean to get her that riled up. It's easy for Nikkei to appeal to the loving side of my nature; the problem being I see that side of me as a weakness. So for my protection, now that the cards are on the table, I continue my quest and my interrogation.

I say, "Calm down, Nikkei, I trust you!" I take her hand in one hand and gently pat it with my other. I work hard at calming her down, and when I think she is, I ask, "What did you eat when you were there?"

It's not really a trick question, but I know what Nikkei likes and figure if Brock supplied that kind of food it is a strong suggestion they may have been getting along better that she says.

Unaware of my new tactic, she wipes the tears from her eyes, sniffles a couple of times, and answers, "It depends, sometimes I didn't! Sometimes Brock would bring me eggs and milk, stuff like that." She looks up into my eyes, and while struggling to hold back tears, says, "Brock told me if I tried to escape or tell anybody what he did, he would kill my mother! That's why I was so insistent she stay at our house with Buttons while we're gone. Clutch, I know it sounds bad, but the guy he had guarding me was so scary I was actually happy whenever Brock would show up and terrified whenever Brock would leave again. I hate that man! All he did was drink, and as soon as he was drunk, he would start fucking with me. He made me cook and clean up after him. I was like his slave! I told you once he fired his pistol at me and the bullet hit inches from my head!"

I carefully asked, "Is that when you wet your pants?"

She shamefully bows her head and says, "Yes."

She had told me parts of that story the day she came home but never the entire thing. I'm now feeling great anger. Nikkei says she wants to kill that man, but I promise, once I find out who he is, I will beat her to it!

I already know I'm going to murder Brock, but before I do, I must find out who this guy is so I can slowly and painfully kill him too. It still has not occurred to me he is a Brother, Big Bart.

I guess I don't need to interrogate Nikkei any longer; I'm the problem here, not her. I must come to grips with myself as a man and either accept what she's telling me as the truth and then get busy cherishing our relationship. Or accept my jealousies as the truth, then get busy bumping her. But I can't do that because I love her and my heart overrides my jealous brain; for that reason, I must accept what she tells me.

We sit for another hour sipping wine; our conversation reverses to a much sweeter subject, sex. We talk about all the weird places we've done the 'Nasty' and then decide to adjourn to the pool and sauna area to see which one will suit us for another session of lovemaking in weird places. We go to our room and change into our swimsuits; we kiss and grope a little, then go to the pool. Wearing cut-off blue jeans, I dive into the pool directly under a large sign prohibiting cut-off shorts and diving! Nikkei, however, is making up for all my shortcomings by sporting a sexy little bikini. No one would dare throw me out knowing she would leave also. That would be a sin against all mankind!

The pool is void of people; we have it all to ourselves. We chase each other around and act like children right up to the point we begin passionately necking. I fondle Nikkei's gorgeous ass. I can't help myself. The bikini she's wearing is driving me nuts. We fool around in the deep end, lots of foreplay. Then finally, hanging on the small ledge that surrounds the deep end of the pool, we fuck. It's sort of a quickie; we don't want to get caught and it's very uncomfortable, so we both hurry, but it's still nice. After that, we sauna for a while, then shower, put on our last change of clean clothes, and head to the hotel bar.

We walk in and sit at this beautiful bar; it's trimmed in solid brass and the entire room has adopted a nautical theme. Across the back bar are four ship like Porthole windows; they are built into the pool's deep end, about four feet under the water! So anybody sitting at the bar has a pretty good view from under the water of people swimming! The bar is totally empty, but Nikkei and I sit stunned anyhow, knowing we could have had an audience watching us spawn in the pool. A pretty bartender comes up to take our order; she was smiling ear to ear. I ordered two beers then say, "Those are pretty cool windows. I'll bet you can see anything anyone is doing in the pool from them, can't cha?"

She smiles and says, "I can . . . . and I did! You two are amazing! What a turn on. If ya wanna party, I get off work in an hour."

She leans down on one elbow much closer to Nikkei and smiles even more.

Knowing we were watched gets Nikkei and I both laughing. Nikkei takes a sip of her beer and says, "We'll think about it!"

Here's the situation: the bartender suggests a threesome while looking and flirting with me because she figures as the male I can influence Nikkei into agreeing. Meanwhile, Nikkei is really who she wants! I don't want her asking and flirting with me as much as she's doing because I'm afraid that Nikkei will become jealous, and that will end any chance of this thing ever happening. So I don't respond as if I'm eager for that reason, but I do like the idea. Nikkei hasn't decided yet. Because the bartender didn't receive a great response from me and not willing to give up, she turns her attention to Nikkei. Now Nikkei is thinking, this girl is very pretty and after me, not Clutch. So her jealousy subsides and she passes the pretty Bartender the plastic room number off our room key!

Whenever Nikkei drinks, she gets horny as hell, and that's usually when her bisexual tendencies emerge. I have told different Brothers about the times Nikkei has tried to get a threesome going between me, her, and another beautiful female. They all, while grabbing their dicks, say, "You're crazy for turning that down, Bro!" But what they don't understand is, the next day when sober, Nikkei is not going to be nearly as friendly. Maybe even violent! We have done many threesomes and even a foursome with other women, and almost every time Nikkei drills me the following day on whether I liked it or not, and if so, how much? It's like she wants me to pick a number from 1 through 10 then compare her to them, via a number. The questions never end; they keep coming for days later! It's not really worth it to me. This one is a little different though, because we don't know this girl and come tomorrow, we'll both be gone and out of her life forever. So I'm gonna go along with it, but I'll pretend not to be enjoying it too much whenever Nikkei is watching. See how the Head Games are for this kind of thing? That's my complaint. I like honesty and no drama, and it's always been my experience what threesomes lack in honesty they make up for in drama.

We get to our room, and within twenty minutes, the cute little brunette knocks on our door. Nikkei lets her in; she's carrying a magnum of champagne and three small plastic champagne cups with the little snap on bottoms. It doesn't take long, about two glasses of champagne before Nikkei and her new friend are lying on the bed kissing. What a beautiful sight. They're both gorgeous and perfectly matched! One's no bigger than the other and they both have perfectly shaped bodies and beautiful faces! These two get busy with one another for a long time, licking and moaning in perfect concert. They're coupled together lying on their sides in the 69 position. I very tactfully sit back and watch. For Nikkei's sake, I don't want to appear overly anxious. This little girl knows what's going on also, and like me, she doesn't push for a third; she waits until Nikkei invites me into the mix. Once Nikkei does, she does it more for her new girlfriend's benefit than mine. Well, all three of us suck and fuck the night away! We each take turns receiving a two tongue, Champagne Tongue Bath, where one lies while the other two, kneeling, gently pour champagne over the eager recipient's body and then slowly lick it off. As the champagne cascades down one's body, it deliberately maneuvers into the most exotic places, those spots that love to be licked. Once again, I could say if given the opportunity, I could spend eternity in this moment, but I figure that's to be assumed!

When we're done and the girls are sleeping I remain somewhat awake. Many men have been set up and have fallen prey to a beautiful woman, just like this one. That's an old Biker trick, using a pretty girl like the Queen on a chessboard, to infiltrate. But she doesn't seem like the Biker type; I think she just fell for Nikkei's beauty—can't blame her for that! But I still don't take any chances. I put my spare Master Lock, the extra I carry for securing my scooter, around the chain bolt on the door, this holds it out away from the door far enough that the chain becomes too short to slide to the round opening that will unlock it. Now I'm the only one that can open the door without nosily breaking the chain lock. In addition, I sleep with one eye open and my .45 under my pillow.

It's funny because at first my over inflated ego told me this girl was wanting me along with Nikkei, but now that we have spent the night together, it's obvious that Nikkei is the one she really wanted. I think Nikkei knew that all along, and that's what kept her jealousies in check, making this encounter possible. Funny how the male ego works.

In the morning, no jealous drama from my fiancée. She gives me a smile, a very pleased content smile, as she sits up and stretches. We all get dressed. Nikkei kisses the pretty bartender good-bye and that is it, she leaves. Well, not exactly. They exchange telephone numbers first.

Nikkei and I pack up and hit the road; we have a long way to travel to get back home, but neither of us is in a hurry. I'm still homesick and I miss my Brothers. I'm anxious to see them, and I hope everything is okay back there, but I don't want to race back either. This is still Nikkei's Road Trip, so I'm taking the long way home for that reason. But another reason is, in twelve hours, I can be in our Club's territory and then will be for the rest of our journey homeward. Therefore, Nikkei and I will be a hell of a lot safer. That never really occurred to me during this entire trip, but after doing a number on that Hang-Off's head yesterday and knowing the dude I saw sitting in the corner booth was probably a Full Patch Member of our rival club, I figure I better play it safe. Of course, I don't mention any of this to Nikkei. I don't want to ruin her good mood; she's still smiling from having her pussy licked for four hours straight by a beautiful brunette bartender!

It's afternoon; the sky is clear and free from clouds. The blistering sun bakes the road, creating wavy blurred water mirages in front of us. I'm riding fast with my pistol carried in its shoulder holster. I'm defending against any chance of a car trying to pull beside me and take a potshot. I have been thinking more and more about the incident at the bar and how easy it would be for that club to be out looking for us. After living as a one percent Outlaw Biker, one learns that while riding forward, to always be looking backward through his mirror. It's times like this I understand exactly what Hillbilly did when reversing his throttle from the right side of his handlebars to the left. Like him, I'm right handed, and if forced to fire my pistol while riding, I will have to completely remove my hand from the throttle. That could suck if I need to shoot and get away at the same time. Maybe I'm just tweaking, but when I get home I may switch my twist grip to the left side of my handlebar.

I'm not worried about the overpasses at this point although they're a good place to be ambushed from. I don't see how anyone could determine when and where I am. But a car pulling up beside me could happen because the word may have been put out to watch for me, and if I'm seen by a passing car ferrying enemies, it could easily turn around and pursue us. It's tricky, because I want to ride hard and fast so I'll know if a car is following, but I don't want to be stopped by the cops either.

I've made up my mind to ride hard to our closest Chapter and stay there for the night. When I get there, I'll call Crusher and tell him I'll be home in a few days.

We pull into a gas station to fill up my bike. Our asses are sore; Nikkei walks into the restroom to "Wash her Hands," and I fill up my tank. As I walk into the station to pay, I notice a car sitting alongside the road with its hood up. It wasn't there when I pulled in; I don't know why and I'll never be able to explain it, but I get the worst Vibe from that car, like I'm looking at the Angel of Death. A cold chill runs through my body.

As we are pulling out of the station, I stop and look hard at the parked car. Although everything looks normal, I must follow my gut feelings. The car is sitting between the expressway's entrance ramp and me. Nikkei, wondering why I'm just sitting, asks, "Clutch, what's wrong?" I don't answer; I just continue to sit and watch. Finally, I pull onto the road, but at the very last second I turn right, opposite the direction of the expressway and the would-be stranded car. I don't give my bike very much gas; I just slowly cruise down the road, my eyes affixed to the image of the parked car vibrating in my mirror. Just as I thought, the hood on the car slams shut and it does a U-turn and is now speeding towards us. That's a big problem! Another problem is, I don't know these roads and where they lead. But I'm on a state route and that's good enough for me. I give my Harley as much gas as it will take. I turn to Nikkei and tell her to take my pistol out of its shoulder holster and shoot any car trying to get past us. She yells back to me, but I can't hear what she's saying at this speed.

I just repeat, "Take my fuckin' gun and shoot!"

We're barreling through corners at one hundred miles per hour plus. Nikkei reaches around and removes my .45 from its holster, but as she does, she drops it! My pistol falls in between my legs; it's just teetering there, not knowing whether to fall onto the road or stay in my crotch. I immediately grab it by its barrel then cram it tightly between my leg and the bike seat. Not sure if the gun is out of danger from falling, I place my clutch hand, left hand, on top of it, holding it in place, then turn and give Nikkei a dirty look.

At this speed, we're committed to these tight corners. I really need both hands on my handlebars and no distractions, but I also need this gun.

The car that I'm sure is following me is completely out of sight now; it couldn't keep up with me through the series of curves I just came out of. I knew that car was trouble. Had I gone the other direction, toward the expressway, I'm sure the two dudes pretending to be working on the car would have ventilated my ribs as I rode past. This has to have come from the bar incident; I couldn't have fucked up worse, wearing my Colors into one of our enemy's bars. It has taken this long for them to catch up to me because they were watching for a set-up, a trap, cautious that Nikkei and I going into their bar wasn't a deliberate act, bait, so they would chase us into a waiting ambush. But you can bet they're out in full force now.

I slow down a tad and regain control of my gun; I lean back and carefully hand it to Nikkei. I tell her we're being chased and not to allow a car to pass without firing. These guys probably have M16's/AR-15's, and 12-gauge pump shotguns, so stopping and shooting it out with them is out of the question.

Again, I'm approaching another series of large winding curves. I enter them at ninety miles per hour plus. I wouldn't want to negotiate one of these corners incorrectly; there's about a sixty-foot-deep gorge on the side of each one. I am in the middle of No-Wheresville in the foothills of a mountain range. There is not a single house or business in sight, only trees and steep, rolling countryside. I've passed many secondary roads, but have been reluctant to turn onto one in the fear it could lead to dirt roads or, worse, a dead end. I haven't seen the car that's following me, but it's assumable they're trying to catch up.

After winding around this hilly road at near one hundred miles per hour, I begin feeling as if I lost that car, or maybe it was never really chasing me after all. I had really only seen it one time just as it spun a U-turn. I eased back on the throttle then turn to Nikkei and say, "Maybe I'm just tweaking, maybe that car isn't following us."

In my entire life, that turns out to be the dumbest thing I ever thought or said.

I often refer to the cops as 'The Blues' because many of them wear Blue uniforms, and just this morning as we were preparing to head home, I told Nikkei this has been a good trip because it's been absent 'Bullets 'N' Blues' meaning; nobody has been shot and nobody has been arrested. I should have Knocked on Wood because once again, that turns out to be one of the dumbest things I ever said. From here on out, it's gonna be nothing but Bullets and Blues.

That car is following me, and it does have two dudes in it from our rival club, both heavily armed and looking to kill me and cut off my Colors as proof of the kill. Nikkei will just be collateral damage to them.

These guys know this area; they grew up in these parts. What they have done, and what I never considered, was they have taken a detour around all the curves I've been riding through and are now in front of me, waiting. What a stupid and deadly mistake I just made, thinking I was in the clear.

These guys position themselves at a long, tall bridge that spans across a deep gorge. They set up a perfect ambush; one dude is dropped off and is hiding in the tall grass at one end of the bridge, the end I am approaching first. The other has parked the car to the side of the opposite end of the bridge completely out of sight.

As I approach the bridge, I'm feeling relaxed until my bike tires are completely on its surface. As soon as my tires touch the bridge, my entire bike begins to violently oscillate from side to side. I don't know why or what is happening. My first thought is I have a flat tire; I'm doing near fifty miles per hour. I bring my scooter down to a controllable twenty miles per hour and try to figure out what the problem is. My bike is still oscillating side to side but I'm able to control it much better now. This bridge is about one-third of a mile long; its surface is manufactured steel corrugation. It has tens of thousands of rectangular holes through it approximately two inches by three inches. They are patterned in a checkerboard fashion. I can see through the bridge to the bottom of the deep gorge. This is the first time in my life I've ever seen anything like this. Now that I'm getting used to the wobble the bridge is transferring to my bike, I'm starting to like it; it's pretty cool. Nikkei and I are about halfway across the bridge when she says, "Clutch, stop the bike. I want to get a picture through the bridge!" Well, there's not a single car in sight and hasn't been for many miles, so I stop in the middle of this really cool but weird bridge.

Nikkei gets off my bike and at that very second the car that has been following us pulls across the end of the bridge, blocking my exit!

"Nikkei," I shout, "get back on the bike!"

It's almost impossible to turn a bike around fast on this bridge. I no longer think it's cool; in fact, I'm cussing it. "Mother Fuckin' Stupid-Ass Bridge!" Finally, I get my bike turned around and Nikkei climbs back on, but just as I'm ready to fly out of here as fast as the bridge will allow, the second dude steps out onto the other end of the bridge directly in front of me, he's holding a pump shotgun! "Fuck!"

With both ends of the bridge blocked and only armed with a pistol, it's easy to figure, "We're Fucked!"

Chapter Nineteen

ROAD TRIP
'FREE BIRD'

Without a doubt, this is the all-time lowest point of my life. My biggest regret is that I could have avoided it. With my lifestyle, danger is always knocking on my door; it lurks behind every corner. But I've grown used to that and have taken it for granted to the point I stopped yielding to it. I should have never been flying my Colors on this trip, never. Because we're at war, anytime only a few, one or two or even three or four Brothers are flying Colors, they need to be followed closely by an armed van, or at least a car being driven by an armed Brother. There's safety in numbers, so if ten or twenty are flying Colors, it has to be somewhat safer. Although the van should always be there, it's not as necessary as when only a few are flying Colors. But I'm too proud not to fly my Colors whenever I want, so I did. Maybe Brock is right; maybe I am too Lovesick and Love Blind to be an effective Brother. I never gave flying our Colors any serious consideration. I guess I just wanted Nikkei and me both to be flying our Colors on this Road Trip, because after the trip I was going to decide who to choose, her or the Club. I didn't want to isolate myself from the Club to the point I became vulnerable to only Nikkei and our relationship. I wanted to keep a constant reminder of who I am, and my Colors on my back do that for me. Also, I was enjoying the idea of not only having, but being with both her and my Club, via Nikkei on the back of my Hog and my Colors on the back of me. Now it looks like I may not have either. After fucking up this bad I deserve everything I get;

Nikkei, on the other hand, does not. But it looks like neither one of us will be given a choice as this situation plays out, we may both be doomed; me because of my sins, and her because of me.

I'm pretty much out of range from the shotgun the dude on one end of the bridge is holding. But the dude in the car, at the other end, has an AR-15 set up to Rock 'n' Roll, full auto, so I'm a sitting duck for him. My pistol is useless against that.

The dude holding the shotgun crouches down behind a large steel girder that supports the bridge, allowing his partner at the other end to freely fire at us without the risk of hitting him. At first I thought he was hiding from me; this was surprising because I don't understand how he can view me as a viable threat from this distance? With that being my last thought, the deadly stage is set and the conscience of my lifestyle begins.

As this terrible situation unfolds, the dude at one end of the bridge that had pulled his car perpendicular to it, is now leaning across the hood on the far side of the car. He is resting his assault rifle for better accuracy and protection to himself. His first barrage is an entire twenty-round clip fired continuously. Bullets are pinging everywhere, sparking off the steel bridge and riddling my beautiful Harley. It is pretty much crazy and uncontrolled shooting, not a single bullet hit me or Nikkei. But it is definitely holding a strong psychological effect on us both. When the gunfire stops, a loud, echoing roar from the repeated firing echoes through the deep canyon walls for a long time; at first I didn't even realize he had stopped shooting. It must have been heard for miles and miles. I can see this guy frantically looking through the car for another full clip; he is throwing empty beer cans and fast-food wrappers out of the car behind himself as he yells, "Where in the fuck is my ammo!" I throw my bike down, then push Nikkei down behind it, and lay on top of her. I desperately look around for an answer out of our deadly situation. I know these guys are not going to stop until they finish what they've started here.

This Hit seems somewhat planned, but for the most part, its pure luck granted to a couple of amateurs. They may be Heavyweights by their own admission, but I'm willing to bet this is their first attempt at murder.

Finding a small olive drab army satchel full of ammo, he reloads another live clip and lights up the second barrage, but this time he is being more careful, squeezing the trigger in short three to five round bursts. One round hits my right arm. This is the first time I have ever been shot. Fucking thing burns! Lying face down, I can see through the bridge. I think if we run toward the dude with the shotgun, which my pistol has a chance against, we may be able to jump off the bridge and roll down the deep gorge. But I don't think I can wait until he reloads again, this guy is zeroing in!

The next five rounds riddle my bike, and pieces of fragmented bullets pepper my face, some piercing deep into my lips. Bullets are sparking everywhere. As they hit my bike, small pieces of my Harley are airborne along with little clouds of dust from the dried bondo used to mold my beautiful machine. If I stand to run, he'll get me for sure. But if I stay here it's just a matter of time; he'll get both of us.

Another five-round barrage goes off; this time a bullet cuts off a piece of my ear. As I reach up to feel the damage, a second bullet blows through the little finger of my left hand, breaking it in half. That's it. I stand and run in the opposite direction from the guy shooting at me, directly toward the dude with the shotgun. Once again he lets out a continuous rate of fire, emptying what's left in that second clip; the canyon is alive with the loud echoing sounds of gunfire. It seems hundreds of bullets are buzzing past me; they are hitting all around the bridge, disintegrating as they loudly crack into the iron that surrounds me. One passes through my hair, blowing it up and out in front of me, like a small hole in a pillow puffing out feathers as you lay your head down; pieces of my locks are pushed hard into the light breeze and like cotton in the wind, freely blowing away. That was close!

My running has drawn all the fire away from Nikkei. It's me they want, but after killing me, they'll probably kill Nikkei so as not to leave any witnesses.

This guy empties the rest of his clip at me as I run, but this time he doesn't have to search for another one to reload; he has more lying beside him on the hood of the car! The few seconds it takes him to reload, I'm able to run and duck behind a large steel girder. He lights up with another barrage; bullets are hitting all around me, pinging and blasting into steel, just as I figured, he has no interest in Nikkei, I'm his trophy. Another bullet hits me in the leg, but this one does not hurt or burn at all; there is much blood however. I am much closer to the dude with the shotgun now, but he is still ducked behind a main steel beam that supports the bridge—I hope! In all the confusion, I lost track of him.

The guy with the AR-15 has stopped firing now; I am worried he may begin firing at Nikkei though, so I lean out around the steel beam I'm hiding behind and fire a couple of rounds at him, trying to keep him focused on me. At this distance I have to aim high, but to my surprise, I hit the windshield of his car, busting it completely out. Glass flies everywhere! He immediately ducks down completely out of sight; after a few seconds he stands and gives me hell. Trying to draw his fire away from Nikkei works well; he empties another twenty round clip at me! But after the smoke clears and the echoing fades, it becomes obvious; I'm out of his line of fire.

As he reloads, Nikkei stands and runs to the other side of the bridge. There is an old rusty steel ladder welded to the bridge to be used for maintenance. She quickly climbs down it and goes out of sight to both me and him.

Well, if Nikkei is safe, my only worry now is the dude with the shotgun and where he is hiding. In all the excitement I completely lost track of him. For all I know he could be directly behind the next closest support beam, only twenty feet away. Other than that, my situation has improved, but it still greatly Sucks! The blood from the gunshot wound to my leg has soaked my boot; I'm creating bloody footprints everywhere I step. I wonder how long I have before I bleed to death.

Suddenly the dude climbs in his car and begins repeatedly blowing his horn. I have no idea why or what he's up to. He starts his car then spins it around onto the road facing away from me and the bridge. At first I thought he was going to drive closer to me. Not knowing where the other guy is, I'm reluctant to step around the far side of the beam I'm hiding behind. This doesn't make any sense to me, why is he just sitting there blowing the horn? But he continues for a long time.

Weak from loss of blood, I slowly slide down the steel girder my back's resting against, until I reach a sitting position, one leg straight out in front of me, the other bent at the knee. I examine my blood-soaked pant leg and then lean around the corner of the beam to watch what the hell this guy is doing. One good thing though; as long as he's blowing his horn, I know exactly where he is! I will never give up, but I'm rapidly losing my ability to mount an adequate defense. I've been outgunned this entire time, but at least I had my strength. Now I'm losing even that!

I keep turning to see if I can locate the guy with the shotgun; I've completely lost track of him! I'm no longer under the threat of being shot by the AR-15. So I lean completely out onto the bridge and look opposite the direction of his car in the hopes of finding the other killer, the one armed with a sawed-off pump shotgun. When I lean out, I see why the dude started his car and why he is so frantically blowing his horn. He is signaling his partner to leave because there is a State Police Cruiser sitting up the road on a hill from the bridge. The cop has his driver's door open and is kneeling down on one knee behind it with a shotgun pointed toward the bridge.

This is great news! I now focus all my attention in that direction. The cop reaches into his cruiser and takes out the radio's microphone. He puts it on Loud Speaker and says, "Drop your weapons and lay on the ground!" His voice echoes through the canyon; and with each repetition grows quieter and quieter until completely silent. A large hawk circles high above, his silhouette etched perfectly into the beautiful blue sky. I am thinking, 'what a beautiful day to die.'

The dude with the shotgun was in fact directly beside me, only a few feet away all along. If not for the cop showing up, he probably would have gotten me. He takes off running for the car at the other end of the bridge. He runs past me only a few feet away; he knew I was there. I point my .45 at him. If he raises his shotgun toward me, cop or no cop, I'm going to give him one in the head. As he passes, we both make eye contact; it's the dude I thumped at the bar. It's funny because as he runs past, I focus on the huge egg like knot on his forehead, the one I gave to him yesterday. His nose has a large Band-Aid across it also. I don't fire because his gun is pointed downward and away from me, and under the watchful eye of the State Trooper, it would be considered cold, calculated murder. He's not a threat to me while running away, so self-defense will not apply.

I wait until both guys are in the car and it speeds off before hiding my gun inside a tight corner of the steel bridge's connecting I beam. I struggle to stand and then step out onto the bridge with both my hands held high above my head. Facing the cop and in total defiance to his order for me to lay down, I walk backward away from him toward Nikkei; now I risk being shot by the police, but I must find my fiancée.

"Nikkei!" I shout, "It's over!"

Suddenly she climbs out of the dark, dirty little crawl space she's been hiding in and runs to me. I put my arms around her and squeeze.

"Are you okay, Nikkei?" I ask.

She says, "I'm not shot if that's what you mean."

She and I both sit down beside my beautiful bike, now riddled with bullet holes, and wait for the cops.

Over a short period of only ten minutes, the cop has been joined by another and another and another. With guns drawn, they slowly drive one cruiser onto the bridge while several other cops are walking beside and behind it for cover. All four doors of the cruiser are open; they are taking no chances.

Nikkei is trying to roll up my pant leg to examine my leg wound; the cops are shouting at her to stop!

She yells back at them, "Fuck you, he's been shot!"

I push her hands away and say, "Nikkei, don't! These cops are ready to shoot us both. So do exactly as they say!"

The cops are advancing down the bridge in "Swat Team" style; there are now many more cruisers on scene, and three more following the first cruiser across the bridge; a show of Total Force.

I look at Nikkei and say with a chuckle, "For the first time in my life, I'm actually happy to see a cop!"

She rolls her eyes and then looks away while slowly shaking her head!

The cops handcuff both of us and secure the crime scene. There has to be twenty-five to thirty cops now. They've dispatched an ambulance for me; Nikkei argues she's fine!

I'm still wearing my Colors; my hands are cuffed to my front as I'm strapped to a gurney and loaded into the ambulance. Nikkei is cuffed and sitting in the back of a detective's car. I'm secured; the sirens come on and off as we go to the hospital followed by many cop cruisers. Oh yeah, there's a detective sitting beside me.

He asks, "Who are the guys that shot you?"

I answer, "I have no idea. I never got a look at any of them, and I don't know why anyone would do this to me."

I'm not gonna tell the cops anything, but the truth is, I really don't know anything; I have no idea who those guys are. I figure it's over the war between our two Clubs, but I'm not gonna tell the cops that. I have broken no laws here and neither has Nikkei, so I'll just keep my mouth shut and call Hillbilly as soon as I can.

I'm wheeled into the emergency room and go directly to the O.R. where I'm plugged into what seems to be a hundred different devices, and that's the last I remember until waking up the following day with Nikkei, Hillbilly, Dealer, and Heavy at my side.

I slowly open my eyes; I'm confused and disoriented from the narcotics. Nikkei is holding my hand; my Colors are neatly folded on her lap. When she sees my eyes open, she immediately stands and kisses my forehead, then says, "Welcome back, Clutch!" She gently lays my folded Colors on my chest.

Hillbilly and Dealer crowd to my bedside. Hillbilly says, "What, are ya gonna sleep your life away? You've been out for fifteen hours, you lazy bum! The doctors say you'll be fine. We've scheduled to have you moved out of this dump and to the hospital in the city, ASAP. We can take better care of you in our own territory!"

Dealer looks at me and says, "There are nearly one hundred Brothers outside right now. Many are Goons from up to five states away! When they heard you had been shot, they all stopped what they were doing and immediately came here. We'll wait until you're moved before asking what happened."

Next Heavy leans forward, laughing, and says, "When Whirly heard you had been shot, he told his workplace he had an emergency and had to leave for a few days. They told him if he did he was fired. So he punched-out his boss and quit! I had to bail him out of jail before coming here. When I did, the cops were practically begging for his release. I think if I had been a little short on his bail money, the cops would have all divvied-in just to get him out of there!"

Everyone laughs. Heavy continues, "He was arguing and threatening everyone in the jail! One dude told Whirly that he better not go to sleep tonight.

Whirly got dead in his face and replied, 'No motherfucker, you better not go to sleep tonight!' And when we got here, he was gonna punch-out a doctor for telling him he was not allowed to see you!"

Again, everyone laughs, but it hurts me to laugh so mine is more of a chuckle.

Wow, how cool is this, to have this many Brothers come to my rescue. I know how tight our Club is and how much we love one another. But to actually experience this many Brothers showing up here so quickly for my help and support—even quitting their jobs if necessary—is so emotionally overwhelming for me I almost shed tears of joy. But I will never do that in front of my Brothers or Nikkei for that matter, so I just one by one ask for their handshakes and then one by one thank them. They all know that's my way of showing my love and thanks at this point in time. Not to exclude Nikkei, I ask her for another kiss, squeeze her hand, and thank her also.

I have Band-Aids and gauze over most of my head and face. My left hand is wrapped tight with gauze covered by an Ace Band-Aid wrap; my leg is done the same way, along with my right arm, which is almost totally numb. There are many police standing around the hallway near the entrance to my room, and a nurse has called a detective to inform him I'm conscious. Hillbilly, Dealer, and Heavy, along with Nikkei's help, had to put up quite a fuss in order to get in here and see me. But as soon as the detectives arrive, they'll all have to step out for a while. That's okay; there is absolutely nothing that can upset me at this point in time. I am in much pain, but overjoyed that Nikkei and I lived through the attack on the bridge, and Nikkei came out of it unscathed. I may be untouchable by anger right now, but you can bet your last dollar my Brothers gathered at this hospital are not, and you can also bet they're looking for some Payback! And the truth be known, so is Nikkei!

The detectives come and go, to my surprise in a short amount of time, and without too much argument. I think they know I'm not going to say anything, and without me having committed a crime, the cops really don't have any kind of lever to use in any way. One thing is for sure, BET has been notified.

The doctors say I don't really have to be moved to another hospital. Because no major organs were hit I can be released from this one in a few days as long as I go directly to a doctor as soon as I get home for follow-up care.

Right now I'm thinking the only follow-up care I need is with Nikkei. I could have lost her on that bridge. I love my Club, but

I'm not willing to sacrifice her for it. I'm pretty sure I'm gonna quit. I was thinking about quitting the Club anyhow. The only problem is, I hate to leave under these circumstances; it makes it look like I'm running. But I will not up and quit just like that. I will take my time and ease out; I'll tie up all my loose ends before I go. Brock is most definitely one of my loose ends. I think I can be out of the Club, with no bad feelings between me and the Brothers in six months. If that's my schedule, then I only have six months to find out who Brock had guarding Nikkei, then kill them both! Weeding Brock from the midst of my beloved Organization will be my secret going away Gift!

Nikkei stays at my bedside for the next three days, the entire time I'm in this small hospital. This is a very small hospital; back home we would call it a clinic. One thing is for sure though; this small hospital is packed tight with Brothers. They are coming out of the woodwork. They have set up their own security system and living quarters in a nearby hotel; security is mainly controlled by Goons, and there is no shortage of them. To avoid conflict with this hospital's administrators, the Club sends in our PR men. Every Brother in our Club has a different talent or skill, a specialty. Some fight good, some are experts in small arms and demolition, and many are walking Harley Davidson encyclopedias. And each Brother has a different skill-set to be used within our Club regardless of how big or small they are, or how smart or even how, not so smart they are. We have Brothers we call our PR men. This entire Hospital/Shooting ordeal is the kind of situation that calls for their use. So, if you look closely through all the Brothers, you'll see our PR men behind the scenes, working their "Public Relations" magic—that's their Skill Set. They have brought large boxes of candy for all the nurses to enjoy and high-dollar three pack, signature series golf balls for the doctors, just to say thanks—you understand! In fact, during every single shift for the last three days, they have had the local pizza shop deliver pizza to the local Sheriff's Post. Again, just our way of saying thanks.

One thing for sure, people that have only read or heard stories about our Club have an entirely different point of view after meeting us. Providing we want them to, they gather a very good opinion about us when it's all said and done. Some cops may say, "It's all Bullshit. These guys are ruthless 1% Outlaw Criminals!" But the truth is, this is how we really are! We wouldn't give the nurses chocolate if we didn't want to say thanks. If we ease some tension by doing that, then so be it, that's a good thing! They're helping me, and my Club's thanking them for that. As far as feeding the cops pizza, it's no more than an act of respect. View it any other way, and the point is lost!

At night when my room is empty of all the Brothers and doctors, Nikkei and I sit quietly and talk. We do some very Heavy-Duty talking. We get more heart-to-heart talking done during the three days I'm lying in this hospital ventilated by bullet holes than we did the entire time we were on our Road Trip.

I tell Nikkei when she was gone, held prisoner by Brock, I made a deal with God; that if he brought her home, I'll do whatever he wants. I told her I prayed often and there's no doubt in my mind God is the reason she came back to me. To my surprise, Nikkei told me, while kidnapped and held at the cabin, for the first time in her life, she also prayed. She asked God, "Please let Clutch be alive, let it be just another lie told by Brock when he says, Clutch is dead!" She too made a deal with God, to please bring her and me back together and she would do whatever it is he wanted from her.

Wow, I never talked to Nikkei about God before, but as it turns out, we both entered into a relationship with him at the same time and for the same reason.

For three days, every night, while my room was empty—void of Brothers, doctors, nurses, and cops—Nikkei and I talked hard about our love for each other, our relationship with each other, our future, and God. For the first time ever, I tell Nikkei I am going to leave the Club. She didn't know what to say or do; she just sits and contemplates what it was I just said. She tells me she once thought I would never leave the Club. She says, "But if you leave the Club over me, you'll end up hating me over it." I've thought about that, but I can never see myself hating Nikkei for any reason.

So I say, "Nikkei, nothing on this planet could ever bring me to hate you for any reason. I won't give you my word because I can't right now, but I should be out of the Club in six months."

I'm finally released from this tiny hospital; its parking lot is filled with Bikers on Harleys, armed Club vans, and many, many cars holding Brothers and Ol' ladies. All the Brothers begin kick-starting their motorcycles at the same time; they loudly rev their motors as their Ol' ladies gracefully climb on the backs of their bikes. The first two bikes slowly pull out, riding abreast, then two more, and two more. This continues for a long time as the parking lot slowly empties. The sound of all these Harleys combined with the commotion of this many Bikers has drawn crowds of spectators; they quietly stand on street corners, watching. The small crowds grow larger and larger. Doctors, nurses, and patients press tightly against hospital windows curiously watching. It's exciting to many; some wish they were a part of it. In a well-disciplined manner, keeping in a tight pack, we slowly empty the parking lot onto the road and make our way home. Like an army convoy, I'm ferried homeward in a Club van, armed to the teeth, led by and followed with nearly fifty of the most hard-core one percent Bikers in the World. They are all ready, willing, and able. Behind the Bikers on Harleys following my van are more Club vans and then a half-dozen cars and such following them. This procession begins with a long string of Harleys riding side by side, then the van I'm in, then another long string of Harleys riding side by side in tight formation, then two more armed vans followed by a group of cars. Oh yeah, there are cops driving in front and behind our long convoy, along with a state police helicopter high above.

The van I'm riding home in has three Brothers with pump shotguns and AR-15's; all three are Goons. As much as Hillbilly, Crazy George, and Dealer love to ride their Harleys, in order to guard me, they have sacrificed their bike rides home for this ride home in our van. I love having my Brothers here in this van guarding me. They don't ease up in the least. Hillbilly is holding an AR-15; it's set up to Rock 'n' Roll. He is steadily watching out the window for any sign of trouble. Dealer is riding shotgun, literally! He's holding a 12-gauge pump shotgun at the ready. There is a bandoleer full of 12-gauge Double-Ought Buckshot across his leg. Crazy George is driving and is monitoring the CB radio; all the vans guarding this convoy are in communication with each other and are talking in code on Citizen Band radios. Our Club has armor plated all our vans. There is plate steel paneled inside all the doors, and the small door windows can easily be pushed out so a rifle can be fired from the van, as the shooter is protected via the steel paneling. It's sort of like a large Roman Shield. These vans are somewhat like scaled down versions of armored cars the banks use. Almost every Chapter has its own van and has armored it in different ways.

This van has six captain seats. Nikkei and I sit quietly in the middle row and her head is tilted onto my shoulder. The loudness of all the Harleys has been baffled by the van, leaving only a deep, thunderous sound that pounds inside my gut, similar to a bass drum. The continuous roar does not monopolize; rather, it is in harmony with the music on the radio softly playing Lynyrd Skynyrd's 'Free Bird.' I love that song! It sets the mood during this very special moment for me—all my Brothers offering such support, Nikkei alive and well at my side, the roaring thunder of fifty Harleys, "Free Bird" playing through the high-dollar stereo system. I close my eyes and thank God.

That song has set my mood, a rather somber one. Right now, I'm with both my Club and Nikkei, but even though I'm with both, I do not have both. In fact, I never will, not without destroying Nikkei or my relationship with my beloved Club. Just like that song, which is about a man leaving, I must also leave, but I will not be leaving my woman. I will be leaving my Brothers. Hopefully, that does not destroy me!

I have my Colors draped over my leg; they cannot be worn in an automobile. I slowly examine them, fondling my Patches. It's the first time I have really looked them over since the shooting. I stare at my Death Head Patch and smile; it reminds me of my Brothers Hillbilly, Dealer, and Crazy George, riding only an arm's length away. My Rag, my Colors, consists of three Patches—a Top Rocker, a Center Patch, and a Bottom Rocker sewn on a cut-off Levi's jacket, no sleeves, no collar. On the inside of my Rag, I have sewn two pockets, one on either side of the front opening. As I feel one of them, I notice a small object inside of it. I reach in and remove a bullet. This is undoubtedly one of the many fired at me on the bridge. I hold it up and examine it carefully. To my surprise, it's in perfect condition. Not even a scratch. How is this possible? I saw bullets sparking and exploding all around me that day, but this one's perfect. It had to of hit something to slow it down enough not to tear completely through my Colors and end up in this pocket; hitting anything that would slow it down that much would have no doubt distorted it, if not destroyed it. What the fuck is going on here? My first reaction is,

BET has something to do with this, and is up to No Good. But logic cancels that idea because Nikkei and I have had possession of my Colors the entire time. Nikkei is sleeping, she hasn't gotten much sleep during the last few days, but I nudge her anyway and ask if she knows anything about this? Still groggy from sleep, or lack of, she opens one eye and says, "Clutch, whatever you have can wait till morning. Now, good night!" Then drops her head back on my shoulder. She must think we're in bed or something, because it's midmorning now.

I hand the bullet to Hillbilly and say, "Hillbilly, look what I found in the inside pocket of my Rag!"

He too examines it carefully and then hands it to Dealer. Crazy George, while driving, watches as Dealer looks at this pristine bullet in amazement.

After a while Crazy George turns to me then says, "That, Clutch, is divine intervention! That bullet was probably gonna hit Nikkei's head until God caught it. He's probably the one who put it in your Rag just to show you what he did!"

He follows his analogy with a slight chuckle and a grin. I look at him very seriously, and then at Hillbilly; he is slowly nodding his head in agreement.

He says, "In all the years I spent in Nam, I never seen anything like that before! That 5.56 round will come apart when hitting anything, even a can! Maybe that one was a dud and didn't have any energy behind it! Or maybe George is right, maybe that is a sign from God." He shrugs his shoulders with a grin and a wink.

It's obvious to me my Brothers don't really see this as Divine Intervention, they're sort of joking around with that idea, but I do. What other explanation is there? Oh, I'm sure stranger things have happened, but never to me. There are probably thousands of scientists that will give a hypothesis as to how that bullet found its way into my pocket undistorted. Science is always trying to discredit theology! But one thing I do know, God is the reason Nikkei survived Brock's imprisonment, and he is the reason she and I lived through the attack on the bridge, so why wouldn't this be a sign from him? As far as I'm concerned, I asked God for a sign, and this is it! What an insult it would be if I was to deny him the credit!

It's a long drive home; we stop for fuel and to eat a couple of different times. Whenever we stop, saddle-sore Brothers come to the van, bringing me beer and good company. We joke and laugh around, but I can't get that bullet off my mind.

Finally, I'm home! Nikkei's mother, Sam, could not make the trip to see me at the hospital, but she called continually, two or three times every day. As I open my door, I'm greeted by her; its spooky how much she reminds me of Nikkei. She's sporting that little girl smile; it's obvious that's where Nikkei gets it; she very carefully hugs and kisses me! Sam has a huge "Welcome Home" banner draped across my kitchen cupboards; my house is filled with Brothers! Even my Pitt Bulls chained around my house are happy I'm home. They are loudly barking in their deep Pitt Bull dog voices and lunging forward high into the air, only to be jerked back by their chains. There are Brothers everywhere.

I'm walking on crutches, my head, right arm, and left hand covered in tight band aids. The doctors couldn't save my little finger; I lost it from the knuckle up. The shot I took in the leg cut through a main artery; the doctors said I'm lucky I didn't lose it also. They never did get all the bullet fragments out of my lips, and a large piece of my ear is missing. Oh well, I never figured on winning any beauty contests anyway.

The Brothers are having a party here tonight in my honor. It's a homecoming party motivated by me surviving the attack. There are two kegs of beer and some prospects will be cooking a 250-pound hog. And a party is just what I need.

After hugging and kissing Sam for a while as my Brothers respectfully give her time with me, I begin hugging all of them. Even though this is a very small amount of what our actual Club membership comprises, it seems an endless amount of Brothers that I one by one hug and am told "I love ya, Bro, glad you made it!" By the time I am done, I have tears in my eyes. Everyone loves being loved.

We all go outside to the Party Pit; there're Brothers from twenty different Chapters here. I'll bet I tell the "Attack on the Bridge" story a thousand times. I always back the story up to the beginning, where it actually started, at the bar one day earlier when I thumped the dude in the head with a homemade black jack. He ended up being the one on the bridge with the shotgun. I'm willing to bet the other guy, the one with the AR-15 assault rifle, is the guy at the bar I thought was a full patch member of the club we are at war with. He had red hair and I'm pretty sure the guy shooting at me had red hair also.

I swear after four beers it's all I can do to stand up; the beer must have Kick-Started the Dilaudids I'm taking. Yeee-haa!

It's getting near dark. Bikers are still pulling down my long drive; some have rode from great distances to come here in my honor. This party is going strong, but not so much me. I tell a Prospect to bring me a blanket, and when he does, I pass out between the beer kegs and pig spit, surrounded by Brothers, where I know I'm safe. Just as I pass out, Bones pulls in with a pack of about thirty-five Brothers from the Mother Chapter and a few other Chapters from Up North and Back East.

As the Guest of honor, the first thing Bones does is come looking for me. When he finally finds me passed out in the middle of the field surrounded by Brothers, he orders three Brothers, not Prospects, to come and guard me against any drunken Brothers accidentally falling into me as I sleep. They were ordered not to drink and to stand in a triangular formation around me and not to let anybody within ten feet of my Dead Ass.

About midnight Nikkei comes with additional blankets and a soft pillow; she covers me, then puts the pillow under my head, and cuddles up next to me. We both sleep there on the cold ground surrounded by partying Brothers until midmorning.

When I wake up, I look around and see there's even more Brothers here now then when I passed out last night, and the party is still going strong. I'm still being guarded by three Brothers, not the same three I started with, but three very large, very capable, very sober Brothers. These three were not ordered to guard me. They took it upon themselves to relieve the first three; they volunteered and they are all three Goons.

Seeing I'm awake, they help me to my feet and hand me an ice-cold beer. Hurting like hell, I pop a couple more pills, down the beer, smack my lips, and say, "Let's do day 2. Yeee-haa!"

Well, Day 2 of my "Welcome home, Glad ya Made it" party has come and gone. In fact, it's been a week since that party. They tell me I enjoyed myself and had lots of fun, but I can only take their word on that. With all the narcotics and beer I eagerly consumed, I really don't remember very much at all.

Whirly is here now. He's been coming to my house every single day, checking on me, and each day he comes, he comes with Road Kill. Those two have become inseparable; they are Thick as Thieves.

A couple of days ago, while out riding together, they stopped in a strange bar. One thing led to the next and a fight broke out. Whirly and Road Kill ended up single-handedly Kicking Ass on the entire bar. No wonder they get along so well; they're both one of the same, tough as nails!

Road Kill and I are sitting alone in my living room having a heart-to-heart talk along with an ice-cold beer. Nikkei and Whirly have driven up to the store for more beer and cigarettes. Road Kill and I have done a lot of talking this week. We are becoming close, and he really has turned out to be a righteous Brother. Once again, today he and I talk seriously about all issues that we've had between each other and our two Chapters. He tells me, at first, he didn't like me. He says, "Probably because of all the shit Brock was saying." He also very respectfully says, "Brock tells a story of you being too lovesick and too love blind to put the Club first." And to him that was believable. Our conversations have been structured around pure honesty even when they reached an emotional level or became painfully true. He said through Whirly he understands Brotherhood more now than ever before and sees Brock's shortcomings in that area. He told me he did not know Nikkei was at Brock's cabin, and then he very seriously says, "Clutch, you and I can never be Brothers if we keep secrets from one another and I can see now I want to be your Brother, so I must tell you what's been bothering me. Big Bart is the guy Brock had guarding Nikkei!" he says. "Big Bart will deny any of it, but I believe Brock kidnapped Nikkei and Big Bart was ordered by him to guard her. But I'm sure Brock will say she came to him willingly."

I stand and give Road Kill a long, tight hug then say, "Thank you, Bro, you truly are a Brother to be honored!"

I tell him this conversation will stay between us and only us.

When I do, he raises his chest along with his voice and says, "It don't matter to me if it does or doesn't! I speak from my heart, so I'll say it to anybody that wants to hear!" He pounds his fist directly over his heart one time.

Well, well now that I know who the second man in Nikkei's disappearance is . . . .

CHAPTER TWENTY

SIT-DOWN

Nikkei and I are lounging around the house when I get a phone call from a detective; he wants me and Nikkei to come downtown in a couple of hours to view a police Lineup. The cops picked up a couple Bikers and believe them to be the two that ambushed Nikkei and me on the bridge. They want us to come and ID the two if possible. I agree to his request. "This sounds like fun!"

Nikkei is driving us downtown to the police station when she asks, "Clutch, you know I love you very much, don't ya?"

"Of course I do, Nikkei, why would you ask that?" I ask.

She says, "On the bridge the day you were shot, I had an overwhelming feeling you died, and just like at Brock's cabin when I thought you were dead, I asked God to save you. Now that he has, I'm asking him to save us both, but this time not from the bullets, but from our lifestyle. I'm asking God to save us through the strength of our love. I believe God intended for us to be together all along, even from birth, because neither of us has the ability to live well without the other. You told me you were gonna leave the Club. I give you my word, Clutch, I will support you one way or the other, whether you decide to stay in or not, but I want you to know now I really hope you quit."

I'm not sure what provoked Nikkei to say that, but for sure her mind is tripping a thousand miles per hour over our lifestyle, the Club, and of course, our relationship.

This police station is huge. Unfortunately, I'm all too familiar with it and know my way around much too well, but my familiarity with this place doesn't keep me from hating it.

We meet with two detectives and talk for quite some time. For a long period, they separate Nikkei from me and question us individually. Finally, Nikkei and I are taken into the police Lineup room and seated. This is all new to me, but one thing is not; I can see many of the detective's questions are being asked because BET has told them to ask. You can bet, ATF's Task Force, Biker Enforcement Team has been lurking in the shadows through this entire incident ever since they heard I was shot.

I'm sitting in a dark room behind a two-way mirror; Nikkei is beside me on this very uncomfortable cold steel bench. There is a uniformed cop standing at attention in front of the entrance and two detectives standing on either side of Nikkei and me. On the other side of the two-way mirror all the lights come on and in walk eight men in a single file line to the lineup area. They are all wearing inmate orange coveralls; this is like looking into a giant aquarium, only it's filled with people instead of fish. The hair on the back of my neck rises when I see the tall dude I thumped at the bar walk in. He is definitely the one that was wielding a shotgun that day on the bridge. It's all I can do not to break through the glass and attack him. Nikkei is holding my hand and begins to squeeze it tightly. I wonder if it's from her anger or if she's trying to calm me. I never told Nikkei I know the guy on the bridge is the same one I hit on the head at the bar. I wonder if she realizes it now. There's another dude in the lineup that's probably the one who was driving the car that day. The one that actually shot me with an AR-15! He has long, thick red hair!

I calm myself then act as if I'm studying the entire lineup. One by one I pause and pretend to be considering each and every suspect. The detectives are watching Nikkei and me very closely, probably for any kind of reaction. Finally I look at the lead detective and say, "No, I'm sure none of these guys are the ones that shot me."

The detective anxiously replies, "Are you positive? Please look again."

I say, "There's no point, I'm positive now!"

I look at Nikkei and ask, "How about you, dear, recognize anybody?"

She turns and hatefully says to the detective, "Like I told ya, I never saw anything!"

Nikkei doesn't feel the need to be nice to the cops; after all, they have harassed her also.

The detective presses an intercom button then leans down and in a disgusted tone says, "Okay, Jim, that's all. Put 'em back in their cages!"

The only thing the cops accomplished here today was to give me a good look at the dudes that shot me. I swear, I will sear their faces into my memory's hoard. Now that I know where they are, my Club will put everything it has into finding their legal names and addresses. We won't fuck with them here in jail though; the cops will be watching for that! Probably, BET pushed hard for this lineup, just so I could get a good look at the guys they think attacked me and my fiancée! No doubt they're Stirring the Pot. They want us at war, killing each other, and that's because the U.S. government is scared to death someday all one percent Bike Clubs may unite. I'm sure the cops know those are the right two guys, but without our testimony, it would be useless to charge them. And I'm also sure BET knew neither Nikkei nor I would say anything.

On our drive home Nikkei and I stay 'In Character,' we pretend to be talking about the lineup as if neither of us recognized any of the suspects. If the cops are somehow listening, and they could be, this will not fool them, but if they are somehow taping us, what we say may fool a Grand Jury.

A month has come and gone since I was shot. I've recovered remarkably well, I must say. I do have numbness in my leg and arm though; they both tingle to the touch. Kind of like when you're outside during the winter so long that your hand becomes frozen and numb, and once inside a warm house, it begins to tingle as it thaws. That tingling is what I feel to the touch! The swelling in my lips has gone away. Nikkei tells me it's not noticeable at all, probably it is. The one-half of my little finger from my left hand that was shot off is very noticeable however. Every now and then I struggle when picking something up and have to compensate by using a different approach to the task. But I must say, if I had to lose one-half of a finger and was given a choice, that's the one I would pick. And I will always have only half an ear; however, all the Brothers say, "It's cool looking!" One Brother tells me, "With only half an ear, you look like a Pirate, one not so good at sword fighting!" Another Brother said, "It gives your head that well-seasoned, lived-in look!" But no matter how it looks, I'll never get it back and have accepted my loss as just one more payment to my Lifestyle.

It's a Wednesday and this is my first week back at work. Heavy took Monday and Tuesday off this week but today he's back and this is the first time I've seen him. He and I are quietly sitting and eating our box lunches together at my workstation. He tells me Brock has been dropping little hints around his Chapter that I am the reason I was shot. Brock said had I not been so concentrated on Nikkei and more on security, the ambush at the bridge could have been avoided. He said Brock slowed down with that rhetoric after Road Kill stood and angrily told him, "Cool it with that kind of talk, Brock! We're at War, and that's why Clutch was shot!"

Heavy and I talk about Road Kill a little. He says, "I like Road Kill, but I still don't think he prospected long enough. Brock let him into our Club too soon and he still has a lot to prove!"

I tell him, "Road Kill told me Big Bart is the one Brock had guarding Nikkei, the one that fired a pistol at my woman, the one that tortured her through mental abuse!"

Heavy stops and thinks about what I just said, and then tells me he and I will discuss it very soon. This weekend at my house; we'll ask Hillbilly, Dealer, and Crazy George to be there.

He angrily says, "There's a debt here that must be paid!" He also tells me to be smart and don't say or do anything about Big Bart until we talk this weekend.

I assure him, "I'll be cool!" He then asks me how Nikkei and I are getting along and, of course, reminds me how lucky I am to have her back. He then follows that statement by telling me how much he still misses his daughter.

I know I should not, but I feel guilty for having Nikkei back knowing he'll never have his daughter, Weird Sally, back.

On my way home from work, I think hard about what Heavy told me Brock has been saying. I smile when rehearsing Road Kill's words to him; he basically told Brock to shut the fuck up! Road Kill is becoming a true Brother. I wonder how he's going to react to Brock's murder, after I kill both Brock and Big Bart.

When I get home I call Hillbilly and tell him to round up Dealer and meet me at my house Friday night. Heavy is going to talk to Crazy George and tell him to be here also.

Friday night arrives soon, probably because I've never quit thinking about our meeting and what to do with Big Bart and Brock. My plan is to try and have them Eighty-Six'ed from our Club and then I can quietly kill them both without violating our Club's Oath of Brotherhood. If I can't have them thrown out, then I'll just have to figure another way to do them in. Problem is, I can't quit the Club until they are taken care of because it will be almost impossible to kill either of them once I'm out and they're still active.

We all sit outside on a melting pot of different-colored steel lawn chairs that surround the burn pit. There are nearly twenty different chairs out here that Brothers have donated for use during our Club parties. Our Harleys are resting in a small group close by; they are randomly clumped together and pointing every which way. The sun has set nearly an hour ago, but there is still a dim orange-red sky stretching across the western horizon, a beautiful sunset indeed. A small fire softly crackles as it burns anonymously; the night air is brisk. We are all wearing our Colors over black leather jackets. After our meeting, we plan to ride to Papa Dadieo's and do some Mild-to-Light partying.

Hillbilly stands. Holding a cold beer in one hand, he slowly looks around my property; his towering silhouette set against the western sky is a reminder of what a huge man he is. He's wearing tight, faded blue jeans with the pant legs rolled up around his high-top, tightly laced black boots. His leather jacket is only zipped up a quarter of the way; his chest is pushing through the open area. He's broad shouldered and muscular. He is wearing black leather gloves with the fingers removed and has a tight bandana wrapped around his forehead holding back his long, thick red hair. An earring sparkles from his left ear; his full red beard is perfectly groomed. As he pans his eyes around my land, Dealer, Crazy George, Heavy, and me all sit patiently watching and waiting for him to say something, to explain what it is he is looking at or thinking of. It's obvious he has deliberately taken center stage.

He enters the Brock-Bart issue slowly by saying, "Clutch, first off I want to thank you for this moment." Still panning his head around my property, he continues, "I love this place, so many parties out here, so many good times. It's impossible for me to stand here and not reflect on all the Brotherhood I've shared right here in this exact spot. Brotherhood is what it is all about. We have set up rules in our Club. Although not many, they must be followed to the letter, or we will have nothing!"

Looking directly at Hillbilly, Heavy gives a deep, approving nod yes, then continues to slowly nod his head in agreement for a long time, and like an echo, his nods become less and less until they slowly fade and stop.

Hillbilly says, "We are here right now because of Brock and Big Bart. We must determine, did Nikkei go with Brock willingly, or did Brock kidnap her? Then what was Big Bart's role, was he just following orders? If so, can he be held responsible? I'm gonna talk as a Goon and officially call this a Goon meeting. Heavy is not an active Goon but was for many years, so I don't think there's any problem with him sitting in. Although Bones has to give the final okay, as the acting Hit Squad and Police Force for our Club, I say if Brock did what it looks like I think he did, then all we do is Pull his Patch and eighty-six him from our Club. Nothing else. After that, Clutch can have him and do whatever he wants, that's none of our business!"

Dealer stands and says, "Clutch, I also want to thank you, although I have not been out here as much as y'all, once I come over to this Chapter, I'm planning on living right here in this exact Spot!"

He loudly emphasizes the word 'Spot' and points his finger straight down then laughs, as we all do. Hillbilly slowly sits down and Dealer continues, "I'm gonna make it real simple. Did Brock violate Clutch? Brock will say no, Clutch will say yes, so it's simple. We must choose who to believe, and I'm casting my vote with Clutch!"

Heavy throws up his right hand and says, "Me too!" Then he looks at Crazy George, who is now standing. George places his hand on Dealer's shoulder and gently presses him down into his chair.

Crazy George looks around my property then says, "Clutch, I partied with your Blood Brother, Kebus, many times out here. I remember the night you were Step 'n' Fetchin' beers for Brothers during a Fourth of July party. You couldn't have been thirteen years old! I remember what you told me that night. You said, 'It's the Fourth of July, celebrate your nation with urination and fornication!' Everyone laughs. He continues, "That was the first time I gave you any notice. That was also the same night we fed you 151 rum and you puked all over lil' Bob's Harley! Do you remember the Ass-Kicking you took for that one?"

I nod my head and smile then say, "I remember!"

He continues, "I like the way Dealer made his decision on how to solve this problem between you and Brock, to either choose one or the other to believe. Although not very scientific, I believe it to be an accurate method. I was Brock's Sponsor, he was my Prospect, and you and he have always been at odds! Clutch, I held back from you for a long time, watching and analyzing whether or not you were running games on Brock. I'm gonna cast my vote for you, Clutch, but I have a lot of history with Brock . . . . so for that reason my vote is scientific. As his Sponsor, I'm the one who helped him into our Club. So he is my mistake. And I correct all my mistakes!"

He sits down and once again Hillbilly stands.

He says, "Well, I'll make it unanimous. I also vote for Clutch! Now, what are we gonna do with Brock? Like I said, we must follow Club rules! So I say we have a Sit-Down with Bones and tell him Brock must go. After that, we'll figure out what to do about Big Bart!"

Everyone nods their heads in agreement, ending the meeting.

The following day Hillbilly and I schedule a Sit-Down meeting with Bones and some other Brothers from the Mother Chapter. Brock will be there; the goal is to get the okay from Bones to Pull his Patch. I'm meeting Hillbilly in one hour; he and I are riding up to a Clubhouse a few hours north of here; it's approximately halfway between us and the Mother Chapter.

I meet up with Hillbilly and we ride to our destination. The ride up here is nice; I love riding side by side with my Brother Hillbilly. I have only been to this Clubhouse a few times, and never to party, always for business. But I got to say, it is set up nice. We walk in and are greeted by the usual hugs. We adjourn to the backyard where Bones and a half dozen other Brothers are sitting at a couple of picnic tables pushed end to end, waiting. Brock comes through the back door followed by his New Bro, Big Bart. I'm now aware that Big Bart was the second man when Nikkei was being held captive, the one that fired his pistol at her. I don't know if he helped kidnap her, but I do suspect he had something to do with that also.

We all sit and the meeting begins. Bones looks directly at me and says, "So what's the problem, Clutch?"

I passionately answer the question, "We all know Nikkei disappeared a few months back. I put the word out for all Brothers to listen for any news about her. Now I hear Brock knew something about her disappearance and never said a word to me about it. So I must ask why."

Then Bones looks at Brock and asks, "Do you know anything about Nikkei, Brock?"

Brock half smirks and says, "I do. About a month ago, she showed up at my place in the city drunk, asking me to forgive her and take her back. When I refused, she threatened suicide!"

Hillbilly should have let him continue, hoping he would hang himself, but he did not. He just suddenly jumps into the conversation by loudly interrupting Brock.

"Crazy George, Dealer, and me found Nikkei chained to the floor at Brock's cabin!"

Hillbilly is not easily rattled, but it's easy to see he's very emotional over this situation.

Brock laughs and says, "What the fuck else could I do with her?"

He looks directly into Bone's eyes and says, "She was out of her mind saying she was going to kill herself! With all the problems I have from Sally's murder, and I know Clutch is Love Blind and will believe anything she tells him, so I put her out there hoping to calm her down! I told Big Bart to stay there and watch her till I could figure out what to do. I was going to call Clutch and tell him what was going on. I was hoping Nikkei would listen to me and just go home! I know the situation with Clutch is touchy. With all respect, he's lovesick and love blind. I knew I had to approach the situation slowly because Nikkei is a conniving liar. I wanted Clutch to see I was only trying to help and then maybe ease some of the friction between us."

When he finishes, I stand and start advancing toward him. Hillbilly grabs my arm and pulls me back down. I just sit and glare.

Bones stares at me for a long time until he is satisfied I'm calm, and then asks Brock, "Well, where did she say she was for the last month?"

Brock looks at him and puts on a very serious, concerned face, answering, "I don't know, Bones, she wouldn't say. I kind of got the impression she was shacked up with some other guy."

This time I do stand up!

Hillbilly stands and grabs me, saying, "Clutch, stop!"

I almost pull my .45 and put one right between Brock's beady little eyes. Bones looks at me until once again I relax and return to my seated position. He sits forward, puts his hands together in a praying manner, his fingertips touching his chin, elbows on the table—he's deep in thought. Bones is 110 percent for the Club and I love and trust him, but he, like many, can be Bullshitted by Brock's genius for lying, conniving, and politics.

After a few minutes of total silence, he says, "When this meeting was called, I knew there had to be a serious problem that we would all have to work hard at solving. But now I can see someone is lying. I know Clutch believes what he is saying. So that only leaves Brock or Nikkei. Let me say this, Brock is a Brother and a President, Nikkei only an Ol' lady, and if Brock is telling the truth, then she's not even that. The problem is, if Clutch goes against the Club for his woman then that's a Rat-Pack offence, maybe even a chance he could be Eighty-Six'ed from our Club for such a thing. But if Brock has violated a Brother's property, Clutch's woman, Nikkei, then that is also a Rat-Pack offence, and he too could be Eighty-Sixed for such a thing. We've had bad blood between Chapters before, but the feud between your two Chapters is almost war. So right now this is what I'm going to do—nothing! That's not to say I do or do not believe what I'm being told by either of you, but we must keep this Club strong at any cost. So you all go back home and stay away from each other until you hear back from me . . . . That's an order! I must do some investigating. One thing for sure, I will get to the bottom of this at any cost, and when I do, and I find out who's lying, nothing will save that person!"

Bones looks directly at me as if that's a warning to Nikkei. Well, at least that's how I took it!

I never even say good-bye; I just walk out, get on my bike, and burn rubber out of there. "I'm going to kill him. Club or no Club, he's dead!" I shout to the wind as I feed my Harley as much gasoline as it can take. I should have known Bones was going to back up a Brother over an Ol' lady. Brock is such a convincing liar. If I'm not careful, he'll turn the entire thing around and I'll be the bad guy!

I'm about an hour into my ride home when Hillbilly unexpectedly pulls his bike alongside of mine. I look over at him; he gives me a smile. As mad as I am, Hillbilly's smile brings warmth to my heart; I return it with a smile. With his right arm he makes a drinking gesture, raising his cupped hand to his mouth; he then points to an up-and-coming exit ramp. I nod yes and we both pull off the expressway and into the parking lot of a large strip joint.

He says, "Come on. Bro, let's go have us an ice-cold beer!"

He and I sit in there for a couple of hours drinking beer and occasionally slipping a dollar bill inside the Dancer's G-string. Although being with Hillbilly has calmed me down, I'm still bitching about Brock. "Can you believe that piece of shit telling Bones the reason he took Nikkei to his cabin was to prevent her from hurting herself! I can eat a can of alphabet soup and shit a better lie than that!"

At one point Hillbilly looks at me and says, "Talking to Bones about Brock was only phase one. If he doesn't Pull Brock's Patch, leaving him to us, then you and I will begin phase two!"

I ask, "And phase two is?"

Hillbilly smiles, leans forward, and quietly says, "Remember the gun you took from under the cop's pillow when taking back Fingers' Colors?"

I lean close to him and grin in a most interested manner and answer, "Yeah."

Hillbilly, still smiling, says, "Well, that's the gun that's gonna kill Brock!"

I slowly and repeatedly nod my head yes, thinking strongly on the genius of that idea as my smile continually grows larger and larger.

After I took that gun from the cop's apartment, I carefully placed it in a plastic bag, preserving the cop's fingerprints that are undoubtedly all over it. I have it stashed in a safe place; Hillbilly and I are the only two humans on this planet that know about it.

Hillbilly and I have a few more beers then we head home. I ride with the comfort of knowing, with Hillbilly on my side, justice will be served.

I get home and dedicate the rest of my evening to Nikkei. I've yet to tell her that this is the New Me, the one that's gonna give himself to her and only her. I figure seeing is believing! The last thing I ever wanted was any of the filth from my lifestyle to boil over onto her, but I know now I can't bring it this close to home without running the risk of that happening.

I have a few days of vacation built up at work and use them to stay home with Nikkei; although I was off work for over a month after I was shot, I figure now that things have calmed down a little, she and I can spend time together, alone. I find every time I look at her it's impossible not to thank God for holding up his end of the deal. I also find I've been searching my heart to make good on my promise to him. I'm kind of stuck though, because I have to kill Brock, and I don't figure that's the way God wants it.

I get a call from Dealer; we have a secret language we use, especially when we're on the telephone. It's constantly changing and we always talk in parables. This time he calmly says, "Hello, Clutch, did you hear I bought a new car?"

I knew then there was a major problem, one for the Goon Squad.

I answer, "No, I didn't, what did you get?"

He says, "A red Camaro."

I say, "Wow, that sounds nice."

'Red' is a Key Word meaning we must meet immediately.

Dealer says, "Yeah, I test drove it for an hour."

An hour is the next key word.

He continues, "I wanted to get Hillbilly's opinion, so I drove it over there but he went fishing."

I say "Okay, but I gotta go. I'll call ya right back . . . . bye."

What was just said is, Emergency meeting; meet Hillbilly and me at the lake in one hour. That may sound corny, but it helps keep us out of jail.

I'd rather stay home with Nikkei, but I have obligations to my Club and I am a Goon. I get to the lake; it is a secluded place where we can see far into the distance if anybody is watching. Hillbilly and Dealer are already there, and Crazy George is pulling in as I do. Our rival Club just shot two of our Brothers from a Chapter Out West. They walked into a bar and opened up. Both Brothers are alive and will recover; the only thing that saved them was both their Ol' ladies had guns in their purses and fired back, stopping the assault. They hit one attacker; he went down but with the help of his partner was able to flee the bar. Our Club is watching the hospitals to see if he shows up at one. The police were never involved.

Dealer says, "Bones wants the Goons to strike back fast and hard before the cops get wind of what happened, and here's how. Our enemies have a bike shop out there. We are going to blow it off the map! That club's chapter holds their weekly church meeting in that bike shop. They use it almost like a Clubhouse. Done right we can destroy an entire chapter with one strike!"

I know for a fact the Goon Squad has a Bazooka stashed out there, and I figure that's what we'll probably use!

Dealer says, "We are going to send two Goons out there from these two Chapters." He looks at me and says, "Clutch, what's your situation at work, can you leave town for a few days, maybe more?"

I answer, "No way, but if I absolutely have to go out there, I'll fake an injury or something."

Dealer turns and says, "How about you, Hillbilly?"

As he smiles, Hillbilly replies, "You can count me in!"

Then Crazy George says, "I'll go with Hillbilly. Clutch, you sit this one out."

I nod my head in agreement. To be honest about it, I'm glad I'm not going, for two reasons: Nikkei and God.

Dealer looks at Hillbilly and says, "Okay, it's settled, you and Crazy George will fly out there tomorrow. We have two other teams flying in, and I'm driving up north tonight to see Bones, then me and Offal will fly out in two days. Clutch, you're gonna have to get them some money from your Chapter's slush fund, okay?"

I say, "No problem, there's plenty of that!"

Finally Dealer says, "Okay then, gentlemen, start your engines!" That is his way of saying we're done with the meeting and it's time to leave.

As we walk to our cars, Hillbilly looks at me and says, "Have gun, will travel!" Followed by a slight smile and a wink. I can see the warrior inside of him has surfaced and is in his element!

On my way home I'm thinking how happy I am I'm not going out there to Take Care of Business, because I want to stay with Nikkei and keep my deal with God. But at the same time, I'm feeling terribly guilty that I'm letting my Club down by not going! But I did not lie; I really can't leave work for any extended period of time right now. Nevertheless; I feel like a punk that just 'betrayed' his Brothers! It weighs very heavily on my heart. I'm thinking, something has to break.

CHAPTER TWENTY-ONE

DEATH DOES COME IN THREES

It's been two days since Hillbilly and Crazy George flew out of town. Offal, a Goon from the Mother Chapter, and Dealer left together yesterday. I hope they're all doing okay. I'm sitting in a small bar a few blocks from where I work. At lunch break today Heavy told me to meet him here; he seemed weird, like he was worried or something. He's been brokenhearted ever since his daughter's murder, but today he seemed worse. Between thinking about our Goon Squad out west and worrying about Nikkei and wondering if Heavy is okay, I didn't get anything done at work today. Such is life!

Heavy enters the bar and slowly approaches the table where I sit and wait. He still wears that weird, consumed look on his face; it's somewhat worrisome but mostly blank, almost zombie like. He sits down with me and monotonically says, "Clutch, we go back a long way together, and I know we both love and respect each other and only want what's best for the Club, and I trust you and your instincts. Two detectives came to my house last night. They said they are doing some follow-up investigating on Sally's murder. You know I'm hip to cop games, and you know, I know how BET loves to Stir the Pot. So I figured that's who sent them. They came right out and said they can't prove Brock killed Sally, but they believe he did. I figured they were just trying to start trouble, but I played along anyhow. I asked why they think that, and after they told me, I'm starting to believe them. So much of Brock's story never made any sense to me anyhow, but after the cops connected all the dots, it's pretty hard not to believe he did it!"

I just sit and listen as he continues, but he is now emotionally charged. "Ya know, Clutch, I loved her mother 100 percent! After she died, Sally was the only thing I had left on that side of my life. I ain't kidding. If you had known her mother, you would see Sally and her were more like twins than mother and daughter! Everything Sally would say or do would remind me of her mother. When Sally got shot, it was just like her mother dying all over again, but worse, coz now they're both gone, and I no longer have either!"

Tears, one by one, grow from Heavy's saddened eyes then liberally roll down his puffy, sorrow-filled cheeks; he's doing his best to stop them, but to little avail. I struggle but can no longer hold back. His tears are too contagious; they begin drawing tears from my eyes also! It's difficult for me to see a Brother in such pain; I'm constantly wiping my eyes with my shirt sleeve as I try to stay focused on what Heavy is saying. It's obvious he is grieving terribly. What's worse, I think Brock did it also, and I feel as if I'm betraying Heavy by not telling him. I don't because I'm afraid if Heavy thinks for sure that Brock killed Sally, he'll no doubt go on a rampage and attack Brock. I'm afraid he'll end up in jail and have the Club after him ta'boot. In the past, the consequences of Heavy's rage have cost him dearly. Even though Weird Sally was his biological daughter, he must put the Club first, so if he fucks with Brock too much he could be Eighty-Sixed from our Club.

Even with all the fear I harbor for Heavy's protection, after listening to him for so long, I feel as if I do not say something, I'm not being loyal to him. Still feeling guilty from not going out west with Hillbilly, and feeling as if I'm betraying my oath of Brotherhood by not telling Heavy what I know, I decide to tell him everything! I want to tell him; 'I too believe Brock killed your daughter!' Also, I want to tell Heavy everything the patrol cop that stopped me that day said! But, just as I begin to speak, Heavy interrupts, and the mood of our entire conversation changes.

He very specifically says, "Clutch, I trust your Gut Feelings, and if you don't think Brock had anything to do with Sally's murder, then I guess I'll just have to accept it. I think I'm just so eager to find her killer I'll believe anything anyone tells me, even if it's the cops!"

After hearing what Heavy just said, I retire the idea of telling him what I believe and retreat to my original plan of keeping what I know about Sally's murder to myself. There will be plenty of time to talk to Heavy about it once I kill Brock. Right now I must keep Heavy believing Brock is innocent of the deed so he doesn't get himself in trouble with the Club.

Heavy and I sit and talk another hour or so, and when I'm sure his emotions are calm I suggest we both go home and call it a night. I must spend all my time the Club hasn't consumed with Nikkei.

Heavy gives me a strong hug and says, "I love you, Bro, I always knew you'd turn out alright!"

On my ride home I'm feeling pretty good about Heavy. I think everything is going to work out all right—I hope!

Heavy is smart as hell; he can usually see straight through any Bullshit story someone is telling him. One thing for sure, right now he's thinking I know more about Sally's death than I'm saying. So he drives his truck over to Brock's house to do a little snooping around on his own!

This can be very bad. If he fucks with Brock, as a President, Brock can have him thrown out of our Club. Under no circumstances can a Brother go against another Brother for something outside Club business, not even if it's because Brock killed his Daughter. If Heavy yells some, maybe stomps around a little, that's different. He could even get away with punching Brock in the nose. There would be big problems over something like that but Heavy wouldn't be Booted from our Club over it! But if Heavy goes nuts over there tonight, Brock will no doubt do everything in his power to have Heavy Rat-Packed then Eighty-Sixed from our Club. This could be bad.

At the very second I'm pulling into my long driveway, Heavy is pulling into Brock's drive. As I'm opening my door and entering my house, forty miles away, Brock is opening his door and welcoming Heavy into his house!

The parallel between our time sequence is ironic because I'm entering a house secure in the knowledge its occupant, Nikkei, is loyal to me. She is one I can trust and one I love. So my night has come to a safe end. Heavy, on the other hand, at the exact same time is entering into a house of unknown. Although Brock and Heavy wear the same Patch and are supposed to share Brotherhood, trust, and love. Heavy knows that's not true and he must be very careful. So his night has not come to a safe end. His night is just beginning, and the memory of this night will ride with us forever!

Heavy gives Brock a hug and enters the house. The small living room is clouded with marijuana smoke. Big Bart is sitting back in a recliner chair; he doesn't bother standing to greet Heavy, rather extends his arm, offering Heavy a lit joint and says, "Here ya go, Bro . . . . you'll like this shit. Just came in from Panama. It's Primo!"

Heavy politely declines and takes a seat on the couch.

Brock is extremely stoned. He is giggling as he kneels down to look through a wooden orange crate full of record albums.

Heavy asks, "Is anyone else here?"

Once again Brock giggles as he turns to Heavy and answers, "Nope, just you, me, Bart, and the Ghost of Sally! She's been floating around here all day . . . . probably wants Fucked! If she's half as good as a ghost as she was as a Mama, that's good enough for me! Coz one thing for sure, Sally never was a Dead-Fuck!"

Big Bart is puffing on a joint when Brock says that. He immediately sits forward letting out a large cough as he gags; all the smoke he was holding exhales at once. A huge cloud of smoke explodes from his mouth; he tries to hold it back by cupping his hand over his mouth, but his coughing is too intense. He surrenders and then holds his chest and laughs as he coughs more; his eyes are watering.

What a terribly disrespectful thing to say, especially to Heavy, Sally's Father! Heavy feels what Brock just said was in poor taste, but doesn't respond. He looks at Big Bart still laughing, then back at Brock who once again has turned away from him, giggling, as he continues to flip through the record albums. Heavy is not sure, but he kind of thinks they're deliberately fucking with him.

Heavy stands and approaches a large broken vase that once belonged to his wife. After his wife died, Sally claimed it for her own, but only after Heavy made her swear she would protect it with her life. Sally had no problem agreeing to his conditions, for she too loved that vase and treasured its memories as much as Heavy himself. Saddened by the vase's condition, Heavy asked, "Brock, what the fuck happened to Sally's vase?"

Once again Brock laughs and says, "Bart used it as a Beer Mug and dropped it when he was staggering drunk. No problem. It makes a perfect ashtray now!"

This sends a surge of anger through Heavy. The hair on the back of his neck stands-up, but he visually shows no outward signs of anger; instead, he simply shrugs his shoulders and calmly replies, "Oh . . . . well, if you don't mind, I'll take it with me when I leave . . . . and I'll owe ya an ashtray!"

Heavy forces out a slight grin and a weak chuckle, then returns to his seat.

Brock says, "Suit yourself, Bro, what's mine is yours!"

Brock doesn't like Heavy at all. Actually, Brock doesn't technically like or dislike anybody! He simply, narcissistically gauges people by how much he can or can't use them. That dictates how much he likes or dislikes them. Heavy is nobody's Patsy, and Brock has never been able to successfully manipulate him in any way; therefore, Brock does not like him. But even worse, Heavy and I have a tight bond and share much love, so Brock sees that as a bad thing and therefore views Heavy as a threat.

Brock's devious brain begins scheming one hundred miles per hour. He sees Heavy being in his house as an opportunity—an opportunity he must seize upon. He mustn't let this chance get away; he figures he must capitalize on it immediately. He thinks this is a perfect time to play with Heavy's emotions over Weird Sally's death enough so that Heavy will react violently against him, then Brock can finally have him Eighty-Sixed from the Club. This is the 'Big-One' Brock's been waiting for!

Although Heavy is tough as nails, and in the Heavyweight category and could easily crush Brock's cranium, Brock is not worried in the least, not with Big Bart sitting there. Between the two of them, Heavy doesn't stand a chance. And once it begins, Brock plans to Thump Heavy! Being Thumped is what we call it when a man is beaten almost to death. When a Thumped individual does recover, they'll never be the same. They may have a speech impediment; maybe they'll walk funny, perhaps slobber a lot. One thing for sure, after a Good Thumpin', they all have some level of Brain Damage. But what Brock and Big Bart haven't considered is, if this is what they do to Heavy tonight, Club or no Club, I will go and kill them both!

So Brock begins carefully and tactfully taunting Heavy. He very skillfully maneuvers every conversation into Sally being dead. He knows this is the area where Heavy is most vulnerable. Well, guess what? Heavy is not so easily victimized. As I've said before, 'Heavy is extremely intelligent,' he's very smart and sees exactly what ol' Brock is up to. So he is determined not to allow Brock to Rattle his Cage. He is here on a mission, a mission to try and figure out if

Brock had anything to do with Sally's murder, and always defaults back to that mission any time Brock approaches a Sore Spot in their conversation. His mission is why he is here, and it keeps him focused and out of reach from Brock's insidious head games designed to provoke a violent reaction from him.

Brock always expected that, sooner or later, Heavy would show up pumping him for information about Sally. He has formulated an array of well-rehearsed answers to a broad range of questions he figures Heavy is sure to ask. He doesn't want to be caught off guard. But tonight is different. Tonight Brock would like Heavy to somewhat believe he killed his daughter, because he thinks that's one sure way to provoke a violent response from an already emotionally challenged Heavy. Brock is now in his element. This is what he does best, and he loves doing it!

Brock turns to Heavy, adopting a concerned look and says, "Heavy, I had a couple boxes of Sally's stuff. But because of the way she was, I figured you wouldn't have wanted any of it, so I threw all of it in the trash!"

He then shrugs his shoulders and squeezes out a smirk.

Angered, Heavy loudly snaps back, "What the fuck is that supposed to mean?"

Brock is pleased by Heavy's response, but far from appeased. He has an agenda tonight and will not stop until he has his way with Heavy. He knows he hit a nerve, and like a boxer that has his opponent On the Ropes, Brock relentlessly continues his advance, invading Heavy's soul where the love for his late daughter resides. But first he must reassure Heavy that none of this is contrived. He wants to relax Heavy so Heavy will lower his guard!

"Whoa, Heavy, I didn't mean any disrespect!"

Brock says with a sneaky grin as he leans back, raising both arms high into the air, hands flat, and palms out. "I just meant she was a little on the weird side. I'm sorry!"

Brock momentarily retreats back a step as he prepares himself for the next assault. He's starting out slow but intends to escalate his attack on Heavy until Heavy snaps.

Heavy's blood pressure just ratcheted up a notch. But he is wise to Brock's efforts to rattle him and is doing everything possible to combat his growing anger. He is trying to stay focused on his mission, but he can feel the burning desire to get up and pound the fuck out of Brock's head. Heavy is smart enough to see for the first time since he arrived that Big Bart, now sitting forward, is obviously preparing to jump on him if and when he jumps on Brock. Now he is wondering if this isn't what all of this is about; to antagonize him to the point he responds violently so Brock and Big Bart can give him a Thumpin'.

Now Heavy begins to zero in on Brock. He smiles and politely asks, "Brock, the night Sally was shot, had you two gone out for dinner earlier?"

The detectives have already informed Heavy that in Brock's statement he said Sally and he ordered in Chinese food, and when the knock came on the door, the Chinese food is what she thought it was, via a delivery boy. But when she opened the door . . . . Ka-Boom! The cops said the restaurant had no record of a delivery to that address, not that night, or in fact, ever!

Brock nervously stands and anxiously goes to the refrigerator for a beer. He opens the beer and, with his back to Heavy, takes a couple of long drinks before turning around to answer. It is obvious to Heavy his question rattled Brock, and Brock is retreating to his Corner to regroup his thoughts. Finally, Brock turns and says, "No way Bro, her and me were in for the night. We didn't want to go out so we ordered in Chinese from that little Gook Joint down the road!"

Heavy had already heard that story secondhand from many others, but this is the first time Brock had personally told him the lie.

Sally hated Chinese food, and as her father, Heavy knows she would never have ordered any for herself, yet Brock contends she did.

Now each one, both Heavy and Brock, have scored a hit on the other, and they both persistently continue to advance their agendas.

Heavy can see his question shook Brock a little, but before he can land another hit, Brock says, "Heavy, did you know Sally had a Heroin addiction and what she was doing to support it?"

With this question, Heavy's temper flares, and as his anger spikes, he gives out an emotional response.

"That was a long time ago . . . . Asshole!" he loudly shouts.

"Remember who you're talking to . . . . Dickhead!" Brock hatefully yells back as he stands and points to the Pres Patch sewn on his Colors.

The small room now becomes tense and totally silent. Heavy jumps up and faces Brock. Big Bart stands and calmly stretches as he sizes up Heavy; he deliberately stays back, out of Heavy's sight. Heavy steps up nose to nose with Brock; they both angrily stare into each other's eyes for a long time. Then finally Heavy says, "I'm sorry, Brock! That was out of line, forgive me!"

Heavy meant none of what he just said to Brock; it was orchestrated as a deterrent to mask the anger now boiling in his soul. He knows if he starts punching on Brock his mission will be over, so his apology is a nice tactical move on his part and a small defeat for Brock. But it's not over yet! Brock doesn't want to take a chance on Heavy leaving, so he opens three beers and proposes to toast to the Club and Brotherhood. Heavy could never turn that one down; it would be a total insult to our Club and all our Brothers. So all three stand and toast the Club; the room calms as they return to their seats.

When Brock is sure he has once again regained control of the situation, he continues his attack. "Heavy, you know I thought the world of Sally, don't ya? Life was good between us, she loved it here!"

Brock is trying to cover up the fact that Sally had a horrible last couple of days living with him.

Heavy very methodically analyzes Brock's every word. What Brock doesn't know is, Sally called Heavy one day before she was murdered and told him she was moving out the following day, the day she was shot. Now that Heavy just snagged Brock in a lie, he questions why Brock is lying; Just because Brock is lying doesn't mean he killed Sally. On the other hand, the lie could be there in an attempt to cover up killing Sally.

Big Bart has been unusually quiet through all of this drama. Heavy is thinking that's because Bart wants him to forget he's there and then if he hits Brock, Bart will have the element of surprise when Double-Teaming him.

Big Bart knows Heavy will not be easy to take down. So he is quietly lurking in the dark corners of this dramatic confrontation. He is hoping by remaining anonymous, Heavy will stay focused on Brock and forget about him. He thinks Heavy is more likely to attack Brock if he believes it's only going to be one-on-one. Big Bart wants Heavy to hit Brock so he can help Brock take Heavy down. But Heavy sees exactly what Big Bart is up to and is only pretending to have forgotten about Big Bart. He figures if this thing does get out of hand and a fight does happen, the first punch

he's going to throw will be a sucker punch into Bart's nose. Big
Bart shouldn't be expecting it as long as Heavy can convince him
he's focused 100 percent on Brock. Heavy is hopeful one sucker
punch will bring Big Bart down! Heavy is an expert at knocking
people out with only one punch. That's always been his first line of
defense, but he knows if he doesn't succeed with that first punch,
he is too big and broad shouldered to move quickly while fighting
two people, and therefore will probably lose the fight. Heavy is
built like a giant rectangle, like a huge concrete cinder block with
a head, arms and legs! If he lands a direct punch, no doubt Bart is
going down for the count. But if he misses, Heavy is too slow and
too muscle bound to fight two guys.

Brock carefully tells Heavy about some changes he made on
the Harley he took from Smack after Smack was Eighty Sixed from
the Club. Smack is the Brother that turned State's Evidence on
two Bikers for kidnapping him. Although off the Sally Subject,
it's a good move for Brock; there were many arguments between
him and Heavy over that bike, much Bad Blood. Heavy feels Brock
never paid for the bike and Brock is obviously rubbing it in. Now
Heavy's anger climbs even higher; he's much madder and Brock
knows it. Now that Heavy's anger has once again surged, Brock
skillfully shifts the conversation back to Sally.

"Yeah, I miss Sally a lot. I think of her often. Sometimes I forget
she's gone until I get home to an empty house. I look around and
just before I call her name, I remember she's dead! Yeah, that's
kind of depressing. She was a good woman, a good cook, and a
great fuck! But there are many things about her I do not miss.
Like when she would get drunk and talk down the Club! Trust me,
Heavy, there were many nights when, had it not been for her being
your daughter, I would have shot her dead!"

Oops! Wow, the room just got quiet! Brock just fucked up, and
Heavy knows it. Knowing he just fucked up, once again Brock
stands for a beer, but this time Brock's last statement has put
Heavy's mind into Overdrive and he won't be so easily distracted
from his mission by a Toast. Now Heavy's anger is suppressed by
the resolve of his mission.

He specifically asks, "Speaking of shooting Sally, when she was
shot, where exactly was she standing?"

Once again Brock throws his flattened hands up above his head and says, "Whoa! Hey! I'm sorry, Bro . . . that was a dumb thing to say. It was only a figure of speech!"

But as he apologized he looks directly into Heavy's eyes and gives a deliberate wink! The wink was obviously a disclaimer to his professed innocence, one designed to provoke Heavy; one that can easily be taken as an admission of guilt.

After seeing that, Heavy nearly climbs out of his own skin. But he shows no outward signs of any additional anger. He's Holding his Mug perfectly, a worthy adversary indeed. He's not the Big Dumb Biker that Brock believes him to be.

He continues his question, "Well, Brock, exactly where was she and where was the shooter?"

Heavy stands and goes to the door that leads outside, the one Sally was shot when opening. Heavy opens the door and says, "Here, come and show me!"

Brock is growing irritated with Heavy's relentless persistence toward The Sally Murder. The truth is, Brock did kill Sally. He had been drinking heavily that entire day; he was also going on day 2 without any sleep from a long Crank Binge. For days Sally had been threatening to move out, but Brock was determined not to allow that to happen. He had blocked her from taking any of her belongings, but on this particular day, she was scared of his behavior and had planned to leave empty-handed then return on a later day to get her property. She figured as long as Brock was this high, he would never let her take any of her belongings and probably would try to stop her from leaving also. Her plan was not to tell him she was going. She planned to just walk out, get in her car, and leave. She planned to go straight to Heavy's house, then call Brock later when she knew she was safe. But Brock became suspicious and an argument ensued, and then, a knock at the door! Knock, knock, knock. "Who is it?" Sally yelled through the closed door.

"Big Bart," Big Bart answered.

Brock yells from the bedroom, "Well, open the fucking door, Sally!"

Sally only opens the door a very small amount; she stands behind the slightly cracked door as she peeks around, and there stood Big Bart holding a twelve gauge Pump shotgun. He entered the small living room, the shotgun strung over his shoulder. He was bringing it as a gift for Brock. It was a gun that had never been registered, and for that reason, a real value to an Outlaw Biker.

Brock and Bart sat drinking beer for hours, yelling for Sally to bring more whenever empty. Brock would yell, "More beer, Bitch!" After a long time, Sally decided she had had enough of Brock's insistence to dominate and humiliate her.

She finally said, "Fuck you, Brock! Get your own fucking Beer!"

She headed for the door to leave once and for all. Brock sprang to his feet, grabbing the shotgun as he did, then blocked the door by standing between it and her. Big Bart, thinking this was amusing, sat in the recliner, laughing.

After debating with Sally for a long while, Brock finally opened the door and stepped out, saying, "If you try to leave here, Sally, I will blow your fucking head off!" as he leveled the shotgun.

Never believing he would, Sally rebutted, "Fuck you, Brock! I'm not afraid of you!"

At first Brock was only bluffing, but when Sally said that, his drunken anger, spurred by no sleep during his two day Crank Binge, destroyed his logic as well as his ability to reason, and as she was attempting to leave . . . . Ka-Boom! Brock gave her one in the gut and Sally died instantly.

Brock and Big Bart cleaned the house, removing all drugs and any illegal firearms, and then Big Bart took the gun that killed Weird Sally and left. Next, Brock called his attorney who came immediately. He and Brock talked for a long time, and once they coordinated Brock's explanation of the killing by setting the proper time sequences and logistics, Brock called the police. When the police arrived and Brock gave his detailed story, they found it to be surprisingly flawless. Although they don't believe him, there is not enough evidence to charge Brock with a crime.

Once again, but this time in a more demanding voice, Heavy says, "Well, come and show me exactly where my daughter was standing when she was shot! Show me where the shooter was, Brock!"

Brock's temper is growing from Heavy's insistent tone of voice. He loudly answers, "All right!" as he walks to the door and stands beside Heavy. Brock is now thinking no way will Heavy ever get out of here without a hard Thumpin', so he is no longer being hospitable.

"Look!" Brock disrespectfully says as he slams the door shut, "Someone knocked on this door!" Just to be an Asshole, Brock loudly pounds three times on the door with his fist! Boom! Boom! Boom! Then turns to Heavy and says, "We thought it was the delivery boy bringing our Chinese food, so Sally opened the door and Bang! That was it, she was dead! I was in the bathroom when this happened!"

Heavy carefully looks at the door and where the shooter had to have been standing, then positions himself where Sally would have had to have been. He does this several times, opening the door, closing, then reopening it, looking outside and inside, methodically challenging the logistic formula of her murder, Brock's version. Brock is standing back watching Heavy reenact Sally's murder; he is occasionally looking at Big Bart and nodding toward Heavy, signaling his disgust!

Finally Heavy says, "Okay, Brock, sorry for all the questions. I just wanted to get it in my head how my only daughter was murdered. I got a fifth of Jack Daniels in my truck; I think I'll go get it. I need a couple stiff shots! We'll all do another toast to our Club . . . . and then one to Sally!"

With his head hung low, Heavy somberly turns and quietly goes to his truck, carefully closing the door behind him.

Brock quickly moves to Big Bart and says, "When that Big Piece of Shit returns, you and I are going to Thump the living fuck out of him! You got it?"

Bart smiles and says, "Cool, I've been waiting a long time for this!"

Brock goes to the bathroom and stands in front of the commode, loudly pissing. Big Bart leans back in the recliner rubbing his two hands together, eagerly awaiting Heavy's return!

Knock, Knock, Knock. "It's Heavy . . . . Open the fucking door!"

Big Bart stands, and as he's walking to the door, leans into the hallway leading to the bathroom where Brock is still loudly pissing and says, "It's Party Time!" He goes to the door then sharply opens it, and there stands Heavy holding a sawed-off twelve gauge pump shotgun, exactly what they used to kill his daughter!

Bart looks at him confused, but before he can say anything, Heavy lowers the gun and lets him have one in the chest. Ka-Boom! A twelve gauge deer slug, point-blank, hits him directly in the heart, blowing it apart. Big Bart throws his hands high in the air as he falls backward, smashing the coffee table into small pieces. Brock is still holding his dick pissing. He thought he would be beating on Heavy soon; instead, Heavy is stepping over Big Bart's bloody lifeless body looking for him. Brock has a .357 Magnum sitting on the top of the toilet; he drops his dick and grabs the pistol, uncontrollably urinating all over himself and the floor. Heavy is looking around the house trying to figure out where Brock is. Suddenly, Brock bursts out of the bathroom and shoots Heavy. Boom! Heavy falls backward, tripping over Bart's dead body. Brock fires two more rounds. Boom! Boom! But misses Heavy with each shot. Both rounds hit Big Bart, one in the head and one in the neck. Heavy rolls toward the kitchen out of Brock's view then gets back on his feet. Just as Brock begins charging down the hallway toward him, Heavy loudly yells, "This one's for Sally" as he jumps out face-to-face with Brock then let go with a single shot, hitting Brock right between the eyes. Ka-Boom! Another deer slug, point-blank! Brain Matter is splattered all over the walls. Brock goes down hard, but as he does, he fires one more round, hitting nothing more than the wall. His body flies backward, busting through the bathroom door and coming to rest half in and half out of the bathroom, his head only inches from the toilet he was pissing in only a few seconds ago. His cheek is lying in his own puddle of urine, now being mixed with an endless pool of his blood.

Heavy slowly walks up and stands over Brock's lifeless body, his smoking shotgun still held at the ready. He looks at Brock's mutilated head and grins, then turns to leave. On his way out, as he's stepping over Big Bart, he reaches out, takes his wife's broken vase and says, "I don't think you'll be needing an ashtray!"

Brock had a genius for scheming and playing politics and that would have been fine, but he was narcissistic and never understood Brotherhood. So ultimately he used his genius for scheming and politics to cover up the fact that he didn't practice Brotherhood. Although he made it far in my Club, it was only a matter of time before this was going to happen. This Club is full of the most Hard-Core 1% Outlaw Bikers in the World. The only way someone can make it in our Club is through pure honesty and pure love. Brock exercised none of these traits; he had brains; in fact, they're now spread all over his hallway. But with all his brains, he underestimated Heavy.

As Heavy stood in that doorway surveying Sally's murder site, he listened to Brock's explanation of how Sally was shot. Number one, Weird Sally would have never eaten Chinese food. That, along with many other discrepancies told Heavy Brock was probably lying, and Heavy was beginning to believe Brock had only one reason for lying—to cover up killing Sally. But when Brock told Heavy where Sally was standing when she was shot, Heavy knew it was a lie. He had personally taught her to never stand in front of a door when opening it. Always keep the door between her and the person she's opening it for, step backwards, following the door as it opens, and then only peek your head slightly around to look and talk. Heavy drilled this into Sally the entire time she was growing up, along with many other Streetwise defensive tactics. So after looking at the door and hearing Brock's lies, Heavy knew once and for all Brock killed Sally, and then he responded.

Brock always felt as if Heavy was the 'Big and Dumb' type, but that's only because Heavy never felt the need to show him otherwise. Heavy's intellect was always playing 'possum around Brock, so Brock never realized just how smart Heavy was. Had Brock been a true Brother, he would have known Heavy for what he really is, and therefore never underestimated him. Of course, had he been a true Brother, none of this would have happened.

It's somewhat funny because, first, we lost Fingers and now Big Bart and Brock. It would seem that maybe 'Death Does Come in Threes.'

Chapter Twenty-Two

THE LAST CHAPTER

I'm lying in bed with Nikkei when I hear Heavy yelling through the intercom, telling me to "Open the Fuckin' gate!" I know from the sound of his voice and the time of night that there is something seriously wrong. So I grab my gun and go down to let him in; when I get there I see blood everywhere.

"Heavy!" I shout. "What the fuck happened?"

He says, "I killed Brock and Big Bart!"

Upon hearing that, I fell back into the gate and then staggered a couple of steps and sat down in the driveway.

I look up at Heavy and say, "Heavy, did anyone see you do it?"

He softly answers, "I don't think so."

It is easy to see this is not the time or place for a long discussion, so I help him to the house and Nikkei begins to nurse his wound. He was hit in the shoulder and the bullet passed through, never hitting any bones. When I'm sure he's okay and the bleeding has stopped, I put Heavy's truck in the back of our old barn, hiding it from sight. After that and while I'm in this portion of the barn, I dig up a gun I have stashed. It's the gun I took from the cop's apartment, the cop that stole Fingers' Colors; then I ride to Brock's house. When I arrive everything looks to be fine, until I open the door. Man, Heavy did a number on both of them! One thing for sure, Brock won't be bothering me anymore! Brock's head looks like a Mack truck drove through it! And in a humiliating fashion, what's left of Brock's head is laying on the bathroom floor touching the toilet, and his dick is partially hanging out of his Levis. This makes no sense to me, but I really don't have time to be analyzing what may have happened here! So I carefully shake the cop's pistol from the plastic bag I've been storing it in and let it fall to the floor, then leave. I hope it's that simple; we have to convince the cops as well as the Club this had nothing to do with Heavy.

I drive straight home and find Heavy in great pain, but he can't go to the hospital because a gunshot wound must be reported to the police. There is a doctor the Club has used in the past; he'll patch up bullet wounds and not report them if he's paid well enough. I have plenty of cash here and can take Heavy there, but I don't know that doctor, and I don't want to involve the Club. If they find out Heavy was shot on the same night as Brock and Big Bart, then Heavy will probably be blamed.

There is also a problem with the two detectives that stirred the pot with Heavy. It will not be hard for them to figure out that one day after they told a Hard-Core One Percent Biker that Brock is the one who killed his daughter and then Brock ends up with a ten-inch hole through his head, who did it! Either way, with the cops or the Club, this could be bad.

I feel like praying. It worked with Nikkei, but I'm not so sure God will help me cover up a double homicide!

But I do it anyway. I simply ask God to 'Help Heavy.'

Here is my plan, it's simple. Get Heavy patched up, he can stay out here with Nikkei and me for a while and then take it as it comes. I think my pull as a Goon can convince the Club the same assassin that shot Sally was originally there to kill Brock; it looks like he came back and finished the job. That's pretty much the popular opinion anyhow, so in that respect, Brock only fucked himself. His story was, 'the person who shot Weird Sally was there for him.' And when the cops find out one of their own guy's fingerprints are all over a gun found at the murder scene, they won't be too eager to pursue the investigation. I don't think Hillbilly will have a problem with what Heavy did; he and I were planning the same thing. If Crazy George suspects Heavy, Hillbilly can make it okay with him. And Dealer has been more or less in limbo on the entire Brock issue. Maybe everything will work out—I hope!

Boy, Ol' Nikkei Snapped-to when she saw Heavy had been shot. Him and her go back as far as him and I. She's been nursing and mothering him for three days now. It turns out the bullet wound was nowhere near as bad as we first thought. Nikkei has a stash pile of penicillin she got from her mother. With that, some rubbing alcohol, and lots of 'Tender Loving Care' Heavy is doing quite well. In fact, I've been jokingly shaking my head in disgust anytime I walk through the living room and see him propped up on the couch with Nikkei spoon-feeding him homemade chicken noodle soup. He just sits-back and smiles. He loves it!

It's been a week since Brock's murder. Heavy has plenty of vacation time built up at work; he's been at my house the entire time. Thanks to Nikkei, he's doing fine. She doesn't know for a fact that he killed Brock, but she does know Brock is dead, and she hasn't shed so much as a single tear over his sudden demise!

In fact, I believe it's safe to say she's quite pleased over the news of Brock's abrupt departure from this world. I figure she suspects Heavy was either in a shoot-out defending Brock or in a shoot-out against Brock. And if so, the one who killed him and Big Bart, because Heavy showed up that same night with a bullet wound, but she hasn't said a word about any of it. She still does not know who Big Bart is by name. She doesn't know he's the one Brock had guarding her at the cabin, the man she hates and has sworn to kill. And I have no plans to ever tell her.

Well, Nikkei hasn't asked any questions about Brock's murder; but the Club sure has. There are plenty of rumors going around, much suspicion, and a lot of talk. Our Club stretches far across the United States; many Brothers from Chapters far away may have met Brock at a National Run or such, but most only know of him as a Member and a President by name only. Very few knew Brock as the conniving, narcissistic prick he truly was; most Brothers only know he was a Brother who was murdered. And for that reason, they're all looking for payback; tremendous anger abounds.

We haven't heard anything from the cops, but you can bet they're lurking in the shadows, along with BET. They know Brock's .357 had been fired four times, so just in case, they've no doubt checked all the hospitals to see if he hit his assassin. They must be scratching their heads over Big Bart having been hit by two of those rounds. One thing for sure, they must be wondering what happened to Heavy. He just up and vanished from their radar!

Hillbilly has returned from Out West and unexpectedly showed up here about an hour ago. He has a pretty good idea about what actually happened to Brock and has been talking with Heavy ever since he arrived. But when he first showed up, he thought I was behind the double murder. Nikkei and I are sitting outside on the porch swing, letting them have their space. To me there's no problem; we are all Brothers and share much love. I will not lie to Hillbilly, and I know he needs to hear the entire story in order to help. Hopefully Heavy can appease Hillbilly's appetite in his quest for the truth, and then Hillbilly and me will never have to openly discuss it.

Brock and Big Bart were buried with full Club honors a few days back. Hillbilly, Dealer, Offal, and Crazy George missed the funeral; they were all still away taking care of business. Heavy showed up at the funeral but left immediately on an emergency; nobody knows what that emergency was. The truth is, Heavy still hasn't healed, and therefore, he and I decided it would not be smart for him to show up with a bullet hole through his shoulder. I'm sure if any of the Brothers noticed him favoring his shoulder or arm, many questions would have been asked. Also, it would not be smart if he didn't show up at all. So showing up and then immediately leaving was the answer. There's also too many cops wondering where he's been, so a personal appearance, even if it was only for a short period of time, shows he's not hiding from anything or anyone.

It's never safe to talk in a house, so after fifteen or twenty minutes, Hillbilly and Heavy take a long stroll through the woods. I know Heavy is now telling Hillbilly everything that happened and why. They return from their walk through the woods with no hostilities toward one other or about the situation. Hillbilly never tells Heavy he and I were planning to kill Brock also, and Hillbilly never mentions a word to me about Brock's death. It's always best if we never say a word to anyone about anything unless it's 100 percent necessary. I already know what happened to Brock, and Hillbilly has to know I do, so it would not be smart for him and me to discuss it any further!

However, there is one loose end that Hillbilly, Heavy, and I tie up, and that happens when Hillbilly throws a set of keys at me. Surprised, and not knowing what he threw, I quickly snag the flying object from mid-air and examine it closely.

"What's this?" I ask.

Hillbilly replies, "That, Clutch, is your Brother's key chain!"

I reexamine the keys then say, "You're right, these are his. What are you doing with Kebus's keys?"

Hillbilly answers, "Heavy gave them to me. He found them in a vase he took from you know whose house! I knew instantly whose they were because I had the Death Head that's attached to the key ring custom made. It's one of four in the word. I kept one for myself, then gave one to Kebus, Heavy, and Dealer for a job we did as Goons years ago. I know Kebus always kept his on this key chain!"

I ask Heavy, "How did they come to end up in that vase?"

He said, "The only thing I can figure is, after the Feds raided the Clubhouse in the city and Kebus was locked up, I personally sent Brock in there to snoop around and pick up a few things I had stashed in the hall closet. He was just a Prospect then and must have found the key chain and figured he needed it more than Kebus, that thieving little bastard!"

Hillbilly laughs and says, "Now, now, we mustn't talk bad about the Dead, even if it's Brock . . . . Rest In Pieces!"

I smile and say, "Well, finally, I never did understand how Brock ended up with a key to my gate, and that always tormented me!"

Hillbilly gives Heavy first and then me, each a strong hug. He says, "Good-bye, Bros, I love you both very much!" But before starting his bike to leave, he also gives Nikkei a tight hug followed by a kiss on her forehead, and then he says, "Thanks for nursing my valued Brother back to strength!"

It seems all kinds of loose ends are coming together, and all kinds of problems are solving themselves. It turns out the gun I planted at Brock's murder site was confiscated by the police during a drug raid one year earlier, then stolen from the police evidence vault. Theft of confiscated weapons and drugs has been an ongoing problem in that police department. Not to mention a real embarrassment for the Sheriff who has to worry about his reelection. Now the cop I took it from has to explain how and why it showed up at the scene of a double homicide with his fingerprints all over it. Bingo! Isn't payback a bitch? He has been quietly dismissed from duty. The papers have been unusually quiet about Brock's murder and any ongoing investigations. As long as the cops figure one of their own was somehow involved, I'm sure the entire investigation will go quietly to the wayside.

Our Club is convinced that cop had something to do with Brock's murder also. There have been many, many rumors going around the police department to that effect. And our inside snitches keep us very well informed on those kinds of issues. That cop had a brother that was Hanging Around our rival Motorcycle Club years ago and did some time in the State Penn over illegal gun sales with that club. That's perfect for us; it couldn't have worked out any better had we planned it that way. Now that cop's supervisors suspect it's possible he had some involvement also. But that really does parallel with the emotional hatred he showed toward our Club. Remember, he's the one that bashed out the teeth from one of our Club's Hang-Around's mouth. Maybe he is involved with our rival Club. Who knows? Oh well, nevertheless, both Brock and the cop deserve what they got. Now that the cop has lost his job and the protection that comes along with being a cop, our Club can finish him off . . . . "You don't fuck with our Colors!"

I haven't technically lied to my Club about what really happened to Brock. I just haven't offered any additional information.

Being untruthful to my Club is not what I'm about. I love and worship pure honesty among all my Brothers. But the situation with Brock's murder and Heavy's involvement is different. I'm not trying to twist things around so that everything fits into a perfect mold created by my own design. But I'll go to my grave knowing the only way I could protect my Club from Brock was to see him dead by Heavy's hand, my hand, or anybody else's for that matter. Dead is dead! I know for a fact, Heavy is only out for the good of our Club, and Brock's insidious, narcissistic ways were hard to detect because of his genius for playing politics. And I'm sure he did not care one iota about my Club, only about what appeased his lust for self-gratification; even if that meant stomping on a few Brothers' toes along the way. So Heavy saved us from him. Wrong or not, I support Heavy to the end over what he did to Brock. And if an occasional 'White Lie' to my Club helps protect him, then So Be It.

One thing for sure, you've heard me say "Brock was not a true Biker!" Well, one easy way to gauge that is simply; how much did he ride? Seems elementary, but that's what Bikers do. After all, riding is the root cause for being a Biker, and he did very little riding. Heavy, Brock's killer, on the other hand, is always on his Harley. In fact, even though his Chapter is on the far side of this huge city, many miles from my house, he always makes it out to my farm on his Putt, wanting to Take-a-spin with me.

The problem I recently accrued is, I no longer have a fucking motorcycle! Mine was shot out from underneath me! But that changed, and this is how and what my beloved Club did for me—God bless 'em all.

After my shooting on the bridge, the police wanted to hold my bike as evidence; I figured I might not see it again for a year or so. Without my knowledge it was finally released to one of our Club lawyers. He had the damage documented, mainly the bullet holes, and the bike was sent to a huge Chapter we have Back East. My bike was there for nearly a month, about the length of time it took me to recover from my bullet wounds. The day it was returned to me, I didn't expect it, and I had no way of knowing it was going to be returned or what my Club had done to it.

It started out a while back when Hillbilly invited Nikkei and me to Papa Dadieo's. Hillbilly, Dealer, Crazy George, and Offal had just recently returned from Takin' Care of Business out west. When we pulled in, the place was filled with bikers from our Chapters Back East along with my Chapter and many other Brothers from everywhere in between. I knew something was up, but had no idea this was a gathering for me. After an hour or so, Hillbilly challenged me to a game of pool and I reluctantly accepted. The pool room is off to the side of a second area of the bar that is usually only opened up as an overflow room when large numbers of people are here, as it is now. We make our way through the crowded bar to the back pool room, but all the lights in that room were off.

Hillbilly said, "Shit, musta blown another breaker! Wait here, Clutch, I'll tell Papa."

As I stood in the darkened entrance way, all the Brothers crowded around me; if I wasn't a President in good standing, I probably would have figured I was going to be murdered. These guys can be a little scary that way.

Finally the lights turned on, and on top of the pool table sat my Harley! At first I didn't recognize it as mine, but I approached it anyhow, who wouldn't? The pool room was now packed with Brothers. As I slowly circled around the pool table checking out my bike, they would step back and let me pass, then press back in after I did. I couldn't fucking believe it; this is one of the nicest Harleys I've ever seen, and it's mine! Buttons had put the last paint job on my scooter; because my bike is a retired police bike he adopted a police scene. It was cop cruisers with their beacons brightly flashing, giving chase to Brothers on Harleys stretched across the entire bike, from fender to fender, beautifully crossing over the large gas tank. Now he has adopted the same theme but this paint job takes place across the bridge where I was shot. And this time my Brothers are riding along with the police, giving chase to the dudes that shot me. Everybody is shooting guns. The cops are firing from their police cruisers, the Brothers are shooting from their Harleys, and one of the bad guys is leaning from the passenger window and shooting a rifle back toward the posse. If one looks closely, it's a M16 and the dude firing it has red hair!

The entire bike has been totally rebuilt. There was concern that BET would put some sort of listening device or maybe even a tracking device in my bike, so I had planned on tearing it down and examining every nut and bolt and then totally rebuilding it anyhow, but my Brothers have done it for me. Each bullet hole has been duplicated by Button's artful hand in their exact location on the bike. He is amazing with an air brush! The bullet holes couldn't look any more realistic! But this time around, there is blood trickling from each one of them!

Finally, I stopped and stood awed, totally speechless, looking for words to express my gratitude, but could never find them. It would have been an insult for me to offer to pay for any of this, so I didn't bother with that, but I did tell all the Brothers gathered, "In celebration of the rebirth of my '65 Panhead, there will be a thank-you party at my house beginning as soon as we're done here!"

The entire room full of Brothers began howling. That party lasted for three days!

It's been a couple of months since Brock was killed. His sudden departure from this world left that Chapter without a President. At their weekly church meeting last week Heavy was voted in as the new Pres! Fuckin'-A! He has healed completely from the gunshot wound he took in the shoulder. One of his first official acts as Chapter President was to give Brock's other new bro, Road Kill, the boot. When Brock died, Road Kill took his bike, which is the same bike that Brock took from Smack when he was eighty-sixed from our Club for turning State's Evidence on the two bikers that kidnapped him. Now Heavy has taken it and is going to auction it back to the Club. The money will go to his Chapter; that's what should have happened to begin with. Heavy told Road Kill he's welcome to come back and prospect, providing he has a Harley to sign over to the Club before he begins.

When hearing Road Kill's Patch had been Pulled, Whirly went on a rampage. He came blasting into my house, yelling at the top of his lungs. He told me our Chapter must take Road Kill in as one of our own and give him his Colors back. I feared this would start-up the feud between our two Chapters all over again. Now that Brock is gone, we're starting to bury the hatchet and I want to keep it that way. I couldn't calm him down; no matter what I said, he would not give up the idea that Road Kill was fucked over by Heavy. He finally stomps out, slamming my front door, gets on his Flathead, and literally throws gravel all over my bike as he peels out of my drive! Not knowing where he is going, I jump on my Panhead and chase after him.

I swear I never realized how fast his bike is. One thing for sure, Whirly is an excellent Bike Rider. I follow him for nearly an hour. We are heading into the city; I figure he's going to Heavy's house. That could turn out bad! With the mood Whirly's in and Heavy being the type that will not take any shit from anybody, I'm thinking, I'm glad I followed. We end up on the far side of this huge city, Heavy's Chapter's territory! Whirly runs down a few side streets and pulls up to an older-type city house, one built during the housing boom following World War Two. At one time, during the late forties and early fifties, this was an upscale neighborhood built to support the mass migration of people coming to this large city for factory work. Now it's as rundown as my nerves after babysitting Whirly for the last couple of hours. I have no idea who lives here or why he picked this house to stop at.

Whirly stomps up the old wooden porch steps and pounds on the dilapidated, old rickety screen door. I'm thinking if he doesn't go a little easier on that door, he'll knock it the rest of the way off its hinges! To my surprise, Road Kill opens the door. He's not wearing a shirt; his body is inked with tattoos. He is holding a .44 magnum in his right hand; he looks at Whirly and nods, then leans his head out and looks around to see if there is anybody else with Whirly other than me. He invites us in, no hugs are exchanged. Whirly and I just enter and sit down in his living room.

This is the first time I've ever been here; it's easy to see Road Kill is a bachelor and likes to party. His old-style front porch is stacked with empty beer-can filled trash bags. Some have fallen over and emptied a large deposit of loose cans directly onto the porch, but then another trash bag has been thrown on top of that. And another and another. No shortage of aluminum here!

In the '70s beer cans had removable cap tabs that pulled completely off when opening the can. Some people drop the beer's Pull Tab back into the can to discard it. Road Kill does not. He has put them together by folding one cap over and locking it onto the next, forming an aluminum beer tab chain. His entire wall just beneath ceiling level has what seems to be an endless chain around the living room. It goes into the kitchen, then back around through a couple of bedrooms, up the steps, and who knows what happens up there. Finally it returns down the steps and comes to an end back in the living room. It had to have taken thousands of beers to create it and must have cost a fortune. He has a large sheet of plywood screwed to the wall that he obviously uses for throwing knives. A large picture of President Nixon adorns the center bull's-eye with a knife scored directly into his forehead. This house is littered with empty beer cans, empty pizza boxes, and marijuana pipes.

As I pan my head around Road Kill's house, amazed by its décor, Whirly anxiously says, "Road Kill, what happened?"

Still holding the pistol tightly gripped, Road Kill throws his arms high into the air and shouts, "They Pulled my Patch! They Pulled my Mother Fuckin' Patch!"

Whirly demands, "Who? Who pulled your Patch!"

Still screaming, Road Kill answers, "It was Heavy's idea, but it took the entire Chapter to do it!"

Road Kill points to his swollen eyes. His knuckles are busted up and he is holding his side when he talks. It's easy to see his ribs must hurt terribly; maybe they're broken? He no doubt fought with all his might to keep his Top Rocker!

Whirly stands and begins pacing around the living room. He stops briefly and asks, "Where's your bike?"

Road Kill shouts, "They took that too!" Road Kill looks directly at me, then ratchets his emotions down somewhat and asks, "Clutch,

I need help here, what can I do? I'd never quit this Club, but it's all I can do not to kill somebody over what they've done to me!"

I pause and stare at him for a long time; I look past all his cuts and bruises, past his loud, violent anger, and into his heart. There I see his real pain, and it's accompanied by great sorrow. This guy is genuinely crushed and heartbroken!

After analyzing this man's true feelings for a long time, I calmly answer, "Road Kill, do not do anything, especially anything stupid, something you'll regret! I give you my word I will go this very second and find out what's going on!"

Whirly stomps his foot down hard on the old wooden floor and yells, "Bullshit! You go get Road Kill's Colors back or I will!"

I spin toward him and angrily fire back, "Fuck You, Whirly! It's not that simple!"

Whirly continues to yell, "Then let's go talk to Bones, right fuckin' now!"

Road Kill steps up to Whirly and hooks one arm around the back of his neck, then says, "Thank you, Brother! I give you my word; I will get my Colors back!"

Whirly has his head down listening to what Road Kill is saying; he then raises it and hooks his arm around Road Kill, pressing their foreheads together tightly and says, "Fuckin' A-Right, you'll get your Colors Back!"

The mood in the room just got calmer. I ask Road Kill, "What was the deal you made for Smack's bike?"

Road Kill walks into the adjoining kitchen, opens the refrigerator, and chucks a beer to Whirly, then one to me, then opens his own, and says, "When I blew the motor in my Panhead, Brock told me he would sell me Smack's Shovelhead for three thousand dollars. He owed me a grand and I gave him a grand in cash. He gave me the pink slip and I agreed to square the rest of the debt in three months. When Brock was murdered, I went over and took the bike out of his garage because I was afraid the cops would do something with it."

I ask, "Who knows you paid two grand and only owe one thousand?"

Road Kill gives a concerned answer, "I don't know. I told Whirly I was getting the bike. We were gonna rebuild it in his basement this coming winter." Whirly finishes his beer, goes into the kitchen, and returns with a beer in each hand and one in each pocket of his Colors. He gives Road Kill and me one, then opens and chugs a beer from his pocket in seconds. He's still madder than hell. He opens the other then returns to a somewhat normal drinking pace—well, normal to him, maybe not the rest of the beer drinking world.

He smacks his lips and says, "If Road Kill says he paid two grand for that Harley, then he paid two grand for that Harley! And fuck anyone that says anything different!" Once again I give Road Kill my word that I'm going to get involved immediately. With that, I give him a strong Biker-type hug and call him My Bro.

I do the same with Whirly. He says, "We're trusting you, Clutch, get it done, fast!" With that, I leave.

I never told Nikkei I was leaving my house or what was going on. I won't talk Club business on the phone, so I call and simply say, "I love ya, and I'll see ya later on tonight!" I also call Heavy and tell him to meet me at a bar not too far from his house in twenty minutes.

I wheel into the bar's parking lot and see many Harleys from Heavy's Chapter. Heavy's pick-up truck is here with Road Kill's bike in the back of it; there's a Prospect standing close by, obviously guarding all the bikes. I enter the bar; the mood is tense. The truth is, Road Kill was given his Top Rocker fast, but the question is, did he earn it? Personally, I think he's going to be a righteous Brother. Many members of his Chapter feel the same and that he should not have had his Patch Pulled. However, many agree with Heavy. I think most of those negative opinions were spawned because Road Kill was Brock's friend and Brock was a conniving asshole, and I think Road Kill is being associated with that.

Heavy knows why I am here; he figures Whirly is on the warpath and sent me. He's right, that's exactly what happened. We talk for hours; I don't try to change his mind after seeing how strongly he supports the decision on Pulling Road Kill's Patch and knowing how stubborn and By the Book he is. He follows Club rules to the letter. One thing for sure, now that Brock is gone, our two Chapters need to heal our relationship and get back to being Brothers that wear the same Patch once again. Whirly wants me to get Road Kill's Colors back and if I cannot, then have him come over to our Chapter and give him a new set of Colors, Fully Patched! Heavy will not give his Colors back to him with the Top Rocker and I cannot intervene by even suggesting that Road Kill comes over to my Chapter. This would cause more problems and create more friction between our two already stressed Chapters.

Heavy simply tells me "If Road Kill wants to come back that's ok, but he'll have to do it in the form of a Prospect! I will honor the deal he made with Brock on the Harley, but he'll have to sign it over to the Club first. Then I'll give him his Colors back, less the Top Rocker and he'll have three months to pay the bike off, with interest!"

There's nothing I can do here. I will not go against Heavy, but Whirly's anger toward the situation will not be solved quite so easily. Fuck! I hate this kind of shit.

Something must be solved soon before Whirly does something stupid. If he does go after Heavy though, I guess I will have to back him up. I don't want to, but I will not leave my Brother Whirly standing alone. That would mean, Brock is dead but the war between our Chapters will continue. I cannot and will not leave this Club like that, in a war between two Chapters. To get out of the Club, I said I had some loose ends to tie up first. Brock was the biggest one, but Heavy solved that problem for me. Now I must solve this problem for Heavy. Once both problems are solved, my Club will benefit, and I will be that much closer to the door.

I leave quietly, but before I go, I give my Brother Heavy a strong hug and promise him I will keep an eye on Whirly. We both know when Whirly is on the warpath, look out! I don't ride home though, rather back to Road Kill's house. My plan is to calm him into accepting the situation and then hopefully he'll calm Whirly into doing the same. There is a certain amount of disgrace that follows having your Patch Pulled, but I think not so much for Road Kill. His situation is different. He's a good man that just fell into a bad situation because of Brock; this situation has come from some of the filthy residue Brock left behind.

I wheel into Road Kill's drive, and to my delight Whirly is not here. Not that I don't love Whirly and treasure his company, but it would be impossible to have the conversation with Road Kill that I intend to have if Whirly is here.

Road Kill meets me at the door and says, "Let's go across the street and have a beer . . . . I'm buying!"

We walk across the street and into a shitty little dive bar infested with old-age alcoholics that burnt out twenty-five years ago. He and I sit at a corner table, both our backs to the wall. Road Kill is still carrying his .44 magnum, and I have my .45 automatic tucked behind my back.

A couple of minutes into our discussion and a beautiful female approaches us. She says, "Hello, Road Kill, hello, Clutch." It's a girl that's been hanging around our Club for a few years and one Road Kill has been fucking on a regular basis.

Not remembering her name I say, "Hello, sweetie, good to see ya again." Road Kill tells her to get us each a cold beer and a shot of tequila, and to Keep 'em Comin'.

It turns out her father owns this dump. Besides her good looks and sweet little ass, I wonder if that's another one of Road Kill's interests in this beauty—that he drinks here for free!

The entire conversation is dominated by Road Kill. He explains how he couldn't live without flying our Colors on his back. While he believes it was wrong to have Pulled his Patch, he will accept it and go back to being a Prospect without any grudges. He says because of Brock's behavior, he understands how Brothers can group him in the same category and he will prove to all our members he is a true Brother. He tells me he had this exact conversation with Whirly and Whirly has accepted the situation and is calm now.

He says, "Whirly is the reason I feel this way. When I saw that he was ready to go to war for me, I knew then this Club is where I belong forever!"

The truth is, he always knew this Club is where he belongs, but Whirly made it more visible than ever. He brought it to the surface.

We finish up our talk and leave the bar; I'm feeling great about what Road Kill has told me. There's no doubt in my mind he'll have his Top Rocker and the title to his Harley back in no time flat. He says he will prove to all Brothers that he is worthy of wearing our Patch. As far as I'm concerned, 'that's a given!'

As I prepare to start my Harley, I turn to him and say, "One thing for sure, you won't be prospecting very hard when you're out with my Chapter! You have my word on that!"

With that we hug, and I split!

I'm feeling great during my ride home. The beauty of my life with Nikkei is now she no longer gets upset when I leave suddenly, like I just did. She has pinned all her hopes to me leaving the Club and is patiently waiting for that to happen. With each Loose End I tie, I grow closer to that day.

Another month has passed and Bones is working on a truce with the Club we're at war with. Both sides are happy with the arrangements, and it looks like we've settled a peaceful end. Both Clubs have set up communications with a few of their members to monitor the Feds. We all know BET, Biker Enforcement Team, will continue Stirring the Pot; they want us at war. One of the largest fears the government harbors is that someday all Outlaw Motorcycle Clubs will unite. Trust me, if this ever happens, it will take the U.S. Army to stop us! Right now, BET is busy Stirring the Pot in the hopes they can prevent that from ever happening. They want us forever at war with each other, in the hopes we'll do all the work for them—we'll annihilate each other. They hope that for every One Percenter killed, they can put at least one in prison for doing it!

With this treaty, all the Feds have done is made both our Clubs stronger. I think finally this will work out. Our rival club also has a thriving drug business. So as not to conflict with each other, we have set up boundaries. As long as we both keep our word, I think it can be said the "War is over!"

It's not conflict that causes War; it's the insistence to resolve conflict that causes War.

Dealer has purchased a small piece of land not far from my house. He traded his Nomad Patch for our Chapter's Bottom Rocker and is now officially a member of this Chapter. After being a Nomad for so many years, he said, this is 'The Last Chapter' he'll ever belong to. In fact, he is the new President! That was made possible because I quit the Club. It was the hardest thing I have or will ever do. When I quit, I handed my Colors to Hillbilly. He said he will personally, always, have them just in case I ever want to come back. He also said, "Clutch, you will always be my Brother, with or without our Patch!"

I kept my deal with God and worship him daily, Nikkei and me both. I was always connected to Nikkei through our strong physical attraction, and once we became an item, our strong physical activities. Also, mentally, she and I have always shared the same sense of humor and the same Biker-type attitude. But now she and I have a third connection, Jesus Christ, and we pray together often. So it has come to pass, Nikkei and I have achieved body, mind, and spirit. And that's a good thing! She is pregnant now and continually argues with her mother Sam over the baby's name. But I think they settled on Kaden if a boy, Kylee if a girl, but you'll have to wait for my sequel to find out for sure. Oh yeah, that little girl's smile of hers is back! Anytime I say or do anything special, I'm rewarded with it! It goes from ear to ear as she looks directly into my eyes; it lasts a long time!

Now Nikkei and I live quietly, far away from our past, totally focused on each other, and I swear there's not a day goes by I don't look at her and thank God for her. She was the life jacket God threw to my One Percent heart as it risked being pulled down by the undertow currents of Hell.

Never forget, the best lies are those cloaked under the truth, and my One Percent heart found the truth in Brotherhood. The lie was from my One Percent mind, which told me One Percenters will never find peace, they have No Choice, they were Born That Way, and they will Die That Way!

I will always be a One Percenter, but through God and his gift, Nikkei, I managed it to rest.

The End.

The Beginning.

It is foolish to believe the Seas will ever Calm,
We must learn to sail in Rough Seas!

—Clutch

CONTACT THE AUTHOR

Write:

Dave Ebert

P.O. Box 42

Annandale, Mn 55302

Email:

dle2010@live.com

Visit:

www.daveebert.com